For the first time in his life,
Leo Friday found himself wishing
he was an extremely rich man.

Then he could afford a woman like Lily Rigby. Her pale green eyes hinted at an easily amused nature. She had the kind of hair that always had a man's fingers itching to loosen it.

But he was here to discover who was robbing Schuyler Kimball blind, not admire Kimball's "secretary."

"Why don't you travel with Kimball?" Leo asked. "Wouldn't that make things . . . easier?"

"I'm needed here on the estate. Modern technology has made jobs like mine infinitely more manageable."

Oh, I don't know about that, Leo thought.

"I have a pager, you can beep me and I'll know if you need me here."

Just then, a realization quickly materialized in Leo Friday's brain, and no amount of trying to tamp it down would roust it.

He already needed Lily Rigby. Badly. Only not quite in the way she was thinking . . .

Avon Books are available at special quantity discounts for bulk purchases for sales promotions, premiums, fund raising or educational use. Special books, or book excerpts, can also be created to fit specific needs.

For details write or telephone the office of the Director of Special Markets, Avon Books, Inc., Dept. FP, 1350 Avenue of the Americas, New York, New York 10019, 1-800-238-0658.

ELIZABETH BEVARLY

Her Man Friday

AVON BOOKS  NEW YORK

AVON BOOKS, INC.
1350 Avenue of the Americas
New York, New York 10019

Copyright © 1999 by Elizabeth Bevarly
Inside cover author photo by Chuck King
Published by arrangement with the author
Library of Congress Catalog Card Number: 98-94816
ISBN: 0-380-80020-9
www.avonbooks.com/romance

First Avon Books Printing: June 1999

AVON TRADEMARK REG. U.S. PAT. OFF. AND IN OTHER COUNTRIES, MARCA REGISTRADA, HECHO EN U.S.A.

Printed in the U.S.A.

WCD 10 9 8 7 6 5 4 3 2 1

*This book is dedicated very fondly to
Cass Johnson, Michael Gregory,
Mark Johnson, and Michael Williams,
four of the smartest, cutest guys
to come down the pike.
Thanks for all the hours of
literate (and literary) conversation,
not to mention all those pitchers of Dark Stroh's.*

ACKNOWLEDGMENTS

I have a few quick thanks to extend on this one. Thanks first to my editor, Lucia Macro, for her limitless patience and understanding, not to mention superior editing skills. Thanks next to all the writers on the Avon Ladies and Desirables e-mail loops for providing me with my daily doses of friendship and reality. You guys have no idea how important you've become to me.

Many, *many* thanks to Laurie Jones for doing that promotional thing you do (and to your lovely husband Bailey for getting me to the airport on time).

Special and profuse thanks go to my two—count 'em two—personal Mother Teresas. Thank you to Teresa Medeiros and Teresa Hill for helping me hold on to my sanity and good humor during a year when those grew increasingly difficult to hold on to. I simply do not know how I would live without friends like you.

Musical inspiration for this book came from the incomparable Brian Setzer Orchestra and their CD entitled *The Dirty Boogie*. I will never, ever, tire of hearing "Jump, Jive and Wail" in the morning. It makes coffee pretty much redundant.

And my apologies to Seiller & Handmaker, LLP, who, thanks to my lousy penmanship, were misidentified in the acknowledgments for my last book. I hope I got it right this time.

And as always, thanks to my husband David and my son Eli for putting up with all the deadline dementia, the quickie meals, and the distracted staring off into space. I owe you guys big. Someday, I promise, I will give you the gift of time. Until then, know that I love you more than anything. Thanks, guys.

ONE

Oh, man. A bunch of wrinkled old white guys wearing two-thousand-dollar suits. So it was going to be one of *those* jobs again, was it?

As he tunneled fingers through his medium brown hair, Leo Friday shifted his weight from one foot to the other, arced his gaze around the U-shaped table that surrounded him, and eyed each of his new employers one by one. But even the fact that he was standing and they were sitting did nothing to relieve his tension. First in line was Versace Man, dressed to the nines in a black pinstripe number that put Leo's faded blue jeans, white T-shirt, and black blazer to shame. Beside Versace Man was Cohiba Man, puffing with much relish on the stump of a fat cigar. Beyond him was—oh, swell—Grecian Formula Man. Did old guys really think they were kidding anybody when they used that stuff? And after that came . . . ew, Halston for Men Man, way too close for comfort. Leo did his best to breathe shallowly.

One by one, he took in the dozen or so members of the board of directors of Kimball Technologies, Inc., the pride and joy of Philadelphia's business community. And he thanked God—not for the first time—that he was self-employed and didn't have to answer to guys like these. Because guys like these definitely lived and played by a different set of rules than Leo did, rules that were doubtless engraved in twenty-four-carat gold somewhere.

Okay, he amended reluctantly, when he recalled that these guys were his newest clients, so he was *technically* self-employed. Unfortunately, being self-employed meant he was also up for hire. Which meant he was pretty much answering to Kimball's board of directors. For now, anyway.

They'd dispensed with the initial formalities, and he'd declined the obligatory cup of coffee. Might as well get on with it. "All right," Leo said half-heartedly. "Give me the particulars."

"Someone is stealing money—a considerable amount of money—from Schuyler Kimball," Versace Man said.

Leo had to admit that as particulars went, that one was pretty substantial. "Can you be more specific?" he asked.

Versace Man shook his head. "No. That's the problem. We don't know how the money is disappearing, or from what branch of the business, or who might be doing the stealing. We only know that there should be quite a bit more money than there is. And we want you to find out where it is, and who's responsible for its disappearance."

A man halfway around the table met Leo's gaze with what the old guy probably thought was a steely glare. Unfortunately, his expression only succeeded in making the man look nearsighted. "And then," he intoned with a voice reminiscent of God's, "we want to you hang the bastard out to dry by his nuts."

Hoo-kay, Leo thought. So Charlton Heston Man

had checked in, had he? Aloud, he said, "That's not much to go on. I mean, Kimball Technologies *is* a multinational, multi-billion-dollar corporation, with holdings in dozens of areas of industry. Couldn't you be a little *more* specific?"

Versace Man plucked at his perfectly knotted necktie, an accessory that had probably set him back more than Leo's poker losings for a whole year. "No. That's the problem. Whoever is doing the stealing is damned good at it. We can't locate the origin of the theft at all."

Grecian Formula Man nodded his agreement. "We only know that the annual report for Kimball Technologies just came out, and although there was a nineteen percent rise in gross earnings, total profits fall short of what they should be. It's a pattern that's been plaguing the company for a few years now—a rise in gross earnings, yet a drop in total profits. This year, however, the discrepancy is a bit too big to ignore. It's causing us some concern."

"How much is 'a bit'?" Leo asked.

The men all exchanged wary glances, as if they weren't sure how much to reveal to the very man who was supposed to uncover the alleged theft. Ultimately, they all turned their attention to Cohiba Man, who puffed once on his cigar, then cleared his throat indelicately before meeting Leo's gaze.

"More than fifty million dollars," he said.

Fifty million dollars? Leo gasped inwardly. These guys were missing fifty million dollars, but they couldn't even say from *where*? Just how much money was Kimball Technologies bringing in annually?

Okay, granted, Schuyler Kimball, Philadelphia's most notorious native son, was one of the world's leading billionaires. Even without doing his research on the company—and the man—before taking on his current clients, Leo knew that much about Kimball. As did nearly everyone else on the planet. And it wasn't like Leo had never been exposed to extremely large sums of money in his time. Recouping massive corporate losses was part of what he did for a living. But this . . .

This was a hell of a lot of money they were talking about. And the fact that it was only a small percentage of Kimball's annual take just made it that much more astonishing.

Leo swallowed hard, pretending he wasn't completely awestruck, and said, "More than fifty million bucks, huh? Gee, that really sucks."

Another member of the board narrowed his eyes and glared at Leo. "Yes, Mr. Friday, it does indeed . . . suck," he agreed. "It's unfortunate. Inconvenient. One might even say ruinous. But that's why we wish to utilize your preeminent faculties and aptitudes. We comprehend that you are unequaled in the business when it comes to unearthing white-collar crime and harvesting the illicit fruits of that felonious labor."

Oh. Wonderful. Thesaurus Man, Leo decided. He shrugged off the compliment—once he understood that it was, in fact, a compliment. Hey, he *was* the best in the business when it came to ferreting out embezzlers, appropriators, abstracters, and outright corporate thieves. With degrees in accounting and finance, and a government background with both the government's General Accounting Office and the FBI, he'd left public service five years ago to start his own investigative agency—one that specialized in white-collar crime, particularly theft.

And boy, had he seen a boom in business, right out of the gate. Today's executives seemed to think their six-figure incomes and full medical coverage and luxury company cars and golden parachutes didn't begin to cover their needs. It never ceased to amaze Leo how greedy people could be. People who had it all still wanted more. And more. And more.

"I'm going to require total and unhampered access to the Kimball Technologies files," he said flat out. That was always the hardest thing the corporate big shots had to get used to—surrendering all their dirty little business secrets. But if these guys didn't give him unlimited access, they'd have to find another man for the job.

Cohiba man puffed once. "You'll have it, Mr. Friday," he said.

Leo arched his brows in surprise. Okay, so maybe Kimball's board of directors wasn't going to be so hard to deal with after all. "And I'll need for all of you to be available to me for questioning."

"Done," Cohiba man agreed without even consulting his colleagues. The other men nodded.

Well, hell, Leo thought. They were taking all the fun out of it. "And I'll require full and unhampered access to Schuyler Kimball, as well," he added.

Cohiba Man shook his head resolutely. "Absolutely not."

Scratch those earlier observations. "Excuse me?" Leo said.

"I said you won't have access to Schuyler Kimball," Cohiba Man repeated. "You're not to bring him into this. He's a very busy man."

Leo eyed the other man warily. "Let me get this straight. I'm trying to find fifty million dollars that someone has stolen from Kimball, but I can't have access to the man because he's too busy to see me?"

"That's correct."

"Excuse me for seeming a bit, oh . . . shall we say

. . . *miffed* about such a development, but I'm gonna kinda need to talk to the guy."

Cohiba Man puffed some more. "No, you won't."

"Why not?"

"Far be it from me to *miff* you, Mr. Friday, but you won't need to speak to Mr. Kimball because Mr. Kimball doesn't know the money is missing, and he's not to know of your investigation. That's why."

Leo squinted as the billows of smoke grew thicker around the other man. "Isn't he the one who's hiring me?" he asked.

"No, Mr. Friday. We—" He gestured down the table. "—the board of directors, are the ones who are hiring you."

Interesting distinction, Leo thought. He'd been under the impression that the board of directors of a company sort of answered to the man in charge. What were these guys? A wandering band of rogue executives? "You want to clarify that for me?" he asked.

Cohiba Man puffed one more time before removing the cigar from his mouth. Then he settled it in a crystal ashtray and folded one hand over the other on the table, an action that told Leo he was in for a serious—and lengthy—monologue.

Just as he'd suspected, Cohiba Man inhaled a long breath, then stated, "The board of directors of Kimball Technologies is hiring you, Mr. Friday, not Schuyler Kimball. Mr. Kimball isn't currently aware of the theft, nor is he to be informed about it. In fact, Mr. Kimball isn't to be informed of your activities at all. He's much too busy to be bothered by something like this. He has the running of his company to see to, not to mention other, more personal, pursuits."

Leo studied the other man in silence for some time, shifting his weight again from one hiking-booted foot to the other as he contemplated what the true nature of *personal pursuits* might be in terms of a billionaire playboy. Then, when his thoughts started to get away from him, lingering far too long on scantily clad women and whipped cream, he shook his head hard and said, "You, uh, you want to tell me how you're going to explain it to Kimball when he finds out that someone— namely me—is poking his nose into every single file in the Kimball archives?"

Leo was really looking forward to the answer to that question, and shifted his weight again as he waited to hear what it might be.

Cohiba Man picked up his cigar and puffed some more. "No, Mr. Friday, I don't want to tell you that. It's immaterial."

"But—"

"Suffice it to say," Cohiba Man cut him off, "you are in no danger of Mr. Kimball discovering your presence or your activities."

"But—"

"And should you make your identity and the particulars of your investigation known to him— either voluntarily or involuntarily—then your work for this company shall be immediately terminated, and you'll never crunch numbers in this town again. Do I make myself clear, Mr. Friday?"

"Crystal," Leo replied without missing a beat.

But he stiffened under the other man's perusal, his back going up fast at the suggestion that he'd never work in Philadelphia again. Right. Like that was ever going to happen, seeing as how he had a national reputation for being the best at what he did. Leo was more than confident of his ability to stay in business, regardless of what these overblown egos thought of their own power.

But if they didn't want Kimball to know about the investigation, then he'd keep it under his hat. He could manage, as long as he had access to—and the blessing of—the board of directors, and the freedom to plunder all of the company files. It might take longer than it would if he'd been able to sit down with the big boss and ask a few questions, but Leo could still do his job quite nicely, thanks, without Kimball's input.

He was about to say something more, to ask the first of many questions, when Cohiba Man started up again.

"Unfortunately," the executive said, "Mr. Kimball keeps some of his records at his estate in Bucks County. Naturally, Mr. Friday, we'll expect you to begin your investigation at company headquarters here in town. But ultimately, this assignment could force you to do quite a lot of traveling, to other cities and countries where Kimball Technologies has holdings. A worst-case scenario would have you infiltrating Mr. Kimball's private residence, but in all likelihood—if you're as good as you claim—that will never come about, because you'll find the source of the theft right away. At any rate, we'll start here and work our way out, shall we?"

We? Leo echoed to himself. Like these guys knew the first place to look for corruption. Then again, some corruption went pretty high up in the company. Just why, exactly, were they so reluctant to let Schuyler Kimball know what was going on?

While Leo was pondering the answer to that question, Cohiba Man added, "And because of the delicate nature of this investigation, it will, of course, be essential that you cover your tracks. No one other than the men present in this room right now is to know your true reason for poking around. *No one.* You'll have to make every effort to keep yourself invisible."

"That goes without saying," Leo said. "And, no offense, but I wouldn't be where I am in this business if I hadn't mastered discretion a long time ago."

"No, Mr. Friday," Versace Man piped up then. "You don't understand. It's not your discretion we're worried about. It's *you.* Your very identity is the problem. You're too well-known, even by some of the company's less, shall we say, important employees. You're not to go by Leo Friday. You're not to be an investigator of fraud. We'll have to come up with another persona entirely for you. This has to look like a simple, standard audit of the books. Period."

Great, Leo thought. This was just great. The wandering band of rogue executives were now Elliot Ness and the Untouchables.

He shook his head imperceptibly. This had happened to him before. A different company, a different board of directors, but the same damned thing. They'd been convinced that his reputation had preceded him, right down to the guys in the mail room, and they'd insisted he play a game of cloak and calculator. And not only had the charade been totally unnecessary, it had been annoying as hell.

"Well, can I at least go by my own first name?" he asked, masking his sarcasm as best he could, and telling himself that was *not* petulance he heard in his voice.

"Leonard?" Cohiba Man asked with a shrug. "I don't see why not."

Leo cringed at the sound of his given name. He *really* hated being called Leonard. No one but his great-aunt Margie got away with calling him that anymore, and the only reason she did was because she was ninety-two years old. Well, that and the fact that, even though at six-foot-two, Leo was a solid one-hundred and ninety-eight pounds, Aunt Margie outweighed him by a good fifty pounds. *And* she watched way too much Championship Wrestling.

"No, not Leonard," he started to object.

But Halston Man cut him off. "Leonard Freiberger!" he exclaimed. "That's who you could be. It would be close to your real name, but not really. And you won't be an investigator. You'll be a . . . let's see now . . . a bookkeeper! Yes, that's perfect. A mousy little bookkeeper who's been hired to double-check the files for a few minor discrepancies. And I think Leonard Freiberger is the perfect name for a mousy little bookkeeper. I went to school with a Morton Freiberger," he added parenthetically. "Trust me. This will be perfect."

"That's interesting," Leo replied blandly. "I went to school with a Butch Freiberger. Son of a bitch beat the hell out of me one day during PE."

Leo also thought about telling Halston Man that he had bookkeeper friends named Trixie LeFevre and Jamal Jefferson, and not a single one with a name like Leonard Freiberger. But the old guy seemed to be having so much fun that Leo didn't have the heart. Unfortunately, when he said nothing to counter the man's suggestion, the other executives, incredibly, seemed to warm to the idea.

"Yes, yes," Versace Man chimed in. "That's a wonderful idea. You'll need glasses, though." He whipped his own pair of delicate, horn-rimmed spectacles from his face and held them out to Leo. "Here, you can wear mine. Don't worry—they're not prescription. They're mood glasses. Women *adore* them on men."

Mood glasses? Leo wondered. Now what market-ing genius had come up with *that* idea? One who had never had to wear real glasses, obviously. Leo should know. He'd been wearing contact lenses for half his life—since he was nineteen years old.

"I don't think—" he began to object.

But this time Grecian Formula Man interrupted him. "And you absolutely must wear tweed," he threw in. "Not the good kind—the Lauren or the Hilfiger—the absent-minded professor kind. Like Peter O'Toole wore in *Goodbye Mr. Chips.* That would suit the charade beautifully."

Leo pinched the bridge of his nose—hard—and tried not to panic. "Uh, I think you guys are getting a little too—"

"It's just too bad we can't do anything about your physical makeup, Mr. Friday," Charlton Hes-ton Man piped up, frowning as he considered Leo from head to toe. "There aren't many bookkeepers who look like football linemen. Perhaps if you slouched a bit . . ."

All right, that was enough, Leo thought, drop-ping his hand back down to his side. He owed it to bookkeepers everywhere to put a stop to this egregious stereotyping ASAP. Otherwise, he'd have Trixie and Jamal up here kicking corporate butt in no time flat.

"Look," he bit out, barely able to contain his growing outrage. "You guys are out of line. There's no reason for me to affect any kind of damned ste-reotype. I'm perfectly capable of handling this as-signment the same way I've handled hundreds of other assignments over the years. Just sit back and let me do my job."

"Oh, we'll let you do your job, Mr. Friday," Co-hiba Man said. "But don't forget who's paying your salary here."

"Fine," Leo conceded sharply. "I'll play by your rules, *to an extent*." He emphasized those last three words as much as he could. "I'll go by another name, and I'll be the simple, lowly bookkeeper doing a perfunctory and very standard survey of the records. But I *won't* be a buffoon."

"We never asked you to be that, Mr. Friday," Cohiba Man said. But he smiled as he puffed his cigar.

Leo shook his head once more, not bothering to be imperceptible about it this time. These guys were flat-out nuts. Too much living in the corporate ivory towers would do that to a person, he supposed.

Fine, he thought. He'd play a part. Whatever it took to get these guys off his back so he could do his job, collect his paycheck, and leave them in the dust. One thing, however, was absolutely certain. He *wasn't* going to go by Leonard Freiberger, and he *wasn't* going to slouch, and he *wasn't* going to wear tweed or mood glasses.

He didn't care who was paying his salary.

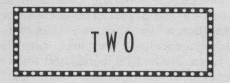

TWO

"Leonard Freiberger, ma'am. We spoke on the phone yesterday afternoon?"

Lily Rigby gazed at the man standing on the other side of Schuyler's front door, blinked a few times in rapid succession, and realized she had no idea what to say in response. His appearance simply left her at a loss for words. She reminded herself that Mr. Freiberger *had* identified himself over the telephone the day before as a bookkeeper, but still . . . She hadn't thought anybody wore that *Goodbye, Mr. Chips* tweed stuff anymore.

"Lily Rigby," she finally said, extending her hand toward him. "I'm Schuyler Kimball's social secretary. It's nice to meet you, Mr. Freiberger."

Actually, she was quite a bit more than Schuyler Kimball's social secretary, she thought. She and Schuyler had, after all, gone to college together. And he had, after all, been her first lover, however briefly. And they had, after all, lived together for years and years and years. But that was undoubtedly a bit more than Mr. Freiberger wanted to know, wasn't it?

So she said nothing further as she extended one

13

hand toward him in greeting, then skimmed the
other over the straight black hair she had wound
into a sleek French twist. She forced a smile as she
catalogued the rest of him, scrambling for a bland,
polite addition to her salutation. When he took her
hand, his fingers closed over hers, virtually swallowing them. He had big hands and a strong, capable grip, and his flesh was warm and rough
against hers.

When she glanced up at his face, it startled her
to realize that beneath close-cropped, medium
brown hair, and behind round, wire-framed
glasses, Mr. Freiberger had beautiful hazel eyes—
not quite green, not quite blue, not quite gray. They
were eyes that reflected intelligence, wit and a generally easygoing disposition, and not a little heat.
His other features were craggy, but pleasant—a
square jaw, full, but finely chiseled lips, a straight
nose, nice cheekbones. Oh, yes. Very nice cheekbones, indeed.

Quickly, she shook his hand and released it.
Then she skimmed her gaze downward, and back
up again, hoping he noticed neither her hasty in-
ventory, nor the reluctant blush she felt warming
her face when she completed it. Because even the
baggy tweed jacket and trousers, even the rumpled
white oxford shirt and outdated tie, did nothing to
hide the solid body lurking somewhere beneath.

Goodness. Mr. Freiberger was built like a Mack
truck. And he probably topped six-feet, though it
was hard to say for sure, considering that nasty
slouch of his. But even with his bad posture, he
towered over Lily. Then again, she stood a mere
five-foot-four in her stockinged feet—on a good
day—and never wore heels any higher than one
inch with her work clothes.

She stepped aside to allow the man entry, wondering again why the board of directors of Kimball Technologies wanted him to go over Schuyler's home files. Something about a problem with last year's tax return, Mr. Freiberger had explained, but honestly. She wished they would have given her more notice for an audit that sounded in no way urgent.

"Come in, Mr. Freiberger," she told the book-keeper, sweeping a hand toward the expansive marble foyer. "I apologize for my hesitation. My mind is elsewhere. Mr. Kimball is out of town this week, so I have my hands full keeping things running on my own."

Not that she didn't run things all by herself when Schuyler was there, too, she added to herself with not a little pique. Ten years had passed since she'd earned her first degree in business and Schuyler had suggested launching Kimball Technologies, but he had always been far too focused on the design work for the company to ever worry about anything else. Like so many other things, the day-to-day tasks here at Ashling invariably fell to Lily, regardless of where Schuyler was.

The bookkeeper nodded his thanks as he gripped his leather satchel more firmly. Then he strode forward, pausing just inside the door. When he passed her, Lily noted that he smelled . . . very nice. Not perfumey, but . . . clean. Earthy. Masculine. Somehow the scent was both wildly inappropriate and strangely suitable for him.

"Thank you, Miss Rigby," he said. His voice, like the rest of him, was a combination of opposites, the gentility edged with a roughness she couldn't mistake. "I'll do my best to stay out of your way this week," he added. "I'll be quiet as a mouse. You won't even know I'm here."

That was something Lily sincerely doubted. Already she was far too curious about Mr. Freiberger. In spite of his clothes, he looked like the kind of man she might meet in a South Philly bar, at the end of the work day and the peak of hockey season, downing beer and screaming on the Flyers to the Stanley Cup. Yet he dressed and spoke and carried himself as if he were an unassuming and inconspicuous . . . well, dweeb.

"Um, that's okay, Mr. Freiberger," she said. "It's pretty quiet around here when Mr. Kimball's not in residence. And we tend to fall into a fairly casual routine, even when he's home. I assure you, you won't be in the way at all."

She closed the door behind him, but not before a breath of autumn scurried inside. The mid-October wind was cool and crisp, already hinting at the winter to come, redolent of apples and drying leaves. The expansive maples and oaks that surrounded Schuyler's estate were ablaze with orange and red and gold, their leaves scattered about the grass like fallen handkerchiefs. Mr. Tooley, the groundskeeper, could scarcely keep up, even with the help of two college boys he had at his disposal. Then again, the house they cared for wasn't exactly your run-of-the-mill estate.

Ashling, the thirty-four-room, twenty-nine-thousand-square-foot Georgian manor that was Schuyler Kimball's primary residence, rested on forty-five acres of prime real estate in rural Bucks County. With its rose-colored brick and lead/copper roof, with its twelve fireplaces and nine bedrooms, with its gymnasium and movie theater, and with its majestic marble gallery that linked the house's two wings, Lily knew Ashling surpassed even Schuyler's expectations for living quarters. The name he had bestowed upon his home was a phonic representation of *Aisling*, an Irish name that meant *dream*. Because to Schuyler, that was precisely what the huge house was. A dream come true.

She supposed there were a lot of people who would consider the residence excessive, particularly for a single man who had made no secret of his confirmed—and womanizing—bachelorhood. Truth be told, Lily was one of them. But Schuyler had worked hard and sacrificed a lot to earn the wealth he claimed. She had seen firsthand how many obstacles he had overcome to achieve his current status, and how many battles he continued to fight every day to maintain it.

And it wasn't like he *did* live here alone. There was a huge staff of hourly workers who filed in every morning to see to the day-to-day running of Ashling. Schuyler's mother, Miranda, and his sister, Janey, were residents. Lily, too, with a handful of servants, lived here full-time, though her quarters were significantly more modest than the family's. And, of course, she mustn't forget Chloe.

As much as she might like to.

As Lily led Leonard Freiberger through the gallery toward the east wing that housed the private living area where Schuyler kept his office, she strove for polite conversation. "Leonard," she repeated. "That's a lovely name. My mother had a chocolate point Siamese named Leonard. Of course, it goes without saying that we always called him 'Leo.' "

She wasn't sure, but she thought the bookkeeper grunted something in response to that. She sighed and tried again. "He was rather neurotic, though, even for a Siamese. There were times when we were convinced he thought he was a Turkish Angora."

Silence greeted the comment from behind, followed by what sounded to Lily like a very weary sigh. She was about to say something more, when finally Mr. Freiberger asked in a flat voice, "Um, why was that?"

Without breaking stride, she replied over her shoulder, "Well, he just thought he was so much smarter than everyone else, you know? I mean, honestly. A chocolate point Siamese. Can you imagine?"

When Mr. Freiberger responded with another lengthy silence, she glanced back to find that he was squinting at her—as if the light in the gallery had suddenly gone dim. Men, Lily thought with no small exasperation. They never did understand cats.

She continued to lead him on their journey, passing the receiving room, the sitting room, the living room, and the atrium, then turned left into the east wing. For some reason, there seemed to be a strange tension emanating from Mr. Freiberger, a tension whose origin Lily couldn't quite pinpoint. So, as always, she fell back on meaningless chitchat to defuse the taut mood.

"I know you drove here from Philadelphia, Mr. Freiberger and work for Kimball Technologies. Are you originally from the area?"

"Not Philadelphia, no," he told her. "Although I've worked and lived in the city for about five years now, I grew up in Maryland, in a small town on Chesapeake Bay called Harborside." She could tell by his tone of voice that he carried a lot of fond memories of his upbringing. And she noted that when he smiled the way he was smiling now, he was almost . . . She sighed involuntarily. Well, he was almost, sort of, kind of . . . handsome.

She began to walk again, but this time strode side by side with Mr. Freiberger, instead of two paces ahead of him. And this time she slowed their pace to one that was much more leisurely.

"It sounds like a wonderful little town," she told him.

"Yes, well, 'little' would be the operative word," he agreed, still grinning, still speaking warmly, still almost handsome. "There's not much there but oystermen. But you're right—it is wonderful."

They entered the living quarters of Ashling, but since they were still in mid-conversation—and since Mr. Freiberger was still looking so almost handsome—Lily slowed their pace even more as they approached Schuyler's office.

"You're from a fishing—or, rather, oystering—family then?" she asked, assuming the obvious.

Mr. Freiberger nodded, lifting a hand to straighten his glasses as he replied, "Yes, my father and brother both are oystermen."

"Why didn't you go into the business, too?"

He shrugged as he said, "There's not a lot of that kind of work left these days. Besides, I showed a proficiency for other things. I wasn't really suited to the family business."

She was about to ask him what kind of other things he claimed proficiency in—and would he, if she asked nicely, show her what they were—but by that time, they had cleared the family room, the library, and the conservatory, and they stood by the door of Schuyler's private office. As Lily opened it and turned to gesture Mr. Freiberger in ahead of her, she marveled again at the incongruencies in the man.

The son of an oysterman. Yet he claimed not to be suitable for that type of work. Strange, because he was clearly in prime physical shape, certainly more than up to the back-breaking labor such a job would require. And something about him bespoke the great outdoors. His complexion was touched with a golden tan, lines fanned out from the corners of his eyes, and his lips were framed by deep slashes that might be genetic, but more probably resulted from exposure to the elements. Certainly it was evident that he spent more than a little time outdoors. Nothing about him suggested the bookishness he projected.

Still, who was Lily to judge appearances? Hadn't she herself been erroneously pegged on more occasions than she cared to admit?

"Any files Mr. Kimball keeps for professional reasons are all in here," she said, once more shaking off her odd preoccupation with Leonard Freiberger.

She entered Schuyler's office behind the bookkeeper and strode immediately toward the massive mahogany desk that sat before an even more massive Palladian window. Of course, Schuyler's personal files were all in here, as well, but there was little chance Mr. Freiberger would be accessing those. Not just because they had little to do with the business, but because they were all protected by passwords and elaborate booby traps that baffled even Schuyler himself from time to time.

"Most of them are on diskette," she added, pulling open a drawer and extracting a stack. "Some are on the computer's hard drive, and a few are filed the old-fashioned way—in filing cabinets." She smiled. "For all his technological savvy, Schuyler still hasn't made his environment completely paper-free. He's not very good with computers, I'm afraid."

Leo nodded as he enjoyed another leisurely study of Schuyler Kimball's "social secretary," noting her slip at using her employer's first name. And, for the first time in his life, he found himself wishing that he was an extremely rich man. Then maybe he could afford a woman like the delectable Lily Rigby.

Her pale green eyes and now-you-see-it-now-you-don't smile hinted at an easily amused nature, her flawless ivory complexion and artfully applied cosmetics suggested good breeding. Her black hair, doubtless long and straight when freed, was wound up the back of her head the way Kim Novak used to wear her hair in all those Hitchcock films from the fifties and sixties—the kind of hairstyle that always had a man's fingers itching to loosen it.

As she leaned forward to boot up the computer on the big desk that was obviously Kimball's central nervous system here at home, Leo took in the rest of her. Her chocolate-brown business suit was professional enough to pass muster at most companies, he supposed, but he hadn't encountered too many professional women— hell, too many women, period—who filled out a corporate uniform quite the way Lily Rigby did. Her straight skirt was just a little *too* tight and a little *too* short, and her waist-length jacket swung open over a top that was a little *too* snug and scooped a little *too* low. A thin, gold chain encircling her neck hosted a bright diamond, one that was a little *too* big for someone on a social secretary's salary.

Social secretary, Leo repeated dubiously to himself. Yeah, right. *Mistress* was more like it. He'd learned enough about Schuyler Kimball, playboy billionaire, to know the man would never have a woman like this in his employ without sampling her personal wares on a regular basis. Oh, sure, the job title was a nice, convenient cover, and giving her a regular paycheck for such a role might make the arrangement more socially acceptable. But there was no way Leo would ever believe that the job description for Miss Rigby's position was anything other than sexual.

"I appreciate Mr. Kimball's accommodating me this way on such short notice," he said aloud, reluctantly slipping back into Leonard mode.

She waved a hand as she typed a few instructions into the computer. "Oh, Schuyler doesn't even know you're here. He's been in Bermuda since Thursday and isn't expected back until next week. And even if he were here, he never troubles himself with this kind of thing. It would fall to me anyway."

Which went a long way toward explaining how someone was robbing him blind, Leo thought. Aloud, he only said, "How much time does he spend here at the estate?"

"Not as much as he'd like," she said as she scanned the computer screen and typed in some more instructions. "He travels quite a bit for the company, and even more for his personal enjoyment. And he has a half-dozen private residences, all over the world. Between his work and his mood swings, he could be anywhere on the planet at any given time."

"Don't you have a hard time keeping track of him?"

Evidently having concluded whatever mumbo-jumbo she had to complete to get the system up and working, Lily Rigby straightened. And Leo tried not to become suicidal over the fact that when she did, her jacket draped down over the creamy swells of her breasts again.

"We're frequently in touch via the phone or e-mail," she said.

"Why don't you travel with him?" Leo asked the obvious. "Wouldn't that make things easier?"

She turned and offered him a knowing smile.

"Well. I'm really needed here at home far more than I am wherever he is. And besides, I don't want to cramp his style, do I?"

Leo smiled back, a bit less knowingly. "Don't you? I'd think that would be part of your job description. If not cramping Mr. Kimball's style, then certainly organizing it."

She lifted her shoulders and let them drop again, obviously unconcerned about that. "There are a lot of women in Mr. Kimball's life," she said in as matter-of-fact a tone as Leo had ever heard, surprising him. "They frequently travel with him. And they often misunderstand my role in the scheme of things. It gets a bit awkward."

Wow, he thought. She was a really understanding mistress if she let Kimball flaunt his other girlfriends so blatantly in front of her. Just how much was the guy paying her anyway? Then again, maybe a cool disposition was exactly what a man looked for in a mistress, precisely so that he could maintain a variety of relationships. Well, a cool disposition *outside* the bedroom anyway, he amended. *Inside* the bedroom, however . . .

Leo let his mind wander freely over that one for a moment, until the images parading through his head became far too explicit, enough so that his baggy tweed trousers began to feel much less baggy. With a none too courteous nudge to his libido, he returned his attention to the matter at hand. Unfortunately, that meant he was looking at Lily Rigby, and those illicit ideas began to creep right back into his brain.

"Naturally," she continued easily as she circled to the front of the desk, clearly oblivious to his salacious intentions for her, "I do travel with Mr. Kimball from time to time. But he and I have both come to the conclusion that I'm generally needed here at Ashling more than I'm needed with him on his travels. I e-mail him his daily agenda, and, as I said, we speak frequently on the phone. Modern technology has made jobs like mine infinitely more manageable."

Oh, Leo didn't know about that. He didn't want Miss Rigby selling herself short. There was obviously a lot to be said for her basic, not-so-technological talents. Or, at least he assumed there was a lot to be said for those. Schuyler Kimball was a connoisseur of only the finest things in life, after all. And Lily Rigby was definitely one of those.

She might not be the brightest bulb on the Christmas tree, he thought, thinking back on that whole cat story she'd told him a few minutes ago. But, hey, a woman didn't have to be a rocket scientist to be good at her job. Unless, of course, he amended, she happened to be a rocket scientist. But that was beside the point. The point was that there were some jobs where little things like, oh . . . thinking . . . knowledge . . . a capacity for understanding . . . just weren't a major concern of employment.

"Well," she said, "if there's nothing else you'll be needing?"

He shook his head. "No. Thank you, Miss Rigby. Everything I need is right here."

"I have a pager," she said, flipping open her jacket again to indicate the little black box fixed at her waist, bestowing upon him another glimpse of her less technological—and extremely sensational—gifts. She gestured toward the telephone on the desk. "If something comes up, just press number one on the speed dial. That will beep me, and I'll know you need me here. Wherever I am on the estate, I can be here in ten minutes at the most."

An unwanted realization quickly materialized in

Leo's brain, and no amount of trying to tamp it down would roust it. He already needed Lily Rigby. Badly. Only not quite the way she was thinking.

He bit back a frustrated sigh. Perfect. This was just perfect. The last thing he should be doing was indulging in libidinous plans for one of Schuyler Kimball's favorite playthings. With any luck at all, he'd be able to wind up his business here at the estate within a few days' time, and then he could forget he ever saw Lily Rigby.

Well, he could *pretend* to forget he ever saw Lily Rigby, anyway.

He watched her go, inhaling deeply as she passed by him because she just smelled so damned good. Like a field full of exotic spices. That he wanted to wallow in. For a long time. Naked. With one final, heart-stopping smile, she reached back to close the door behind herself, and then Leo was left alone in Schuyler Kimball's personal, private realm.

Immediately, he loosened his necktie, as uncomfortable in the idiotic persona of Leonard Freiberger as he had been when he first ventured out on his relentless pursuit to find the missing Kimball millions. He still couldn't remember how he'd been talked into submitting to this particular requirement of his employment, this wearing of the geek. But there it was just the same—Leo Friday, who had once seriously considered pursuing a career as a professional hockey player, who had fought in Golden Gloves competitions as an adolescent, whose nickname in high school had been Bloody Friday. He sighed with much gusto. Now he was lame Leonard Freiberger. And a beautiful woman had seen him that way.

Dammit.

After shrugging out of his jacket, he rolled his shirt sleeves to his elbows, then tossed his leather, satchel-style briefcase onto the desk and unbuckled it. From inside, he withdrew a stack of his own diskettes that were rubber-banded together, then set them next to the ones Miss Rigby had placed on the desk. That done, he folded himself into Kimball's comfy, throne-like desk chair, wheeled himself over to the computer, and went to work.

After weeks, months even, of virtually circling the globe for the board of directors of Kimball Technologies, Leo had uncovered nothing remarkable. Certainly, there had been discrepancies here and there in the records, a few things that didn't add up. But those instances hadn't been anything that he wouldn't normally find within a corporation the size of Kimball's. And none of them had been the result of any criminal or fraudulent behavior. Certainly none of them had added up to anything even remotely resembling fifty million dollars. In most cases, they had occurred due to human error. In one or two more, it had simply been the push of a wrong button.

Coming here to Kimball's estate was a last resort. Leo knew it. The board of directors knew it. If he didn't find anything here, then he was, as the students at St. Francis in the Fields parochial school used to say, S.O.L.

That was why he was confident that there *was* something here. And that was why he suspected that not only did Schuyler Kimball know about the missing funds, he was doubtless responsible for them. Naturally, Leo had voiced those very suspicions to the board of directors, but they had all but shouted him down before he'd even finished justifying his feelings.

It was impossible, they had assured him, that

Kimball could be the one funneling the money else-where. And not just because Schuyler Kimball was a complete tightwad, a man who didn't spend money on anything other than himself. But because there was no way he would filter money anywhere, unless it was into a personal account. And if the money were going into a personal account, then why would he be so secretive about it? It was *his* money, after all.

Leo still didn't have an answer to that. But he intended to find one. As far as he was concerned, there were all kinds of reasons that a man might keep a secret bank account, few of them legitimate or ethical. Nevertheless, he'd been hired to find out what had happened to fifty million dollars last fis-cal year. And that was what he would do. After that, whatever happened would be between the board of directors and Schuyler Kimball. Frankly, it was none of Leo's concern who did what with Kimball's money, so long as he found it, as he had been hired to do.

Unfortunately, there were a lot of people in the company who were doing what with Kimball's money, something that had significantly hampered Leo's search. Every office at every outpost of Kim-ball Technologies claimed someone who had the authority to okay the transfer or spending of funds. At least there was always a ceiling on how much those people entrusted with money could spend, but even at that, there was way too much room— and opportunity—for error. And for doubt. And for theft.

So far, there was no one other than Kimball whom Leo suspected of dabbling in a little creative bookkeeping. Still, that didn't rule out the possi-bility completely that there might be a thief at large. But if it *wasn't* Kimball doing the funneling, then there was *some*one, *some*where, who was. And if it wasn't Kimball, then whoever was doing it had no right to do it, something that made the perpetrator a sneaky, finkish little crook. And if *that* was the case, then there was a good chance that the thief was someone right here at the estate, right under Kimball's nose. So Leo rehearsed in his head again what little he knew about the inhabitants of Ashling.

Anybody who knew their way around a computer could find a way to "update" a file in a manner that was in no way legal. There were scores of daily workers who pretty much roamed freely about Ashling. There were doubtless regular visitors—many of them Kimball's colleagues and employees—who might use their visiting time for a little recreational stealing. Kimball's mother and sister also lived here with him. And who knew what kind of family dynamics—i.e., dysfunctions—were indigenous to the Kimballs of Bucks County?

Too, as reluctant as he was to do it, Leo had to keep Kimball's social secretary, the delicious Miss Rigby, under consideration. Maybe she wasn't as quick as a brown fox, but she was the mistress of a man who made women a recreational sport. She might feel like a woman scorned and all that. She might even have an accomplice up her sleeve—or under her slip. Who knew what her real story was?

He made a mental note to find out more about the personal lives of the people living and working at Ashling. Then he crossed his arms over his chest and leaned back to watch in silence as row upon row of numbers appeared on the computer screen in front of him. Somewhere in Schuyler Kimball's well-tended, high-tech, state-of-the-art, billionaire world, there was a rat stealing millions of dollars worth of cheese. And even if it took Leo the rest of the year to do it, he was going to find that rat.

And then, cool as a wheel of Edam, he was going to trap it.

THREE

Lily was in the kitchen, stealing a few moments to brew herself a much-needed cup of tea, when she heard the scream. And not one of those run-of-the-mill, oh-great-what-now kind of screams, either. But a truly horrific, straight-from-the-darkest-part-of-the-soul scream.

And she muttered, "Oh, great. What now?"

As usual, a second scream quickly followed the first, and she rolled her eyes heavenward, giving her tea bag a few more quick dips before withdrawing it from the cup to squeeze out the excess with her fingers. As she licked those clean, she used her other hand to add two teaspoons of sugar and a healthy dose of milk to the brew. The third scream—right on schedule—came just as she finished stirring, and she sighed wearily, knowing her much needed cup of afternoon tea would be cold by the time she returned. Again.

She took a moment to shrug back into her suit jacket and tuck her feet back into her shoes, then made her way toward the stairs at the back of the kitchen. Predictably, a fourth—and hopefully final—scream serenaded her as she began her ascent to-

ward the back of the house where her own room
was. Her room, and Mrs. Puddleduck's room, too.

Of course, Mrs. Puddleduck's name wasn't really
Mrs. Puddleduck. It was something else that only
sounded like Puddleduck, but Lily could never remember what it was. At any rate, Schuyler had
hired the woman a few months ago—against Lily's
recommendation to the contrary—to be Chloe's
nanny. Even though, at fourteen, Chloe was a bit
too old to have a nanny. Even though what Chloe
really needed was a companion of equal measure.
Like a wolverine, for example. Or that masked
butcher from the "Halloween" movies. Or Her-
mann Goering. Someone along those lines.

"Coming, Mrs. Puddleduck," Lily called out
mildly as she topped the last stair that led to her
and the nanny's quarters, hoping that would prevent another bout of screaming. Nevertheless, she
hastened her stride toward the other woman's
room. Which was good, because she was opening
her mouth for yet another bellow just as Lily entered.

The apartment was nearly identical to her own,
painted a creamy shade of pale yellow, with ivory
lace curtains covering both of the floor-to-ceiling
windows that looked out on the garden behind the
house. A huge, oval-shaped, hooked floral rug
spanned the entirety of the room, not quite ob-
scuring the honey-toned hardwood floor beneath.
The furnishings were simple but beautiful—a full
bed with an embroidered ivory-on-ivory coverlet,
a dresser and bedside table, a rocking chair and
armoire, all crafted of exquisite bird's-eye maple.
The mid-afternoon sun spilled through the windows to cast a warm, golden light over it all, dap-
pling the room with lacy shadows.

Yes, Lily noted with a fond smile, not for the first

time, this room at Ashling was pretty much exactly like her own. Well, except for that small slimy ... thing ... surrounded by a pool of clear, pungent ... stuff ... in the middle of the other woman's bed.

She approached it cautiously, striving for a sympathetic smile at the quivering nanny, but there were times when Lily found it difficult to be sympathetic toward the other woman. She looked to be only in her fifties, but she dressed and acted like a centenarian. A boring, stuffy, self-defeating centenarian, at that, and not one of those eccentric, fun-loving centenarians who jumped out of airplanes and drank whiskey and called octogenarians "Sonnyboy" or something like that. Still, Lily supposed no one was perfect. And who knew what kinds of things lurked in Mrs. Puddleduck's background, after all? She might very well be the way she was today because of episodes like this very one.

Lily turned her attention back to the bed—to the *thing* surrounded by *stuff* on the bed—and tried to identify it. Funny, it did seem familiar somehow, but she couldn't quite place where she had encountered such a thing before. She had tilted her head to one side in an effort to contemplate it from another angle when Leonard Freiberger, having evidently heard the screams, too, came crashing into the room.

She was amazed he'd been able to pinpoint the source of the outburst from Schuyler's office two floors and a couple of hallways below. That showed real investigative talent. She'd only known to come here herself because, well, this sort of thing had happened at least once a week since Chloe Sandusky had come to live with them. Who else could have been screaming *but* Mrs. Puddleduck?

The nanny *du jour* was always Chloe's favorite target.

"Hello, Mr. Freiberger," Lily said as she turned to greet him, wondering if being exposed to Chloe's habits on his first day at work would prevent him from returning tomorrow. Goodness, she hoped not. She was reluctant to replace the nanny, even though she and the other woman hadn't much agreed on anything, especially where Chloe was concerned. (And there had also been that business about Mrs. Puddleduck thinking that Clarence Thomas had told the truth.) But Lily *really* didn't want to have to replace Mr. Freiberger. She rather liked him.

"Miss Rigby," he replied, his even timbre of voice at odds with the expression of stark horror etched on his face. "May I ask what all that screaming was about?"

"Oh, by all means," Lily told him.

He hesitated for a moment, waiting for her to explain, and when she didn't, he added, "Uh, then . . . what was all that screaming about?"

Lily sighed. "I'm afraid Mrs. Puddleduck has been the victim of a little prank."

"A little prank?" the nanny repeated. "A little *prank*? You call that . . . that . . . that *thing* on my bed a little prank? And it's *Poddledock*," she added. "I wish you would remember that."

Her question directed Mr. Freiberger's attention to the bed, and his expression of stark horror was immediately replaced by one of vague repugnance.

"*What*," he said, pointing toward the offending item, "is *that*?"

With what she hoped was an encouraging smile to both of them, Lily covered the remaining length of the room in a half-dozen strides and extended her hand toward the thing on the bed. But before she could touch it, Leonard Freiberger moved in from behind her and caught her hand deftly in his.

"Maybe you should let me," he said.

She noted then that he looked different from the way he had appeared earlier at the front door. He'd shed his jacket, loosened his tie, and unbuttoned the top button of his shirt. He'd also rolled his sleeves up to his elbows, and she couldn't help but notice that he had some very good musculature for someone whose primary activity in life was pushing pencils. Even with number two lead, a man must have to push an awful lot of them to get muscles like that.

She also noticed that he wasn't wearing a wedding ring, but that was really neither here nor there.

More than his physical appearance, however, something else was different—his entire demeanor since this morning seemed to have gotten somehow . . . larger. That was the only way Lily could describe it. Although she'd already thought him tall and broad, suddenly he seemed even taller and broader. He wasn't slouching anymore, but there was more to his expansion than that. He just seemed . . . larger. All over. More self-assured. In every way. Just *more*. More than he had been before. Lily had to force herself not to take a step backward in an act of self-preservation.

"It's all right," she told him, shaking off the odd realization as she tipped her head toward the mess on the bed. "I have a lot of experience with this kind of thing. I know what I'm doing."

She patted his hand with her free one, trying to ignore the warmth and roughness of his skin, the kiss of the coarse hair growing there. Then—very reluctantly—she removed his hand from her own. Behind his glasses, his eyes narrowed, but he allowed her to go forward alone, shrugging off his concern for her welfare quite literally. So Lily leaned over the bed and, without an ounce of fear or concern, poked the small, slimy thing with her finger.

"Oh, I know what this is," she said as a flashback from tenth grade biology class hit her square in the head. It was the unmistakable aroma of formaldehyde that did it. "This is . . ." She threw what she hoped was a heartening look over her shoulder. "Well, to be precise, it's part of a pig."

"Uh, precisely which part?" Mr. Freiberger asked.

She picked up the offending item between thumb and forefinger, turning it first to the left, and then to the right. "I do believe it's the spleen. In fact, I'm sure of it. I recall dissecting one in high school, myself. It was really quite a fascinating experiment. I had no idea that a pig spleen was actually capable of—"

A sound from behind—actually two sounds: a gasp and a thump—halted Lily's observation, because it alerted her to the fact that Chloe's nanny had fainted. So she replaced the pig part on the bed, then sighed as she spun around.

"Oh, dear," she said. Then, trying her best to reassure the other woman, in spite of her lack of consciousness, she added, "It's only a biological organ. We all have a spleen, after all. There's absolutely nothing to be afraid of, I assure you." Turning to the bookkeeper, she added, "Mr. Freiberger, if you could look in the bathroom there behind you, I think you'll find some ammonia capsules in the medicine cabinet. Would you fetch them, please?"

He was gazing at her in much the same way one might look when the porch lights were dim, but he did as she'd requested. When he returned, Lily asked him to see if he could rouse the nanny while she washed her hands. By the time she rejoined them, the other woman had begun to come around. Together, they managed to bring her to a sitting position on the floor.

"Are you all right, Mrs. Puddleduck?" Lily asked when the other woman's pupils had returned to their normal size. Well, sort of normal, anyway. Kind of. "Would you like a cup of tea, or perhaps one of your muscle relaxers? I'll be happy to get you either one."

Feebly, the other woman shook her head. "What I would like, Lily, is two weeks' severance pay and a damned good reference from Mr. Kimball. And it's *Poddledock*," she added with surprising force for someone who had just regained full consciousness.

That, of course, was what Lily had been afraid the other woman would want. In spite of that, she said, "You knew the job was dangerous when you took it. I did warn you that Chloe isn't your average fourteen-year-old."

"You told me Chloe was a handful," the nanny said. "You never mentioned that she was prone to this kind of mischief and mayhem."

"Yes, well, I never said a handful of what," Lily offered halfheartedly.

Unfortunately, she knew the nanny's objections were perfectly well grounded. Lily was absolutely certain that, deep down, Chloe Sandusky was a good kid. But the girl had indulged in so much, well, mischief and mayhem, since coming to Ashling, that even Mother Teresa would have felt taxed.

In a last ditch effort, however, and with as much cheerfulness as she could muster—which, granted, wasn't much—she pointed out, "Chloe's actually quite a remarkable child. I mean, think about it.

This all shows real promise for a career in veterinary medicine."

"Or a career in serial killing," Mr. Freiberger added in a flat voice.

Lily threw him what she hoped was a chastening look. "Wake up and smell the formaldehyde, Mr. Freiberger. It's clear that Chloe performed the operation in a controlled environment like biology class, and didn't just take advantage of a defenseless creature while skulking about the farmlands with her friends, the Children of the Corn."

In response to her assurance, he only arched one eyebrow in silent query.

Lily lifted her chin smugly. "Chloe is what some people would call a gifted child," she began in the girl's defense.

"She's what other people would call a menace to society," he countered, his gaze never flinching.

Lily was about to speak again, but before she could comment, Mrs. Puddleduck began to rouse herself. She stood silently, wavered a bit, smoothed out her dress, wavered a bit more, and then made her way to the closet with all the imperiousness of a czarina. Well, a czarina who was completely whacked on laudanum, anyway. Without a word, she withdrew a suitcase from inside, opened it on the floor, and began to jerk her clothes from the hangers above. She didn't bother to fold them, only tossed them one by one into the suitcase at her feet.

Even though she knew it would probably be pointless to try to make amends, Lily offered, "In light of today's, um, incident, I'm sure we could talk Mr. Kimball into giving you a little bonus for your troubles." She bit back a derisive chuckle. Even Publisher's Clearinghouse didn't have enough money to pay a nanny for Chloe Sandusky.

The other woman spun around and glared at her.

"No, thank you," she bit out through gritted teeth.

"How about if you just take a little time to think about it, hmm?" Lily tried further. "A few days off? Paid, naturally."

But the nanny shook her head and went back to her packing. "No, I think I'll check into that prison matron position I saw advertised in the paper last Sunday. That should be an enormous improvement over this place."

Lily sighed. "Well, naturally, you'd know what's best for your career."

The other woman expelled a strangled sound, but said nothing more.

"Truly, I wish you'd reconsider," Lily tried again. She did *not* relish the prospect of interviewing potential nannies for Chloe. She might spend weeks trying to find someone else. And she had a million other, more pressing, things to do than search for an appropriate companion for Chloe. "Let me talk to Mr. Kimball to see what kind of permanent future arrangements we can make," she said.

Mrs. Puddleduck hesitated in her packing. "I'm assuming you mean permanent future *financial* arrangements?"

"Of course," Lily assured her.

"Significant ones?"

"Well, you are already earning far more than the average nanny. Let's not get greedy."

The other woman spun around and thrust her fists upon her ample hips. "I am *not* greedy," she said. "And Chloe is *not* a nanny's typical charge. The girl is a menace."

"But a gifted menace," Lily reminded her.

"Nevertheless, if Mr. Kimball wants me to continue working with her, he's going to have to make it worth my while. Call it hazardous duty pay, if you want. Because that's exactly what it will be. That girl needs a drill instructor, not a nanny."

"Well, I do appreciate all the work you've put in with Chloe," Lily said. "I know it hasn't been easy."

That strangled sound erupted from the nanny again, then she said, "You might want to tell that to Mr. Kimball. And don't forget to include the part about me deserving a bonus. A *big* bonus."

"I'll do my best," Lily told her, "but you know how Mr. Kimball feels about bonuses."

Mrs. Puddleduck's expression pretty much illustrated her feelings without a word spoken. Which was just as well, Lily thought, because that kind of language really wasn't appropriate coming out of the mouth of a nanny.

Lily sighed. "I'll see what I can do about increasing your salary. And your bonus, as well," she added when she saw the other woman open her mouth to remind her.

"I'll give him one week to . . . you know . . . see to my needs," the nanny stated quite forcefully. Then she stared down at her half-filled suitcase with what was obviously *much* regret. "I need a drink," she muttered. And before Lily had a chance to object—happy hour didn't begin until six o'clock, after all—the other woman had left the room.

Oh, well, she tried to console herself. At least she had managed to keep Mrs. Puddleduck from joining the ranks of Chloe Sandusky's former nannies—a place in dire need of a twelve-step recovery program if ever there was one. She only prayed that she would be able to talk Schuyler into opening his tight fist long enough to eke out a few more dollars per week for the woman.

"What was that all about?"

Lily started at the question. Until Mr. Freiberger had uttered it, she had forgotten he was there. Well, almost forgotten, anyway. There was that small matter of his forearms having totally consumed her thoughts. She turned to look at him, only to find him standing with his weight rested on one foot, his hands hooked loosely on his hips, his intense scrutiny warming parts of her body that really had no business warming in polite company. Oh, and she also noticed that his forearms were still way too sexy.

"That," she said, "was just the latest in a series of troubling developments here at Ashling."

"I see," he said. "And who exactly is Chloe? Other than a juvenile delinquent, I mean?"

Lily supposed that if he were going to be working at Ashling for any length of time, he was going to have to be made aware of Chloe's existence sooner or later. Doubtless, there was some kind of OSHA regulation about such a thing.

She opened her mouth to explain, but the words didn't quite make it out because she was too busy studying the changes in Mr. Freiberger. With his dweeby jacket gone and his ugly necktie all askew like that, he looked quite fetching. His hair was rumpled in a way that was almost sexy, as if some woman had been clutching great handfuls of it in her fingers while he buried his head between her—

Goodness, but that was an uncharacteristically lascivious thought she was having. Lily's eyes widened in shock as the graphic image materialized in her brain, but no amount of coaxing would roust it. She shook her head once to clear it, but unfortunately, the image of Mr. Freiberger, um, doing that . . . to her . . . came bouncing right back to the forefront of her brain again. She swallowed with some difficulty and made a mental note to have a date with someone. Anyone. Soon.

"Chloe is Mr. Kimball's ward," she said, telling herself she must have imagined the huskiness her voice seemed to have suddenly adopted.

"His ward?" Mr. Freiberger echoed doubtfully.

But Lily wasn't going to offer up specifics of the arrangement to a total stranger, so she only reiterated, "Yes, his ward."

"What? You mean like Batman and Robin?"

She narrowed her eyes at him in confusion. "Batman and Robin?"

He nodded. "Yeah, you know. Like Bruce Wayne's young ward, Dick Grayson?"

Lily shook her head. "No. To the best of my knowledge, Mr. Kimball and Chloe have never donned Spandex and fled from a secret underground entrance to Ashling in a re-engineered Pontiac to rid Gotham City of its unsavory elements."

Leonard Freiberger offered her a look that was less than tolerant. But he said nothing.

"Actually," she told him, spurred by his silence, "the situation is more like *Jane Eyre*."

"Come again?"

"You know," Lily went on, "the part about Mr. Rochester's ward being the offspring of a French opera girl? Only with Chloe, her mother wasn't a French opera girl. She was a, uh, a cabaret dancer. But she was originally from Versailles, Indiana, for what it's worth."

Mr. Freiberger's eyebrows shot up at that. "You mean she was a stripper?"

Lily suddenly wondered if she was due for a manicure, and dropped her gaze to the backs of her hands. "Yes, I believe that is, in fact, what they're called in this country."

"So Chloe is Mr. Kimball's illegitimate daughter by a stripper from Indiana?"

Lily continued to study her left cuticles. "Well, I never said *that*."

"You didn't have to."

"I didn't?"

"It was that *Jane Eyre* reference that did it. Just because I'm a bookkeeper, Miss Rigby, doesn't mean I haven't read books."

She glanced up at that, only to find that Mr. Freiberger was glaring at her. "I didn't mean to imply that—"

"Chloe's secret is safe with me," he interrupted her. "If that's what you were worried about. The last thing a fourteen-year-old girl needs is to have talk like that circulating about her."

Actually, talk like that was the least of Chloe's worries, Lily thought. But there was no reason to tell Mr. Freiberger about all that. "Thank you for your discretion," she said instead.

"How long has she been living here?"

Lily couldn't imagine why he would be interested in such a thing, but she told him, "About a year and a half now."

He nodded slowly, and she got the feeling it was because he was thinking hard about something. And although she was reluctant to interrupt him, it suddenly occurred to her that the two of them were alone in Mrs. Puddleduck's room, and his forearms really were quite, quite sexy, and she hadn't had a date in quite, quite some time, so it would probably be better for them to retreat to their previous positions pronto, mainly because Schuyler's office and the kitchen were in two separate wings of the house, and at the moment, Lily felt an intense need to be far, far away from Mr. Freiberger and his forearms.

So she said, "Would you like to come to the kitchen for a cup of tea?"

Thankfully—at least, she *tried* to convince herself that she was thankful of the fact—Mr. Freiberger declined her invitation. "Thank you, Miss Rigby, but I really should go back to my work. I was right in the middle of something very interesting when I heard Mrs. Puddleduck scream."

Lily nodded. "Some other time then."

He dipped his head forward a bit in acknowledgment. "I think I'd like that."

A whiff of formaldehyde reminded her that there was one last matter to which she needed to attend. After glancing briefly over her shoulder, she said, "I'll, uh, I'll have Mr. Tooley, the groundskeeper, see to the, uh, the spleen. Perhaps he could put it in the compost bin. I'll need to order a new mattress, as well." Until then, she thought, the nanny could claim one of the guest rooms.

"Disposing of the evidence?" Mr. Freiberger asked. The look on his face suggested that he was only half-joking.

Lily expelled a restless breath. "Look, I won't lie to you. Chloe is more than a handful. But deep down, she is a good kid. She's just had some rough breaks, you know?"

"What kind of rough breaks?"

Unwilling to divulge the particulars of Chloe's young life to a man she'd just met—after all, even juvenile delinquents were entitled to some privacy—Lily only said, "Let's just say she has a lot of issues to work out, shall we? Despite what Mrs. Puddleduck said, Chloe's not dangerous."

If nothing else, Lily was certain about that. Even after a life fraught with insecurity, instability, and perhaps even subtle abuse, Chloe Sandusky was, in essence, a good kid. She was just crying out for attention, and, as a gifted child—as an *extremely* gifted child, Lily amended—she was simply much more effective than other kids at going about such a thing.

"I'll hold you to that," Mr. Freiberger said.

Oh, goody, Lily thought. And then maybe he'd hold her to himself.

She bit back a sigh at the thought and extended her arm toward the door, indicating he should precede her. But he only smiled and mimicked her gesture, suggesting that she should go first instead. So Lily strode forward with the bookkeeper right behind her. And, with no small effort, she somehow managed to keep from following him when they parted ways at the foot of the stairs. Instead, with a brief nod to his forearms—uh, to him—she returned to her cold tea, and warm thoughts, in the kitchen alone.

FOUR

At the foot of the stairs, Leo kept his gaze trained on Lily Rigby until she was completely out of sight. Not so much because he didn't trust her, but because she had a way of walking that a man simply could not ignore. Yeah, a walk that could start fights and stop traffic, no doubt about it. And he just didn't see any reason to deny himself the simple pleasure of watching her.

In that snug skirt and those smoky stockings, she was, in a word, *very hot*. Okay, so that was two words. One word just wasn't enough for a woman like that. A woman who, one minute, was throwing looks his way that would outgun a flame-thrower, then the next minute was unflinchingly inspecting a pig's spleen, then the next minute was coming to the defense of a young girl who obviously had some serious problems. *Issues*, Lily Rigby had called them. *Felonies* was probably more like it.

And then another thought struck him when he recalled Miss Rigby's revelation that Kimball's young ward had been at Ashling for about a year and a half. That meant the industrious Chloe had come to live here right around the beginning of last

fiscal year. And if Miss Rigby was to be believed—
something on which Leo's mental jury was still definitely *out*—then the troubled Chloe was also a
gifted child.

Well, my, my, my, he pondered as he forced his
feet to move in the direction of Schuyler Kimball's
office. Presuming that the girl's gifts weren't homicidal in nature, or spawned by a chemical imbal-
ance in the brain, then Kimball's ward might
warrant a bit of investigation herself. Just what
were they teaching kids in computer science class
these days anyway? Seeing as how he hadn't uncovered much of anything else so far today, maybe
he'd just try a new tack and see where it led him.

Leo made his way quickly back to Kimball's office—well, as quickly as he could, considering the
fact that Kimball's house was roughly the size of
Rhode Island—and rifled through his briefcase until he located his telephone directory. Then, snatch-
ing up the phone, he dialed his good buddy Eddie
Dolan, a man who was connected in ways that no
one operating within the parameters of the American justice system ought to ponder. Eddie Dolan,
who could find out anything about anybody . . . for
a pretty hefty fee.

Good thing Eddie owed Leo a big favor. Normally, he'd never be able to afford the price Eddie's
superiors charged, which generally consisted of
five figures. Or a selected body part. Depending on
one's relationship with the guy and his . . . employers. Not to mention the size of one's debt.

The phone rang a good half dozen times before
being picked up at the other end, and then a few
more moments passed before a gravely voice muttered in greeting, "Whattaya want?"

"Whoa, Eddie, have you been reading Martha

Stewart books again?" Leo asked. "Your telephone etiquette has come a long, long way."

There was another moment of silence in which Leo envisioned Eddie squinting blearily at the phone as he tried to figure out just where the hell he'd woken up anyway. People who did their business during the hours when most people—people who *weren't* involved in questionable lifestyles— were sleeping, tended to be pretty sleepy and incoherent at . . . Leo glanced down at his watch. Oh, say, three o'clock in the afternoon.

Finally, though, Eddie's voice sounded from the other end of the line. "Leo?" he grumbled. "That you?"

"Yeah, it's me."

"Whattaya want?"

Leo chuckled. "I need some information about some people."

"What people?"

"Schuyler Kimball, his immediate family, and the various and sundry persons he has working for him at his estate."

"Ooo, well, la-di-da," the other man replied. "And what is it you want to know about His Highness, the King of Kimball and all his royal subjects?"

"I'll take whatever you can get," Leo told him.

"That means you want me to get all the dirty, lowdown, under-the-rug stuff you couldn't get on your own, being the upright, forthright, do-right kinda guy that you are. Right?"

"Right."

He heard the other man sigh heavily at the other end. "Well, you know, Leo, that kinda information isn't easy to come by. I might hafta rough somebody up."

" 'Rough somebody up'?" Leo repeated dubiously. "You couldn't rough somebody up if your life depended on it. You always get roughed up yourself before you can get your licks in."

"It's still gonna cost ya," the other man said, ignoring Leo's remark. "I can give you the friends and family rate, naturally, but it's still gonna be expensive."

"Nuh-uh," Leo said. "No way. You owe me, pal. Big time. And I'm collecting."

"I owe *you*?" Eddie asked, his voice tinted with confusion. "For what?"

Leo smiled. Okay, so it had been seven years ago. But he was sure the incident was still quite fresh in Eddie's memory. And it would only take two words to bring those recollections to the fore. "Walla Walla," he said.

At the other end of the line, there erupted a feral growl of discontent. "Oh, *man*. You're not gonna bring that up again, are you?"

Leo expelled an incredulous sound. "*Again*?" he echoed. "What do you mean again? I haven't brought it up since it happened. Hell, I wish I could forget it happened. You're the one who always wants to relive the incident every time you cuddle up with Jack Daniels. And, yeah, you're damned right I'm going to bring it up," he added, picking up steam. "I nearly got my butt shot off that night. And for what? Because you couldn't keep it zipped."

"Hey, Leo, she was a beautiful woman," Eddie pointed out.

"She was also a *married* woman."

"Yeah, well, we all have our little idiosyncrasies."

"Eddie," Leo said, striving for patience. "Being married to a mob boss is *not* an idiosyncrasy. It's a terminal condition, often fatal."

"Yeah, yeah, yeah, so you've said. About a million times." He hesitated a telling moment before adding in a voice rife with lasciviousness, "You know, she still calls me sometimes."

Leo shook his head. "Like I said. Terminal. *Fatal.* You better watch yourself, pal."

"Oh, sure," Eddie replied. "At least until I even things up between us, right?"

"Right."

"Okay, fine," the other man relented. "Tell me what you need, and I'll get back to you when I can. And then we'll be square, got it?"

"Got it. I need everything you can find," Leo told him frankly. "Everything on everybody."

"Gotcha."

"And call me at home when you get it, okay? I'm going to be out of the office for a while."

"No problem. Gimme a coupla three days or so. I'll be in touch."

Leo dropped the phone receiver into its cradle, then spun back around in his chair to face the computer. He nearly leapt out of his seat, however, when he realized he wasn't alone in Kimball's office. A tall, willowy, attractive brunette with wide blue eyes had joined him at some point. She was wearing a pale, whispery, flowered dress, dainty white gloves, a ridiculously large straw hat, and a very suspicious expression.

"Uh, hi," he said in greeting, wondering how long she'd been standing there.

"Hello," she responded in a voice that was as pale and whispery as her dress. But she said nothing more.

Leo arched his brows in silent inquiry, and when she continued to remain silent, he asked, "Uh . . . can I help you?"

The woman shook her head, then turned sideways, lifting her chin and closing her eyes to strike as melodramatic a pose as was ever struck. "No. I'm afraid no one can help me," she told him. "But thank you for asking."

"You're welcome," he replied automatically.

She turned her head again then, and opened one eye just enough to study him, with an intensity that made Leo more than a little uncomfortable. And all the while, she kept her thoughts to herself, whatever they might be. He was struggling to think of something to say himself, something that might either generate conversation or, better still, make her go away, when she finally lowered her head, opened her other eye, and parted her lips, as if she were about to speak.

But another few moments passed before she finally asked, "Do you know what the word 'didactic' means?"

As questions went, it wasn't one Leo heard often, nor was it the traditional ice-breaker for conversation. Nevertheless, he answered, a bit cautiously, "Uh . . . It generally describes something which offers instruction, right?"

She expelled a sigh of clear disappointment. "Yes, that's right," she answered sharply, as if angry that he'd been correct. Then, brightening some, she asked further, "Can you spell it?"

Again, the question wasn't exactly a standard one for two people who had just met, but he found himself stating, without hesitation, "D-i-d-a-c-t-i-c?"

Her mouth formed a disgruntled moue. "How about the word 'quisling'?"

Leo gazed back at her in silence, suddenly wanting to ask a few questions of his own. But all that emerged when he spoke was, "You want the definition or the spelling of 'quisling'?"

Once again, she lifted her chin a fraction, as if in challenge. "Both," she stated in a voice that suggested she didn't think he was up to either task. Then, to emphasize just that, she added in a voice tinted with haughtiness, "*If* you think you can manage it."

Leo's back went up at the very idea. As if. "Okay. Quisling. Q-u-i-s-l-i-n-g. Noun. One who betrays his country by aiding its hostile occupants." Somehow, he managed to refrain from sticking out his tongue and concluding with a snotty, *So there*.

The woman narrowed her eyes at him suspiciously. "What's your IQ?" she asked warily.

Some of the snottiness crept out anyway when Leo replied readily, "A hundred and forty-two. What's *yours*?"

But instead of answering his question, the woman let her entire body go limp, and she expelled a very loud, very rude, sound of disgust. "Oh, *great*," she muttered, rolling her eyes heavenward. "Terrific. Another one. Well that's just *fine*."

Then she spun around on her heel, and with pale, whispery sounds, strode quickly out the door. She was some distance down the hall when Leo heard her call out further, "Mother! There's another one in the house! Would you *please* talk to Schuyler about this?"

The sister, Leo realized. Jane Kimball. He should have figured that out right off, as she bore a strong physical resemblance to her brother. And if rumors were to be believed, she shared his eccentric behavior, as well. As far as Kimball's renowned super-genius intellect, however . . .

Well, suffice it to say that that particular matter was still in question.

Leo wondered again how much of his conversation with Eddie she'd overheard, then decided she must have come in on the tail end of things and missed out on the specifics. Which was good. Because he didn't want anything to prevent Eddie from completing his search. Hey, if Leo's experiences today were any indication, the results would provide some kind of interesting story, he was sure.

Shaking his head at what was promising to be a very strange reality, Leo went back to work.

His day brightened considerably a little later, when he heard a soft knock at the door. It was followed by the appearance of Miss Rigby, who entered Kimball's office looking as cool and elegant— and as hot and sexy—as ever. She was also, he noted with no small amount of distraction, carrying a silver tray laden with all kinds of fragile china . . . tea . . . stuff.

"Four o'clock," she said as she entered. "Tea time. Would you care to join me, Mr. Freiberger? I brought coffee, as well, if you'd prefer that instead. And there's more than enough for two. I just think it makes the day so much more enjoyable if one can take a little break from one's work in the afternoon, don't you?"

Tea time, he repeated to himself. Now there was an activity he'd indulged in exactly zero times in his entire life. He eyed the delicate tea cups, rimmed in gold and painted with red and yellow roses, and he wondered if he would have to undergo hormone-replacement therapy if he picked one up in his bare hand. Because surely it was detrimental to a man's testosterone to come into contact with something like that, wasn't it?

In spite of his misgivings, however, he replied,

"I'd be delighted, Miss Rigby. A break would be very welcome. Thank you for thinking about me."

She smiled becomingly as she placed the tray on Kimball's desk and went about rearranging things more conveniently. The little teacups sat on little saucers with little spoons, and beside them were little plates hosting little sandwiches and little cookies. It was all so . . . *dainty*, Leo thought, squelching a vague shudder of distaste. He must really be consumed by lust for Miss Rigby if he'd go to such extremes just to spend a little time in her presence.

And if this was the way he was behaving on day one, then God alone knew what he'd be reduced to in a week's time. He'd probably end up alongside her in the kitchen, cutting the crusts off those little sandwiches, and wearing an apron with cats on it.

"Coffee, definitely," he said adamantly.

She flinched a bit at his order, and he realized he must have spoken more loudly and forcefully than was necessary. Before he could explain or apologize, however, she finished pouring and asked, "Would you care for cream or sugar?"

"No, just black," he stated proudly for the benefit of his testosterone.

When she extended the cup toward him, though, he hesitated a moment before taking it, then switched it from one hand to the other as he tried to figure out just how to hold the damned thing. Ultimately, he set both cup and saucer down on the desk, telling himself it needed to cool. Then he launched himself into a much-needed stretch, arching his back and curling his arms upward, flexing everything he needed to flex after spending hours in a chair that had been adjusted to the body specifications of someone else.

Oh, *boy*, that felt good.

Evidently, Miss Rigby thought so, too, because as he completed the action, Leo heard her utter a sigh of contentment much like his own. He snapped his gaze to her face when she did, but her expression belied nothing of what she might be thinking. Instead, she appeared to be even more indifferent than usual as she lifted her cup to her lips for an idle sip, and he figured he must have just imagined that soft sound of satisfaction.

"So . . ." she began slowly when she lowered the cup. "How's the search coming? Have you found the problem you were looking for?"

He shook his head. "Not even close. But that's not surprising. I was pretty much resigned to the fact that it could take several days. Possibly even several weeks, depending on the state of Mr. Kimball's files."

She sipped her tea again, then said mildly, "Mr. Kimball's files are a complete mess. You'll be lucky if you can find his sangria recipe in there."

Leo smiled confidently. "Oh, I bet I could find it."

She smiled indulgently in return. "Oh, I bet you couldn't."

He chuckled, then turned back to the computer. In less than five minutes, he had pulled up a screen. "One three-liter box of cheap red burgundy," he began. "One liter citrus soda, one can frozen peach juice concentrate, juice from one jar maraschino cherries—add cherries, too . . ."

Miss Rigby jumped up from where she had perched herself on the edge of the desk and rounded the big piece of furniture until she stood behind Leo. "How did you find that?" she demanded. "I've practically turned the computer upside down looking for that recipe."

He glanced over his shoulder at her and grinned cockily. "Well, Miss Rigby, I'm just that good."

The look she gave him in response struck him as odd. For some reason, she seemed worried about something. Certainly his comment could have been taken as sexually suggestive—and, naturally, that was the way he had intended it—but still. She didn't have to look *that* anxious.

Her lips parted fractionally, as if she were about to put voice to her concerns, but all she said was, "Quick, print it up. I'm hosting my garden club next weekend."

He pushed the print button, and immediately, the laser printer hummed with activity. Miss Rigby set her tea down on Kimball's desk and went to retrieve her prize, but her expression, as she scanned the recipe, still seemed significantly worried.

"Is there a problem, Miss Rigby?" Leo asked, curious about her reaction.

For a moment, he didn't think she'd heard him, then she jerked her head up and looked at him. "What? Oh. No, no, there's no problem at all." Her face cleared then of its clouds, and she smiled, but somehow the gesture seemed forced. "I'm just trying to remember if we have any maraschino cherries, that's all."

Somehow, Leo doubted that was really what was on her mind at the moment. After all, what kind of self-respecting billionaire would run out of maraschino cherries? It was unheard of. No, he'd wager that Miss Rigby's apprehension came from something else entirely, something that had nothing to do with sangria.

"Can I—" he began.

"Have a cookie? Why certainly, Mr. Freiberger," she cut him off. She circled the desk again and reached for the plate where someone had artfully arranged a half-dozen different varieties of baked goods. "Mrs. Kaiser is particularly proud of her springerlies," she said as she extended the plate toward Leo. "I'm sure you'll love them."

Hoo-kay, he thought. It didn't take a genius to figure out that she wanted to change the subject. And speaking of geniuses, that reminded him of something he wanted to ask her about.

"So what's the deal with Mr. Kimball's sister and IQs?" he asked as he closed the program housing the billionaire's sangria recipe and reached for a cookie.

Miss Rigby chuckled. "You've met Janey, then, have you?"

He nodded. "A little while ago. She gave me a spelling test."

The secretary perched herself on the edge of Kimball's desk, a posture that resulted in the hem of her already short skirt shrinking even more. Somehow, he suspected the gesture was deliberate, that by revealing a little extra thigh, Miss Rigby was hoping she might make him forget all about her odd reaction to the sangria recipe.

As far as Leo was concerned, she succeeded. Really, really well.

"Did you pass the exam?" she asked.

"Of course," he told her, reaching for his coffee again, but keeping his gaze trained on the smooth skin of her thigh. Wow.

"Janey suffers from second child syndrome," Miss Rigby said after sipping her tea. "And when the first child is someone like Schuyler, well ... Needless to say, Janey was somewhat overlooked in her youth. Not only was Schuyler a hellion, but her IQ, you see, is terribly, *terribly*, just above average, something that didn't alarm her teachers or her mother into taking drastic measures with her."

"And what's so terrible, *terrible*, about being just above average?" Leo asked. Frankly, there had been times when he was growing up that he would just as soon have been terribly, terribly just above average himself. It would have made things a hell of a lot simpler. For everybody.

"Absolutely nothing," the secretary said, reaching for a cookie that was—somehow he contained his shudder of disgust—pink. "But Janey seems to feel diminished by it. She's the only one in the family who doesn't rank genius, and it bothers her enormously. Even Schuyler's mother, for all her . . . eccentricities—"

"Eccentricities?" he interjected. "What kind of eccentricities?" This ought to be good.

Miss Rigby sipped her tea. "Well, for example, right now, Miranda is in her room having tea, too, except that her companion is much less, um . . . substantial than my own tea companion is."

"Substantial?" Leo asked curiously, not certain he liked the sound of that.

But Miss Rigby only nodded without elaboration.

"As in . . . skinny?" he asked.

This time she shook her head. "As in . . . not there."

"Not there?"

She sighed fitfully. "Well, all right, if you must know, she's having her tea with Hedy Lamar."

"Oh."

"At any rate," Miss Rigby hurried on, "in spite of that, Miranda Kimball is, in fact, a card-carrying member of Mensa. Mensa just doesn't like to advertise the fact, that's all."

Leo nodded, but his thoughts circled back to Janey Kimball instead of her mother. His own brothers had certainly used his accelerated IQ as an excuse to beat the hell out of him on more than one occasion. Oh, but only in the nicest possible way, naturally, and only for his own good, and only because they loved him so much. Their animosity had only been compounded when Leo wound up being the first—and so far, only—Friday who had attended college, and that was only because he'd earned full scholarship privileges, and *that* was only because of his stratospheric test scores.

The rest of the family—except for his mother, of course—had always kept their distance from Leo in one way or another, simply because he wasn't much like the rest of them. This in spite of all his efforts to fit in, efforts which had, one after another, backfired bigtime. Still, he thought, of all the things that might cause alienation among family members, smarts wasn't a very bright one.

And speaking of not very bright, that reminded him of something else he wanted to ask her about.

"And just what, exactly, is it that *you* do for Mr. Kimball, Miss Rigby?" he asked, voicing what was really uppermost in his thoughts today. "Aside from stealing his sangria recipe, I mean."

She had bitten into the pink cookie, but gagged a little as he completed his question. The gag, however, resulted in a gasp, the gasp segued into a cough, and the cough turned into a full-blown dry hack. With no small effort, she reached for her tea and downed a hefty swallow in an effort to halt what was fast becoming a serious respiratory failure.

Okay, Leo was fully aware that he made women nervous sometimes. He was bigger than the average guy, and, all modesty aside, not a bad-looking sort. It wasn't unusual for a woman to react to him with some degree of attraction, mixed with a healthy dose of wariness. But he couldn't ever recall making one gag and hack until tears squeezed from her eyes.

"Miss Rigby?" he asked, standing. He reached across the desk and opened his hand over her back to give her an idle pat.

But instead of helping, the action only seemed to increase her discomfort, because she jumped up from the desk and took a few steps backward in retreat. Holding up one hand palm out in surrender, she enjoyed another healthy sip from her tea. Gradually, she got her coughing under control, then she dragged a finger beneath each eye to swipe away the moisture that had collected there.

"I'm sorry," she mumbled roughly. "I . . . That bite just went down the wrong way."

"Boy, I'll say it did."

She cleared her throat one last time, then returned to her seat on the desk. This time, however, she tugged her skirt down before sitting.

"I'm, uh . . . I'm Mr. Kimball's social secretary," she said, her voice still a little ragged from all the coughing. "I'm sorry. Didn't I tell you that earlier? I could have sworn that I did."

"Oh, you told me your title," he said. "I just wasn't sure what all that involved. Why a social secretary would be any different from a regular secretary and everything." He sipped his coffee and waited for a reply. When he didn't receive one, he added, "I mean, just how many *secretaries* does a man need, you know?"

Lily eyed Mr. Freiberger with what she hoped was a benign expression. However, benign was the last thing she felt at the moment. For one thing, considering his aptitude in finding Schuyler's top secret sangria recipe a few minutes ago, this man was obviously no ordinary lowly bookkeeper. He clearly knew his way around a computer better than the average pencil pusher. She'd spent the better part of the summer trying to figure out where Schuyler had hidden that recipe, and she'd never been able to find it.

Of course, neither had Schuyler, when she'd asked him to locate it, but that wasn't saying much. Schuyler frequently misplaced his files, especially the really important ones. In fact, his master's thesis from college was still out there in cyberspace somewhere, where he had accidentally jettisoned it shortly after completing it—he had been trying to access an adult-oriented bulletin board at the time. Fortunately, Lily had had the foresight to store the work on diskette before allowing Schuyler use of the modem. For someone who was so astoundingly brilliant, Schuyler Kimball had absolutely no idea how to get around a basic home computer.

But there was more than Mr. Freiberger's amazing facility with computers that bothered Lily. She still couldn't shake the feeling that he wasn't presenting himself in a way that was particularly, oh . . . honest. His frumpy awkwardness had only lasted as long as it had taken him to overrun Schuyler's office, and now, suddenly, he was like a man who was in total control. Of his professional role, of his thoughts, of his surroundings. Somehow Lily couldn't quite put aside the sensation that he was trying to overrun her, too.

But what was genuinely mind-boggling was that, truth be told, she really wouldn't mind being overrun by the man. And that, furthermore, she kind of wanted to overrun him in return. It made no sense. Certainly she had experienced immediate attractions to men before, and she'd enjoyed one or two intimate relationships in her life. But those relationships had come about *after* she'd gotten to know the men in question, not the moment she had opened the door to them. She didn't know the first thing about Leonard Freiberger, except that she didn't think he was being honest about something. Yet she found herself responding to him on a level that was anything but professional.

And now he was asking the oddest questions. Wanting to know the most unusual things. Giving her looks that went well beyond suspicious and into outright accusation. What on earth was going on?

When she remembered that he was still awaiting a response to his question about what she did for Schuyler—and how could he have possibly made such an inquiry sound so blatantly sexual?—she lifted one shoulder and let it drop in what she hoped looked like a careless gesture. Even though careless was the last thing she felt at the moment.

"I run things for Mr. Kimball here," she said simply. "I keep things organized, keep track of what needs to be taken care of. Although he also has a secretary at his office who attends to the things that come up there, I make sure that all the things that need to get done here at Ashling do in fact get done. And sometimes, when it's needed, elsewhere."

"Elsewhere?"

"At Mr. Kimball's other residences," she clarified. "As I mentioned, I do travel with him from time to time. This time of year, however, with the holidays coming up, I tend to keep close to Ashling."

"Mr. Kimball celebrates in a big way, does he?"

"You could say that."

"Lots of parties?"

"Well, lots of guests," she said, evading the question.

"And just how did you . . . oh . . . get this position with Mr. Kimball?"

Once again, he'd made a simple word like *position* sound sexually charged, and it finally, finally hit Lily that Mr. Freiberger thought she played a much different role in Schuyler's life than social secretary. She almost laughed out loud at the suggestion, so appropriate was it in its own strange way. Still, she supposed that the kind thing to do would be to set him straight. Well, straighter, anyway. There was no reason to tell him the entire truth. It would only serve to get her into trouble.

"Mr. Kimball and I have known each other for some time," she began. "Since college, in fact. I met him, oh, let me think . . . It was twelve years ago, I guess. I was nineteen at the time, trying to beat the Xerox machine in the school library into submission because it had stolen my fifteen cents. Schuyler came up behind me and fixed it in a snap. I was immediately taken with him. He's a very arresting individual on first contact. And, naturally, I was impressed by how mechanically capable he was."

"Oh, I bet that was what impressed you."

She narrowed her eyes at Mr. Freiberger's tone of voice. But his expression was completely impassive, so she had no idea if he had just made a disparaging comment or not. Deciding to give him the benefit of the doubt—for now—she continued.

"We remained friendly throughout college—"

"Oh, I'll bet you did."

"—and when he started up his business," she continued crisply, pretending—but not very hard—that she hadn't heard his comment, "Schuyler was nice enough to offer me a position."

"A really interesting position, too, I imagine."

"And since I had few other prospects at that point," Lily continued on valiantly through gritted teeth, "I was happy to take him up on his offer."

"And what an offer it must have been."

There, she was finished. And she congratulated herself for not slapping Mr. Freiberger silly during all his adolescent commentary. She'd explained her history with Schuyler all nice and simple and to the point, *and* she'd done it truthfully. She was rather proud of herself for that. Well, pretty truthfully, she amended. She may have left out one or two little things. But she'd covered all the major points. Well, most of the major points, anyway.

Before Mr. Freiberger could demand a more thorough explanation, not to mention ask her another question she really didn't want to answer, Lily leapt up from the desk again.

"And speaking of my work for Mr. Kimball," she said, "I really should be getting back to it. I'll be happy to leave the tea things here for you, if you think you'll be wanting more."

"Oh, I'll definitely be wanting more, Miss Rigby."

There it was *again*, she thought. That tone of voice that let her know he was talking about something significantly different from what she was talking about herself.

But all she said in response was, "Fine. Then I'll just . . . leave these here, shall I?"

"Fine."

She turned to go, but something made her hesitate. Not that Mr. Freiberger said anything that might have halted her progress, but she sensed somehow that whatever business the two of them had was by no means finished. So she pivoted easily around again to face him, and wasn't exactly surprised to see him lift his gaze from where it had been—right at fanny level.

"Was there something else?" she asked.

He shook his head slowly, his expression a complete blank. "Why no, Miss Rigby. Not today. Did I give you the impression that there *would* be something else?"

She opened her mouth to respond, then decided she'd be better off if she kept quiet. So with a silent shake of her head, she turned again and made her way out of Schuyler's office. Somehow, though, she was beginning to suspect that Mr. Freiberger's stay at Ashling was going to result in a lot more than a simple discovery of some minor income tax infraction. And furthermore, somehow, she got the distinct impression that income taxes were the last thing he'd come to investigate anyway.

She only wished she could figure out what it was, exactly, that he *was* looking for. And she wondered if she should alert Schuyler to the fact that there was something funny going on. Immediately, she dismissed the idea. Schuyler would tell her she was being silly. And, perhaps, she was. In many ways, he had always known her better than she knew herself.

Even when the two of them had been students, Lily had known, as had everyone else who had ever come into contact with him, that Schuyler Kimball wasn't normal, that he knew things, could see things, could understand things, that no normal human being would be able to process. His IQ was off the charts, his brilliant mind the eighth wonder of the modern world. Only one thing had ever even come close to equaling it—his ambition. These days, people referred to Schuyler as *driven*. As a student, however, he'd been *consumed*.

As a student, he'd also been very poor. Then again, so had Lily. Back then, neither of them had been able to afford any more than the basic necessities of life, and often, they'd gone without even those. In fact, their shared poverty had probably been what had initially bonded them so quickly, even though it was something else entirely that fueled their friendship today.

But by the time Lily had met him, poverty had been a constant companion of Schuyler's, from the day he was born. She, on the other hand, had enjoyed all the benefits of excessive wealth until shortly after her sixteenth birthday, when her father's business had failed—miserably—and the Main Line Rigbys had lost everything. She and Schuyler had often joked about how they'd both come from entirely different backgrounds only to end up in exactly the same place—with less dollars than sense.

In spite of that—or, perhaps, because of it—he had always placed infinitely more importance on money than she ever had. He had determined early on that he would make a fortune someday that was truly obscene, and that he would spend it entirely, frivolously, selfishly on himself. Lily, in turn, had pointed out that the billions he intended to keep as his own, the billions with which he intended to indulge himself so shamelessly, could instead be used to feed and clothe and make warm people who needed and deserved it far more than he did. But whenever she reminded him of that fact, Schuyler had always scoffed at her, had always responded the same way.

"Lily. Darling," he had always said on those occasions. "Someday, if someone puts billions of dollars into your hands, then you can take it and spend it on all the bleeding-heart social programs you want to spend it on. But until that day comes . . ." He had always left his statement unfinished, his meaning clear.

And always, in response, Lily had offered up the

same reply. "Fine, Schuyler," she had always told
him then. "Someday, if someone puts billions of
dollars into my hands, then maybe I'll do exactly
that."

Her steps slowed as she thought again about
Leonard Freiberger and the work he claimed to be
doing here at Ashling. And for just the briefest,
slightest, most faltering moment, something else to
worry about nudged its way into her brain. And
for that moment, Lily wavered a bit in her conviction.

No, she finally decided. Mr. Freiberger would
never uncover all of that. Although she still questioned his reasons for being at Ashling, whatever
he was up to, Lily could handle him.

FIVE

Although he would have sworn such a thing would be impossible, Leo's second day at Ashling turned out to be even stranger than the first. Not just because he was slowly coming to realize that Schuyler Kimball's files were, as Miss Rigby had readily assured him, a mess—even for an eccentric billionaire—but because Leo met the rest of Kimball's family and constituents, starting with the illustrious, the mysterious, the felonious . . . Chloe.

"I'm up!" a female voice shouted from outside Kimball's office as Leo struggled to break into one of the billionaire's many booby-trapped personal files. "Lily?" the girl continued, her voice moving into double-digit decibels. "Did you hear me? I said I'm *up!*"

She rounded the office door just as she shrieked out that last bit, coming uncomfortably close to shattering Leo's eardrums. The potential loss of hearing, however, didn't concern him nearly as much as the prospect of being arrested did. Arrested for the crime of . . . of . . . of being in a room with a minor who wasn't dressed the way a minor should be when she was in a room with a man who wasn't a minor.

Or something like that.

Because Chloe, in addition to being all the other things Leo had begun to suspect she was, was also, evidently, an exhibitionist. Fourteen, he reminded himself as he took in her attire. She was only fourteen years old. That didn't stop her from dressing like a Frederick's of Hollywood model, though. Or perhaps, more accurately, *un*dressing like one.

Normally, Leo would consider something like red vinyl, platform thigh boots to be pretty much the focal point of a woman's ensemble. Unless, of course, they were paired with the other thing that Chloe—almost—had on. What appeared to be a dress was made—sort of—from something brief and purple that looked like what Leo's sister called crochet. From waist to neckline, the garment *should* have been laced up the middle with red satin ribbons, but Chloe had evidently gotten bored with that particular chore before completing it. Because the laces hung free, the dress open, well below the neck.

But Leo barely noticed that particular aspect of her attire, because the moment he realized it, he jerked his gaze back up to the girl's face. Unfortunately, moving his gaze to her face made him no less uncomfortable. Because Chloe, he realized much to his distaste, was into that body piercing thing. Big time. Each ear sported a good half dozen earrings . . . and things. A silver circle winked from her left nostril, a gold one from her right eyebrow. For a moment, he wondered why she hadn't bothered mutilating her lips, too, then he realized that they were probably too full to be pierced with anything smaller than a Hula-Hoop.

Her hair was an absolute riot of mahogany curls

that she clearly had trouble containing, and her face was obscured by far too much makeup— enough so that, had he not already been told she was fourteen, he would have sworn she was in her twenties. All in all, Chloe was absolutely nothing like he would expect a fourteen-year-old-girl to be. Unless, of course, she was involved in activities like, oh, say, leaving pigs' spleens on the beds of unsuspecting nannies.

She seemed to be as surprised by Leo's appearance as he was by hers, because she stopped dead in her tracks the moment she laid eyes on him, an expression of stark, raving terror overtaking her features. Before he had a chance to wonder why a girl who'd jabbed her own face repeatedly with sharp objects would be afraid of him, her fear evaporated, to be replaced by an attitude of . . . well, attitude.

"Who the hell are you?" she asked.

Nobody spoke to Leo with such utter disregard. Nobody. He rose from his seat behind Kimball's desk, flexed every muscle he possessed, and glared at her with all the lack of concern he could muster. It was a pose he'd affected many times with excellent results, always reducing his victim to full, blithering idiot status. Yet Chloe didn't so much as flinch. Amazing.

"So?" she spurred in a tone of voice one might use when addressing a cabbage.

"Fri . . . Freiberger," he said. "Leonard Freiberger." Then, showing her the same total disrespect she'd shown for him, he asked, "Who the hell are you?"

But instead of answering his question, she said, "No, I didn't mean who the hell are you. I meant, *who the hell are you*?"

Leo bit back a growl and reminded himself that

she was nothing more than a mouthy fourteen-year-old girl, and that he was, for all intents and purposes, nothing more than mousy little book-keeper Leonard Freiberger. And although Leo Friday wouldn't tolerate this kind of crap from some teenage girl—even if she did sport more hardware than Sears—Leonard probably would. So he forced himself to relax a little.

"I'm a bookkeeper for Kimball Technologies. And you are?" he tried again, already pretty certain of the answer he would receive. She had to be either Chloe or a harbinger of ill fortune. And his money was on the former. Pretty much.

"I'm Chloe," she said. "I'm Schuyler Kimball's *daughter*," she added in a voice that made clear she was in no way happy about that particular fact. "Not that he'll ever admit to it, the prick."

Having absolutely no idea how to respond to that, Leo chose to remain silent.

"Where's Lily?" Chloe asked. "What did you do to her?"

Not nearly everything I'd like to do, Leo thought. Aloud, he said, "I haven't done anything to her." *Yet.* "I don't know where she is."

"Well, when you see her, tell her I'm up."

He narrowed his eyes at the girl. "Up? Up where? In your room?"

She rolled her eyes in a manner he suspected was endemic to all fourteen-year-old girls, regardless of where they stuck their jewelry on their person. "Just tell her I went out, okay, Einstein? And that I'll be back whenever."

Enough was enough, Leo thought. Not even a mousy, little bookkeeper with a name like Leonard Freiberger would put up with this much crap. Unable to help himself, he snapped, "Hey, tell her yourself, Lolita. I'm busy."

"Yes, do tell me yourself," a third voice piped up.

Leo snapped his attention to the door, where Lily Rigby stood, her posture, if possible, even more menacing than young Chloe's. Her outfit today was as borderline professional as it had been the day before, her charcoal-colored skirt a little *too* fitted, topped by a berry-colored sweater set that was a little *too* clingy. Dressed as she was, with her hair wound up the back of her head again, she reminded Leo all too uncomfortably of Audrey Hepburn, for whom he had always harbored a major, *major* lustfest.

Tiny as she was—nearly a foot shorter than he, and certainly a good eighty or ninety pounds lighter—Miss Rigby was clearly a force to be reckoned with, something that Chloe seemed to realize immediately. Because as mouthy and militant as the girl had been to Leo, at the arrival of Schuyler Kimball's secretary, her posture became almost meek. Which was interesting, considering the fact that, even at fourteen, she, too, was taller than and outweighed Miss Rigby by a significant amount.

"Uh, hi, Lily," she said. But she dropped her gaze to the floor and didn't turn around.

Miss Rigby considered the girl in silence, seemingly oblivious to Leo, whom she had yet to acknowledge. She strode slowly and purposefully into the room, her attention focused intently on the young hooligan, her gaze sweeping up and down the girl's body with unmistakable disapproval.

"Don't you 'Hi, Lily' me, young lady. Just what do you think you're doing dressed like that?"

Chloe glanced down at her get-up, then back up at Miss Rigby, injecting a confidence into her posture that was dubious at best. "Me and Lauren are up, that's all," she said. "Not that it's any of your business."

Miss Rigby arched her eyebrows incredulously, her mouth dropping open at the slight. "I *beg* your pardon," she said in a clipped voice. "Don't you *dare* speak to me that way."

"Um, sorry," Chloe muttered, dropping her gaze again. And strangely, she did seem to be genuinely apologetic.

"You are not *up* today," the secretary answered imperiously.

God, Leo loved that tone of voice from a woman. It was just so cool, so commanding, so controlled. So *hot*. It made a man itch to say—or do—something that would shatter her self-control. Involuntarily, he reached up to loosen the tie at his throat, then remembered that he'd already done that earlier. So he inhaled as deeply and imperceptibly as possible to steady his pulse, releasing the breath on a slow, silent, not quite steady sigh.

"You are not *up* this week, for that matter," Miss Rigby continued in the same tone, still addressing Chloe, but sending Leo's pulse rate into triple digits. "You'll be lucky if you are *up* for the rest of this year after that little stunt you pulled over the weekend. And as far as Lauren is concerned . . . You know how I feel about that girl. She is *not* a good influence."

Oh, and God forbid someone who was as pure and untainted as Chloe obviously was should fall in with the wrong crowd, Leo thought. But he said nothing, only watched the by-play, impressed by Miss Rigby's success with the girl.

"In your room," she commanded. "Now."

"But, Lily," Chloe whined.

Miss Rigby steeled herself for battle, and through gritted teeth, stated without so much as a hint of doubt, "Don't you front me, girl dude. I know the real. Your stilo today is *off*."

Whoa, Leo thought, even more impressed. Miss Rigby appeared to be fluent in Teenspeak. How very extraordinary.

"You are *so* harsh," Chloe muttered.

"Go to your room, change your clothes and wash your face," the secretary told her, reverting back to standard English usage. Her voice softened some, however, as she added, "And get rid of the hardware. Schuyler called and said he's coming home tonight, and you know how he feels about all that."

"Oh, epic," Chloe grumbled. "Like it matters what *he* thinks."

But she reached for the hoop in her nose and deftly removed it, an action that quite frankly made Leo's flesh crawl. He glanced away when he saw her go for the one in her eyebrow. But not before a shudder of distaste wound through him.

"Now go upstairs and change out of that outfit," he heard Miss Rigby say again. "Where did it come from, anyway? I thought we gave all of your mother's things to charity."

To charity? Leo echoed to himself. What self-respecting charitable organization would take such things? Unplanned Parenthood, maybe, or Promiscuity International, but that was all he could think of.

And then it occurred to him that if they'd given all of her mother's things to charity, then it could only be because Chloe no longer had a mother who needed things. For the first time, it occurred to Leo that maybe, just maybe, all this piercing behavior—both verbal and physical—might be the result of a kid who was lost in more ways than a kid should be. When he glanced at the pair again, Chloe had turned around, so her back was to him and she was facing Miss Rigby.

"I just wanted to keep a few of her things, all right?" she said with what was obviously only a half-hearted effort to recapture some of her earlier antagonism. "So sue my ass, why don't you." But there was absolutely no venom in her voice now.

Miss Rigby's expression eased up some then, and her voice gentled when she told the girl, "Just go upstairs and change, all right? Schuyler will be home in time for dinner, so try to find something appropriate to wear."

Without another word, and with a docility Leo wouldn't have guessed she could manage, Chloe left the room. Her exit was anticlimactic, almost disappointing, really. Somehow, there should have been discordant music and pyrotechnics and the rumble of faraway thunder. Certainly, at the very least, there should have been a puff of smoke and a lingering smell of sulfur. But all that was left in the girl's wake was an awkward silence and unsatisfied speculation.

Lily Rigby, too, remained behind, but her attention was focused on some point on the wall behind Leo. In any case, she didn't look at him square on, and fidgeted almost imperceptibly, as if it were she, and not Chloe, who had just behaved abominably.

"Chloe has, um, well, she's been having trouble at school lately," Miss Rigby announced lamely, as if that explained everything.

Oh, now there was a news flash, Leo thought. "Has she?" he replied blandly, thinking that he'd heard this conversation a dozen times on "Leave It to Beaver" reruns, but he couldn't recall a single episode where the Beave had been called to the mat for body piercing or red vinyl, platform thigh boots.

Miss Rigby nodded. "The headmistress of her school has been trying to arrange a meeting with Mr. Kimball for some time now, but they can never seem to get their schedules to coincide."

Meaning, Leo thought, that Kimball didn't have even the smallest interest in the fate or welfare of his ward.

"Chloe hasn't had an easy time of it," Miss Rigby added, still obviously trying to cover for the girl. "She's actually surprisingly well adjusted, all things considered."

Leo hesitated only a moment before responding, " 'All things' being that she's lost her mother, and found a father who evidently doesn't want to claim her."

Miss Rigby did turn to face him then, but her expression belied nothing of what she might be thinking. "Did Chloe tell you that Mr. Kimball is her father?"

Leo nodded.

Her gaze remained steady and unflinching as she said, "Yes, well, Mr. Kimball doesn't necessarily agree with her on that particular assumption."

He wasn't sure why he cared, but Leo heard himself asking, "And just what does Miss Rigby think?"

She dropped her gaze to the back of her hand and inspected her fingers with a thoroughness that few manicurists would bother to perform. It was the same gesture she'd completed the day before, when she had skirted the issue of Chloe in the first place.

"What I think in that regard, Mr. Freiberger, is not important. Whatever is or is not, Mr. Kimball has taken on the care and feeding of Chloe until a time when she is able to manage those things herself. We do our best with her. Unfortunately, our best has met with mixed results."

"We? Our?" Leo repeated. "I wasn't aware that Chloe was your responsibility, too."

Her rapt fascination with her cuticles continued as she told him, "There's more to Chloe than the side you just witnessed. And in spite of what you may be thinking about her, she deserves something better than what's she's received from life. Her mother was an alcoholic, and from what I gather, she dated men who were anything but pleasant, some of whom made overtures toward Chloe that were anything but fatherly. To put it far more politely than it actually was." She dropped her hand to her side and met Leo's gaze intently. "Let's just say that, speaking as a human being, I'd like to see her happy."

From the expression on her face, he knew that any further query he might request into the matter of young Chloe would be in no way tolerated. So he kept the numerous questions he had about the girl to himself. She was a troubled kid who was undoubtedly bound for more trouble before there was any improvement in her life. A rebel without a cause, a kid without a country, a searcher without a clue. The oldest story in the world, and all that jazz.

She was none of Leo's concern. So he nudged his curiosity about Chloe to the back of his brain, and focused on Lily Rigby, who was infinitely more interesting anyway.

"How's your search coming?" she asked, nodding toward the computer on Schuyler Kimball's desk. "Have you found the problem?"

He shook his head. "Not yet."

"I thought you said it would be a routine search of the files," she said. He hoped he only imagined the thread of suspicion that laced her voice.

"It is routine," he assured her, striving for a blandness he was nowhere close to feeling. "But Mr. Kimball has an awful lot of files here. And as you said, they're in a bit of a mess."

She nodded, but didn't pursue the matter. "How long do you plan to be today, Mr. Freiberger? As you undoubtedly heard me tell Chloe, Mr. Kimball will be returning to Ashling tonight by dinner time. If you'd like, I can see that an extra place is added, so that you have a chance to speak to him about all this. I don't know how receptive he'll be, however. It takes him some time to . . . decompress . . . after he's been traveling. He may very well take his meal in his room."

There was no way Leo would turn down an invitation like that. Not just because he was eager to make Schuyler Kimball's acquaintance, and not just because, even after only two days on site, he'd become completely caught up in the little daytime drama that was the billionaire's life. It wasn't even because he was starting to feel a little hungry.

No, the real reason Leo wanted to stay for dinner at the Kimball estate was actually quite ordinary. Having come from rather meager beginnings himself, he was just naturally curious to see more of how the other half lived. He wanted to find out if money really could buy happiness. He wanted to see if a man who claimed more assets than some sovereign nations picked up his fork the same way everyone else did. And he wanted to know if the man's appetites were any more exotic or unquenchable than a normal guy's were.

But more than that, deep down inside, Leo had to admit that the biggest reason he wanted to have dinner at Ashling, the real impetus that spurred him on, the actual explanation for his desire to stay . . .

Well, it was because Lily Rigby would be there, too.

SIX

Deep down inside, Lily had been hoping that Leonard Freiberger—what on earth had his parents been *thinking* to name him that?—would decline her invitation to remain at Ashling for dinner. And really, when she got right down to it, she had no idea why she'd extended such an offer to him in the first place.

Schuyler hated having guests for dinner, even people he considered close friends—*close* being a relative term, naturally, seeing as how Schuyler fairly drove people away in, well, droves. And where common workers like Mr. Freiberger were concerned . . . Heavens, Schuyler would just as soon entertain a rabid badger as he would a laboring drone for Kimball Technologies. He was bound to be unhappy to discover a lowly bookkeeper sharing his dinner table. And he would likely take Lily to task for including the man.

So just why, precisely, had she included him?

Unfortunately, she was no closer to an answer to that question now, as she considered her options for appropriate dinner wear, than she had been when she'd issued the invitation to Mr. Freiberger some hours before. Even more vexing than that, however, was why she was feeling such angst over what to wear. Although Schuyler, for some reason, insisted that everyone Dress for Dinner—with a capital D . . . no, *two* capital Ds—whenever he was in residence at Ashling, Lily had never given much thought to what she put on. She only had two dresses that were appropriate, anyway, and she generally just alternated between the two.

Tonight, however, neither held any appeal for her. The long-sleeved, black velvet cocktail dress that she'd always considered timeless and elegant suddenly seemed dated and unremarkable instead. And the dark green, off-the-shoulder number that had served perfectly for whatever formal occasion presented itself, now seemed a bit too revealing.

Maybe it was time she did a little shopping, she thought, and spent a little money on herself, instead of squirreling it all away, as had become her habit. It had been so long since she'd splurged on something luxurious and unnecessary, for the simple purpose of making herself feel good.

Somehow, though, Lily couldn't quite bring herself to part with her money for frivolous pursuits. Certainly, there had been a time in her life when she wouldn't have given a thought to doling out hundreds of dollars for a new dress that she would wear only once. But those days were long gone, never to return. Because they'd taught her a lesson she would never forget.

Her father's financial woes had begun while Lily was still in junior high school, but Harrison Rigby hadn't told his family about the downturn until it was too late to bring it back around. Instead, he'd spent years trying to recover all by himself, then had panicked when things hadn't gone according to plan. Ultimately, he had waited too long, had tried too little, had lost too much. And before any of them had known it, everything they'd owned was just . . . gone.

Everything.

Seemingly overnight, the Rigbys had fallen from swimming amid the cream of the Main Line social elite to stumbling along with the tired, the weak, the poor, the hungry. They'd pretty much become the wretched refuse Lily had studied about in her American history class. They'd been booted from their roomy six-bedroom home in Ardmore *and* their Center City townhouse. They'd watched as the cars and boats were repossessed one by one, had stood by helplessly as every privilege they'd come to take for granted had been jerked right out from under them.

At the lowest point, things had gotten so bad that the Rigbys had found themselves living in a homeless shelter, eating the kind of food they would have tossed out before. Such had been their lot in life for three full months. Lily had gone from wearing DKNY off the rack to DAV cast-offs, and she'd left the posh Emerson Academy for a public high school in a *very* questionable Philadelphia neighborhood. Her friends had disappeared as quickly as her lifestyle, and she'd learned fast and hard that life, if left untended, could become a very dark and ugly place.

Ultimately, her father had found another job— albeit one that held far less prestige and paid much less than his last—and they'd gradually improved their standing. Now her parents lived in a middle-class suburb of Philadelphia, and both of them had jobs that, if they weren't high-paying, at least provided them with the necessities required to make life livable. But the Rigbys would never, ever again be wealthy. And Lily had sworn a long time ago that she would never, ever again fall into the kind of poverty they had suffered for those short, yet all-too-long, months.

On the contrary, she was determined to recoup the family losses. Like Schuyler, she had attended Harvard on an academic scholarship, and she had chosen a double-major of economics and business, specifically to boost her earning potential on the outside. She'd vowed years ago to dedicate her life to recapturing the good name of Rigby—and the Rigby fortune—that her father had lost. Not because she wanted to relive the excesses of her youthful life, but because she'd come to learn that there were far more important things that money could buy than big houses, silk dresses, and imported cars.

It could buy food to fill an empty belly, and blankets to warm a cold back. It could buy courage, and it could buy dignity. Lily had met too many people in her time at the shelter who'd had none of those things. For a while, she'd been one of them herself. Ever since college, her ultimate goal in life had been to found, fund, and manage a vast organization whose sole purpose was to lend a hand to the people who needed help.

Schuyler, of course, thought her intentions were ridiculous. Which was actually kind of odd, seeing as how he'd come from exactly the kind of family that would benefit from the type of foundation Lily had always envisioned. His father had abandoned his mother, his younger sister, and him when Schuyler was barely three years old, and the three of them had spent much of their lives living as refugees. He'd never had a place to call home for more than a few months at a time, had made the circuit from shelters to halfway houses to the street and back around again. Hunger, insecurity, and fear had been his constant companions while he was growing up.

Yet as an adult holding an MBA from Harvard that enriched his BS in mechanical engineering from MIT, as a man who had worked and sweated and sacrificed to build an empire from nothing, Schuyler scorned everything that smacked of welfare. He was a staunch Republican and conservative, and he showed nothing but contempt for people who had fallen on hard times. Although he spent lavishly on things to enrich his own lifestyle, he was otherwise a parsimonious hoarder of every nickel he made.

And for the life of her, Lily couldn't imagine why he would want to deny someone who was needy the basic essentials of life. Especially since he knew firsthand just how terrifying and soul-emptying such a way of life could be.

As she always did when pondering the puzzle of Schuyler Kimball, Lily sighed and pushed her troubling thoughts away. She'd made a promise to him a long time ago, and he had made one to her. So far, they had both stuck to their words with no problem. Schuyler was a big boy now; it wasn't up to Lily to be his conscience. It wasn't up to her to remind him what was right and what was wrong. It wasn't up to her to tell him what a big, fat jerk he could be sometimes.

Nor, she told herself further as she considered her options for dress again, was it up to her to be Leonard Freiberger's ... anything. She snatched the black dress from its hanger and tossed it onto the bed, then went about changing her identity from social secretary to dinner hostess. Because even though, technically, it was Schuyler who owned and operated Ashling, he and Lily really had a partnership in that respect. Schuyler owned the estate. Lily operated it. It was an arrangement that worked out quite nicely.

As she made her way back downstairs to Ashling's generous dining room, she realized she still wasn't certain whether or not Schuyler would be joining the rest of the household for dinner. She knew he was home and had been for over an hour, had in fact known that from the moment he'd set foot in the house. Not just because he'd screamed, "Lileee! Darliiing! What happened while I was gone?" the moment he was inside the front door, the way he always did when he returned from a trip. But because the entire estate seemed to hum with energy and activity whenever Schuyler was in residence. It was as if there was simply too much to the man for his body to contain it all, so whatever it was that made him Schuyler spilled out over everything—and everybody—else.

He was, quite simply, a remarkable human being. Everyone knew that. Especially Schuyler. And there was no point in anyone trying to dissuade him of the idea.

The dining room, when Lily entered it, shone like an African landscape at sunset. Its sweeping paneled walls of bird's-eye maple glowed like warm honey beneath the gentle light of a spectacular chandelier reigning over the room—a massive, ornate oval of pale gold glass that spanned the length of a banquet-sized table. The three dozen chairs lining the table were upholstered in faux leopard, the expansive rug beneath it patterned in a surprisingly realistic-looking zebra stripe. On the walls where men of lesser conscience would have mounted dead animals, Schuyler had opted for tribal decorations instead—masks, carvings, textiles, and seemingly primitive, but very elegant, weaponry.

Although Schuyler himself had never hunted in his life—the sight of blood and the mere suggestion of violence generally made him throw up—it didn't prevent him from being caught up in the whole Ernest Hemingway/Teddy Roosevelt manly man sort of thing that seemed so popular with testosterone-driven units these days. And he had been to Africa on a number of occasions, though he usually viewed the vistas from a climate-controlled Land Rover driven by someone named Omar, while he and someone of the feminine persuasion sat in the back sipping martinis and listening to the soundtrack from *The Lion King*.

All of that, however, was immaterial, because mystique, to Schuyler, was everything. Well, mystique and mood were everything. Mystique and mood and money. And image, too. Okay, so maybe mystique wasn't quite *every*thing. But it did count for quite a lot where Schuyler Kimball was concerned. And Ashling reflected mystique—and mood and money and image—in every room.

The table, Lily noted as she approached it, was set with very fine china for eight instead of the customary six—a population of less than one quarter its capacity—and she wasn't much surprised to realize that someone else, in addition to Mr. Freiberger, would be joining them tonight. A woman, no doubt. With big hair, big bosoms, big assets . . . and a very tiny brain. Schuyler never came home from a trip alone. And he never brought with him women who indulged in activities as unnecessary and mundane as thinking.

"Miss Rigby."

Lily's own thoughts were interrupted by the quiet summons, and she spun quickly around to find Mr. Freiberger standing framed by the entrance to the dining room. He'd donned his icky gray tweed jacket again, and had straightened his ugly blue necktie, but he still looked adorably rumpled.

Well, maybe not *adorably* rumpled, she amended. It was, after all, rather difficult for a man who evoked notions of a construction crew on a hot day to appear *adorable*. And not exactly rumpled, either. No, what Mr. Freiberger appeared to be, she decided upon further inspection, was rather sexily mussed, as if he'd just tumbled out of bed after a raucous and very satisfying experience.

"Good evening, Mr. Freiberger," she hastened to greet him, before the image in her head could proceed any further and become more graphic.

Oops. Too late.

Just like that, a *very* graphic image exploded in her brain, so graphic that she saw quite clearly what Mr. Freiberger wasn't wearing, and who he had tumbled before leaving his imaginary bed. And Lily was absolutely certain she'd *never* seen herself smiling quite like that before.

"I'm so glad you could stay for, um . . . dinner," she said, stumbling over the last word.

Even across the expanse of the dining room, she saw his smile turn sexy, and she wondered if he'd guessed what she'd been thinking about. "I wouldn't miss um-dinner for the world," he told her, his voice laced with an unmistakable intent.

Oh, dear. Evidently he *had* guessed what she'd been thinking about. Well, some of it, anyway. She doubted he could have figured out that part where the two of them had been coiled around each other, doing something she'd always wanted to try, but had never had the nerve to even—

"The others should be along shortly," she hurried on, battling with questionable success the heat that was fast creeping up from her belly to her breasts and all points beyond. "Whenever Mr. Kimball is in residence, we always dine at precisely seven o'clock."

Mr. Freiberger took a few idle steps forward, the soft scuffing of his shoes on the hardwood floor the only sound in the otherwise silent room. "And when Mr. Kimball isn't in residence?" he asked. "Whatever do you do then, Miss Rigby?"

Just how the man made the question sound sexually charged, Lily couldn't have said, but somehow, it came across as exactly that. Mr. Freiberger seemed to be suggesting that Schuyler performed a service for her that gave the designation of *social secretary* a whole new meaning. It was that spark of something speculative in his eyes, she finally decided, a speculation that overflowed into the even timbre of his voice.

Ever since he had shown up on Ashling's doorstep, Mr. Freiberger had played fast and loose with Lily's libido, and she couldn't for the life of her figure out why. Oh, certainly, beneath all that *Goodbye, Mr. Chips* bookishness, there was an odd kind of sexual heat burning and churning, but still. The man was a bookkeeper, a very small cog in the very large machine that was Kimball Technologies. No one of Leonard Freiberger's capacity should exude such an air of authority and command. Nor should he be able to rev up her motor with a simple look. But her motor had most definitely been revved. And she couldn't help but wonder just what Mr. Freiberger planned to do once he got under her hood.

"I beg your pardon?" she said, cursing herself for the faintness and uncertainty she heard in her voice. "What did you mean by that?"

He shoved his hands deep into his pockets, then lifted his shoulders and let them fall in a shrug that was nowhere near casual. Because his gaze remained firmly fixed on Lily's face—or, more specifically, on Lily's mouth—and his eyes were lit with a dark and intriguing fire. "What do you mean, what did I mean?" he asked, a naughty—and very knowing—little smile dancing about his lips.

She opened her mouth to respond with something flirty and fun that she would doubtless later wish she hadn't said—mainly because she didn't have time for flirty and fun these days, no matter what her treacherous libido seemed to think. And even if she *did* have time, she was in no position, thank you very much, to take on someone of Mr. Freiberger's evident . . . um . . . prowess. But she was spared the response because Janey Kimball chose that moment to flutter in with her mother in tow—something that prevented her from saying much of anything at all. Because Janey, God help them all, was clearly in a snit.

Lily supposed that if she tried very, very hard, and was very, very patient, she might someday be able to convince Schuyler's sister that the earth and moon and stars in fact did *not* revolve around Janey Kimball. But really, what was the point? To dissuade the woman of such notions would only make her that much more irritable—and, therefore, more irritat*ing*—and why unleash such a creature on an unsuspecting public?

"Janey," Lily said when the other woman breezed past her without so much as a nod of acknowledgment. "Have you met Mr. Freiberger? He works for your brother."

Then, not wanting to exclude Schuyler's mother—well, Lily often wanted to exclude Miranda Kimball from things, but it would be frightfully impolite to do so—she turned her body to include the other woman in the introduction, as well. "Mrs. Kimball," she added, "this is Leonard Freiberger, an employee of Kimball Technologies. Mr. Freiberger, Mrs. Miranda Kimball and Miss Jane Kimball."

"Mrs. Kimball," Mr. Freiberger stated formally, dipping his head first toward Schuyler's mother in greeting. "How do you do?"

Miranda lifted a hand to press her fingertips lightly against her temple, then sighed with a melodrama that put her daughter's affectations to shame. Her attire, too, rivaled Janey's in the Golden Age of Hollywood department—a flowing, silver lamé caftan with matching turban, and enormous rings on each of her fingers. Norma Desmond had nothing on Miranda Kimball in the wardrobe department, Lily thought. And not in the insanity department, either.

"I'm afraid I'm not well at all, Mr. Freiberger," Miranda said in a much-put-upon voice. "But thankfully, Montgomery has come to help me with my problems. He's been very helpful."

Somehow, Lily refrained from expelling a rude snort of disbelief. She couldn't stop what she knew would come next, however, and steeled herself for Mr. Freiberger's inescapable query, followed by Miranda's insipid reply.

"Montgomery?" he asked.

Miranda nodded. "Montgomery Clift."

To his credit, Mr. Freiberger only arched his eyebrows in mild surprise. "Montgomery Clift is a guest at Ashling? Forgive me, Mrs. Kimball, but I was under the impression that Montgomery Clift was, uh . . . somewhat incapacitated these days."

"Oh, no, Mr. Freiberger," Miranda assured him. "He's not incapacitated. He's dead."

After only a slight hesitation on his part, God bless the man, Mr. Freiberger replied, "And you don't consider death an incapacitation?"

Miranda tittered prettily. "Oh, no, certainly not. In fact, there's nothing more liberating. Why, in death, one can travel anywhere."

"And I believe," Lily interjected quickly, before Miranda could start off on the whole astral plane thing, "you've already made the acquaintance of Mr. Kimball's sister, Jane."

Beside Miranda, Janey sighed with much impatience. "Yes, yes, we've already met," she agreed shortly, carelessly sweeping a gloved hand down the front of her pale yellow chiffon dress.

Chiffon *gown*, Lily corrected herself automatically, not dress. Janey never wore dresses—only gowns. Gowns and gloves and big ol' hats that could put a person's eye out if they weren't careful, like the vast, botanically enhanced one she was wearing at the moment. Honestly, Lily thought, she might as well plant shrubbery in that thing.

"He's one-forty-two," Janey continued with a quick gesture toward Mr. Freiberger, using the same tone of voice she might use if stating that he were currently covered with slugs. "I have nothing to say to him. Nothing at all."

Then she spun around again and made her way to the bar on the other side of the room. With a watery smile, Miranda followed her daughter, which was just as well, Lily thought, because they both became much more tolerable after a cocktail or two. Well, after *Lily* had a cocktail or two—or ten—anyway.

She couldn't quite mask her surprise—nor her interest—when she turned back to Mr. Freiberger. "Are you really one-forty-two?" she asked before she could stop herself. "That's extraordinary."

He eyed her in confusion for a moment. But before she could elaborate, he suddenly nodded his understanding. "Oh, the IQ thing," he said modestly. "I thought she was talking about my weight. Which is actually one-ninety-eight. It's all solid rock, though," he hastened to add, his voice reflecting his concern that she might find the number excessive where poundage, other than of the mental variety, was concerned.

Solid rock, Lily reiterated to herself. Right. To think that she might need a reminder of such a thing.

"Schuyler's IQ is one-hundred-and-ninety-seven," Lily said, wondering what made her offer up the information. It wasn't as if the two men were competing, after all.

But Mr. Freiberger evidently didn't see it quite that way, because he straightened to an even more impressive height than usual and said, "Oh, yeah? And can he bench press his IQ the way *I* can mine?"

She smiled, striving for a benign expression. "I have no idea, Mr. Freiberger. I would think not, seeing as how Mr. Kimball prefers swimming and tennis over brute force athletics."

He seemed to deflate some at her suggestion that she found brute force unappealing. But even deflated, Leonard Freiberger was quite an intimidating specimen of manhood.

Unable to help herself—he did look so dejected, after all—Lily added, "I myself, however, think that there may be something to be said for brute force on occasion."

Mr. Freiberger brightened some at that, straightening to his full height once again. "Oh, yeah?"

She managed a brief nod and congratulated herself for not acting on her impulse to leap into his arms and claim him as her very own personal love monkey in the most basic, primitive way imaginable, with her own show of brute force. "So long as it's performed in moderation, naturally," she added faintly.

"Well, that goes without saying," he agreed.

For some reason, she suddenly began to grow warm again, and decided that it might be wise to discontinue their discussion—at least while other people were present. So instead, she gestured over her shoulder toward the bar and asked, "Would you care for a cocktail before dinner, Mr. Freiberger?"

"That would be nice, thank you, Miss Rigby. Scotch, if you have it."

She smiled again. "Why, Mr. Freiberger. You forget whose home you're in. Don't you read the papers? Schuyler Kimball has *every*thing."

Leo watched with much interest as the delectable Miss Rigby spun around and made her way across the dining room—*dining room* being a deceptive term, as far as he was concerned. *Veterans Stadium* might have been a more accurate one. With a single, quick assessment, he'd come to the conclusion that the square footage on the room where Schuyler Kimball took his meals was larger than that of Leo's entire townhouse.

He shook his head in silent disbelief. In addition to having an IQ up there with da Vinci's, the man had more money than God. Eleven billion dollars. That was what Schuyler Kimball was worth. Certainly Leo had already known that before coming to Ashling, but witnessing the physical evidence of such enormous wealth was more than a little awe-inspiring. The idea that one individual could possess *billions* of dollars was almost incomprehensible. To think that the man could spend ten *billion* dollars and still be a billionaire . . . To think about what ten *billion* dollars could buy . . . To imagine how many people could be fed and housed and clothed with ten *billion* dollars, and Kimball would *still* be a billionaire . . .

It just wasn't right, Leo thought. He didn't care how hard Kimball had worked or how talented and gifted the man was. There was no reason to hoard all that money, when it could do so much for so many and still leave Kimball a fat and sassy cat. The man should be ashamed of himself, for God's sake, not spreading a little bit around for others to enjoy. And on top of that . . .

On top of that, Leo had actually just bragged to a woman that he could bench press his IQ. He groaned inwardly. What a moron. He should have his IQ rechecked. Because ever since coming to Ashling, he'd felt it slipping away little by little. And whenever Lily Rigby walked into a room, well . . . His IQ went right out the window.

He couldn't remember the last time he'd felt it necessary to try and impress a woman in order to win her over. Usually, women responded to him with enthusiasm right off the bat, with absolutely no coaxing from the studio audience. And although he definitely sensed interest on Miss Rigby's part, there was something else in her that held her aloof. It was something that also prevented him from acting on his desire to get to know her better.

Partly, in spite of her clear interest, he suspected there was something going on between her and Kimball, however superficial the relationship seemed to be. And he was also hesitant, he had to admit, because, well, at the risk of coming off as an intellectual snob—which, when he got right down to it, he was—Lily Rigby just wasn't as smart as Leo was. And he really preferred women who could keep up with him in the contemplative arena. Not that she was particularly shallow, mind you—well, not *too* shallow—but that whole cat thing from their initial encounter was never far from his thoughts.

Plus, as much as he hated to do it, he still had to view her as an unknown quantity where the missing Kimball millions were concerned. He didn't really think Lily Rigby had anything to do with the money's disappearance—thanks to that cat business—but at this point, he had no leads, and it would be foolish to rule out anyone. Miss Rigby was as likely a suspect as anyone, he supposed.

Yet even at that, something held Leo in check where she was concerned. As gregarious and chatty as she was, there was something standoffish in her nature that warned anyone—male or female—not to get too close. It was almost as if she were hiding something she feared others would discover about her. Then again, Leo had encountered that kind of thing in women before, and it had only made him work that much harder to win them over.

Miss Rigby, he was beginning to think, would be no different in that respect. Ultimately, he was going to want to figure her out, to dress her down and study her thoroughly, until he knew once and for all what made her tick. Because in spite of all his misgivings, she was, quite simply, too tempting to pass up.

He did his best to hide his interest as she made her way back across the room. And given the size of the room, it would probably take her half an hour to make the journey, so Leo took his time drinking in the sight of her. Where her snug little suits and sweater sets had fairly scorched his insides, the black velvet number wrapping her body now set off little explosions throughout. With its long sleeves and modest length, the dress shouldn't have been revealing. But the scooped neck fell just low enough to display the upper swells of her breasts, and the hourglass shape made the most of Miss Rigby's numerous—and dangerous—curves.

For a small woman, she was lush as hell, he thought. And something inside him that was already strung way too tight grew even more taut.

"Johnnie Walker Blue Label over ice. Is that all right?" she asked as she extended the glass toward him.

An exceptional Scotch that, last time he'd checked, ran one hundred dollars a bottle? Leo thought. Gosh, he guessed he'd just have to make do, wouldn't he?

"That will be fine, Miss Rigby. Thank you."

When he curled his fingers around the glass, somehow—he couldn't *begin* to imagine quite how—his hand wound up completely covering hers. They spent a few moments volleying for possession of the glass before Leo finally lifted his free hand to shift the drink there. But even after he'd managed a successful trade off, their fingers remained tangled for another moment more. And as he worked—but not too hard—to free himself from the delicate trap she posed, it occurred to him that in addition to being small and lush, Miss Rigby was also very, very soft. And warm. And tempting.

Oh, boy.

He was just about to forego his personal freedom, to succumb to the urge to tighten his fingers in hers and pull her forward, when she somehow managed to disengage herself from the snare. Without so much as a *Mother-may-I*, she took a giant step backward, curling both hands around her own drink, as if the cut crystal tumbler were a talisman to ward off evil. Her cheeks were stained with pink, though whether the blush was a result of embarrassment or something else entirely, Leo couldn't have said. But relief coursed through him at the realization that he could unbalance her the way he had. Hey, why should he be the only one here who'd lost his equilibrium?

Unsure exactly what kind of comment might be appropriate following what had felt like foreplay for some reason—very public foreplay, at that— Leo lifted his drink to his lips, filling his mouth with the smoky, mellow Scotch that lesser men had never before tasted. And as he rolled the liquor around on his tongue before swallowing, as he savored every last trace of it spilling into his belly, he decided there was a lot to be said for having billions and billions and *billions* of dollars.

As the liquor warmed his insides, his spirits, his very soul, Leo turned to say something else to Miss Rigby. But she'd directed her attention elsewhere, to a point behind him, and every last ounce of her being seemed to be focused on whatever—or who-ever—that was. Before he even turned around, Leo knew.

Schuyler Kimball had come down to dinner.

SEVEN

Leo had expected the billionaire to be larger than life, but the man who entered the dining room wearing a faultless black tuxedo—and an even more faultless blonde—looked to be ordinary enough. All right, so Kimball was reasonably good-looking, Leo conceded. If you were one of those women who went for a man who was tall and well built, who had ruggedly handsome features . . . jet-black hair and ice-blue eyes . . . a square jaw, strong mouth . . . and one of those cool, shaken-not-stirred dispositions about him. But only if you were the kind of woman who went for a man like that. Immediately, he turned to look at Miss Rigby, whose gaze was still fastened on her employer, and he frowned.

Evidently, she was one of those women.

Because she seemed to have forgotten that Leo was even there, so focused was she on Schuyler Kimball. He looked for traces of jealousy or resentment on her part where the faultless blonde was concerned, but he detected neither. On the contrary, Miss Rigby didn't seem to notice Kimball's companion any more than she noticed Leo.

Instead, she simply watched intently as her employer crossed the dining room toward where the two of them stood.

When Leo turned his attention back to Kimball, his frown deepened. Because the billionaire, too, was clearly far more interested in his secretary than he was in the *extremely* well-endowed, tightly sheathed-in-red woman at his side, the one who had fastened herself so steadfastly to the man that she appeared to be trying to absorb through osmosis. Kimball's gaze never wavered from Miss Rigby as he paused before her, leaned forward, and, to Leo's amazement, brushed a chaste kiss on her cheek that she in no way tried to discourage.

"Lily. Darling," he said as he pulled back, his attention still fixed on her face. "Who on earth have you invited to join our little soiree this evening?"

Leo's amazement compounded. He honestly hadn't thought Kimball had even noticed him. But now the billionaire turned to inspect him, letting his gaze wander over Leo's person from head to toe. And for the first time since coming to Ashling, Leo worried that his cover was blown. Because Schuyler Kimball, for all his reputed eccentricities and self-absorption, seemed capable of staring right down into a person's soul to find every little dirty secret that person held locked inside.

It was more than a little disconcerting.

Adjusting his glasses with feigned disinterest, Leo decided not to bother with the slouch he'd been ordered to maintain. Because even slouching, he'd still be taller than Kimball, if only by an inch or two. For some reason, the realization brought Leo some measure of reassurance.

"Leonard Freiberger," he said, extending his hand.

But instead of acknowledging the gesture—or

Leo, for that matter—Kimball turned back to Miss Rigby. "Lily. Darling. Who is this man? More to the point, what's he doing in my dining room?"

"He works for you, Schuyler," she said simply, showing no sign of intimidation where her employer's clear dissatisfaction was concerned. "He's an employee of Kimball Technologies. A bookkeeper. Evidently, there have been some problems with some of your files or something, and Mr. Freiberger is trying to get it all straightened out."

She turned to Leo, giving him the perfect opening to explain the fabrication of facts that was his sole purpose for being these days, but before he could utter a single syllable to explain his mission, Kimball slashed a hand through the air, closed his eyes, and shook his head. Vehemently.

"I don't want to know," he said adamantly. "Don't *even* bring up business to me tonight. It's the absolute last thing I want to have on my mind right now. No business discussions tonight," he reiterated adamantly. "None. I need a drink."

No sooner had he uttered the declaration than someone pressed into his hand a martini glass filled nearly to the brim with something frosty and clear. His mother, Leo noted. Miranda Kimball was still looking after her boy, God love her.

"Thank you, Mother," Kimball said before lifting the drink to his lips for a long, hefty quaff. He sighed with undisguised glee after he swallowed. "Oh, that helps." He sampled the drink again, this time with a bit less gusto, then, almost as an afterthought, turned to his—hoo, boy, was she built— companion. "Everyone, this is . . ." He hesitated, thinking, then glanced down at his date. "I'm sorry, sweetheart, but I seem to have forgotten your name."

Leo couldn't help the soft sound of incredulous

surprise that escaped his lips at Kimball's disregard for the woman at his side. He'd known some real pricks in his life, but Schuyler Kimball put them all to shame. Leo didn't even know the woman who accompanied the billionaire, but he was ready to declare pistols at dawn on her behalf. No one should be treated so shabbily.

But she didn't seem at all surprised or bothered by Kimball's—to put it mildly—faux pas, and she won Leo's admiration when she simply smiled at everyone and said, "I'm Valerie. Hello."

Kimball nodded as recollection evidently dawned. "Valerie," he said, disengaging himself from her to sweep his free hand carelessly over the small crowd that had gathered to welcome him home. "This is everyone. Everyone, this is Valerie. We met . . ." Another hesitation, then Kimball turned to the woman again. "I'm sorry, sweetheart, where was it we met?"

Leo's fist clenched involuntarily at the second slight perpetrated against the undeserving Valerie, but she seemed to be not at all concerned with the rude dismissal.

"We were first introduced in the back seat of your limo," she said simply. "Right after you gave Miss Wisteria your platinum card and told her you only needed me for one night."

"That's right," Kimball said with a slow nod, lifting his drink for another sip. "It's coming back to me now."

Janey Kimball pushed through the throng and eyed Valerie with a look clearly meant to put the blonde on the defensive. "Do you know how to spell *scopophilia*?" she asked Kimball's . . . date.

The billionaire rolled his eyes heavenward and expelled a hiss of discontent. "Mother, I thought I told you to keep Janey away from the *Oxford En-*

glish Dictionary. Am I going to have to lock up every book in the house?"

"Do you know how to spell it?" Janey demanded again, though she threw her brother a look of grave concern when she heard his threat.

"Sure," Valerie replied easily. Then she made good on the assurance by quickly and accurately fulfilling Janey's request.

"Do you know what it means?" Janey asked further.

"Yes, I do," Valerie told her. "But something tells me you don't, asking the question in mixed and polite company this way."

Janey furrowed her brow with more concern. "What's your IQ?" she asked anxiously.

Valerie lifted a hand to the permanent wave of silky blond that swept across one eyebrow. "It's a hundred and thirty," she replied. Rather smugly, too, Leo thought. "I pull in a hundred more an hour than the other girls do, thanks to that."

Kimball gaped at his escort. "It's *what*?" he demanded. "I told Miss Wisteria specifically that I *didn't* want a woman in that range."

Valerie shrugged off his displeasure. "You also said you wanted someone who could, um . . ."

She pushed herself up on tiptoe and whispered something into Kimball's ear that immediately had him smiling. And also shifting his weight from one foot to the other and back again, as if trying to dislodge something from his pants.

"And I'm the only one who can do that right," Valerie concluded as she returned to her regular stance. "Miss Wisteria figured you'd think that was more important than the IQ thing."

Kimball tugged impatiently at his tie and shifted his weight again. "Miss Wisteria was absolutely right."

Janey frowned in clear consternation. *"Mother,"* she growled to the woman beside her. "Are you going to talk to Schuyler about this or not?"

Leo turned to the billionaire, curious as to whether or not he would indeed make good on his threat to lock up all the dictionaries, suddenly thinking it a very good idea. But Kimball only sipped his drink again and ignored his sister. Likewise, his mother said nothing in response to her daughter's question, just looked a bit pained around the eyes.

Leo shook his head once again in disbelief. At the family. At Kimball's ... date. A hooker? he wondered. Billionaire Schuyler Kimball, who looked like one of Hollywood's most successful leading men, had been reduced to hiring a hooker to be his companion for dinner?

Well, naturally, Kimball had probably hired her for more than just *dinner*, Leo thought further, but still. He'd always kind of liked to think that once a man reached a certain level of success in life— like, oh, say ... *billionaire*—he stopped having trouble getting dates. And why the hell would Kimball bother with a hooker when he had Lily Rigby waiting for him at home, looking at him like ... like ...

He turned his attention to Miss Rigby—again— and frowned—again.

Like *that*.

Okay, so Valerie might have one or two qualities that Miss Rigby lacked. Like, for instance, Valerie would probably be able to perform page seventy-two of *How to Leave a Man Groaning with Satisfaction Every Time* correctly. But was that really important when there was another woman around who obviously had *feelings* for you?

Well, yeah, okay, page seventy-two was pretty important, Leo backpedaled. But still. Surely it was in bad taste to bring a hired woman home to one's family and social secretary, even if one was an eccentric billionaire. Or was Kimball a billionaire eccentric? At the moment, Leo couldn't quite decide which word should be the adjective and which should be the noun.

He was spared having to ponder the quandary further, thanks to the entrance of Chloe the Magnificent. And the befuddlement that had dogged Leo for oh, about two days now, ascended to the next level. Because where before Chloe had been a surly, snide nymphet of indeterminate criminal potential, there was now a quiet, unassuming young woman of almost startling beauty and grace in her place.

Without all the hardware and makeup, Chloe's face was fresh and youthful looking, her complexion smooth, ivory, and flawless. She had somehow managed to contain all that dark hair in a short braid fixed at the end with a plain white ribbon. Her attire, to Leo, seemed appropriate for the teenage daughter of a billionaire—whether or not that was what Chloe was. A simple, sleeveless white satin dress, accessorized by a string of pearls and white satin flats. He could scarcely believe she was the same juvenile delinquent he had met that afternoon.

Then, "So we gonna toss chow or what?" she asked, spoiling the image completely.

Mrs. Puddleduck stumbled in behind her then, her face red, her knuckles white, her mouth open to utter language that was undoubtedly blue. Leo couldn't help but wonder what had transpired between the two to create this kinder, gentler version of Chloe. To her credit, however, the nanny curbed whatever words—or expletives—she had been about to utter when faced with the crowd before her. But he noticed that she was eyeing the bar on the other side of the room with *much* affection.

Beside him, Lily Rigby smiled at the pair with what appeared to be genuine warmth. "Aren't you going to say hello to Mr. Kimball, Chloe? Mrs. Puddleduck?"

"That's Poddledock," the older woman returned. But she covered the distance necessary to greet her host—who replied with a benign "Hello, Mrs. Puddleduck"—then she hastened over to the bar to pour herself what looked like . . . a double Stoli straight up.

For a moment, Leo suspected that Chloe was going to stand firm and reply that hell, no, she wasn't going to say hello to Mr. Kimball, why the hell should she? Then she dropped her gaze to the floor and moved slowly forward, pausing a good foot away from her . . . whatever it was Kimball was.

"Hey, Mr. Kimball," she said softly.

"Chloe," Kimball replied without looking at her. Then he enjoyed another sip of his martini and gazed at a trio of masks on the wall. "Lily, darling, one of those is crooked. See to it, would you?"

"Certainly, Schuyler," Miss Rigby replied readily. "I'll have Mrs. Skolnik take care of it first thing tomorrow."

Evidently satisfied that everything was right in his world again, Kimball spun around and made his way to the head of the table to claim a chair that was much larger—and more thronelike—than the others. And wordlessly, everyone else in the room followed suit. Leo waited until the others had been seated to figure out where he should place himself, then was delighted to discover that the only vacancy was beside Miss Rigby.

He wondered if she had done that on purpose, or if the seating had simply been a result of necessity. Because on her other side was Chloe, who clearly needed an additional handler, and beyond Chloe, Mrs. Puddleduck. To Leo's left, claiming the head of the table, was Kimball, and directly opposite Leo, on Kimball's left, was Valerie. Beside Valerie was Janey Kimball, and beside her, as far from Kimball as she could be, was his mother.

Just how accurately, Leo wondered further, did the dynamics of their dinner seating reflect the politics of the Kimball family? It didn't escape his notice that he and Kimball were the only two men present, nor did he miss the fact that they were both seated in the traditional places of honor at the table. This in spite of the fact that Leo was a virtual stranger, and, in his guise of bookkeeper, was more than likely the one with the lowest income. Doubtless Mrs. Puddleduck was pulling in a bundle for taking on the care and feeding of Chloe, and as for Valerie, well . . . It went without saying that if her usual customers were of Kimball's ilk, she was pulling in a lot more than a lowly bookkeeper would be.

So clearly it was gender rather than wealth that Kimball valued more in a person. Yet he lived in a house surrounded by women. Then again, he spent much of his time away. Interesting. Leo still couldn't quite dissuade himself of the idea that Kimball and Miss Rigby had more going on between them than the usual employer/employee relationship. Yet it was Leo, not Miss Rigby, who was sitting at Kimball's right hand. And it was a prostitute, not a friend or family member, sitting on his left.

Interesting, indeed. Suddenly, Leo wasn't quite so put off by the idea of hanging around Ashling for a few more days. There was just no telling what might develop among such a cast of characters.

*   *   *

Enthroned as he was at the head of the table, Schuyler Kimball could survey his court with all the cool detachment of a ruthless, omnipotent czar. And at the moment, he was wondering, as any self-respecting despot would be, how prudent it would be to exile his family—nay, his entire household—to the island of Elba. Then again, ultimately, Napoleon had escaped from Elba, hadn't he?

Ah, well. Another perfectly good plan dashed before getting fully under way.

At the very least, Schuyler was wondering why he had bothered to come home. He'd been having as much fun in Bermuda as he would likely be having anywhere else. Plus, the beaches were so breathtakingly lovely there, and the servants so wonderfully obsequious. What had possessed him to think he might be needed here? That he might be comfortable here? That he might be welcome here?

Even Lily, darling Lily, had annoyed him tonight, bringing home her stray without asking Schuyler's permission first. Whoever, whatever, this man was who had come between them—both literally and figuratively, considering the seating arrangement Lily had designated at the table—he didn't work for Kimball Technologies. Not that Schuyler was familiar with every last man, woman, and drone who worked for him—*au contraire*. But Leonard Freiberger was no lowly bookkeeper; that much was obvious.

Nor was there anything of the team player about him, something that rather hampered the whole odious concept of Team Kimball, a corporate policy conceived by his board of directors—or rather *bored* of directors, as he liked to think of them. Still, as long as the bored of directors were happy, as long as they were under the misguided notion that they were the ones running the business, Schuyler could find his own fun, and never the twain should meet.

For some reason, then, his gaze was pulled toward Chloe, who simply sat staring sullenly at her tiramisu and looking exactly like her mother. Well, except for her eyes, which she had clearly inherited from Schuyler. He drew in a deep breath and released it slowly, wishing he'd been more careful in his youth. Ah, well. There was nothing for it now but to make sure the girl was cared for, and God knows he'd done his best in that respect. Mrs. Puddleduck, for all her regimentation, seemed to be doing an adequate job with the girl. With any luck at all, Chloe would avoid the pitfalls her mother had been helpless to miss.

Having noted that everyone had just started eating their dessert, Schuyler stood and asked, "Everyone finished? Good. I, for one, am ready to call it a day." He extended his hand toward the piece of cheesecake seated to his left, for which he had paid a bundle, and which he intended to enjoy for his own dessert. "Veronica?"

"Valerie," she corrected him mildly as she stood. "If you want to call me by a name other than my own, it's going to cost you another fifty dollars."

"Fine," he said. "Put it on my tab."

He was so intent on the night that stretched before him—Veronique had assured him, after all, that she could perform perfectly page 72 of *How to Leave a Man Groaning with Satisfaction Every Time*—that he almost didn't notice the commotion outside the dining room as he approached the door. He was reaching for the doorknob only to have the door burst open on him before he could move out of the way.

Before he realized what was happening, a

woman had barreled through that door and right into him, knocking him backward with enough force to send him sprawling onto the floor on his fanny. And the only reason Schuyler decided to forgive her for such an egregious transgression was that she came falling forward, too, landing in a sprawl right on top of him.

He noticed right away that she was even more lushly built than Vanessa was. But where the call girl's attributes were doubtless the result of surgical enhancement—they were just too damned perky, in Schuyler's opinion, to be anything other than cosmetically enhanced—this woman's gifts were obviously there because Mother Nature had decreed it. Just to be certain, however—and because he knew he could excuse his behavior as a result of his surprise and the fall—he quickly copped a feel to reassure himself. Oh, yes. They were definitely real.

Well, my, my, my.

He was about to go in for another touchdown— or, perhaps more accurately, another feelup—but the woman anticipated him and deftly struck his hand out of the way. Hastily, she scrambled off of him and stood, tugging her sweater—a shapeless, colorless bit of drab—down over her equally unremarkable skirt. Schuyler, too, stood up, automatically brushing off his tuxedo and running a quick hand through his hair, tending to himself before turning his attention to the woman.

When he finally did look at her, he had to bite back a mutter of disappointment. Because as erotic and exotic as her erogenous zones below the neck clearly were, everything above was obviously— and thoroughly—contained.

The woman's hair was probably a rich red auburn, he thought, but it was hard to tell, seeing as how it was pulled back into a tight . . . *tight* . . . bun-thing on the back of her head. Big, tortoiseshell-framed glasses obscured what were probably amazing, luminous brown eyes when not hidden. Her mouth was pinched, something that prevented him from telling much about her other features. But somehow, he suspected that when she let her guard down, when she opened herself up, this woman would doubtless be . . .

He sighed fitfully. Oh, who was he kidding? The woman appeared to have no sense of style, humor, or beauty whatsoever. And just because he was a connoisseur of fine feminine flesh didn't mean he could make a silk purse out of a sow's ear. What-ever the hell that meant.

All in all, he decided pretty quickly that he didn't like the woman and had no use for her in his life. And, just as quickly, he decided he also wanted her to go away so that he could experience the hired—albeit plastic—bounty of Victoria in-stead. He opened his mouth to tell the woman ex-actly that, but before he could say a word, she grabbed him by the bow tie and tugged him for-ward. Hard.

"Mr. Kimball?" she inquired in a tone that was the absolute picture of politeness, her voice soft and lovely, and tinted with just a hint of the Geor-gia peach debutante thing—a feature that rather compromised her aggressive manhandling of his upper person.

Still, no need to be hasty, he thought. He was familiar enough with the works of the Williams—Faulkner and Tennessee—to know that these southern belles could be formidable foes. So, every bit as courteously, he replied, "And who, may I ask, wants to know?"

She jerked her hand upward, an action that

nearly cut off his breath, then continued in that Miss Antebellum Manners voice, "I'm Mrs. Beecham. Mrs. Caroline Beecham. I'm the headmistress of the Van Meter Academy. That's Chloe's school, in case you've forgotten. And Mr. Kimball, you and I need to have a little chat."

With a gentleness that surprised him—considering the fact that he was currently being attacked by a madwoman—Schuyler lightly circled the madwoman's wrist with sure, but careful, fingers. "That's going to be rather difficult, don't you think, Mrs. Beecham, with you trying to crush my windpipe and all. Do you mind?"

Instead of releasing him, she nodded. "Yes, as a matter of fact, I do mind. I'm afraid I won't be letting go until you promise me fifteen minutes of your time. Frankly, Mr. Kimball, it's been terribly difficult to get past your sentinel, and I'm at my wit's end. At this point, I am by no means averse to . . . unconventional tactics."

He was more likely to call them homicidal tendencies himself. He narrowed his eyes at her. "Sentinel? What sentinel?" Although, now that he thought about it, he rather liked the idea of having a sentinel. A sentinel might come in handy for situations like, oh, say . . . this one, for example. He'd have Lily look into hiring him one tomorrow morning.

"Uh, I think by 'sentinel,' Mrs. Beecham would be referring to me."

As if conjured by his thoughts, Lily appeared at Schuyler's side, seeming to be not at all surprised by the fact that there was a woman attempting to squeeze the breath right out of him. But then, that was Lily. Darling Lily. Always grace under fire. Especially when she wasn't the one who was under fire.

"Mrs. Beecham has been trying to meet with you for some time now," Lily said. "And I'm afraid I may have—inadvertently, of course—given her the impression that you weren't interested in talking to her."

"As well you should," Schuyler said. "Because I'm *not* interested in talking to her."

It bothered him more than he cared to admit that, instead of responding to his statement, Lily turned her attention to the Valkyrie who was still trying to make a Venetian blind out of him.

"Mrs. Beecham," she said in that no-nonsense voice of authority. "I apologize if I did, in fact, give you the wrong impression over the telephone the other day. Mr. Kimball has been out of the country for some time now, attending to business. That's why he hasn't responded to your requests to see him. Not because of . . . uh . . . that other thing I mentioned." More confidently, she concluded, "I'm sorry if I didn't make that clear to you initially."

Mrs. Beecham eyed Lily cautiously, but she loosened her grip some on Schuyler's tie. Mind you, she didn't remove her fingers completely, but at least he was able to inhale a deep, calming breath. When he did, Schuyler was treated to the scent of the tightly bundled Mrs. Caroline Beecham. And he found it very interesting indeed to discover that she smelled of hot summer nights, bluesy saxophones, and the crackle of something spicy and bad for you hissing on the grill.

Well, well, well.

"That's not what you told me the other day, Miss Rigby," she said, her attention flickering from Schuyler to Lily and then back again.

And as he studied her more intently, Schuyler realized that, even through the lenses of her glasses—or, perhaps, because of them—she really did have quite amazing, luminous brown eyes. They were the color of fine bittersweet chocolate, ringed by a wealth of ridiculously long, dark lashes. They were also, he noted further, smudged beneath by faint purple crescents. And he wondered what it was that left her tossing and turning, unable to sleep in her bed at night.

"Yes," Lily continued with obvious reluctance, "Well. You, um . . . You did call several times, didn't you?"

With clear discomfort, she glanced down at the back of one hand. Uh-oh, Schuyler thought. She only did that when she was trying to hide important—or embarrassing—information. This ought to be good.

"And that last time you called," she continued with a blitheness he could see was completely feigned, "you, ah . . . you were rather worked up, after all. And you did catch me on something of a bad day, you see. And—"

Mrs. Beecham interrupted, "You told me Mr. Kimball would rather skip naked in the surf with an oversize version of Bermuda Fun Barbie than be bothered with whatever problems Chloe was having at school."

Lily perused one cuticle in particular and sucked in her cheeks tight, as if she were trying to keep in whatever words were threatening to escape. Schuyler wanted to laugh, but didn't know whether it should be with derision or genuine humor. Certainly what she'd told Mrs. Beecham was true. But, hey, what man wouldn't want to skip naked through the surf with Bermuda Fun Barbie—or, as Schuyler had actually been, with Tourist Guide Barbie. Still, there was no reason to go broadcasting it to every Tom, Dick, and Mrs. Caroline Beecham, was there?

Ultimately, he opted to simply let Lily dig herself out of this one. Mrs. Beecham was something of an interesting enigma, after all, one who, under other circumstances—like maybe if she *hadn't* tried to strangle him by way of an introduction—Schuyler might have liked to get to know better. Deep down, he supposed he didn't mind if she knew he liked frolicking naked in the surf. There might come a time in the future when such knowledge on her part would come in handy.

"Yes. Well." Lily cleared her throat and gazed benignly at the backs of *both* hands now—*as well she should*, Schuyler thought indignantly. "Although it's true that I may have said something to that effect—"

"Actually, Miss Rigby, those were your exact words," Mrs. Beecham interjected. "I'm quite good at remembering things like that, and you distinctly said 'Bermuda Fun Bar—' "

"Yes. Well." This time Lily was the one to interrupt. "Those may indeed have been my exact words, but I, um . . . I was obviously mistaken. Mr. Kimball was actually attending to some business overseas, and not, uh . . . frolicking naked with anyone."

Schuyler nodded. "That's exactly correct, Mrs. Beecham," he lied. "And I wasn't even attending to business with Corporate Fun Barbie, the way I would have liked to have been."

Mrs. Beecham's expression changed swiftly at the announcement, going from murderous—albeit courteous—intent, to stark, raving, embarrassment in no time flat. Immediately, she released his tie and took a step backward, then dropped her head into her hands. "I'm sorry," she mumbled. "I am so sorry."

As quickly as she had succumbed to the need to

hide, however, she lifted her head, squared her shoulders, and once again assumed the pose of a fighting Valkyrie. "I've been under some pressure myself lately, Mr. Kimball. Not that such a thing excuses my behavior tonight, but . . . I do apologize." Before he could accept or decline that apology, she hurried on, "And it is imperative that I speak with you as soon as possible. Why not tonight, since I'm already here?" She nodded toward someone behind Schuyler. "Chloe could join us, seeing as how she's here, too, and this concerns her."

He eyed Mrs. Beecham with warning, deftly rearranging his bow tie until it was, once again, perfect. "No," he said with a conviction that in no way invited contradiction. "Not tonight. I've just finished dinner with my—" He hesitated, then forced himself to say it outright, concentrating very hard so that he didn't trip over the word. "My family. And right now . . ."

He gave his tie one final tug for good measure, then spared as lascivious a look as he could manage for Valentina. The call girl still stood by his side, watching the by-play with as much interest as one might show for a pictorial about anthrax.

"Right now, I have other plans," he continued without removing his attention from his escort, who brightened considerably as a result. "You, Mrs. Beecham, may call my secretary tomorrow and make an appointment to see me at a time when I'm available. Until then . . ."

He tossed her a final—and very careless—scrap of attention as he strode by her. "Until then, I have some personal business to attend to."

He thought that would be the end of it, but he heard Janey cry, "Wait! Mrs. Beecham!" and he hesitated, fearing what would come next.

True to form, Janey asked her standard question of greeting when faced with a new acquaintance. "Mrs. Beecham," she said, "can you spell *evapotranspiration*?"

Schuyler closed his eyes and waited to hear what Mrs. Beecham's response would be, though why he cared, he honestly couldn't have said.

"Well, of course I can spell evapotranspiration," Mrs. Beecham replied. He had to hand it to the headmistress. She didn't even sound surprised by the question. "E-v-a-p-o-t-r-a-n-s-p-i-r-a-t-i-o-n." Then, before Janey could get her licks in, she added, "Evapotranspiration. Noun. The transference of moisture from the earth to its atmosphere by water's evaporation and plants' transpiration. I minored in biology," she added by way of an explanation.

"What's your IQ?" Janey asked further.

Schuyler waited, hoping, for some reason, that Mrs. Beecham would reply that her IQ was nothing out of the ordinary, that she only knew about evapotranspiration because she was an avid gardener. Unfortunately, what she said was, "One hundred and eighty-five, why?"

One hundred and eighty-five? he repeated to himself, shocked. Amazed. Intrigued. Oh, *fine*. She *would* have an IQ large enough to compete with her . . . other endowments. Dammit.

"*Mother!*" Janey exclaimed. "When are you going to talk to Schuyler about—"

"Janey?" Schuyler interjected without turning around, and with a surprisingly tepid tone.

For a moment, she didn't respond. Then, in a very small voice, she asked, "Yes, Schuyler?"

"Go to your room."

"But—"

"Go to your room. And your library privileges are suspended until further notice."

"But—"

"You will write an essay entitled 'Why I Won't Harass My Brother's House Guests About Their IQs Anymore,' and you will place it on my desk tomorrow morning."

"But—"

For the last time, he hoped, Schuyler turned to Vivian and conjured the most licentious smile in his arsenal. Strangely, though, he felt as if he were rousing the smile not for Viveca, but for Mrs. Beecham. Stranger still was his realization that he was no longer as interested in page seventy-two of *How to Leave a Man Groaning with Satisfaction Every Time* as he was in the hidden chapters of the headmistress.

Because as he dipped his head in farewell to the entire dinner party, his expression lingered only on her. And he hoped she knew what she was missing out on by being so damned intelligent and tightly bound. Unfortunately, somehow, Schuyler suspected that *he* was the one who was missing out on something. And that maybe, just maybe, he wasn't quite as smart as he thought.

EIGHT

Oh, God, oh, God, oh, God, oh, God. When was it going to stop?

As she did every night, Caroline Beecham awoke from sleep at precisely 3:22 a.m., to find that she lay curled in a tiny ball, in her tiny bed, in her tiny bedroom, in her tiny apartment. 3:22 a.m. She rolled over in her bed and tried to think of something—anything—else.

Unfortunately, when she did that, the first thought that wandered into her head was of Schuyler Kimball.

Of course, that wasn't surprising, seeing as how she'd been thinking about him a lot over the past week. Ever since she had barged into his home and grabbed him by the throat, only to discover that she was making a really big mistake—not to mention a really big fool out of herself—in the process. All things said and done, she supposed something like attempted homicide on a man *would* rather permanently etch the intended victim's image into a woman's brain.

Oh, God, had she actually done that? she asked herself for perhaps the hundredth time since it had happened. Had she truly snatched up Schuyler Kimball—*Schuyler Kimball!*—by the throat and threatened him?

She groaned and rolled over in her bed again. The glowing red letters on her clock read 3:24 now, and she felt her heart rate slow some in response to the realization that she had survived 3:22 a.m. for one more night.

Her slowing pulse accelerated again, however, when she recalled once more her escapade with Schuyler Kimball. She had called his secretary the first thing the following morning to set up an appointment to see him. After much hemming and hawing and alleged rearranging of his schedule, Miss Rigby had managed to pencil Caroline in for an impressive twenty minutes the following Saturday morning—which was only a few hours away from right now. Caroline swallowed hard as she rehearsed yet again what she intended—what she needed—to say to Mr. Kimball.

They were losing Chloe. And he had to help her bring the girl back. It was that simple.

Never had Caroline met a more remarkable child than Chloe Sandusky, but every day the teenager was slipping farther and farther away. Caroline was beginning to fear that, unless there were some vast and immediate changes made to the girl's life, she would be lost to them forever. And the world— yes, the world—might potentially suffer as a result.

Simply put, Chloe Sandusky was the most gifted, most brilliant, most incredibly minded person Caroline had ever met. And having worked with gifted, brilliant, incredibly minded children for more than a decade now, that was saying something. Yet no one but her seemed to care about Chloe. Even the teachers at Van Meter—who'd been trained to deal with gifted, and often difficult to manage, children—had pretty much washed their hands of Chloe.

Because in addition to being the most brilliant child Caroline had ever met, Chloe was also the most self-destructive. There could be any number of reasons for that—and, having finally met Mr. Kimball, Caroline could easily conceive of one really *big* reason—but that didn't mean she was ready to give up on Chloe. Not yet. Not now. Not ever, if she could help it.

Unfortunately, that was less and less up to Caroline, and more and more up to Chloe. And if Chloe didn't give a damn about her future—or her present, for that matter—then how was Caroline supposed to help her?

The words she had rehearsed so meticulously to recite to Schuyler Kimball tumbled through her head, sounding stilted and stunted and sterile. Twenty minutes, she reminded herself. That was all the time she had to save a girl's life. Twenty minutes to convince a man who may or may not be her father that Chloe Sandusky's was a life worth living, a brain worth nurturing, a soul worth saving. God alone knew what the girl was capable of achieving if given even a tiny injection of self-worth. She might become a research scientist who would ultimately rid the world of disease. She might become a composer who created music to calm even the most restless spirit. She might become a leader who ran a government that would bring peace to a weary planet.

But none of that would happen unless someone could make Chloe understand how very important she was. Not just as a brilliant individual, but as a decent human being. Caroline had tried so hard to make the girl see how amazing and abundant her gifts were. But Chloe would be blind to those gifts forever unless someone else—someone she cared about more than she did the headmistress of her school—pointed them out to her, and praised her for possessing them.

Caroline flopped over onto her back again and tried not to look at the empty space on the other side of the bed, the space that had been empty for almost a year now. Instead, she thought about the morning to come. Twenty minutes, she reminded herself. How could she find enough words in that brief span of time to save the life of a child who didn't consider herself valuable enough to rescue?

The moment his secretary led her into Schuyler Kimball's library, Caroline knew she was about to undertake a battle for a lost cause. To say that the billionaire looked uninterested in her arrival would have been a gross understatement. In fact, as he closed his book and rose formally from a leather-clad sofa, what he looked to be was hostile. And immediately, instinctively, she shifted into self-preservation mode.

Strangely, though, she recognized at once that the reason her defenses leapt so utterly to alert *wasn't* because of his clear animosity toward her. Antagonistic parents—and guardians—were part of the terrain where her job was concerned. But Caroline was fully confident in her ability to manage such situations when they arose. She was, after all, a professional. No, the reason every last one of her personal shields hurtled up now was, she was certain, to keep her safe from Schuyler Kimball as a man. Because Caroline Beecham, for all her self-assurance as an educator, was in no way confident of her abilities as a woman.

Particularly when she was faced with a man like this.

She found it odd that someone who worked at home would bother dressing in a power suit, complete with Windsor-knotted tie. She would have thought that would be one of the perks of self-employment—billionaire self-employment, at that—the freedom to wear whatever one wished when performing one's job. Schuyler Kimball had so much power and so much money, she couldn't conceive of a single person who might tell him what to do. Had she been in his place, she would have worn her pajamas every day.

Yet here he stood, in his own home, looking as if he had just risen from the head of an executive boardroom table. Then, for some reason, it struck her that perhaps this was the only way Schuyler Kimball could maintain his authority over his personal empire. By treating it the same way he would his professional one. Still, he seemed out of place here, dressed as he was. And certainly all the more formidable. She had rather been hoping she might catch him between tennis sets, when he would be more relaxed, more exhausted, more malleable. And, naturally, more amenable to seeing things her way.

Ah, well, she thought as she took a reluctant step forward. Might as well get this over with. Tally ho. Half a league onward. Mine eyes have seen the glory, and all that.

"The headmistress of Chloe's school is here, Schuyler."

Miss Rigby's announcement from directly behind her made Caroline flinch, simply because, for an instant, she had completely forgotten that she and Mr. Kimball weren't alone in the room—or in the universe, for that matter. What was worse than her reaction, however, was the fact that he had obviously noticed her quick recoil, because he smiled slightly, almost, she thought, triumphantly.

"Thank you, Lily darling," he replied coolly, his gaze fixed not on his secretary, but on Caroline.

No one moved for a moment, then the soft click of the door closing behind her made Caroline flinch again. Because then she and Schuyler Kimball truly were alone—in the room and in the universe. For twenty minutes. Whether she liked it or not.

In light of his unmistakable antagonism, she inhaled a deep breath, threw back her shoulders, and smoothed a hand quickly down the front of her beige knit dress. The loose-fitting, nondescript, long-sleeved sheath wasn't, perhaps, the most efficient armor in the world. With a man like Schuyler Kimball, she probably would have fought the battle more effectively if she had donned a hula skirt and halter top. But Caroline had learned long ago that if she wanted others to see past the outer shell that had always betrayed her, then she would have to learn to disguise it as best she could.

Evidently, she thought, as Mr. Kimball flicked a hasty—and indifferent—glance in her direction before turning away, she had succeeded well in that this morning, at least. As always, though, the victory felt hollow at best.

"Mrs. Beckwith, isn't it?" he asked as he approached her, focused not on her, but on the rows of books he slowly passed.

"No," she replied easily, unwilling to lose her composure in light of his games. A man like him, she supposed, would always want to have the upper hand. Nowhere was it written, however, that she had to let him have it. "It's Mrs. Beecham."

He kept coming until a scant foot of space separated them. But instead of halting to face her, he seemed to become preoccupied by something else and moved to her left, covering the half dozen feet between him and a wall completely obscured by books. He scanned the titles idly for a moment, until locating whatever had caught his interest. Withdrawing the volume, he opened it to the table of contents, then leaned one shoulder insouciantly against the shelf from which he had pulled the book and began to read.

She waited in silence while he finished his stalling tactic, suddenly none too eager to get on with the reason for her visit. Frankly, she found him far more interesting to watch than she did to talk to. She wondered if he ever stopped thinking, or planning, or scheming. For long moments, neither of them spoke, and Caroline congratulated herself for her patience. Then, as absently as he had taken an interest in the book, he lost it again, closing the volume and reshelving it with much care.

But still he maintained his indifferent posture. With one shoulder pressed to the shelf, he stuffed his hands nonchalantly into his trouser pockets and met her gaze with a look that was, at best, incredibly bored. "And, I'm sorry . . . what is your position again?" he asked. "I've forgotten what it is you said you do."

She smiled dryly. "The hell you have."

A flicker of something—surprise?—lit his eyes for a moment, then dimmed again. "A teacher, or something, right?"

Caroline took a few steps toward him, thinking it might be best if she could at least appear to be on the offensive here. "I'm the headmistress of Chloe's school, the Van Meter Academy. Where," she added, biting back the sarcasm that spurred her, "your young *ward* is currently enrolled in the program for extremely gifted children, studying literature, music, art, science, and philosophy. Or at least she would be, if she made it to class more than a handful of times a week and completed the required assignments."

Mr. Kimball nodded slowly, seemingly lost in thought. "That's right," he murmured, his voice as soft and smooth as velvet. He met her gaze levelly again, mischief sparking his eyes this time when he did. "How could I forget? That's one of my favorite words in the English language, after all."

She eyed him with confusion. "What word?"

He smiled the way he had smiled at his . . . *play-mate*—she hesitated to use the word, though she wasn't sure why, seeing as how that was essentially what his dinner companion of the week before had been. "*Headmistress*," he said, enunciating the word with much relish. "I love that word. It just seems to encompass so many wonderful things, doesn't it?"

Instead of rising to the bait, Caroline ignored the remark. There was no reason for her to resort to adolescent comments. Especially since Mr. Kimball seemed more than capable of providing enough for both of them.

"Your ward, Mr. Kimball," she said, moving a few more slow steps forward, until she, too, could lean a careless shoulder against the bookcase, albeit a shelf lower than where he'd settled his own, "is an extremely gifted young woman. I don't know if you honestly realize just how gifted."

His lips flattened into a line of clear disapproval where the change of subject was concerned. "My ward, Mrs. Beecham, is a troubled kid whose mother should have done better by her," he replied.

"Maybe it's her father who should have done better by her," Caroline returned without hesitation. "It takes two to generate a life, after all. Why do people have so much trouble remembering that?

Why is it always the mother who fails a child, and not the father, hmmm?"

But Mr. Kimball didn't rise to her bait, either. He simply stated blandly, "Chloe is doing just fine, in my opinion, all things considered. Yes, she can be difficult at times, but she's by no means any worse than a number of children her age. I don't see where you need to trouble yourself with her welfare. Will that be everything? Lily can show you out."

Caroline inhaled a deep breath, releasing it slowly as she tried to keep a lid on her anger and decide how to proceed. Finally, ignoring his invitation for her to beat it, she said, "I have been working with gifted children for nearly twelve years, Mr. Kimball, ever since earning my master's degree in child development. But I've never met a child like Chloe. Ever."

"Yes, well, you wouldn't be alone in that regard," he interjected dryly. "She's certainly one of a kind."

Caroline ignored that comment, too. "There are a lot of gifted children in the world," she continued, striving to keep her voice even, hesitant to succumb to the passion she felt for her subject matter. Something told her that Schuyler Kimball would react to passion—any passion—in a way she wasn't prepared to deal with right now. "Musically gifted children," she went on, "linguistically gifted children, intellectually gifted children, emotionally gifted children, kinetically gifted children. But I've never met a child who combined so many gifts in one single package. Chloe is gifted in virtually every way imaginable. She could do or be anything she wants. Anything. Do you understand what I'm saying?"

For a long moment, the billionaire didn't respond. He only stared at Caroline as if giving great weight to some very important matter. In many ways, he seemed not to see her at all, so absorbed was he in whatever had claimed his attention. His entire being seemed to hum with the process of dissemination, as if he were some sophisticated bit of machinery filing and sorting what she had just told him, drawing conclusions no mortal human would ever be able to fathom.

Although she didn't alter her seemingly careless pose any more than he did, ultimately, Caroline had to look away. She suddenly wished she had kept her glasses on instead of leaving them in the car, even though they were only necessary for close-up work like reading and driving. At this point, she thought, any barrier, anything that might give the impression of distance between them, would be welcome. Such intensity on Mr. Kimball's part, such focus, such utter fixation . . . It made her nervous. It made her anxious. It made her . . .

God help her, it made her *hot*.

She had been totally unprepared for Schuyler Kimball a week ago, and she was no more ready for him now. And it wasn't just because of the simple matter that he was an extremely handsome, rawly sexy, man. Certainly she'd met plenty of handsome, sexy men in her time, and had been married to one for nearly ten years . . . before losing him.

But Mr. Kimball's appearance went beyond dark good looks. There was something compelling about him. Something commanding. Something charismatic. It was something she'd never encountered in another human being before. He was the kind of man who could tell a person to do something outrageous, something ridiculous, something dangerous . . . and that person would do it without a thought for the repercussions of the action.

He was the kind of man who, if he had a mind to, could honestly *own* another person, heart and mind, body and soul. Maybe that was why Miss Rigby had granted Caroline an audience with him of only twenty minutes. Because to spend any longer than that in the man's presence was to risk losing oneself forever.

He shifted his position slightly then, and she brought her head back up to glance at him. But only long enough to note that he had removed one hand from his pocket and was absently rubbing his open palm over his roughly shadowed jaw. There was something strangely intimate about the gesture, though, and she forced her gaze away again, focusing on the flame-colored trees that dotted the vast landscape outside the big Palladian window behind him.

"Look," he said softly, a bit wearily, "I'll grant you that Chloe is brighter than the average child, but—"

"Her IQ is off the charts, Mr. Kimball," Caroline interrupted him. "Higher, I'll wager, than even yours."

He thrust his chin up defensively at that, and Caroline realized with no small degree of surprise that she'd just inflicted the first blow of battle. So Schuyler Kimball's own armor wasn't quite as impenetrable as he let on. The recognition that he wasn't, in fact, omnipotent, as everyone seemed to think he was, offered her some small measure of reassurance.

"She's nothing at all like the average child," Caroline continued, taking advantage of his silence. "In fact, Chloe's nothing like anyone. If you could put Einstein, Mozart, and Da Vinci in one person, Mr. Kimball, you would end up with Chloe Sandusky. It's that simple. And believe me, she's smart enough to know it. Can you imagine what that must be like? To be fourteen years old—*fourteen years old*—and to be as brilliant as she is, and to look the way she looks, and to have no idea—*no idea*—where you fit into the scheme of things?"

Mr. Kimball's chest expanded with the silent and lengthy breath he inhaled. His eyes grew turbulent, his mouth hard when he replied, "Yes, Mrs. Beecham. Believe it or not, I can, to some extent, imagine what that must be like."

She shook her head. "No, I don't think you can." She held up a hand when he opened his mouth to object. "I'm familiar with what kind of man you are," she told him. "Everyone is. A brilliant, analytical mind, a child misunderstood and all that. But that's the point—you're a man. Even when you were a boy, your potential was still seen as a man's potential."

"When I was a boy, Mrs. Beecham," he interrupted her, "no one saw any potential in me at all."

He didn't even try to disguise the bitterness in his voice, and for the first time, Caroline realized that perhaps he and Chloe had something more in common than she'd initially surmised. Still, she thought, Chloe was at a far greater risk than Mr. Kimball ever had been. There was no question about that.

"Chloe obviously isn't male," she continued, dropping her voice to a quieter, gentler pitch. "Nor is she even an unattractive female," she added with a soft, sad chuckle, "which is what most people expect to find when a female person is vastly intelligent.

"Chloe matured early in as many ways as there were," Caroline went on intently. "She should have started receiving the proper attention the moment she was born to prepare her for what lay ahead. And once she entered puberty, she should have had a strong female role model to guide her through the hazardous waters. Yet prior to coming here, the only influence she ever had in her life was her mother, who, I don't think I need to remind you, made her living as a stripper."

"An exotic dancer," the billionaire corrected her halfheartedly.

Caroline surrendered to a little sound of derision. "Chloe doesn't talk a lot about what her life was like then, but her mother, quite frankly, didn't seem to give a damn about her."

"Yes, well, she's not living with her mother anymore, is she?" Mr. Kimball pointed out.

"No, that's true," Caroline agreed. "Now she's moved into a big, beautiful estate, and her guardian is a hugely successful, very wealthy, very prominent businessman. Who," she added pointedly, "doesn't seem to give a damn about her."

His eyes turned absolutely stormy at that, and for a moment, Caroline honestly feared he would lunge at her, in much the same way that she had gone after him at dinner that night a week ago. Quickly, she steeled herself for the press of roughly one hundred and seventy-five pounds and nearly six feet of solid flesh. And, oddly, for just the briefest of moments, she almost found herself looking forward to it.

But Schuyler Kimball evidently had better control over his own emotions and reactions than she did her own, because, although a muscle twitched once in his jaw, he didn't move an inch.

"I don't have to give a damn about her," he said coolly. "I have people to do that for me, and they get paid a pretty penny for it."

Caroline was so taken aback by his response that

she had no idea what to say. She'd never met anyone who could be so heartless, who could be so clearly proud of his inhumanity. As rigid and distant as Mr. Kimball had come across, she hadn't expected him to be like this when grilled about his feelings for his . . . ward. Startled by the discovery that he was, in fact, a cold-hearted son of a bitch, the only thing she could manage by way of a reply was, "You bastard. You cold, selfish, stupid bastard. You have no idea what you've just thrown away."

Immediately, she regretted the words. Although the accusation was perfectly understandable coming from a woman who was concerned about the welfare of a child, it was anything but appropriate coming from the headmistress—or, rather, the director, she decided to call herself now—of the exclusive and conservative Van Meter Academy.

That wasn't the main reason why she regretted the statement, however. The main reason she regretted it was because, the split second after she uttered it, that lunge she had been expecting earlier on Mr. Kimball's part did in fact materialize.

Before she even realized what had happened, he had her pinned against the bookcase behind her, his entire body pressed into hers, his face a scant inch from her own. One of his forearms was braced against a fat leather volume beside her face, his hand fisted tight just above her head, while his other hand gripped fiercely the shelf at her shoulder level. When she tipped her head back to look at his face—frankly amazed by her ability to do so—she saw that a single lock of jet-black hair had fallen over his forehead, giving him the look of a very dangerous man.

But his eyes were what jolted Caroline the most. Because a dark and angry storm roared rampant within them, one she suspected had been raging unchecked for a very long time.

The shelves behind her bit into her back, and instinctively, she arched forward to alleviate the discomfort. Instinctively, too, she opened her palms over his shoulders, as if that meager show of objection might honestly stop him from doing whatever he intended to do. His breathing was ragged and uncontrolled, pushing and shoving his chest against her breasts, and every time their bodies made contact, she felt the rapid-fire beating of his heart that mirrored her own exactly.

His heat, his energy, his very soul, seemed to surround her, enveloping her, drawing her closer to him, even though the two of them were already as close as they could physically be. Somehow, she felt as if he were reeling her inside him, absorbing her, joining her to him, and it was with no small effort that she struggled to keep herself independent of his command.

Curling her fingers tightly into his shoulders, she made a halfhearted effort to repel him. But he only seemed to come closer when she did, and to her utter mortification, she realized she was pulling him toward herself instead of pushing him away. But as she felt herself weakening, about to surrender, he abruptly let her go. Not that he moved his body away from hers—on the contrary, physically, he seemed to be closer than ever. But a door slammed shut somewhere deep inside him, and in every other way that counted, he released her, as if he'd encountered something in her essence that simply did not mix well with his own.

Still leaning his body provocatively into hers, he parted his lips in what promised to be a bitter retort. But for a long time, he said nothing. He only held her there, pressed to the bookcase, not quite against her will, and searched her face for the answer to some very important question that she couldn't recall him having asked her.

Finally, in a voice that was soft, serious, seductive, he said, "I've been called many things in my life, Mrs. Beecham. But 'stupid,' I'm afraid, is not one of them."

She felt the hand above her head drop down to her hair, felt his fingertips skim softly over the tresses until he wound a dark auburn curl around his index finger. Only then did Caroline realize that, at some point during their—she wasn't sure what to call whatever was happening between them—their . . . encounter, the wide clip that had secured her French twist in place had slipped. Now bits of hair tumbled down around her shoulders, and Schuyler Kimball had decided, as he undoubtedly had for so many other things in his life, to claim some of them for his own.

His touch sent a sizzle of heat spiraling across her scalp and down her neck, and she shut her eyes tight in an effort to dispel the sensation. She swallowed hard in an effort to alleviate the dryness that had overtaken her mouth, but all that did was magnify the rapid rhythm of the pulse pounding against her throat. So she opened her eyes again, hoping that staring her nemesis in the face might offer her some measure of strength, however meager. But Schuyler Kimball, too, seemed to notice the irregularity of her heart rate, as his attention was fixed intently on the slender column of her throat.

"Although," he went on in a voice that was longing, leisurely, lascivious. He sighed, still gazing at her neck the way an amorous vampire might. "I don't know what else to call the impulses traveling through my brain at the moment, but *stupid*. You seem to have me at something of a disadvantage,

Mrs. Beecham. Congratulations. I don't think anyone's ever managed that before.''

She had *him* at a disadvantage? Caroline wondered wildly. Hey, he wasn't the one pinned to a bookcase under pounds and pounds of pure, pulsing male. She opened her mouth to say something that might defuse what was fast turning into an explosive situation. But he removed his other hand from the bookcase and skimmed his fingertips lightly along her throat, an action that dispelled any hope she might have of ever speaking again. Deftly, he dipped his fingers into the delicate hollow at the base of her neck, then ventured out to trail the backs of his knuckles slowly along her collarbone and back again.

And when he did, she couldn't stop the not-quite-silent murmur of pleasure that whispered out between her lips.

At that soft, sensual sound, he halted his caress, lifting his gaze to her face. And that was when Caroline forgot all about Chloe Sandusky's well-being. She had no choice but to forget about the girl, even if only temporarily. Because she knew that if she didn't start thinking about her own well-being instead, she would be lost in a far worse way than Chloe would be.

With one final squeeze of her fingers into his shoulders, and without a word of explanation, Caroline pushed Schuyler Kimball away. She didn't know where she found the strength or fortitude to manage such a thing, but she wasted no time as he stumbled backward in his surprise. Not caring how ridiculous, how desperate, how terrified she must look as she fled, Caroline hastened to the door and escaped the library as if flames were licking at her heels.

She would never be able to recall quite how she

found her way through the vast, infinite house to the front door. Miss Rigby had deposited her coat and purse on a bench in the massive foyer, and Caroline snatched up both in one hand as she passed them. But it wasn't until she had cleared the half-mile-long drive to the estate that she dared to inhale a lengthy, calming breath. And when she did, her nose and lungs were filled with the scent of Schuyler Kimball. The scent he had transferred to her in his nearness, the scent that clung to her still.

And all she could do was think that now, he was inside her, too.

In the library, Schuyler braced both hands against the bookcase before him, tried to steady his own breathing, and wondered what the hell had just happened. One minute, Caroline Beecham— *Mrs.* Caroline Beecham, he reminded himself brutally—had been accusing him of being a stupid bastard, and the next, he had been looking to make her pay for it.

Why? He had no idea. He couldn't imagine a reason to make her pay for such a thing. It wasn't as if he disagreed with her on that score, after all.

His thoughts were thankfully interrupted when his darling Lily entered the library. He sensed more than saw or heard her arrival, and when he glanced up to greet her, he saw that she was in warrior mode. The expression she wore was dark and unforgiving, and her black wool suit was almost austere. And it would have been, too, on another woman—a woman who *wasn't* soft and sensuous and splendid. Lily, however, made the ensemble look sleek and elegant, even when she stood as she did now, making no effort to disguise her utter disregard for him.

"She's a nice woman, Schuyler," she said resolutely, not bothering to identify Mrs. Beecham with anything other than a pronoun. "And she cares about Chloe. Which is more than I can say for some people. You leave the woman alone. Or you'll answer to me."

Without awaiting a response to her threat—after all, they both knew exactly what she was talking about—Lily turned and strode out of the library. Schuyler watched her go with a half-smile playing about his lips, daring himself to defy her. Because, hey, there were infinitely worse things in life than being answerable to Lily Rigby.

And Caroline Beecham, he thought further—*Mrs.* Caroline Beecham—was proving to be far more interesting than he had planned.

So darling Lily was just going to have to deal with that. Some things in life were worth risking one's friends for.

Holding fast to the memory of Mrs. Caroline Beecham's near capitulation, Schuyler went back to his books.

NINE

Having cautioned Schuyler the best way she knew how to leave Caroline Beecham alone—well, the best way she knew how that *didn't* involve the use of a Louisville Slugger—Lily decided that she needed, and deserved, a day off. It was Saturday, after all, and she was tired of working on Saturdays. Besides, October was fast drawing to a close, and she'd scarcely had a chance to leave the estate to enjoy her favorite season. Soon the trees would be stripped bare of their bright fall foliage, and winter's chill would be nipping at her nose. And once hibernation and the holidays set in at Ashling, there would be little chance for her to venture out.

Air. She needed air. She needed to fill her nose and lungs with the pungent scent of autumn, needed to feel the kiss of the brisk wind on her face, needed to remind herself that there was more to a day's passing than the little dramas that took place inside Ashling.

What Lily needed was a life. Unfortunately, on days like this, when she felt as if she were tending to other people more than she tended to herself, life seemed to be racing past her without stopping to even explain its rush. How had she arrived where she was, having planned none of it? she wondered, not for the first time.

Not that she was unhappy—not really—but she wasn't entirely happy, either. She felt as if she'd spent the bulk of her adult life making plans for the future, thinking that after this happened, or that happened, or something else happened, *then* she could get on with the business of living. But always, something else seemed to intrude first, hindering her progress, keeping her from enjoying the plans she made. It had never once occurred to her to enjoy the here and now.

Now, however, *here*, it was beginning to occur to her. She only hoped that *now*, it wasn't too late.

For some reason, such a realization made her think again about Caroline Beecham. And as Lily started for her bedroom to change her clothes, she couldn't quite rid herself of the notion that Schuyler hadn't fully appreciated the vehemence with which she had offered her warning some moments ago. Mrs. Beecham *was* a nice woman. That was the first reason Schuyler should leave her alone. And Mrs. Beecham *did* care about Chloe. That was the second reason Schuyler should leave her alone.

But the third, and perhaps most important, reason was that Lily suspected there was something going on with the woman right now that made her far too fragile to handle someone like Schuyler. Lily had no idea what that something might be, but Mrs. Beecham was clearly going through a rough time of it. She looked more tired than Lily had ever seen anyone looking in her life. She seemed defeated. She seemed hopeless. She seemed lonely.

She was easy pickings for someone like Schuyler. And Schuyler, damn him, had been in a surly mood ever since his return from Bermuda, and had clearly been spoiling for a fight. It would be just like him to take advantage of the weakness and fragility of a woman who, at another time, under other circumstances, would probably be a worthy adversary for him. As much as Lily cared for him, there was no getting around the fact that there were times when Schuyler could be a complete . . . a complete . . .

She sighed fitfully as she searched for the right word. A complete butthead. There, that would do nicely.

Goodness, she thought as her low heels pounded the black and white checkerboard of Italian marble that made up the endless length of Ashling's gallery. She was in something of a surly mood herself today, wasn't she? Normally, she didn't mind being Schuyler's keeper. Or Chloe's keeper. Or Janey's keeper. Or Miranda's keeper. Or even Mrs. Puddleduck's keeper. It was part of her job, after all. And she'd been doing it long enough now that it was almost second nature to her. Today, however, she wished the various and assorted Kimballs would just grow up and learn to take care of themselves.

Especially Schuyler. Honestly. He was thirty-five years old and, for all intents and purposes, headed up a multi-billion-dollar empire. One would think it would be all right to leave such a man alone for one morning. But *noooo* . . .

Lily had wandered off for less than fifteen minutes, and look what had happened. He'd gone after a perfectly nice woman who deserved to be heard and heeded where the care of one Chloe Sandusky was concerned. Lily made a mental note to call Mrs. Beecham herself and arrange for a meeting with her at the school later this week. How could she expect Schuyler to look after the girl when he wouldn't even look after himself? As always, the responsibility would fall upon Lily.

Her thoughts spurred her dark mood, dogging her as she covered the distance of the house, reinforcing her conviction that she needed to get away for a while. But it was only when she closed her bedroom door behind herself that she finally, finally realized what had actually put her in such a foul mood today. It wasn't her concern for Schuyler. Nor was it her concern for Chloe or Caroline Beecham. It wasn't even because of the unsteadiness of her own feelings this morning. No, what had her feeling off-kilter and irritable this beautiful autumn day was really quite obvious.

She missed Leonard Freiberger.

It was Saturday, so he wasn't working, and Lily, quite simply, missed him. She missed greeting him as she had every morning for more than a week now, and chatting with him as she accompanied him to Schuyler's office. She missed the borderline lascivious looks she caught him throwing her way on those few occasions when they met during the day, and she missed the innuendo in their conversations when they broke for tea and coffee every afternoon. She even missed being suspicious of his motives and wondering what he was up to, even though she had double-checked to make sure he was indeed here at the behest of the Kimball Technologies board of directors. She just plain missed his presence at the estate.

And now it appeared that he wouldn't be coming back. Yesterday he had informed her that, having found nothing in Schuyler's files here, he would be taking his search for the income tax problem elsewhere. Then he had gathered up his pert little files, had rubber-banded his cute little computer disks, had adjusted his darling little glasses, and smoothed out his adorable little ugly tweed suit. And with a quick goodbye and an awkward handshake—*handshake*, Lily recalled with much disappointment now, thinking that a man who had starred front and center in her sexual fantasies for a week should be good for at least one heart-stopping grope—he'd left Ashling to return to work in Philadelphia.

And Lily had been feeling oddly dejected ever since, as if she'd been dumped by a lover.

It made no sense, her reaction. In spite of their daily chats, she didn't really know the man all that well, after all. Yet as she changed out of her suit and into her off-duty uniform of well-worn jeans and thick, oversized, berry-colored sweater and hiking boots, she couldn't quite stop her thoughts from lingering on the man. And then, suddenly, somehow—she really, truly, honestly didn't mean to—she found herself going to her closet and pulling out the Philadelphia telephone directory, and flipping through the white pages until she located *F*.

Or, more specifically, until she located *Fr. Fr . . . e*. Let's see now . . . *Frederick, Freed, Freeman, Frehse, Freibaum* . . . Ah ha. *Freiberger*, there it was. All three of them.

Lily frowned. But no Leonard Freiberger. Not even an L. Freiberger. Well, that didn't help at all, did it?

She slammed the phone book shut and replaced it in the closet. It would figure that he would have an unlisted number. He had, after all, fairly exuded the warning, *No Trespassing*. And *Keep off the Grass*. And *Access Denied*. That sort of thing.

And then she was overcome once again by the feeling that Mr. Freiberger had been trying to hide something during his brief sojourn at Ashling.

What? She couldn't imagine. But her instincts had cautioned her to beware.

Before leaving, she quickly checked her e-mail on the state-of-the-art laptop that perched on her writing desk, to make sure there was nothing pressing that needed her attention. Not that she'd expected anything, seeing as how it was Saturday and Schuyler was home, but there was always a chance for the odd development that might require her input. Satisfied, however, that there was nothing she needed to attend to for the rest of the day, Lily donned a knit cap the same color as her heavy sweater, grabbed her backpack and a new romance novel she'd been looking forward to reading, and headed down to the kitchen to pack herself a lunch to take with her. Might as well make a day of it, she thought.

Today was hers, she told herself further, as she reached for the keys to what she'd always considered, not the SUV—the sport utility vehicle—but the SAV—the suburban assault vehicle. Jingling the keys merrily in her hand, she headed toward the four-car garage behind Ashling. She wasn't going to worry about anything today, she promised herself. Not Schuyler. Not Mrs. Beecham. Not Chloe. She wasn't even going to worry about Lily.

And she certainly wouldn't worry about Mr. Leonard Freiberger and what he had been up to during his time at Ashling. Not for all the money in the world.

Funny how life worked out sometimes, Leo thought as he lay beneath a big pile of large, sweaty men. He had just been thinking about Lily Rigby—not so surprising, really, seeing as how he'd been thinking about little else lately—when, lo and behold, a woman should appear who looked exactly like her.

Well, not *exactly* like her, he amended as he grunted and tried to push himself up on his elbows, only to be thwarted by the most massive of the large, sweaty men. With a muffled *oof*, he fell back to the ground, tasting dirt, and eyed the woman again. No, this woman wasn't wearing a no-nonsense business suit and striding purposefully through a huge estate as if she were the queen of all she surveyed, the way he'd come to think about Lily Rigby. Instead, this woman was clad in faded jeans and a sweater made of some soft, fuzzy . . . stuff . . . and she was lying on her stomach in the grass with her legs bent backward and upward. She was reading a book—and was really, really involved in it, too, if the look on her face was any indication—beneath a tree not fifty feet away from where Leo had just been soundly sacked in his role as weekend quarterback.

Call him crazy, but there was just something incredibly sexy about a woman wearing big ol' hiking boots. Maybe it was because hiking boots were traditionally something he'd always viewed as utterly masculine, and seeing them on a woman who was anything *but* masculine just made her seem that much more feminine. Then again, he thought further, Lily Rigby could be wearing waders and have a duck sitting on her head, and Leo would still think she was sexy as hell. Especially if that was *all* she was wearing. Hmmm . . .

With one final shove, he pushed upward, freeing himself from the last of the large, sweaty men. "Get *offa* me," he grumbled to his buddy Nelson as the two men struggled to stand. He arced his gaze around at the five other men who met weekly for a game of football in Fairmont Park. "Jeez, you idiots, I thought this was just supposed to be a friendly game. College rules, not prison rules."

"Sorry," Nelson said without an ounce of apology. As always, however, anything the man said came out sounding like a death sentence.

Nelson stood eye to eye with Leo, but outweighed him by a good thirty pounds. With his dark skin and shaved head, and eyes as black as thunder, he was a menacing-looking sonofabitch. He'd been drafted to the Eagles once upon a time, but an injury had forced him into extremely early retirement. Which was just as well, because he was doubtless making a lot more now as a stockbroker than he would have made playing second-string ball.

He cracked each one of his knuckles in turn—slowly—and smiled evilly. "Felt like we were losing you there, man. Needed to bring you back around. You been awfully . . . *distracted* lately."

Well, no shit, Leo thought. A woman like Lily Rigby living in your brain and taunting your libido night and day sorta left a man preoccupied. But he didn't offer any explanation. Instead, he turned to gaze at the source of that preoccupation, became even more preoccupied than usual, and smiled with *much* preoccupation.

Yep, that was definitely Lily Rigby. She was definitely wearing some incredibly sexy denim and sweater stuff—not to mention those haunting hiking boots—and she was definitely so wrapped up in her book that she wasn't paying any attention at all to her surroundings. He could sit there all day watching her, he thought, and she'd never even know it. But hey, where was the fun in that?

He glanced down at his Georgetown sweatshirt and jeans and noted they were only a little bit muddy and grass-stained. Likewise, he was only marginally fragrant from his athletic endeavors of the last hour. So he bent to retrieve the driving cap he'd been wearing to ward off the day's chill and settled it on his head backward, where it had been before Nelson had tried to turn him into a bag of mulch. Damn. If only he'd had the foresight to wear his glasses instead of his contacts, he might just be able to pass himself off as lame Leonard Freiberger.

"I need a pair of glasses," he said, so focused was he on that one thought.

"What for?" Nelson asked.

Only then did Leo realize he'd spoken aloud. He didn't want to have to explain his reasons to a bunch of guys who would hound him relentlessly about his double life and his attraction to the delectable Miss Rigby. Nor could he offer an honest explanation anyway, even if he wanted to, seeing as how he had taken a blood oath for the sake of Kimball's board of directors.

So all he said was, "Long story. It's not that big a deal."

"Here," Mike, one of the other men, piped up. He pulled off his own tortoiseshell-rimmed spectacles and held them out toward Leo. "Take mine. They're not real. They're mood glasses."

Leo scowled at his friend. "Oh, God. Not you, too." But he reached for the glasses anyway. "What is it with this stuff?" he asked as he donned them. "I can't believe anybody who doesn't have to wear these things would actually choose to wear them."

All the men gaped at him. "Chicks dig 'em," they said as one.

Leo rolled his eyes. "Just pretend you don't know me, okay?"

Nelson chuckled. "Like we don't do that all the time."

Leo emitted a rude sound of disgust in response, and turned his back on the men. When they realized he was approaching Miss Rigby, however— hey, they were smart guys; they recognized a man in heat when they saw one—they all began to laugh themselves silly and offer him, oh . . . etiquette instruction . . . that was dubious at best.

Suddenly, he felt as if he were back in sixth grade, and all the boys in school knew about his crush on Marianne Gianelli, and how he was leaving the football field to go over to where the girls were playing Josie and the Pussycats, just so he might get a whiff of her Love's Baby Soft cologne.

It was humiliating, he thought, that a thirty-eight-year-old man could be reduced to hormone-driven prepubescence by the simple sight of a woman in hiking boots. Man. He was a disgrace to his gender. Even if they were really sexy hiking boots.

As he drew nearer to Lily Rigby, however, his humiliation vanished, because there was something about the look on her face as she rapidly, rabidly, turned the page of her book and continued to read. Seeing that expression made him feel much better about the potential for what might lay ahead.

In the time it took her to finally notice him, he had dropped down onto the grass beside her, had leaned on one elbow and stretched his legs out before him, feigning an idleness he was nowhere close to feeling. And even after she did look up, it still took a moment for her eyes to focus, a moment he used to drink in the sight of her.

If she'd put on makeup that morning, it had long ago vanished. And somehow, the absence of cosmetic enhancement only made her that much more attractive. Her eyes were clearer somehow, her mouth more luscious. The cool wind had stained her cheeks and the tip of her nose pink, giving her the appearance of an innocence he suspected wasn't quite an illusion. For all her businesslike efficiency, there was still something very human and approachable about Lily Rigby. And even though he couldn't quite define what that something was, Leo decided that he liked it. In fact, he liked it a lot.

Her hair was tucked up under a knit cap, save the long bangs brushing her forehead, bangs that she'd always combed to the side before. The fringe of black only added to the suggestion of youthful innocence about her, and for the first time, he wondered if she was younger than he had originally guessed. Thanks to her air of command at Ashling, he had assumed that she was in her early thirties. Now, however, he wondered if she had yet to even see thirty at all.

He told himself to say hello, but as he opened his mouth to do so, she seemed to suddenly recognize her surroundings. Her eyes widened in surprise when she realized who he was, and she hastily sat up, shoving her book behind her back. It was, to say the least, an incriminating gesture. He could only imagine what she didn't want to get caught reading. Probably some gruesome true crime thing about relentless slaughter, he guessed. That was about the only thing he could think of that would be unlike her.

"Mr. Freiberger," she said. But there was little welcome in her voice when she said it. "Where did you come from?"

He jerked a thumb over his shoulder, to where his friends were still gathered. There was no sense denying he knew them, seeing as how they were all pointing at him and doubled over with laughter. He didn't *even* want to think about what kind of speculating they were doing back there. "I'm here chaperoning a bunch of slackers who wanted to play football today," he said. "How about you? What brings you into the big city?"

"I . . . I decided to take the day off."

"It's Saturday," he pointed out unnecessarily. "Everybody should be taking a day off today."

"Yes, well, I imagine there are a lot of restaurant and retail and hospital workers who would agree with you, but I don't see them out here running around the park."

"Touché," he said. "But you're not a retail or restaurant or hospital worker, are you? Doesn't Mr. Kimball give you weekends off?"

Her gaze darted away as she said, "It depends on what's going on with Mr. Kimball and Kimball Technologies."

Leo shrugged, using the gesture to try and see what book she was hiding behind her back. But what he said was, "The stuff going on with Kimball Technologies doesn't seem like it should affect a social secretary's duties." He tried to hide the smile he felt threatening as he returned his attention to her face, but knew he didn't quite succeed. "I mean, come on, Miss Rigby, just how much of Mr. Kimball's business do you actually handle, anyway?"

She smiled, too, not quite benevolently. "Why do I get the feeling, Mr. Freiberger, that you don't think I'm particularly bright?"

He arched his eyebrows in surprise and had no idea what to say in response to her charge. So he said nothing.

"Because that's exactly the feeling I get from you sometimes," she added. "That you don't think I do much . . . thinking. That you believe my job for Mr. Kimball doesn't require much . . . thinking. That

most of my time is spent doing things other than
. . . thinking."

"You think so?" he asked evasively.

She nodded. "Yes. I do."

"Well, gosh, Miss Rigby, I never meant to give
you that impression," he said, still scrambling for
an honest explanation that wouldn't insult her. Unfortunately, he thought, being honest about something like this would definitely insult her. Because
truth be told, she told the truth.

"No, I'm sure you never meant to give me the
impression that you don't think I'm very bright,"
she said. "Nevertheless, you don't think I'm very
bright, do you?"

"I never said—"

"No, and I don't suppose you ever would," she
interjected. "Not that it's really very important
what you think of me anyway."

It wasn't?

"And in spite of your miscalculations, Mr. Freiberger—or perhaps in light of them," she amended
easily, "you might be surprised how much weekend work I have to do for Mr. Kimball."

Yeah, he probably would be surprised, he
thought. Especially if that weekend work actually
involved work. Well, work that couldn't be performed in a horizontal position, anyway. Although
there was a lot to be said for doing it standing
up . . .

Deciding he really didn't want to think about
something like that right now, he asked impulsively, "What are you reading?" Then, before she
had a chance to answer, he reached behind her in
an effort to snag the book from her hand.

"Nothing," she said, angling her body to hinder
his progress. "I'm not reading anything."

"Oh, come on," he cajoled as he reached for it

again. "I know you have a book back there. I saw you reading it. You were really interested in whatever it said, too. Just what kind of book is it?"

She grinned, turning her body more resolutely to prevent him from locating his quarry. "Oh, all right, if you must know, it's Heidegger," she told him. *"Being and Time.* I find it absolutely riveting."

Heidegger? he thought. She'd heard of Heidegger? But . . . but that was impossible. She wasn't particularly bright. Okay, he conceded, so maybe she'd enrolled in Philosophy 101 in college for a humanities credit. That would make sense. Assuming, of course, that she'd gone to college. Did they offer programs for social secretaryism at any of the universities?

"Don't give me that," he said, pushing his thoughts aside. He reached for the book again, lurching forward to rope his arm around her shoulder, hoping that might facilitate his hunt. "Nobody ever found Heidegger riveting. Not even Mrs. Heidegger. And you were definitely interested in whatever this is."

"It's *nothing*," she repeated more adamantly this time, turning her body even more to thwart him.

"Yeah, yeah, yeah. I've read a few books like that myself. Come on," he echoed. " 'Fess up."

With one final lurch forward, he felt the book in his hands. Unfortunately, his final push sent him right into Miss Rigby, who lost her balance and landed backward. Leo snaked out his other arm to catch her, but the result was that Miss Rigby was on her back and Leo was on top of her.

For a moment, he forgot all about the book that he had managed to free from her grasp and held firmly in his own. All he registered was the way her face was barely an inch away from his, how her pupils expanded to nearly eclipse the green of her irises, and the way her lips parted in surprise at their landing. Then, gradually, a few other things registered. He noted the way her lush breasts felt pressed against his chest, and the way her legs, tangled with his, were such an incredibly comfortable fit. And then he felt the rapid-fire pounding of her heart that perfectly mirrored his own.

Then he heard the sound of faint, masculine laughter from behind them, and it was Marianne Gianelli all over again. Quickly, he scrambled off of Miss Rigby and parked his butt firmly on the grass. She, too, wasted no time righting herself, scuttling backward to settle herself against the tree trunk, and well away from Leo.

"Uh, sorry about that," he said.

She nodded quickly. "No problem. Can I have my book back? Please?"

Only then did he remember what had started this whole thing, and, remembering all the trouble he'd gone to to get it—not to mention the wonderful reward he'd received as a result—he held up the book to inspect it. He frowned when he noted the flowers and girlie stuff on the front cover and realized it wasn't what he'd thought it was. Instead of grisly, bloody, true crime, it looked like Miss Rigby's reading preferences were as dainty and innocent as she appeared to be herself.

"Looks good," he lied halfheartedly. Then he flipped open the cover and saw the colorful illustration inside that included two semi-clad people with a raging ocean and stampeding army off in the distance. The man's face was nuzzled against the woman's ample breasts, and she appeared to be *this* close to having a shattering orgasm. "Whoa. Looks *really* good," he amended as he began to flip through the pages.

"Mr. Freiberger," she said with clear objection, reaching for the book.

But in his quick perusal, Leo's attention had lit on the word *nipple*, and there was no way he was going to give the book back just yet. Scanning the rest of the paragraph, he realized that *innocent* and *dainty* were the last words he'd use to describe Miss Rigby's reading preferences. *Raging fever of desire* was a more accurate description. Especially since it was right there in print, in the paragraph that followed the nipple business. And after that . . .

Good God. It was page seventy-two of *How to Leave a Man Groaning with Satisfaction Every Time.*

"Can I borrow this when you're done with it?" he asked, still not looking up from the highly erotic prose. He wondered if there were many men who realized the kinds of things women were learning from romance novels, then thought maybe he should start a campaign to enlighten his gender. It could only benefit everyone.

"Are you serious?" she asked, punctuating the question with a soft laugh.

"Hell, yes, I'm serious," he assured her, turning the page to read more. He wanted to see if Melinda would achieve . . . satisfaction from her lover, Beauregard. *Whoa.* Yes, she did. Several times, in fact. Way to go, Beauregard. Leo made a mental note to try that trick himself next time he—

"It's even better if you start from the beginning and do it a little more slowly."

He glanced up from the book to find Miss Rigby smiling at him. So he smiled back, hoping that in that single gesture, he managed to convey everything he was feeling at the moment—all the heat, all the hunger, all the lust, all the longing, all the fire, all the fury, all the—

"Reading, I mean," she qualified.

Reading? Just like that, his thoughts fizzled. He nodded slowly. "I knew that," he assured her.

But her soft chuckle told him she didn't believe him at all. And that was when Leo decided that yes, it would no doubt definitely be a good idea to start at the beginning, as she had suggested, and to go slow, to see where things led. Because so far, with Lily Rigby, the path had been a bit winding. Now, however, Leo was beginning to think it was time to straighten things out.

"So, Miss Rigby," he began, glancing back down at the book in his hand, "you got plans for the afternoon? I, uh . . . I promise I'll go slow."

TEN

There was little in life that Leo could imagine dreading more than having to face Kimball's board of directors again. The only thing that made this incident worse than the first time was what had made it worse last week, too—on both occasions, he'd had to come clad in his persona of Leonard Freiberger.

And as he had the week before, when he'd given them his first report about the status of his work at Ashling, Leo felt strangely vulnerable, strangely violated, and thoroughly sick to his stomach. Not just because he had to be Lame Leonard Freiberger, but because he knew he was failing at the job he'd been hired to do. And failure, in any form, was something to which Leo was totally unaccustomed.

What was worse was that his inability to find the missing Kimball millions wasn't the only place where he was failing these days. He'd struck out with Miss Rigby last weekend, too. Although she'd agreed to accompany him to a little coffee shop near the park, the only thing he'd managed to get from her was a brief span of idle conversation, the kind of chitchat that two vaguely acquainted people might share.

And even though he was confident that his acquaintance with Miss Rigby had gone beyond the *vaguely* stage—that sprawl in the park had kinda clued him in to that fact—he could tell that she was still holding back from him. Just what all she was holding back, he wished he knew. But somehow, he was confident that she didn't speak as freely with him as she did with others.

Like Kimball, for example, he thought grudgingly.

But his grudge was interrupted by a booming remark from Charlton Heston Man, who demanded, "Do assure me, Mr. Friday, that you haven't been standing up straight like that when you've been at Mr. Kimball's estate."

Leo bit back a growl of discontent. "No, of course not," he said, striving for a bland expression. "In fact, I've been doing these slouching exercises I read about in *Men's Health* magazine. I do them every morning, as soon as I get up, and they've already taken a full two centimeters off of my original height."

The other man eyed Leo suspiciously, clearly not sure whether he was to be believed or not.

"Honest," Leo said without a single smirk. "I also bought some special shoes."

Charlton Heston Man nodded slowly. "Good," he muttered, though he sounded considerably less Moses-like than he usually did. "Keep up the good work."

Leo refrained from comment.

"Nice glasses, Mr. Friday," Versace Man piped up cheerfully. "Ralph Lauren?" he guessed.

"Wal-Mart," Leo told him.

The other man appeared utterly shocked. "Truly?"

Leo nodded.

Versace Man scribbled a note on the pad before him as he muttered, "I had no idea."

"So what do you have for us today, Mr. Friday?"

This time it was Cohiba Man, speaking from behind a faint haze of cigar smoke, his expression as bored as ever, his voice offering no indication of what he might be expecting.

"Not much," Leo said.

"Not much?" echoed Thesaurus Man. "Nothing? Nought? Cipher? *Rien*?" he quoth further.

"Nada, zip, zero, zilch," Leo threw in for good measure.

"That was what you told us last week," Halston Man said shortly.

"Yeah, well, that's what you're getting this week, too," Leo snapped back. "Because I still don't have anything of significance to report."

"What's the problem?" Cohiba Man asked.

"The problem is that there are still a handful of files in Kimball's computer that I haven't been able to access, that's what. Unless you'd be interested in the man's top secret sangria recipe."

"Oh, I would be," Halston Man said, lifting a finger.

"I'll e-mail it to you," Leo promised shortly. He turned his attention back to Cohiba Man. "Aside from that, though, after two weeks of trying, all I've found in Kimball's other files at the estate are the kinds of things I'd expect to find there. What I've discovered that's business related is pretty mundane stuff. Although there are some financial records, they're all standard information, and none of them appears to have been tampered with, anyway. Certainly none of them has indicated that there's anything suspicious going on."

"Have you tried Mr. Kimball's laptop?" Cohiba Man asked.

Leo nodded. "After he returned from Bermuda, it was the first thing I did. And lemme tell ya, you're gonna get billed double for that day, because not only did I have to sneak around the man's private quarters to access it, but his laptop is a mine field of totally incoherent files. It's like the guy doesn't know the first thing about using a computer, which I find kind of odd, because he's such an alleged industrial wizard."

"Mr. Kimball's technology is mechanically oriented, not computer-oriented," Versace Man said. "And how do you know that what appears to be a mine field of incoherent files isn't actually some brilliantly designed booby trap device to keep people out of those files?"

Leo rolled his eyes. "Trust me. I know. It's my job to know. Nobody's brilliant enough to make files look that stupid. Kimball's no neatnik when it comes to his personal computer files, though, that's for sure. And his business ones aren't in great shape, either. Frankly, I don't know how the guy runs his business with things in the kind of shape they're in."

"Oh, please, Mr. Friday," Versace Man said. "It couldn't possibly be as bad as you say."

Before Leo could comment on that, Cohiba Man cut him off.

"So what, exactly, does all this mean, Mr. Friday?"

Leo hesitated before responding. Oh, God. He'd just been addressed by his own name for the fifth time in a row. He nearly dropped to his knees and wept with joy at hearing it. His ecstasy was short-lived, however, when he realized he had no idea how to answer the man's question.

"It means . . ." He sighed fitfully, running a hand restlessly through his hair. "It means my work at Kimball's estate isn't finished yet, I guess."

Cohiba Man nodded, but he didn't look happy at all. "Then I suppose you'll be returning to Ashling now."

Returning to Ashling now, Leo repeated to himself. Why did that sound so much like, *Last night, I dreamed I returned to Manderley?*

"But just so you know, Mr. Friday," Cohiba Man added with a substantial puff of fragrant smoke, "you're on a timer now."

"What?" Leo asked, certain he'd misunderstood.

"We can't afford to let this investigation go on indefinitely," he said. "We can't wait around forever. We're going to need to set some parameters."

"Parameters?"

"Circumscription," Thesaurus Man piped up. "Rubicon. Boundaries. Time frame."

"I *know* what parameters are, you—" Leo curled his hands into tight fists. "Look, I told you guys from the get-go that this could take some time."

"Mr. Friday, it already *has* taken some time. Too much time." Cohiba Man doubled his own fists on the table and leaned forward in a pose that was surprisingly menacing, considering he resembled the Pillsbury Doughboy. "And now, you're going to wind things up, and find out once and for all *what the hell is going on.*"

If he hadn't seen it himself, Leo would have thought those last words had been uttered by Charlton Heston Man, so God-like had they been.

"And how do you suggest I step up the pace, huh?" he demanded, reaching the end of his own none-too-long fuse. He couldn't quite hide the frustration that had been building for weeks when he said, "I've tried everything I know to get to the bottom of what's going on with Kimball's files. I've looked everywhere I can possibly look to find out where fifty million bucks might have disappeared, and where it might show up again. I don't know what else to do."

It was true. Never in his entire career had Leo found himself up against a wall like this one. He had tried every maneuver in the book—and had invented one or two new ones—trying to breach Kimball's private records, trying to figure out how someone could steal fifty million dollars from one place and put it in another. Either the man was even more brilliant than Leo suspected, or else Leo had missed something somewhere along the line. And the thought that he may have missed something somewhere really didn't set well with him at all.

Plainly put, Leo Friday was just too good at what he did to ever make mistakes. He *didn't* make mistakes. Ever. At least, he never had before. Whatever was going on at Kimball Technologies, whoever was stealing tens of millions of dollars annually . . . He bit back a ragged sound. Well, whoever was doing it was smarter than Leo was.

There. He'd admitted it. For the first time in his career, he was working against someone with a superior intellect. Which was yet another reason to suspect Schuyler Kimball of the act. Of course, from the start, Leo had suspected the billionaire was the one who was behind the amazing disappearing millions. And there wasn't a human being alive who was more intelligent than Schuyler Kimball. In spite of that, Leo resented the whole notion of being outsmarted.

And he still hadn't proven for sure—or at all—

that Kimball was the one stealing the money from himself. There continued to exist an outside possibility that there was someone else behind the theft, someone who was in no way entitled to the money. Now all Leo had to do was figure out how to outsmart the sonofabitch. Which he could probably do eventually, if he could just finger who, exactly, the sonofabitch was.

"What about Miss Rigby?"

Leo blinked once, uncertain who had even posed the question, so lost had he been in his thoughts. "I beg your pardon?" he said.

"What about Miss Rigby?" Cohiba Man asked.

"What about her?"

"Have you checked her files? You might find something there." This time it was Versace Man who asked the question.

"Why would I want to check her files?" Leo said. "Do you really think I'm going to figure out who's filtering fifty million bucks annually by trying to find out where Kimball's next tea party is taking place?"

Cohiba Man shook his head. "No, Mr. Friday. But Miss Rigby has been with Mr. Kimball for a long time, and is privy to other areas of his life. It's not beyond the realm of possibility that he may have entrusted her with some of his responsibilities."

Oh, right, Leo thought. Like keeping track of his tennis balls and which call girl was due at the estate that evening.

"You never know, Mr. Friday," Cohiba Man added in a voice that was rife with speculation. Evidently, Leo wasn't the only one who wondered just what, exactly, the *duties* of a social secretary involved. "Perhaps Miss Rigby might shed some light on what's going on. Not that you need to ask her anything specific, mind you. But, through her, you might be able to discover a few more things about the situation than you know now."

Through her? Leo echoed to himself. Now why did that sound like a really pleasant activity to undertake?

"Check Miss Rigby's computer," Cohiba Man said. "See if you can find anything there."

Leo's lips parted fractionally in surprise, and he narrowed his eyes at the man. "What did you say?"

"I said check Miss Rigby's laptop. You might find something there."

For a moment, Leo didn't—couldn't—say a word. Never in his life had he felt more stupid than he did at that moment. Why had it not occurred to him earlier that Miss Rigby would have her own computer, and her own files? Like, oh, say . . . on day one? Of *course* Lily Rigby would have a computer, he thought now. Even if it was just to keep track of Kimball's social engagements. And hadn't she herself stated that she kept in touch with the billionaire through e-mail? She certainly hadn't checked it from Kimball's big computer in the office, because Leo had been in there every day. And even with Kimball in residence, he suspected she would need the use of a computer on a fairly regular basis. It made sense that she would have one at her disposal.

But where?

And how was he supposed to gain access to it, when he hadn't even been able to access the woman yet?

Not that he was honestly expecting to find anything significant among her files regarding the missing money. Hey, after all, Miss Rigby was no rocket scientist—or computer programmer, for that matter. But there still might be something in her files that would direct Leo to another place to look.

"Uh . . . okay," he said, trying to mask his utter humiliation at having been so sideswiped by Miss Rigby's physical attributes that it had never occurred to him to investigate her professional ones. "I can see where it might be beneficial to check Miss Rigby's computer. I'll do that right away. As soon as I figure out where she keeps it."

"Oh, it's in her room," Halston Man offered. "On the left-hand side of her writing desk, which is just across from the door. It's actually kind of easy to miss, because she has a few Beanie Babies stacked on it. Prance, Pounce and . . . Snip, I think. She likes cats."

Every man in the room turned to look at Halston Man, but he seemed not to understand why. "What?" he asked. "What's wrong?"

"How do you know so much about Miss Rigby's room?" Leo asked.

The other men nodded in silence.

Halston Man smiled and swiped a hand negligently through the air. "Oh, we trade books from time to time, and on occasion, when I've been at the estate, she's offered me free access to her book shelf. We're both *huge* Anya Seton fans. And," he added a bit sheepishly, "I'm the one who gave her the Beanie Babies. When you're a collector, you frequently wind up with duplicates, you know."

Leo nodded but decided not to comment. Evidently, the other members of the board of directors were inclined to do likewise, because no one said a word.

"Uh, fine," Leo finally managed. "I'll, uh . . . I'll check it as soon as I can."

"Good," Cohiba Man said. "Because you have two weeks to find out who's taking that money, how they're doing it, and where the money is going. Two weeks. Do I make myself clear?''

"What happens if I don't find it?" Leo asked.

"Oh, you'll find it, Mr. Friday." Cohiba Man swept his gaze down the length of the table, where each of the other members of the board was nodding his head in slow agreement. "We have faith in you. Because if you don't find the missing money, as I said before, you'll never work in this town again. And that, I promise you, is a threat you should take seriously."

For some reason, Leo was suddenly inclined to agree with the man. Not just because Cohiba Man had uttered his assurance with such conviction, but because Leo was getting the impression that the board of directors knew something that he didn't know himself. Like, for example, lots of other boards of directors, all across the country. Other boards of directors who might be persuaded to hire somebody other than Leo Friday for any future investigative needs they might have. Because, frankly, Leo was beginning to doubt that he was, in fact, the best in the business.

And for that, as much as anything else, he vowed to find the thief. "Two weeks," he repeated. "Fine. In two weeks, gentlemen, I promise you . . . you'll have your culprit."

Lily was already having a bad day when the doorbell rang downstairs and nearly shattered what fragile grip on her sanity she had left. A lack of sleep the night before had caused her to awaken with a terrible headache and a volatile disposition, and nothing—absolutely nothing—had gone right since. Chloe hadn't shown up at school—again— and Mrs. Puddleduck was complaining about her salary—again—and Miranda was wandering through the garden with Claude Rains—again—and Janey was in a snit—again. And Schuyler . . .

Ooh, Schuyler. Lily gritted her teeth hard. Well, suffice it to say that Lily was *this close* to throttling the life right out of him. Again.

And now the numbers on her laptop computer screen were making no sense whatsoever. And no matter how hard she tried to make them do what she needed them to do, they simply and adamantly would not cooperate. And that, she decided, was going to present a bit of a problem for a bank deposit she desperately needed to make.

The bellow of the doorbell downstairs again precluded her from fixing that problem anytime soon. With a final, longing look at the tea that sat cooling near her laptop, she rose from her writing desk and hastened from the room, to respond to the summons that was seemingly acres away from her present position. And as she hurried down the gallery, it occurred to her, not for the first time, that they really should hire someone to see to the more simple aspects of running Ashling—like, say, answering the door, for example.

But they so seldom had visitors at the estate, particularly unannounced visitors, that she supposed it did seem rather unnecessary. Still, as she strove to catch her breath before opening the door, Lily decided that it might be nice to have such a luxury anyway.

And speaking of luxuries . . .

She bit back a wistful sigh after she opened the door. Because, as if conjured by magic, Leonard Freiberger stood on the other side.

She was still trying to catch her breath from the marathon she had just run, but somehow, Lily was fairly certain that wasn't the only reason for her lightheadedness. Mr. Freiberger looked much as he had that first day he'd come to Ashling—round wire-framed glasses, rumpled suit, slouchy demeanor. Except that this time, there seemed to be a steeliness in his gaze that hadn't been there before. There was also, she noted as a slow curl of heat wound up tight in her belly, a familiarity to his smile that hadn't been there before.

"Mr. Freiberger," she greeted him, battling the warmth that radiated from her midsection, spreading to parts of her that scarcely warranted warming in broad daylight like this. "How nice to see you again."

Oh, lame, lame, lame, Lily, she chastised herself. But what was she supposed to do, say what was on her mind? The last thing Mr. Freiberger needed to hear was her breaking into a rousing chorus of, *You're just a hunka hunka burnin' love.* She'd never been able to carry a tune, after all.

"Miss Rigby," he replied easily. Somehow, though, she got the feeling that he'd wanted to say something else in greeting.

She told herself she must be imagining the—what? . . . affection? Oh, no, surely not—that she sensed in his voice, but she didn't try to convince herself *too* hard. She *did* try hard, however, to convince herself that that *wasn't* suspicion in his eyes. Unfortunately, he seemed to be very suspicious of something indeed.

But she decided not to think about that right now. Instead she only absorbed the sight of him as he stood there in the pale yellow light of midmorning, and wondered what he would do if she leaned forward and licked him from head to foot.

"Ah . . ." she began eloquently. "What are you doing back? I thought you said you wouldn't find the problem here? That your work at Ashling was finished? That you should doubtless direct your search at company headquarters?'' And why was she suddenly speaking exclusively in the inquisitive tense? Was that really necessary?

Leo was inclined to tell Miss Rigby that he had thought all that, too. But all he did was stand there staring at her, letting his gaze rove hungrily all over the not-quite-forgotten terrain of Lily Rigby. Wow. She looked even better than he'd remembered. And he'd remembered her as looking pretty damned good.

She still hadn't let down her hair, though, he noted, disgruntled. Someday, he was going to have to do something about that. But not today, unfortunately. Because today he had other things that commanded his attention. He couldn't just stand here looking at Lily Rigby and wondering what she had on under that stark, conservative gray suit that did absolutely nothing to make her look either stark or conservative.

Probably something lacy and sexy, he thought. He'd read somewhere that women who were required to wear suits and such to work often enjoyed wearing impossibly frilly underthings beneath. Peach, he'd bet. Something lacy and sexy and peach colored. One of those little half-thing bras that a woman's breasts fairly spilled free from, and skimpy little bikini panties. With a garter belt. Yeah.

But he couldn't think about that right now, he reminded himself, because he had other really, really important matters that he needed to concentrate on instead. So he shoved aside the image of Lily Rigby in all her decadent lingerie glory and tried to remember what, exactly, it was that he was supposed to be concentrating on.

Or maybe black, he thought. Lily Rigby in black underthings, to go with her gray suit. Yeah, that's the ticket. Black satin. Oh, yes. He could *definitely* see her as the black satin type. Especially with those smoky stockings hugging her long, lean legs. Black would suit her to a—

But then, he had other things to think about today, he reminded himself yet again, this time with a brutal shove to his libido. Still his eyes lingered on Lily Rigby's face and form, however, and still his thoughts lingered on her underwear. Now, what was it he was supposed to be thinking about again? Something about a billionaire or somebody. Schuyler Whatzizname . . . Kimball. Yeah, that was it. Kimball Technologies and . . . What? Some missing money? To the tune of like . . . fifty million dollars . . . ?

Oh, yeah. Now he remembered.

He remembered Charlton Heston Man nearly busting a blood vessel before Leo had finally concluded his business with the board of directors for Kimball Technologies. And he remembered Halston Man leaving in a remarkably well choreographed huff. He recalled Thesaurus Man labeling him a cretinous, low-browed stupe, and Cohiba Man, through a haze of blue smoke, ordering him back to Ashling, pronto, where he would remain banished until he broke open those files and found out what was inside, or died trying. Leo only hoped he could do it without Schuyler Kimball looking over his shoulder and breathing down his neck.

Of course, Lily Rigby would be doing that, too, but for some reason that didn't bother Leo quite so much as having an eccentric billionaire—or billionaire eccentric; he still hadn't decided which—breathing down his neck. In fact, Miss Rigby breathing down his neck—or on any other body part she might want to respire upon—was actually something Leo found himself rather looking forward to.

Then he remembered that he was going to have to infiltrate her room and violate her personal space at some point in the near future, and a wave of guilt lapped at the edge of his brain. He reminded himself that he had no choice, that he had a job to do, and only two weeks left to do it. Still, invading a woman's personal things—without her knowledge or consent, at any rate—didn't set well at all with Leo.

Even if, at some point while trying to infiltrate her computer files, he might accidentally happen upon the drawer where she kept her underwear. And even if then, maybe, by accident, an article of lingerie might, oh . . . leap into his pocket or something. He still felt a little guilty about the whole endeavor.

"I think I may have missed something in my original investigation," he told Miss Rigby, pushing his errant thoughts aside for now. "My superiors thought it would be a good idea for me to have one more look. Just to make sure I didn't miss anything."

Like, for example, he thought further to himself, what Schuyler Kimball's social secretary wore underneath those not-quite-businesslike suits of hers.

"I see," she said. "Well, if there's anything I can do to help you, please don't hesitate to ask."

Leo smiled. Oh, he wouldn't.

For a moment, they only stood there gazing at each other, both of them obviously thinking about something totally different from what they were talking about. Finally, Miss Rigby seemed to remember that it was up to her to invite Leo inside. Deftly, professionally, she did just that, stepping aside and sweeping an arm inward in a silent indication that he should enter. As he passed her, Leo inhaled deeply, enjoying again that singular scent of hers, the one that just opened up so many possibilities.

And he was suddenly very grateful to the board of directors who were timing his every move. Because, hey, without them, Leo would have to be an honest man. And honest men just didn't enjoy their thoughts nearly as much as guys like him did. Nevertheless, he was going to have to come clean with Lily Rigby someday.

Someday, he reiterated to himself. But not today.

ELEVEN

Leo's gratitude to Kimball's board of directors grew by leaps and bounds the following day, even as he was slaving away, sitting at Schuyler Kimball's desk, staring at Schuyler Kimball's computer screen, trying to get past one of Schuyler Kimball's allegedly brilliant booby traps, so he could break into one of Schuyler Kimball's personal files. He hadn't yet found an opportunity to take advantage of Miss Rigby . . . uh, Miss Rigby's lap . . . uh, Miss Rigby's laptop, so he was trying instead, one more time, to access those last few files of Kimball's.

But instead of focusing on the task at hand, Leo was lost in a fantasy of his own making, one that involved Miss Rigby—naturally—and today's choice of lingerie—red—and the kitchen pantry he'd visited once, to help her retrieve a box of tea from the shelf where it was stored—on top.

And even though he told himself he should instead be fantasizing about a way to get into Miss Rigby's bedroom—to find her computer, naturally—there had just been something about that darkened pantry . . . The isolation, the close confines, the lack of light, the mingling aromas of cinnamon and coffee and chocolate chip cookies. Yeah, maybe if he could find an excuse to go to the kitchen for something . . . And maybe if he could lure Miss Rigby there in the process . . . And maybe if he could figure out some way to get her to follow him into the pantry . . . Then maybe, just maybe . . .

"Mr. Freiberger?"

Leo snapped guiltily to attention at the sound of her voice, certain she must have deduced exactly what he'd been thinking about all morning. But when he turned toward the office entry, there she stood as cool and professional as ever, wearing a straight, tobacco-colored skirt that rode a good two inches above her knees, and a cognac-colored sweater cropped right at her waist. Both garments fit her like a second skin, and for a moment, all Leo could do was stare at her, his thoughts neither cool nor professional. Interestingly, she only stared back at him, and said nothing more about why she'd come.

"Uh . . . yes, Miss Rigby?" he finally managed to get out, proud of himself for not drooling even once when he uttered the question.

She lifted a hand to her hair, smoothing it lightly over the sweep of black that was twisted up the back of her head in that Kim Novak way again. In spite of the casualness of the gesture—well, casual for *her*, Leo thought, seeing as how *she* couldn't possibly know how her sweater rode up to reveal a brief glimpse of creamy flesh when she did that— she was clearly nervous about whatever she had to say to him. But, hey, nervous was good, Leo decided. Because that meant the two of them were in sync.

"I . . ." she began. "That is . . . Would you . . . I mean . . ." She sighed fitfully, gazed upon him fully for a moment, then averted her eyes anxiously again. "I could use your help," she said softly. "If you have a moment to spare."

A moment? he thought. A moment? Oh, he could probably spare a moment. Or two. Or ten. Or the rest of his life. Whatever.

Immediately, he stood, ready to climb whatever mountains, and swim whatever seas, and cross whatever deserts, and slay whatever dragons she asked him to. Then he remembered that he was pretending to be someone he was not, and that he had been about to break and enter into one of Kimball's private files, so he seated himself down again to mask his treachery before taking off on his heroic journey.

Some epic hero, he chastised himself as he rose once again. *Leonard Freiberger*, he thought further with disgust. *What a ratfink that guy was turning out to be.*

"I'll be happy to help," he told her, adjusting his glasses. "What's the problem?"

"I need you in the . . . in the kitchen pantry," she said.

Something inside Leo went *zing*. Truly. *Zing*. How very odd.

"The, uh . . . the kitchen *pantry?*" he echoed, just to be sure.

"Yes," she said, still clearly anxious about something. "The pantry."

Trying not to rush *too* much, Leo circled to the front of the desk and approached her. "May I ask, exactly, why you . . . *need* me . . . in the pantry?"

She nodded once quickly, then glanced down at the backs of her fingernails in that way she had of doing to hide her nervousness. Oh, *boy*. This was going to be *great*.

"There's um, there's something in the pantry I

need your help with," she said. "It's . . . well, it's rather personal."

The zinging inside Leo accelerated into a loud *vroooom*. "Oh?" he asked, pretending he had no idea what she was talking about as he pondered exactly which garment to start with. The zipper on her skirt seemed the most likely place to begin, but there was a lot to be said for that tauntingly short sweater, and—

"In fact, it's almost embarrassing to have to discuss it with you this way," Miss Rigby continued, oblivious to his intentions. "But I . . . I . . ."

"You . . . you . . . ?" he prodded.

She finally looked at his face again and inhaled a deep, wistful sigh. Wistful was good, he thought. He could do a lot with wistful. "Well, there's something in the pantry I need you to get for me," she finally confessed.

The vrooming inside Leo screeched to a halt as he realized he had been a bit premature in his plans for her clothing. "Tea?" he asked halfheartedly.

"Um, no," she said. "Not tea."

The zinging geared up again.

"Actually," she told him, "it's . . . it's a bug."

Pfft. So much for the zinging. So much for the vrooming. So much for the zipper on her skirt. There was nothing like the introduction of entomology into a seduction attempt to pretty much send it over a cliff. "A bug?" he asked.

She nodded. "Yes, rather a large one." She lifted her hands to hold them about an inch or so apart, then, when she looked up and noted his disinterest, moved them until they were about five inches apart. "It's about this big," she said. "With long antennae that are quite . . . unpleasant." She shivered for effect. "It's very . . . quite . . . um . . . really icky."

"A bug," he said again.

"A big, icky bug," she clarified adamantly. "I tried to find Mr. Tooley, to see if he might take care of it, but he seems to have left the grounds."

"All right," he said, resolved to his new role in life as exterminator. "Show me where it is."

He kept an eye on Miss Rigby as he followed her to the kitchen, enjoying without a trace of guilt the dance of her hips as she walked—well, hell, he ought to get some kind of reward for what he was about to do. Then, when they arrived at their destination, he crossed to enter the pantry alone, while she remained steadfastly on the other side of the room. He noted the offending creature immediately. It was hard to miss, seeing as how it sat brashly on the wall beside a box of Cocoa Puffs, taunting any and all comers. Plus, he had to admit, it was pretty big. And more than a little . . . icky. Involuntarily, Leo fought off a major wiggins.

"You got a baseball bat?" he called out over his shoulder.

"No, I'm afraid not," she replied, her tone of voice indicating that she hadn't realized he was joking.

Then again, he thought, eyeing the bug once more, maybe he wasn't exactly joking. He thought about asking for a Colt .45, but what came out was, "How about a fly swatter?"

"On the door behind you," she told him.

He claimed the weapon and disposed of the insect as quickly and neatly as possible—which, in the long run, turned out to be neither quick nor neat. Then he exited the pantry, still armed with the fly swatter, his dead quarry sheathed in a shroud provided by Brawny paper towels. Somehow, the brand name made him feel that much more heroic, and he straightened to his full, bug-slaying height as he approached Miss Rigby.

She shuddered again as he passed by her and made his way to the trash can, but before he could dispose of the corpse, she reached out a hand to circle her fingers shyly around his wrist. His pulse leapt at the contact, and when his gaze met hers again, he saw that her eyes shone with gratitude and something else he probably shouldn't ponder. And damned if that zinging didn't kick right in again.

"Mr. Freiberger?" she asked, her voice a soft caress.

"Yes, Miss Rigby?"

"Could you . . ." She batted her eyelashes at him quite prettily. "Could you . . . would you . . . take it out to the big can outside?"

"Of course," he said chivalrously. "I'd be delighted."

When he returned from completing his task, the kitchen was empty. The pantry, however, was not. The door stood open, and Miss Rigby was inside, straining to reach something from a shelf that was laughably beyond her reach. She had one leg extended elegantly behind her, and as she pushed herself higher on tiptoe and thrust her arm upward, her sweater crept above the waistband of her skirt to reveal once again that soft, brief span of tender flesh beneath.

For a long moment, Leo only stood there enjoying the view and the way his blood crashed through his body, dizzying him, heating up parts of him that really hadn't required heating for some time now—ever since Miss Rigby had asked him to join her in the pantry, in fact. As if she sensed the inappropriateness of his thoughts—inappropriate for anyone who *wasn't* currently pondering the taste of a woman's torso, at any rate—she turned

to find him—oh, he might as well just admit it—
ogling her.

"Need some help?" he asked.

Still reaching upward, she opened her mouth to
respond, and somehow, he knew that she was going to insist that no, as a matter of fact, she didn't
need any help, that she was *this close* to reaching
all by herself the box that was still a good three
inches shy of her grasp. So before she had the
chance to say anything—he didn't want to be responsible for her telling a lie, after all—Leo strode
forward into the pantry to offer his aid—or something—anyway.

The moment he stepped inside the pantry, the
already confined space shrank to virtually the size
of an electron. In hindsight, he supposed that for
maximum efficiency, he should have asked Miss
Rigby to come out before he went in. But then
where would have been the fun in that?

Lily's breath caught in her throat as she felt Mr.
Freiberger step up behind her, his entire body
shadowing hers—and then some. She told herself
that there was nothing untoward in his gesture, despite the intimate posture, and that he was only
trying to be helpful, despite the raging inferno he'd
ignited in her belly. Any inappropriate ideas she
might be entertaining at the moment—and my, but
they were becoming more and more inappropriate
with every moment that passed—were entirely of
her own making.

He certainly did smell good, she thought, clean
and rugged and masculine. His warmth surrounded her as he reached up over her head, his
arm brushing against the one she still extended upward. He'd rolled the cuffs of his white shirt back
to his elbows, and she cursed herself for not having

had the foresight to push her own sleeves back before summoning him.

Especially when he leaned forward some more, an action that rubbed his arm all along the length of her own, creating what she was sure must be a delicious friction, if only her flesh were bare to enjoy it. She did very much enjoy, however, the feel of his entire upper torso pressing into her back as he plucked from the shelf the box of tea cookies she'd tried to reach herself. Much to her relief, after completing the action, he didn't immediately pull back. Although she couldn't see what he was doing back there—and she was much too polite to ask— she was almost positive he bent his head down toward hers a bit and . . .

Sniffed her hair.

And that was when Lily's superior intelligence told her that there might have been more to Mr. Freiberger's offer of help than she'd originally thought. Well, her superior intelligence told her that, and also the fact that she felt the hand that wasn't reaching up for the tea cookies settle, very possessively, on her waist.

Yep, guys like Galileo had nothing on Lily when it came to recognizing overtures of a personal nature. And a man's fingers creeping under the hem of a sweater to strum delicately along a woman's bare flesh? Well, she was pretty sure that *that* was definitely an overture of a personal nature.

It was also a damned nice feeling.

"Mr. Freiberger?" she said, scarcely recognizing the deep, leisurely timbre of her voice.

"Hmmm?" he answered from behind her, still unmoving, save the soft, deliberate, back and forth motion of his thumb over her skin.

"Um, may I . . ." She swallowed hard as her

body's temperature began to rise. Fast. "May I ask what you're doing?"

"I'm helping you," he said in as matter-of-fact a voice as she'd ever heard, as if he weren't currently wreaking havoc with her senses and turning her insides into tapioca. Really hot tapioca. "With that thing you wanted me to help you with," he clarified further.

Now, how could he have known about that thing? Lily wondered. She'd never spoken of that thing—that incredibly erotic, sexual fantasy thing—to anyone. Then, it dawned on her that he wasn't talking about the fantasy thing. He was talking about the bug thing. Wasn't he?

His little finger dipped below the waistband of her skirt.

Well, perhaps not.

As he continued to stroke her bare flesh, leisurely, delicately, seductively, the hand that gripped the tea cookies moved lower, depositing them on a shelf at Lily's shoulder level. The hand, too, deposited itself there, something that rather hampered any effort she might make to pass by it and leave the pantry.

Had she wanted to pass by it and leave the pantry.

Which, of course, she didn't.

Not yet, anyway.

Not until she fully understood exactly what Mr. Freiberger had in mind. However, that might be difficult to decipher, she thought, if he remained so stonily silent.

The hand at her waist crept toward the front then, his thumb still skimming just below the hem of her sweater, his little finger still exploring below her skirt, halting when he reached the smooth expanse of skin above her belly button. A little explosion detonated inside her beneath each of his fingertips, their fires spreading through her entire midsection. Lily opened her mouth to repeat her earlier question, but his fingers splayed open wide, an action that brought his thumb to settle over the front closure of her brassiere.

Okay, she was pretty sure she could tell now what Mr. Freiberger had in mind. Voicing his intentions at this point would be a tad redundant, so it really wasn't necessary for her to ask him again what they might be.

But there was something else that prevented her from speaking aloud any of the numerous questions tumbling through her brain. For some reason, she received the definite impression that he didn't want them to speak, and for some reason, she didn't want them to, either. So she only stood still, waiting to see just how far he planned to carry out this ... whatever it was. Waiting, too, to see just how far she planned to let him carry it.

Leaning her own body backward, Lily turned her head to press her cheek against the soft cotton of his shirt. Inhaling deeply, she grew intoxicated by the dark, masculine scent of him, grew dizzy with the sensation of his bare hand opening over her bare belly. He dipped his head lower, but stayed far enough back that she couldn't see his face, then brought his other hand to join the first at her waist. Uncertain what to do with her own hands, Lily only continued to grip the shelf she had grabbed in surprise when Mr. Freiberger had initially touched her. And she waited again to see what he would do.

What he did was dip his entire hand under the fabric of her sweater, scooting it gradually higher until he cradled the lower curve of her breast in the L-shape created by his thumb and long forefinger.

The heat in her belly exploded again, spreading warmth throughout her entire system, and her breathing grew shallow at a time when she most needed it, dizzying her further. She opened her mouth to offer some kind of reaction—though she wondered honestly if it would be one of discouragement—but he pressed his other hand lower, to the hem of her skirt, which he slowly, slowly, oh . . . so slowly, began to urge up along her thighs.

This was utter madness, she thought. Where on earth had all this come from? Certainly she and the bookkeeper had been making eyes—and other body parts—at each other since his arrival. But nothing had prepared her for this kind of encounter. She felt wanton and languid and easy, and was fully tempted to succumb to his overtures right here, right now, right quick. It was a sensation Lily had never experienced before, and she felt drugged by it, as if she had no control whatever over her actions.

Oh, well done, Lily, she congratulated herself. She'd just blamed her responses to the man on a convenient narcotic reaction, and now she could let it go at that. *Bravo, darling. You've just relieved yourself of all responsibility for your actions. Do carry on.*

Turning to face him, she told herself to do just that. In fact, she got so far as cupping one hand over his rough jaw, roping her other arm around his neck, and pushing herself up on tiptoe to . . . do something—she wasn't exactly sure what. He, in turn, hooked his fingers together at the small of her back, the barest hint of a smile playing about his lips, as if he were just waiting for her to say, *Go.*

Lily opened her mouth to give him exactly that command. But what actually came out was, "Mr. Freiberger, would you care to join me for tea and cookies?"

The smile on his lips fled completely, to be replaced by an expression of unmistakable and total bemusement. Lily couldn't help but smile herself. He looked utterly dejected, like a six-year-old boy who'd just been told the family wouldn't be going to Disney World after all.

"Tea and . . . cookies, Miss Rigby?" he said with just a trace of hopefulness touching his voice, as if she might be defining the word *cookies* in something other than its traditional meaning.

She nodded, curling the fingers of one hand lightly over his nape, knifing the others idly through the silky hair at his temple. "I have a lovely Earl Grey that Mr. Kimball brought me from England last month. Not to mention some Peek Freens custard cremes to go with."

The hands linked lightly at her back tightened, pulling her forward. Clearly, Mr. Freiberger intended to ignore her invitation to tea, and invite himself to something else entirely unless she put a stop to it.

"Truly, Mr. Freiberger," she said as he drew her close and lowered his head to hers, "as . . . promising . . . as I find this little interlude, it really isn't a good idea."

He pulled back slightly, but didn't release her. The look in his eyes shifted from playful affection to grim acceptance. "Because of Mr. Kimball?" he asked.

Lily nodded. "I'm afraid so."

For one brief moment, he tugged her close again, pressing his body into hers with enough force to send her heart rate propelling to the stratosphere. He was just so wonderfully . . . hard, she thought. So deliciously . . . hot. So very, very . . . *very, very* . . . male.

"Because you and Mr. Kimball are intimately involved?" he demanded.

The question surprised her almost as much as his proprietary claiming of her had. Still, she knew she shouldn't be surprised. It was a common misconception by nearly everyone, after all, that she and Schuyler were still involved, even though it had been more than a decade since the two of them had been intimate. There was no reason for Mr. Freiberger to assume otherwise, she told herself. What bothered Lily was that he had. And in doing so, he was obviously under the impression that she was the kind of woman who, in addition to sleeping with her boss, would let that boss's bookkeeper put his hands on her cookies. So to speak.

Which meant it would be necessary to educate Mr. Freiberger as to the proper way of doing things at Ashling.

Opening her own hands lightly over his chest, she gently pushed him away. But she couldn't quite make herself release him entirely and continued to press her palms into that hard, hot, male chest. For some reason—well, she was fairly certain she knew *what* reason—she didn't want to let him go.

"No," she said simply. "Not because of that. There's nothing like that between me and Mr. Kimball. But he does like an occasional afternoon cup of tea, too, and would doubtless show up in the kitchen just when you and I were getting to the good parts. His timing has always been frightfully bad."

Mr. Freiberger blinked three times in rapid succession, as if a too-bright flash had just gone off in front of his face. But all he said in response was, "Oh."

So Lily continued, "Therefore, I think, perhaps,

it might be wise for us to continue with our little, um . . . discussion . . . in more promising surroundings. Like, for example . . . your place."

Mr. Freiberger blinked again. "Oh."

"Say . . . tomorrow night?"

"Uh, yeah. Yeah, we could say that."

"Could we also say sixish?"

"Fine."

"Well then. I'll see you there."

"O-okay."

There, she thought. That ought to correct any misconceptions he might have about her relationship with Schuyler. The big doofus. Honestly. The things that men assumed. Somehow, Lily managed to make herself release Mr. Freiberger, and, with obvious reluctance, he let her do it. She took a moment to rearrange her clothing and smooth a hand over her hair, then, with a faint smile, she turned and strode out of the pantry. She spun hastily back around, however, when she remembered something of rather significant importance.

"Oh, and, Mr. Freiberger?" she asked.

Still looking quite flummoxed, he said, "Yes?"

"It might be helpful if you'd leave your address on Mr. Kimball's desk, where I can find it."

He nodded, but his mind had clearly already moved on to other things. "Consider it done, Miss Rigby," he said softly.

"Fine. Then I'll see you tomorrow night."

"Yes. You will."

Lily stumbled a bit at the sound of his assurance, then quickly recovered and moved forward. For some reason, when he'd said, *Yes. You will*, Mr. Freiberger had seemed to be talking about something other than seeing her tomorrow night.

How very interesting, she thought.

*   *   *

As Leo rounded the corner toward Kimball's private rooms and left behind the wide gallery, not to mention the kitchen pantry—which he wouldn't mention, because mentioning it meant he replayed over and over again that incredibly erotic encounter with Miss Rigby, which in turn made him feel something that was really quite unmentionable, so he just wouldn't mention it—he tried hard not to think about what the two of them had just done. Later, he promised himself. He would think about all that later. Much later.

But not *too* much later.

Unbidden, though, the memory of how her smooth, silk-covered thigh had felt beneath his fingertips unfolded in his brain. He recalled the scent of her, the sound of her, the heat of her, and just like that, he started to get hard. So, as quickly as the memories collected, he scattered them to the far corners of his brain.

Later, he told himself again.

Fortunately, he was distracted by the sound of music coming from the direction of, of all places, the music room. The music room was across and down a ways from Kimball's office, so Leo had to walk right past it if he wanted to return to his work at the billionaire's desk. Something about the lilting piano piece slowed his stride as he passed, but when he glanced into the room and saw Chloe seated at the bench, he stopped dead in his tracks.

She had her back to him, but even if she hadn't, he suspected she wouldn't have noticed him watching her. The sun spilling through the window beyond her winked off the ring in her eyebrow, and splashed with gold the wild, dark tresses tumbling around her shoulders. She was dressed in a pair of massive, baggy, extremely disreputable blue jeans—actually, the garment appeared to be a series of shreds and tears that were joined, kind of, by denim—and a short, blood red sweater. Her head was turned in profile, her eyes were closed, and her fingers skimmed easily, confidently, along the keyboard. She appeared to not even be paying attention to what she was doing, as if the piano were simply an extension of her body, and the activity she was performing was as natural and as essential a practice as breathing.

Her choice of clothing was utterly at odds with the music that flowed from her fingertips. The music was soft, gently cadenced, pleasantly complicated. Nothing at all like its creator. Nevertheless, Chloe seemed to be transformed, transcended even, by it, turning soft and gentle and pleasant herself. Leo was even able to overlook the facial jewelry for the moment, because he became so caught up in the sounds so subtly surrounding him.

Whatever the piece was she was playing, it was, quite simply, beautiful. He was by no means an expert on classical music, so he had no idea who the composer was. Still, he mused, it might be worth investing in a couple of CDs by the man. Even to his untrained ear, there was something about the piece she was playing that was simply too wonderful to ignore.

"Is that Bach?" he asked as he took a step into the music room. "Or Beethoven?"

The moment he began to speak, Chloe started stumbling over the piano keys as if her fingers had suddenly become paralyzed. She leapt up from the bench, spun quickly around to face him, and, just for a moment, had that look of stark terror on her face that she had worn the first time he'd encountered her. As she had done then, however, she immediately masked the fear, injecting in its place a fair amount of adolescent insolence.

"Do you get off on scaring the shit out of everybody?" she demanded in that grating tone of voice that put Leo's back up faster than fingernails on a blackboard would. "Or is it just little girls you like to spook?"

He held up both hands, palm out, wondering why he'd even bothered to try to be civil with the kid. "Forget it," he told her as he began to back up again. He had better things to do with his time than defend himself against a young girl whose greatest enemy was herself. "Just forget I asked. Forget you ever saw me. If you'll excuse me, I'll be on my way."

He had turned to leave, had, in fact made his way through the door, when Chloe called out after him, almost tentatively, he thought, "It wasn't Bach *or* Beethoven."

Very slowly, Leo pivoted back around, wondering if this was some kind of trick. For a moment there, Chloe had sounded almost nice.

"It was Sandusky," she told him.

Leo shook his head slightly. "Never heard of him."

"Sandusky's not a him," she said, still looking a bit uncertain about what she was doing. "Sandusky's a her."

He arched his brows in surprise. "No kidding. I didn't even know women were allowed to compose music in those days."

There was a slight hesitation before Chloe replied, and for some reason, Leo got the impression that she was taking great care in choosing what to say. "Sandusky didn't compose it in those days," she finally said. "She composed it just now."

This time Leo dropped his mouth open in surprise.

"Sandusky is me," she added unnecessarily,

scrunching up her shoulders in a rare show of modesty.

"You?" he asked. "You wrote that?"

She nodded.

"Just now?"

She was clearly becoming more than a little self-conscious, obviously disconcerted by his vehemence, but she nodded again, more slowly this time.

Leo forced himself to relax. The last thing a kid like Chloe needed was to have someone gawking at her as if she were the eighth wonder of the modern world. "It, uh . . . it was really good," he said lamely.

And even at that lame compliment, Chloe smiled. A shy smile. A smile of gratitude, of satisfaction. It was a smile that nearly took Leo's breath away, because when she smiled like that, she looked just like . . . just like . . .

Just like a fourteen-year-old-girl who'd done something she was really proud of, something that made her feel good about herself. Imagine that. Chloe could be a normal human being after all.

She thrust her hands behind her back, an action that brought into stark focus the gold hoop glittering in her navel, and only then did Leo remember what kind of a kid she was—namely, an unconventional one. However, even at that, when she dipped her head forward and swayed her body to and fro, he thought for a moment that she might actually say "Aw, shucks" and stub the toe of her shoe—her really big, really ugly shoe—against the huge Aubusson rug that spanned the floor beneath her feet. Then, as quickly as she had turned human, Chloe seemed to recall that she was, in fact, a surly adolescent, and, just like that, the facade went back into place.

"Yeah, well, you don't have to sound so surprised about it," she snapped with a toss of her head that sent her curls flying. "It's not like I'm an idiot here. Unlike *some* people."

But Leo wasn't going to take the bait as easily this time. "No, you're certainly no idiot," he said calmly. "On the contrary, Miss Sandusky—"

Her head snapped up again at his formal address, and she eyed him warily, as if she were trying to figure out whether or not he was being sarcastic or insulting in his formal address.

"I'm sorry I interrupted you," he said further, before she had a chance to verbally assault him. "I hope I didn't blow your concentration and make you forget what you were doing."

Her expression turned puzzled for a moment, then cleared. "Oh, I never forget," she said. She pointed to her forehead. "It all goes right here and stays. I'll be able to find it again when I need to. It's kinda like a filing cabinet."

Leo hid the smile that threatened when he noted Chloe's use of common English. Obviously she could communicate with anyone if she tried. "You seem to have a rare gift," he told her. "I hope you don't neglect it."

She stared at him for a long time without changing her expression, as if she couldn't quite figure him out. Well, that made two of them, Leo thought. Because he sure as hell didn't know what to think about her now, either.

Dipping his own head forward, he murmured, "Miss Sandusky. It was nice chatting with you. Please, by all means, continue with your playing. I myself have to get back to work, and your music would be a welcome accompaniment."

"Maybe I don't feel like playing anymore," she

said. But there was no venom, no surly adolescent anger, tainting the comment.

He wondered if she had intended for the remark to have a double meaning, then decided that, even though she was obviously brighter than the average kid, she probably hadn't.

"Well, then," he said. "I suppose that will be my loss, won't it?"

She studied him in silence again, until the moment began to stretch taut, making Leo feel more than a little awkward. So with another hastily offered, "Miss Sandusky," he spun around again and made his way out, pushing thoughts of Chloe Sandusky and her *oeuvre* to the back of his brain. The last thing he needed right now was to be bewitched, bothered, and befuddled by a child genius.

Because God knew he had plenty of other things to bewitch, bother, and befuddle him right now. His phony identity. Kimball's booby-trapped files. Fifty million missing dollars. Lily Rigby's delectable underwear. Man, his work never seemed to end.

Seating himself in front of Schuyler Kimball's computer one more time—for all the good it would do—Leo went back to work.

TWELVE

Schuyler still couldn't quite figure out how his darling Lily had talked him into this one. Although he'd been paying the bills for the Van Meter Academy ever since Chloe Sandusky had come to live with him, he'd never even glimpsed the place in person. Or, rather, in edifice. Or, more accurately, in mausoleum. Because that was exactly what the place looked like. Only not an expensive mausoleum where Joe Dimaggio might send roses to a tragic blonde for all eternity, but a cut-rate mausoleum where people took their pets to be entombed.

Hesitant to get out of his car, even though his driver, Claudio, would be watching every step he took, Schuyler stole a few moments to gaze at the dilapidated building that overlooked Fairmont Park in the heart of Philadelphia. Some distance across the vast expanse of green space, high up on a hill on the other side, glowing like an amber jewel in the setting sun, stood the Philadelphia Museum of Fine Art. The Van Meter Academy was like a smaller version of that building, complete with frieze and columns and wide marble stairs—except that the Van Meter Academy was . . .

Schuyler twisted his lips in distaste. Where the museum was pristine and beautiful and in very good shape, the school Chloe attended was . . . He sighed again. Was in shape that was considerably . . . less good.

Thinking back, he supposed he probably should have checked the place out before enrolling Chloe, but the Van Meter Academy had come so very highly recommended by everyone he'd spoken to. And besides, he really hadn't wanted to be bothered with the matter of the girl's education any more than he had to be. Still, for what he was paying for this place, it ought to be gilded in gold, its steps encrusted with precious gems. He couldn't imagine where the money would be going otherwise.

He uttered a sound of discontent, then tapped on the smoked glass separating him from his driver. "Claudio," he said, "I'm ready to go in now."

Within seconds his door was swept open from outside, and Schuyler unfolded himself into the warm-hued, red-tinted light of early evening. He buttoned up his jacket as he went, his gaze still fixed on the Romanesque-looking structure before him. "Keep an eye on things, will you?" he asked the driver, as he always did whenever he left the security of his limo.

Claudio was, of course, much, much more than a driver, as anyone who gazed upon the hulking six-foot-six, two-hundred-and-fifty-pound man would probably surmise. His various roles, in addition to chauffeur, included bodyguard, navigator, storyteller, shrink, astrologer, meteorologist, and, at the odd moments when the occasion arose, he made a damned fine margarita. Schuyler would be lost without him. Claudio was almost as important to the billionaire as Lily was.

Almost.

"No problem, Mr. Kimball," Claudio replied.

He closed the door behind Schuyler and followed him up the stairs, buttoning his own double-breasted blazer as he went. To the untrained eye, the two of them might well have been visiting educators or fathers of two of the students. Except that educators didn't usually wear Ungaro suits, and fathers of students didn't generally carry MAC-10 pistols under their jackets.

Not that Schuyler was armed. Good heavens, no. He paid other people good money to be armed for him.

Six o'clock marked the end of the working day for most people, but evidently not for Mrs. Caroline Beecham. Because six o'clock was the time Lily had designated—no, *threatened*—Schuyler should show up at the woman's office. Actually, what she had told him was that if he didn't attend this meeting with the headmistress—he savored the word as it unrolled in his mind—then Lily would, quite simply, emasculate him.

Of course Lily hadn't actually *said* she'd emasculate him. Oh, no. She'd used *infinitely* more colorful language than that. Sometimes he wondered why he kept her on, the surly wench. Lucky for her she was so damned darling. Not to mention essential.

He found Caroline Beecham's office easily enough, seeing as how it was right inside the front door, straight ahead, with a sign that looked freshly painted proclaiming DIRECTOR in big, black letters. So Schuyler strode toward it, indicating Claudio should wait for him on a bench outside, one normally reserved, he supposed, for recalcitrant gifted children.

As he lifted his fist and rapped three times in quick succession on Mrs. Beecham's door, Schuyler wondered how many hours Chloe had passed on that bench. Probably not as many as he'd spent on a similar one when he was fourteen. Of course, he hadn't been able to attend some tony school for gifted kids when he'd been a gifted kid himself. No, he'd had to make do with the public school system instead. No one had even realized, when he was fourteen, what he was capable of accomplishing. No one had cared to find out.

In fact, no one had given much thought to Schuyler at all in those days. Not until he'd been tested just before college. And even then, no one had really encouraged him beyond filling out endless reams of scholarship applications. It wasn't until, oh ... all that wonderful money had started flowing in, that people began to pay him much mind. But once they'd all begun to understand exactly what he was capable of creating, once they'd realized his inherent value could potentially rise right into the ten-figure range ... Well, by golly, then suddenly *everybody* was interested in Schuyler Kimball.

Lily, of course, hadn't been like the others then. Nor was she now. Her interest in him had far predated any kind of promising future he might have. And her interest in him had never been financial in nature. Well, not really. Not the way the others had been interested.

The door opened then, and Mrs. Caroline Beecham greeted him with all the enthusiasm of a dirt clod. "Mr. Kimball," she said, taking a step backward. "I'm pleased—and not a little surprised—that you could make it this evening."

He tugged at a shirt cuff that refused to behave itself. "Yes, well, Lily said if I didn't come she'd take a meat cleaver and hack off my . . ." He hesitated. Lily had also made him promise not to say anything sexually suggestive. Not that what she'd threatened to do to him was by any means sexual, but it had sort of involved his—

"She said if I didn't come," he continued quickly, "she'd . . . do mean things to me."

Mrs. Beecham blushed furiously, but pretended not to. Then she stepped formally aside, extended her hand formally toward the interior and said, quite formally, "Won't you come in?"

The last time he'd seen her, Schuyler had thought she dressed with remarkable blandness. Now, he realized he'd been wrong in that assessment. In fact, Caroline Beecham dressed with remarkable invisibility. Had she not spoken, he might not have seen her at all. The dress she wore wasn't quite beige, nor quite brown, but something blindingly unattractive in between. Its high neck, long sleeves, and hemline well below the knee hid the better parts of her body, and her big glasses hid everything that was left.

Well, not quite everything, Schuyler noted, dropping his gaze just below her neck. He smiled with what he was certain was utter licentiousness. There wasn't much she could do to hide *those*, after all.

Why a woman who was built the way she was had pursued a career in education, of all things, when she could have been making a fortune taking off her clothes in Vegas, Schuyler would never know. There was just no accounting for some people's ambitions, he supposed. He wondered how she could sleep at night, having passed up all that.

Then he noted again the smudges of purple under her eyes, and he realized that, in fact, she didn't sleep at night. Not well, anyway. And he found himself wondering what kind of nighttime ruminations would haunt a woman like Caroline Beecham, curious as to whether they were anything like his own.

He doused the heat of his smile until it was a mere cocky grin, then, with a final nod to Claudio—who unbuttoned his jacket enough that his shoulder holster showed—Schuyler entered Caroline Beecham's domain. It was a boring domain, he noted right off, with boring brown carpet, boring brown drapes, and boring beige walls. Even the books lining one wall all seemed to be bound in brown and gray and black. He felt as if he'd just stumbled into an old sepia-toned movie, so lacking in color was the room—and the woman who rushed to put her big, ugly brown desk between them.

Damn, he wished he'd gone to Happy Hour at Ciboulette instead.

Caroline studied Schuyler Kimball from behind what she had hoped would be the safety of her big brown desk and felt her heart sink. She had told herself that in having him on her own turf, she would be able to manage the situation better, might, in fact, be able to actually control it. She bit back a brittle laugh. That was a good one. Being in control of Schuyler Kimball. She wondered if there was a creature on the entire planet who'd be able to manage him.

Ah, well. She had his attention for the moment—not to mention an alarm button on the floor behind her desk that rang in the school's security office, should she need someone to help her subdue an overly difficult student or billionaire.

"As I said, Mr. Kimball," she began experimentally, proud of herself for keeping her voice on an even keel, "it was good of you to come."

He chuckled without humor. "And as *I* said,
Mrs. Beecham, I had little choice in the matter."

She studied him thoughtfully for a moment, trying to pinpoint what had gone wrong the last time
the two of them had been alone, and how to keep
it from happening again. But all she could think
about was the fact that he had the bluest eyes she'd
ever seen in her life, and that his mouth was so
full, and so ripe, and so inviting, that it made a
woman want to completely forget about herself
and her position and her future and her past, and
just—

"Mr. Kimball," she tried again, reining herself in
before she ran headlong into disaster—or Schuyler
Kimball. Whatever. "As we discussed not long ago,
Chloe's not doing well at school. Not because she
isn't up to the demands of the curriculum, but because she simply doesn't seem to give a damn
about the curriculum. Or herself, for that matter.
And I wondered if you might be able to enlighten
me as to why she isn't receiving more support at
home. Because I think even the smallest indication
on the part of her loved ones that they do indeed
care for her could make all the difference in the
world where her performance is concerned. Both at
school and in other areas of her life."

"How do you know she isn't receiving any support at home?" he asked. But, as always, his expression remained completely impassive, and she
had no idea what he might be thinking. "What
makes you think her loved ones don't show her
that they care?"

"Well, for one thing, you don't seem to be home
much, do you?" she pointed out.

He dropped a hand—and his gaze—to his necktie, focusing on rearranging what looked like an

already perfect Windsor knot. "What would *my* presence at Ashling have to do with Chloe's performance at school? There are plenty of other people who live there," he added, glancing up again.

For some reason, though, it struck Caroline that he sounded rather pained when offering the observation. As if the other people who lived at Ashling belonged there, and he didn't. Then the import of what he'd said hit her square on, and she stared at him open-mouthed, wondering if he was just taunting her, or if he was really that stupid. "There are those, Mr. Kimball, who believe that a parent's input where their offspring's education is concerned, is rather, shall we say . . . *important*."

"Yes, we can say that," he agreed amiably enough. A little *too* amiably, Caroline thought. "What we can't say are the words 'parent' and 'offspring.' Because it seems to have escaped your notice—*again*—Mrs. Beecham, that Chloe has been assigned by the courts as my ward. Not my daughter."

Caroline nibbled her lip thoughtfully as she considered how to proceed, but when it appeared that Mr. Kimball was taking far too great an interest in the action, she stopped. "I think, Mr. Kimball," she began, "that a brain like Chloe's comes along only once in a generation. Am I making myself clear?"

He shook his head. "Not really, no."

"To deny that she's your daughter is pointless. There could be no two people with brains like yours who are unrelated by blood."

"Ah, so you're an expert on genetic analysis now, is that it, Mrs. Beecham?"

"No, I'm not," she confessed readily.

"You must be an expert on me, then."

She chose her words carefully before speaking. "When Chloe came to Van Meter," she began cautiously, "I, of course, already knew who you were. One would have to have been living in a closet for a decade not to know you. But since meeting Chloe, I've read whatever I can find that concerns you. So yes, I suppose you could call me an expert—"

"Or maybe a groupie."

She ignored his interjection and continued, "Chloe may not resemble you in physical features— except for her eyes, of course, which are exactly like yours, Mr. Kimball, something I doubt even you would deny—but her brain is . . . Astounding. That didn't come from her mother. It came from you."

"Or some other unsuspecting sap," the billionaire bit off grudgingly. "And by the way, Chloe's mother wasn't nearly as brainless as you people seem to want to make her out to be. She could scheme and plot with the best of them."

"But then, we were talking about Chloe, weren't we?" Caroline continued, refusing to deviate from the course.

The billionaire sighed heavily, though she had no idea how to interpret the sound.

"Would you like to see Chloe's classroom?" she asked impulsively, wondering what possessed her. After all, Chloe herself was so rarely in the room, it could scarcely be called hers. Still, she was starting to feel a little restless, and walking seemed like a very good idea at the moment. It would prevent her from acting on other impulses that not only made absolutely no sense, but which were totally inappropriate to boot.

"It occurs to me," she went on as she moved back around to the front of her desk, not waiting for a reply from Schuyler Kimball, "that, although Chloe's just begun her second year here at the Van

Meter Academy, you've never visited the school, have you?"

"Yes, well, as you pointed out yourself, Mrs. Beecham, I'm not home very often." He lapsed into thoughtful silence for a moment. "I suppose I could pay someone to visit the school for me from time to time . . ."

"You're here now," she pointed out unnecessarily, ignoring his jibe. "Why don't the two of us take a walk, and I'll tell you a little bit about the school?"

He shoved his hands deep into his pockets, clearly none too thrilled to have to undergo a tour. In spite of that, he said, "Wonderful. Maybe you can tell me where all my money is going. Because it certainly isn't going toward the upkeep of this place."

"No, it's not," she agreed readily, something that clearly surprised him. "Oh, don't worry—the building is perfectly safe. But we're not overly concerned with cosmetic perfection here, Mr. Kimball. Every nickel we can squeeze goes toward the edification of our students. And as expensive as you think the tuition is, I assure you, it's scarcely enough to cover costs. Education comes at a high price in these days of technological wonders. And an institution like ours can't afford to be left behind."

She extended her arm toward the door, indicating Mr. Kimball should precede her, but he only glanced back at her with an expression that said, *You've got to be kidding.*

Then he extended his own hand toward the door and said, "I never forget my manners, Mrs. Beecham. After you."

As if she believed *that* for even a second. In spite of his alleged courtesy, Caroline really didn't like the idea of walking ahead of Schuyler Kimball. Mainly because she knew he'd be back there ogling her. It wasn't any misguided sense of vanity or conceit that made her feel that way. Simply because Caroline didn't have any vanity or conceit. And even an eccentric like Kimball should be interested in something other than a too-rounded woman in an unattractive, colorless dress. But Schuyler Kimball was obviously the kind of man who went for anything in estrogen.

"When Chloe first came to Van Meter," she said as she exited the office and tried to pretend she didn't notice the *huge* man with the gun who stood up to shadow Mr. Kimball. She should have realized a man worth that much money would have a bodyguard . . . or pet gorilla." She seemed as if she would do fairly well. For the first week or two, she seemed to be a pretty enthusiastic student. But gradually, she seemed to lose interest. In school, in the few friends she'd made, in herself."

"And what, pray tell, Mrs. Beecham, would be your explanation for such a thing?"

Caroline ignored the petulance in his voice and decided to instead be heartened by the fact that he'd at least asked a question about Chloe. Maybe he wasn't quite so cold-hearted as she thought.

Maybe.

"I've thought about it a lot," she said, "and I'm inclined to believe that, when Chloe first came to Philadelphia from Las Vegas after her mother's death, she really did want to start her life anew. There's no doubt that she was terrified of the prospect of coming to live with you, Mr. Kimball—"

"*Me?*" he asked incredulously, his steps faltering as he did. With no small effort—and very little success—he tried to cover his gaffe. "Why would she be terrified of *me*?"

He seemed to be genuinely puzzled, Caroline marveled. Unbelievable. "Well, just a shot in the dark, Mr. Kimball, but maybe because she was leaving everything she knew, everything that was familiar—regardless of how dubious the comfort of those things might have been—and going to live with a man whom she'd never met before in her life, a man who had never once illustrated any desire to make her a part of his life."

"I didn't even know about Chloe until I was notified of her mother's death," Kimball told her, his voice edged with resentment. "How the hell could I have, when her mother never said a word to me about her?"

It was as close as he had come to admitting Chloe was his daughter, Caroline noted. And something in his tone when he spoke suggested that perhaps he wasn't quite as convinced of his nonpaternity as he let others believe.

"Regardless," she continued, softening her own tone when she did, "the girl was scared. Yet she seemed to be honestly willing to start over."

Kimball eyed her warily, but Caroline sensed he really was starting to take an interest in Chloe. "Why do you say that?" he asked.

"Because of some of the things she said to her friends and teachers—and to me—I sincerely believe she wanted to put her past behind her and use this opportunity to . . . reconstruct herself, if you will. I think she was hoping that you would acknowledge her as your daughter, and that by doing so, she might be able to claim an identity other than the one to which she'd been forced to mold herself, thanks to other people's perceptions of her. But no one here—no one in her family, at any rate—seemed willing to give her the benefit of the doubt. You viewed her from the start as a troubled, difficult adolescent girl who had little hope of changing, so that's what she decided she would be."

"And I suppose your teachers only reinforced that," Kimball surmised.

"Not at all," Caroline countered. "Our teachers are the best in the country, Mr. Kimball. We pay them well in the hopes that they'll stay on here at the school—that's part of where your money goes. In addition, however, we have a cooperative program here that invites considerable teacher participation. Despite our efforts with Chloe—and I assure you we have made efforts—she has slipped beyond our sphere of influence."

He hesitated only a moment before asking, "Why is that, do you think?"

"Because the way she's viewed and treated at home is infinitely more important—and holds infinitely more impact—than the way she's viewed and treated here. And at home, she simply isn't getting what she needs."

Caroline paused as they approached Chloe's core classroom, then she opened the door for them to enter. On the other side was a standard issue classroom circa 1942, little changed from its original state, save the addition of a few computer terminals and Formica-topped tables that were at least twenty years old. The evening sunlight spilled through the floor-to-ceiling windows opposite, in spite of their smudges and grime, tinting the room with gold and orange, colors that continued in the autumn-themed bulletin board on one wall. The chalkboard bore evidence of recent—and not quite thorough—erasure, and a few errant motes of dust danced and spun in the long sunbeams.

"Oh, God," the billionaire murmured beside her

before he strode quickly to the center of the room. "It's as if I never left."

Startled by his remark, Caroline followed him in. But she stopped well short of where he stood himself. "What are you talking about?"

But he didn't answer her right away. Instead, he closed his eyes and inhaled a deep breath, holding it inside himself for a moment.

"Mr. Kimball?" she urged him. "What is it?"

"That smell," he finally said. "That smell of chalk and floor wax and dust. If I close my eyes, I can almost make myself believe that I'm in seventh grade again." His eyes snapped open. "Although now that I think about it, why on earth would I want to be in seventh grade again? I despised school."

"Did you?" Caroline asked.

Kimball turned to the big, silent man standing just outside the classroom, looking in. "Close the door on your way out, would you, Claudio?"

Without a moment's hesitation, the man reached in and pulled the classroom door forward until it clicked shut, exactly as the billionaire had commanded. Only then did Schuyler Kimball turn to Caroline again.

"Yes. I did. I loathed and detested every moment I had to spend in the hallowed halls of education."

She studied him in silence for a moment, thinking that yes, a man like him would have doubtless had a very unsatisfying educational experience. When Schuyler Kimball was growing up, there had been few programs for gifted children that worked well, and even fewer teachers who tried to identify students who were light years ahead of the others. As a result, many children who should have been in accelerated learning programs were instead misidentified as troublemakers, and even slow learners on occasion. Too many had gone without the guidance they should have received.

And a child with a brain like Schuyler Kimball's, one that would have commanded constant—and very challenging—stimulation, would have probably been labeled difficult, at best. Mainly because he doubtless *had* been difficult as a child without the proper stimulation to keep him challenged or entertained. She could certainly believe that he'd not had an easy time of it at school.

"I wish I had been your teacher," she said suddenly, as surprised to hear the admission as Kimball appeared to be.

He arched his dark brows speculatively. "Do you, Mrs. Beecham?"

She nodded, realizing it was true. "Yes, I do."

He took a few steps toward her. "You doubtless would have handled me with kid gloves. Would have taken extra special care to coddle my big brain, is that it? Then you could have exploited it for all it was worth."

She shook her head. "No, I would have been worse than a Marine Corps drill instructor, exercising your big brain with the most demanding mental calisthenics I could manage."

She smiled warmly, feeling, for the first time since meeting him, as if she might actually be able to get along with him. Because for the first time, she began to understand what kind of person he was. Namely, a normal one. With normal feelings. And normal failings.

She took a step toward him, then thought better of it. No need to get overly confident, after all. She still wasn't the kind of woman who could hold her own with a man like him. Nevertheless, she couldn't help adding teasingly, "Had I been your teacher, Mr. Kimball, you would have had no satisfaction from me."

This time Kimball was the one to smile, but the warmth in his was of a completely different variety than the kind hers had held. *Warmth,* she echoed to herself derisively. *Fire* was more like it.

Slowly, he covered the rest of the distance between them, until he stood in the perfect rectangle of light that tumbled through the window behind her. "Oh, I'd have had satisfaction, Mrs. Beecham," he said. "Eventually."

Once again, just like that, the two of them were on entirely different wavelengths. Caroline couldn't quite keep herself from taking a step backward to preserve the distance she required between them. At least, she *tried* to take a step backward. But Schuyler Kimball reached out a hand and circled her left wrist with sure fingers, tugging her forward again.

"Mr. Kimball," she began to object.

But he lifted her hand and studied her fingers, then asked, "Where's Mr. Beecham? You call yourself 'Mrs.' but you're not wearing a wedding ring. Why is that?"

Caroline dropped her gaze to both their hands and inhaled a shaky breath, hoping it might slow the rapid pulsing of her heart that had kicked in the moment he had touched her. But when she transferred her attention back to his face, her heart rate nearly tripled.

Without breaking eye contact, she told him, "I don't wear my ring, because it's with my husband."

"And where is your husband?" Kimball asked.

"He's, um . . ." She swallowed hard and furrowed her brows in an effort to ward off the emotion she felt rising. "He, uh . . . I buried him almost a year ago."

The billionaire's expression changed not one whit at her revelation. As always, he appeared to be bored by life in general and people in particular. But his voice was a little rough when he asked, "Your husband is dead?"

For a moment, Caroline hesitated. Then, slowly and silently, she nodded.

"You lost him?"

"Yes," she managed to whisper.

"You loved him?"

"Yes."

For a moment, Kimball said nothing, only gazed at her with that maddeningly bland expression. Finally, very quietly, he said, "I see."

"No, Mr. Kimball, I doubt you do," Caroline replied just as quietly.

She had hoped he would release her hand now, and that they could go back to the safer subject of Chloe's education. But Schuyler Kimball apparently wanted to keep things right where they were, because although he did indeed let go of her wrist, he opened his hand against hers, palm to palm, his fingertips extending above hers a good inch. Had she wanted to, Caroline could have pulled her hand away from his.

But she didn't want to.

It was the first time a man had touched her tenderly in almost a year. Although there had been touching that morning in Kimball's office—oh, had there been touching, she recalled with a shiver now—it had been rife with tension and uncertainty and demand. This time however, there was only gentleness. Softness. Solicitude.

And it was almost more than she could bear.

"What happened?" Kimball asked, not moving

his hand from hers, not moving at all. He only continued to hold her gaze with his, and all she could do was try not to drown in the dark, dark depths of his blue, blue eyes.

"His name was Harry," she said. "Harry Beecham. And he . . . he, ah . . ." She inhaled a deep, unsteady breath and released it slowly. "He . . . was wonderful." She cleared her throat with some difficulty before continuing. "He was a police officer, and he was killed in the line of duty. They called me one night—one morning—at three-twenty-two to tell me he'd been shot when he interrupted a robbery attempt. He, uh . . ." She swallowed again. "H-he was killed instantly. That was eleven months ago. A week after our tenth anniversary."

Caroline had to consciously stop herself from releasing all the words that wanted to come after those, telling Kimball more than he wanted to know. Thoughts of Harry were never far from the very front of her brain. She wanted to tell Schuyler Kimball that Harry had coached Little League, that they'd tried to have children, but had never had any success, that her husband had grown up in South Philly, that they'd vacationed every summer in Cape May, that more than anything else in the world, Harry had loved Clint Eastwood movies—the old ones by Sergio Leone—Killian's Red beer, "Cheers" reruns, and pizza with extra green peppers and black olives.

Her thoughts and memories were a jumble of images and emotions she could never quite hold onto long enough. Harry had just been such a wonderful, regular guy. And even eleven months after losing him, Caroline didn't know what she was going to do without him.

"You miss him," Kimball said, curling his fingers

between hers until their hands were joined.

Caroline closed her eyes and nodded, then mimicked his action, closing her fingers over his hand, too. It just felt so good, this simple human contact. There was nothing demanding, nothing complicated, nothing untoward in his gesture. And Caroline appreciated his mere closeness, his innocent touch, more than he could possibly know. It had just been so long since she had had anything like this. With anyone.

So long.

"Yes," she said softly, barely able to form the word. "I miss him."

"You're lonely," Kimball added, more quietly than before.

"Yes. I am." When she opened her eyes, two fat tears tumbled down her cheeks, but she knew any effort to stop them would be pointless. She blinked, and he came into focus, and she realized there was something in his eyes, too. Not tears, but something else. Something that told her he understood. "I'm surprised, Mr. Kimball, that you seem to know so much about something like that. I would have guessed . . ."

He expelled a rueful chuckle, cutting her off, but with the knuckled index finger of his free hand, he lightly brushed her tears away. "Looking at you," he said, "is like looking in a mirror. Mrs. Beecham . . . Caroline," he amended, "you and I, I'm afraid, are two of a kind."

"No," she said quickly. "No, that's not true at all. You're . . ."

"What?"

She shook her head, able to say only, "You're different. From me, I mean." *And from Harry Beecham, too.* "We're not two of a kind at all."

"Isolation is isolation," he said, smiling sadly as

he cupped her cheek in his hand. "Whether it's self-inflicted or not is immaterial. It's still . . ."

"What?" she asked when he left the observation incomplete.

"Unpleasant," he finished with profound under-statement.

Caroline, too, lifted her hand, thinking she would move his away, but her traitorous fingers closed over his wrist and stayed there. Another tear streaked down her cheek, and he nudged it away with the pad of his thumb. Beneath her own thumb, she felt his pulse quicken, and she realized he was as confused and uncertain about all this as she was.

And then she remembered that their reason for being there wasn't because she was lonely. Or because he was lonely. Or because they were trying to define what, exactly, was going on between the two of them, anyway. There was nothing going on between the two of them. It was that simple.

The reason they were there was because a young girl needed something more in her life to get her back on track. Caroline reminded herself that she was an educator, first and foremost, and in forget-ting that, she had let one of her students down.

"Chloe," she said quietly. "We were talking about Chloe."

As if the name were an incantation, that single word broke the odd spell that had descended, and Caroline managed to release Kimball's wrist and hand and take a step away. When she did, what-ever strange illusion had appeared in his eyes van-ished, and his features reverted to the expressionlessness she'd grown accustomed to see-ing.

For a moment, she wondered if maybe she had just imagined the entire encounter, if maybe she had read something into their conversation that hadn't been there at all. Then she recalled the gentleness of his fingers against her face, and the tenderness of his palm against hers. She remembered how lonely and confused he had looked himself. And she realized she had imagined none of it.

Maybe he was right, she thought. Maybe they really were two of a kind. But that was no reason they had to have any more to do with each other than was absolutely necessary. No reason to rush off on a pointless pursuit.

"Chloe," she said again. "We need to talk more about her, Mr. Kimball."

For a moment, she thought he would refuse, then, with clear reluctance, he nodded. "Fine," he said, sounding very, very tired. "We'll talk about Chloe. But please," he added, "at least call me Schuyler. So few people outside my family do."

It was a bad idea, Caroline thought. But if it would help get him to talk about his daughter, she'd do it. "Fine. Schuyler," she said, surprised to realize that his name wasn't so difficult to say at all, even more surprised to discover that she liked the way it felt on her tongue. "If you'd like to come back to my office, I have several suggestions for how we might go about helping Chloe."

THIRTEEN

The afternoon following that profoundly erotic, but not quite satisfying, grope in Schuyler Kimball's pantry found Leo battling no small army of anxiety as he prepared for Lily Rigby's arrival at his front door. He'd left Kimball's estate early in the day—still having discovered jack about what he needed to discover—just so he could come home and get the place ready for Lily Rigby. But as he looked around, feeling strangely helpless, he wondered if he could possibly ever be ready for something like that.

He didn't worry that the place offered any incriminating evidence of what he currently did for a living—namely, lying, sneaking around, and misrepresenting himself to a beautiful, luscious woman who may or may not have something to hide herself. In fact, his turn-of-the-century Chestnut Hill townhouse looked better than it had looked in some time. Maybe, he thought, it looked a little *too* good. A lowly bookkeeper for Kimball Technologies, Inc. probably wouldn't pull in enough in salary to live in Chestnut Hill, let alone have acquired all the electronic wonders that made a single man's life worth living, the way Leo had. Like that state-of-the-art sound system in the corner and that satellite TV system front and center. And the earth-toned leather furnishings and contemporary patterned rugs—not to mention a few pieces of original artwork—were probably also beyond the income of a working stiff like Leonard Freiberger.

Leo was even worried about what he was wearing. What he was *wearing*, for God's sake. He still couldn't believe he'd been reduced to standing in front of his closet, wondering what Miss Rigby would be wearing, concerned about giving off the wrong impression. Would they be staying in, or going out? If they went out, would they go someplace casual, or formal? If they stayed in, just how casual would the situation be? Jeez, next he'd be subscribing to *Seventeen* magazine and reading articles with titles like "Cool Ways to Hang with Your Hottie" or "Fashion *UGHS!*" Ultimately, he'd donned a pair of charcoal gray corduroys and a wine-colored sweater. There. Let her deduce whatever she wanted from that. At least he'd found some clean underwear.

For a moment, Leo wondered if he could pawn himself off as the laboring black sheep of a wealthy family. Then he remembered he'd already told Lily Rigby that he came from a long line of oystermen on Chesapeake Bay. Hmmm . . . Maybe he could tell her he'd just been kidding about that. Rich families were always eccentric that way, weren't they? Lying and sneaking around and misrepresenting themselves? Hell, he'd fit right in.

He sighed heavily. He'd worry about explanations when Miss Rigby called for them. His best hope for the moment was that she would be as uncertain and confused about what was supposed to happen tonight as he was, and wouldn't even notice that his home was way beyond the means of a lowly bookkeeper.

And while he was on the subject, he thought further, just what *was* supposed to happen tonight?

What the *hell* had he been thinking to let Lily Rigby come over to his place? Leo wondered, not for the first time since yesterday afternoon—or even the hundredth time, for that matter. Obviously he *hadn't* been thinking. Not with his brain, anyway. His brain, after all, had a superior intellect that caused him to think and reason before acting. The rest of his body parts, however, weren't so favorably endowed. Well, one part was pretty favorably endowed. Just not with any amount of smarts, that's all.

A knock at the door interrupted his thoughts, a good hour too early for it to be Lily Rigby. When he opened the door and saw Eddie Dolan standing on the other side, Leo was amazed to realize that he'd completely forgotten about calling the guy two weeks before. Man, this whole Kimball thing had him way too preoccupied. What was worse, though, was that he wasn't preoccupied with this whole Kimball thing.

"About damned time you got back to me," he chastised the other man anyway. No need to let Eddie think Leo was falling down on the job. "Just what the hell took you so long?"

Eddie pushed past him, unconcerned, a fat file folder tucked under one arm. "Hey, I ain't even gettin' paid for this," he reminded Leo. "You're lucky I took the time out of my busy schedule to bother."

Leo closed the door behind the other man with a dry chuckle. "So, is your schedule busy lately with a blonde, a brunette, or a redhead?" he asked.

Eddie wiggled his eyebrows playfully. "All of the above."

Leo laughed harder. That was Eddie. The consummate ladies' man. Which was actually kind of surprising, because he wasn't the usual stereotype. Oh, he wasn't a bad-looking sort, in a dark, brooding kind of way. But Eddie wasn't the sharpest knife in the drawer, either. Sure, he had a knack for ferreting out all kinds of information about people, but when it came to disseminating that information, well . . . Eddie was much better cast as a hunter/gatherer than as the village wise man.

And then, of course, there was that tendency of his to commit crimes like distortion, fraud, and petty theft. Which, Leo couldn't help but note, wasn't that far a cry from lying, sneaking around, and misrepresenting oneself.

Ah, well. No one was perfect.

"I brought what I could find on the royal family," Eddie said, flopping himself down on the sofa. He unbuttoned his dark, double-breasted blazer, then hiked his feet up on the brass-and-glass coffee table, ankles crossed. "The royal *pain* family, ya ask me," he added parenthetically. "Man, what money will do to people. It's a crime. They should give it all to me."

"Yeah, yeah, yeah. Just tell me the abbreviated version of the story for now. I'll read over the whole file later."

Eddie eyed him with a critical study. "You got plans tonight, loverboy? Am I . . . intruding?"

"Not yet," Leo told him. "But you will be if you don't hurry up. And get your feet off the table, will you?" he added, slapping the other man's Gucci loafers as he passed. "I just dusted in here."

"Ooo, well, *excuuuuse* me, Mr. Clean," Eddie said, straightening as he lowered his feet back to the floor. "I didn't mean to leave fingerprints."

Leo let that one go without comment, then watched as Eddie thumbed through the file. When he noted the quick passage of text and photos and a variety of documents, then more text and more photos and more documents, he uttered a mumble of resignation. Looked like he'd be up late reading tonight, he thought. Unless, of course, he was up late with Miss Rigby. At which point, of course, *reading* would be the last thing on his mind. Unless he was reading her—

As quickly as the erotic images began to erupt in his brain, Eddie's rusty voice squelched them. "I'm gonna assume you already know the obvious about King Kimball," he said. "The poverty-stricken beginnings, the brilliant mind, all that cutting-edge technology he invented, the business he built from scratch—"

"Yeah, yeah, assume away," Leo said, interrupting him. "I don't want the *People* magazine version. I want the ground-in dirt, too."

Eddie smiled with satisfaction. "Okay. Did you know he used to boink his social secretary, one Miss Lily Marie Rigby, of the Main Line Rigbys, on a regular basis?"

Leo winced at Eddie's command of the vernacular—*boink*, after all, didn't come close to what he suspected Miss Rigby was capable of doing—then snapped to attention at the wealth of information in Eddie's one simple question. "Used to? You mean he doesn't still? And Lily Rigby is from a Main Line family? Are you sure?"

"Yep and nope and yep and yep," Eddie replied. "She and Kimball lived together when they were in college, but evidently the *hot-hot-hot* went out of that relationship a *loooong* time ago. And the luscious Miss Rigby did, in fact, grow up in the lap of luxury, a member of one of Philadelphia's oldest and most illustrious families—until her old man blew the family fortune when she was in high school."

"Whoa, whoa, whoa," Leo said, dropping onto the sofa opposite Eddie. "What are you talking about?"

Obviously delighted to have Leo at a disadvantage, Eddie said, "Got any beer? I gotta wicked thirst been doggin' me all afternoon. And this is a *great* story."

Leo rose and made his way to the kitchen. Over his shoulder he called, "It better not be more than thirty minutes great. I need you gone by then."

"No *People* magazine version, I promise. I'll give you the *TV Guide* Fall Preview capsule review, instead—how'll that be?"

"Fine. Just get on with it."

Leo grabbed a beer for them both, relishing the wet hiss of each cap that signaled their opening, then returned to his seat on the sofa. Eddie enjoyed a healthy swig of the brew as he loosened his Valentino necktie, clearly gearing up for what he had to reveal. Then he leaned back comfortably, one arm folded behind his head.

"Once upon a time," he began, "there was a little princess named Lily Rigby who had everything a girl could ever want. Rich mommy and daddy. Big house on a hill in Ardmore. Sports car. White cotillion dress. You name it. Then, one day, when she was sixteen, her daddy lost everything. Now, mind you, Mr. Harrison Rigby was one helluva of a businessman. Talk about your self-made millionaires. He just panicked, and waited too long to try to recover. Something that sort of left his family, oh . . . Destitute."

Eddie smiled, as if proud of himself for using a word like *destitute* correctly.

"Anyway," he continued, "the Rigbys move into a homeless shelter in Philadelphia for a few months, and—"

"A homeless shelter?" Leo echoed, nearly choking on his beer. "Miss Rigby lived in a *homeless* shelter when she was a teenager?"

At his question, Eddie, too, nearly strangled on the slug of beer he'd pulled into his mouth. Wiping his chin with the back of his fist, he sputtered, "Jeez, Leo, you actually call her 'Miss Rigby?' What the hell have you been doing out at that estate for the last two weeks?" He arched his dark eyebrows in thought, as if something had just occurred to him. "Unless, you're using the 'Miss' part as a shortened form of 'Mistress,' in which case, I gotta hand it to ya, big guy, 'cause I ain't *never* had the nerve to let a woman dress up in black leather and tell me to—"

"Just get on with the story, Eddie."

Eddie shook his head, clearly disappointed in Leo's diminished sense of adventure. Then he shrugged, enjoyed another swallow of beer, and continued. "Okay, so Princess Lily may be poor, but she's got a brain on her that won't quit. Her IQ is a hundred and forty-seven, did you know that?"

Leo stiffened. Miss Rigby's IQ was higher than his? By five points?

"So she gets into Harvard on the Big Brain Scholarship, where she meets Schuyler Kimball, another penniless geek, whose way through the ivy halls is being paid by the Biggest Brain of All Scholarship. Are you still with me, Leo?"

"Oh, you bet." But somehow, he hadn't quite

moved past the fact that Miss Rigby was smarter than he was.

"I guess when two big brains meet like that, their libidos can't be far behind," Eddie continued, "because the two of them shacked up the whole time they were in school together."

Leo choked on another swallow of beer. "*Shacked up*?" he repeated, his version a bit louder than Eddie's. "Miss Rigby and Kimball lived together for that length of time?"

"*College* time, too," Eddie clarified. "And you know how randy those years are, Leo. They musta been at it like rabbits."

Leo shook his head slowly in disbelief. Well, why was he so surprised? he asked himself. He'd *known* there was something more to Miss Rigby's relationship with Kimball than simple employment. He'd *known* that her feelings for the man went far deeper than a social secretary's should. He'd *known* that. And he was always, *always*, right about these things. So then why did he suddenly feel so cheated by the knowledge? *Why*?

Because, dammit, he'd wanted to be wrong about it, that's why.

"What else?" he asked, hesitant to hear any more, but knowing he had little choice. Not only was all this essential information, but when you got Eddie Dolan started on a story like this, it was impossible to shut him up until he was through.

Eddie swallowed some more beer before continuing. "The two of them have stayed together since college," he said, "but not always in the romantic sense. Nobody seems to know for sure exactly *what* their relationship is, but it doesn't look like they do much boinking these days. Not with each other, anyway. King Kimball certainly seems to be on the boinking tour of all the capitals of the world, but

Princess Lily doesn't seem to be boinking anybody at all." He eyed Leo with much interest. "Unless you know something I don't know. Which isn't likely, seeing as how *I'm* the one with the big fat file folder. And you don't show up in there until almost the last page."

Leo opted not to answer that one. He did still have a long night ahead of him, after all. In spite of everything he was learning about Miss Rigby and her employer, he wasn't entirely ruling out some potential for boin . . . uh . . . for romance.

Eddie frowned with clear disappointment at Leo's unwillingness to expound upon the level of boinking at the Kimball estate. With a sigh of resignation, he tipped the bottle to his mouth again before continuing. "At any rate, King Kimball and Princess Lily just seem to be good friends now. She's worked for him in one way or another ever since he started the business. She's got an MBA and all that, so I guess it makes sense that he'd hire her."

An MBA? An *MBA*?

"But she's not using her MBA in the capacity of social secretary," Leo said with some distraction, having a bit of trouble getting past that MBA business. "If that was what she wanted to be when she grew up, then she should have majored in something like hotel management. Why would a woman with an advanced degree in business, not to mention a massive IQ, waste her talents working as a social secretary? Especially for Kimball and his household? He'd be better off employing a zoo keeper or a circus ringleader in that capacity."

Eddie shrugged. "Maybe he's the one who dumped her, and she just wants to be with him however she can. Maybe she's just trying to preserve the fading bloom of a love that wilted long ago. Some women are like that, ya know, Leo. Pining after men they can't have, men who don't want them anymore. Deluding themselves into thinking that if they diminish themselves in one area of life, they'll have gained so much more in another area of life.''

Leo eyed the other man warily. '' 'Preserve the bloom of a love that wilted long ago?' '' he repeated incredulously. ''What the *hell* are you talking about? What would you know about any of that stuff?''

''Hey,'' Eddie cried indignantly, straightening to a sitting position. ''I watch 'Oprah,' too, ya know. And I think women like that are tragic. I feel their pain—I really do. And I think somebody oughta publish a directory of women like that, so those of us who would appreciate them could call them up on Friday nights. It would save a hell of a lot on nine hundred numbers.''

Leo shook his head and somehow refrained from comment. ''Miss Rigby's too smart for that. I don't get the impression at all that she's suffering from a case of unrequited love where Kimball is concerned.''

Involuntarily, he recalled the scene from the afternoon before, those all-too-brief moments when he'd lost control of himself and succumbed to his desire to simply touch her. He remembered the way her scent had taunted him, and the way her soul had beckoned to him. He recalled the heated, silky flesh beneath his fingertips when he'd stolen up under her sweater, and the whisper of fabric as he'd urged her skirt up her thighs. He recalled the look in her eyes when she'd turned to him and tangled her fingers in his hair, and the way her heart had pounded beneath his thumb when he'd settled it on the front closure of her bra.

So close. They'd been so close . . .

He bit back a groan. On the contrary, unrequited love for Schuyler Kimball was the last thing Miss Rigby seemed to be suffering from these days.

"Okay, so she and Kimball were an item once upon a time," Leo conceded reluctantly.

"A *hot* item," Eddie interjected. "A *steaming* item. A *spontaneous combustion* item."

Leo ignored him. "And okay, so she comes from money," he added further, collecting his thoughts.

"*Buckets* of money," Eddie elaborated. "*Olympic-sized swimming pools* of money. *Grand Canyons* of—"

"And, okay, so she's . . . she's . . . she's above average in intelligence," Leo tossed out further, unwilling to wait around while Eddie dug a pit for the Rigby fortune the size of the Pacific Ocean.

"Oh, I think you're understating the facts most egregiously there, Leo, old man," Eddie interrupted again. "A hundred and forty-seven on the noodle scale, well . . . That's even higher than *you*, pal." At Leo's sharp look of censure, he added, "Though I'm sure she can't bench press her IQ the way you can."

The realization brought little comfort.

What brought even less comfort was the fact that Miss Rigby had a few hidden aspects to herself that Leo hadn't anticipated at all. She was irrevocably tied to Schuyler Kimball—in a way that no one seemed capable of defining, a way that went beyond what most people enjoyed together. She came from a moneyed background—one she had lost at an age when she'd probably been most enjoying the benefits of wealth. She laid claim to an enormous intellect—that she kept concealed and didn't use to its potential.

Where Leo had been hoping that Eddie's snooping might provide a few answers, it appeared that the man's findings were only going to launch a host of new questions instead.

And a host of new suspicions, too, he realized. Because if Lily Rigby had come from money—buckets of money, Grand Canyons of money—only to have watched it disappear, well . . . she might just be looking for a way to recoup her father's losses, and her own. And if she was as smart as it appeared, then she'd certainly know how to go about siphoning off fifty million dollars from her employer, not to mention hiding it somewhere that no one would find it. Not until she'd found a nice little hacienda on the Brazilian coast somewhere, anyway. And, hey, who better to steal money from than an ex-lover who may have spurned her?

But this was Lily he was thinking about here, he reminded himself. Lily. *Lily*. She couldn't possibly be capable of something like that.

Could she?

No, certainly not.

Leo's thoughts left a bad taste in his mouth, so he lifted the beer for another swallow, in the hopes that it would both cleanse his palate and numb his brain. Unfortunately, it was going to take more than one lousy beer to do that. He glanced down at his watch. In forty-five minutes, Lily Rigby would be knocking on his front door. And if he'd thought he was ill prepared to greet her before, he was thoroughly unready now.

Only one thing to do for it, he thought. He was going to have to do what countless other men before him had done for the sake of king and country, what people throughout history had done in order to preserve honor, and integrity, and fidelity. He'd have to engage in that activity that kept the status quo safe. He had no choice. There was no way to avoid it. He would do what he had to do.

Namely, turn tail and run like hell.

FOURTEEN

When Lily arrived at the address Mr. Freiberger had left for her on Schuyler's desk, she was surprised enough by her surroundings that she double-checked everything to be sure. But this was definitely the place where she was supposed to be. Schuyler must be paying his bookkeepers a lot more than she'd realized. Either that, or else Mr. Freiberger was a big fat liar.

Because this street of pristine, spotless, honey-colored brick townhouses was no low-rent district. On the contrary, the tree-lined, cobbled sidewalks and the potted chrysanthemums on stoops and in window boxes—not to mention the Jaguars and Mercedes parked along the curbs—attested to how much pride the residents took in their homes. And in their cars. And in their social standing.

Mr. Freiberger, Lily had noted before—only in idle curiosity, naturally—drove a cherry-red, vintage Mustang convertible, just like, oh . . . the one parked in front of this particular house. Keenly, she observed that it was yet something else to clue her in to the fact that she had, indeed, arrived at the right address. His choice of car hadn't surprised her at all initially. She'd imagined him rebuilding the classic vehicle from the ground up, reveling in his weekend endeavor, slaving away in some suburban garage, all hot and shirtless, and sweaty and grease-stained, with his bare biceps pumping under the strain of wrench and tire jack, and his bare back slick with perspiration, and . . . and . . .

Well, she'd just had a pretty good idea of how he spent his spare time, that was all.

But now she wondered if he drove the car not because it had been affordable once upon a time, but simply because he liked vintage cars. Because if Leonard Freiberger could afford this kind of real estate, then he could certainly afford to drive a vehicle of a much higher monetary class.

Still, she was glad he didn't. The Mustang suited him perfectly. This house, however . . . She sighed as she studied the address again, and wished she knew for sure what was going on.

Smoothing a hand over the long, baggy white sweater that she'd donned over a full, blue printed skirt and boots, she extended a hand toward the doorbell to push it. But before she completed the action, the door was jerked open from the other side, and Marlon Brando nearly ran right over her.

Oh, wait. Not Marlon Brando. He hadn't been that svelte since *On the Waterfront*. No, this was just someone who looked a lot like him.

"Excuse me," Lily said as she tried—without success—to step out of his way.

But the man evidently had his mind on other things, because he just kept coming until he'd nearly toppled her, catching her at the last possible moment before she would have tumbled backward down the steps.

"Oh, Miss Rigby," he said as he righted her, surprising her. "I'm sorry. I didn't see you there."

Right behind Marlon came Mr. Freiberger, who, upon witnessing the scene, smacked his open palm against his forehead. Hard. And then he grumbled something under his breath that sounded a whole lot like, "You idiot."

Well, all right, Lily thought huffily, she would confess that she was just a tad early, but that was no reason for him to go off like that, now, was it? Okay, so maybe thirty-five minutes was just a tad more than *just a tad*, but still . . .

"Hello, Mr. Freiberger," she said coolly as Mr. Brando, with one final check to be sure she could stand on her own, released her on her own recognizance. She skimmed a hand down her sweater, then patted it back over the hair swept up into what she had hoped was a sophisticated look. Because suddenly she felt anything but sophisticated. Being called an idiot by a man one had just come to fool around with rather did that to a person. "Look, I admit I'm just a tad early," she went on, "but that's no reason to resort to name calling."

He eyed her in obvious confusion for a minute, then shook his head hard once, as if to clear it. "No, no," he quickly denied, "I wasn't calling *you* an idiot. I was calling *him* an idiot. He nearly knocked you down." He turned to Marlon Brando with a frown and added, "You idiot."

But the other man only smiled in return. Smiled knowingly, too, Lily thought, something that roused her suspicions even more because he also knew her name. She was about to ask him just how he'd come by that information, seeing as how *she'd* never seen *him* before in her life—except in *On the Waterfront*, of course—but the dark-haired man stuck out his hand in greeting.

"Eddie Dolan," he told her with a smile that was dazzling, and really kind of sexy, if you went for that dark, brooding, I'm-gonna-make-you-an-offer-you-can't-refuse kind of thing, instead of that rumpled, tweedy, *Goodbye, Mr. Chips* kind of thing.

"Mr. Dolan," she replied with a quick nod, shaking his hand once before releasing it.

She opened her mouth to ask him how he knew her name, but Mr. Freiberger cut her off with a hastily offered, "Eddie is my, uh... my, um... That is, he's... Ah..."

"I'm Leo's astrologer," he announced, his smile growing unmistakably mischievous now.

Lily arched her eyebrows in surprise, then trained her gaze to Mr. Freiberger. "Astrologer?" she asked him. *Leo?* she asked herself. Then, immediately, she decided she approved of the moniker. Somehow, that name suited him much better than Leonard did.

But instead of answering her, Mr. Freiberger—Leo, she corrected herself—only grumbled something unintelligible under his breath again. So Lily turned her attention back to Mr. Dolan. "How did you know my name?" she asked him.

His dazzling smile dimmed some. "Uh... I... That is..." He furrowed his brow in thought for a moment, then quickly replied, "I'm, uh, I'm Leo's psychic, too. Yeah, that's it."

"A psychic astrologer?" Lily asked dubiously.

The man nodded.

"How extraordinary." *And how suspicious.* "Do you charge for each service, or is it an all-inclusive package?"

Eddie Dolan shrugged in a way that no self-respecting astrologer *or* psychic would ever dare. "Depends on the client's needs," he said.

"Really?" she asked. "And just what are Mr. Freiberger's needs?"

The man chuckled. "Oh, Leo. He's got needs, all right, lemme tell ya."

"Eddie . . ."

The threat in Mr. Freiberger's warning—or was it a warning in Mr. Freiberger's threat? she wondered before completing the thought. Well, no matter. In either case, threat or warning, his intent was unmistakable. Simply put, if Mr. Dolan continued with his description of Mr. Freiberger's needs, then Mr. Freiberger would hurt him. Badly.

"And what have the stars—and you—predicted for Mr. Freiberger's immediate future?" Lily asked, wondering what exactly made her pose the question. Other than her own curiosity about just what on earth the evening ahead was supposed to hold.

Mr. Dolan's smile turned into a supernova at her question. "Lemme think on it a minute," he said. He furrowed his dark brows, as if consumed by great concentration. "Oh, okay. Here it comes. I see a dark stranger."

"Really?" she asked again, running a hand over her—dark—hair once more.

He nodded, then lifted a hand to his head, pressing his fingertips against his temple. "Yeah. Yeah, it's comin' in real clear now. I see a dark stranger about . . . five-foot-three?"

"Five-foot-four," she corrected him.

He nodded, pressing his fingers to his temple again, feigning a semi-trance. "And I also see candlelight," he continued. "And a bottle of wine—good stuff, not the screw-off-cap kind Leo usually serves—and a cozy little table for two."

"Eddie . . ." Mr. Freiberger—or rather, Leo— muttered menacingly.

There was that threat/warning again, Lily noted. But just as before, Mr. Dolan seemed not to notice or care. Because he continued in that dreamy, trance-like voice, "A little Johnny Mathis on the stereo—'Misty,' naturally—a couple of slow dances . . ."

Lily smiled. "Do go on," she told him.

The psychic astrologer closed his eyes, as if it might improve the vision. "And then after that, I see . . . handcuffs," he said, opening his eyes and dropping his hand back to his side.

"Handcuffs?" Lily asked.

He nodded. "And also a can of Criscoe and a Twister game. But that could be my own immediate future intruding a little there. Sometimes that happens to psychics, ya know."

Lily's eyebrows shot up at that. "My goodness, Mr. Dolan, you do seem to have an amazing gift, to see all that detail."

He shrugged off the compliment. "Yeah, well, I have a lot of free time on my hands, Miss Rigby."

"Yes, well, that's rather obvious, isn't it?"

"Beat it, Eddie," Mr. Freiberger—Leo—said succinctly. "Miss Rigby and I have plans."

"Yeah, I'll say you do. Do you even remember where you *put* your Twister game? If you want, I could stay and help you out with—"

"Go . . . away," Leo—yes, definitely Leo—said, more adamantly this time.

Eddie Dolan, psychic astrologer to bookkeepers, lifted a hand to his forehead again, this time in salute. "Miss Rigby," he said. "It was nice meeting you. Leo," he added, turning to his . . . client. "Don't do anything I wouldn't do."

Now why did Lily suspect that that left the field wide open?

"Have fun tonight, kids," Mr. Dolan tossed over his shoulder as he headed down the steps. And then, singing what sounded like "Strangers in the night, shoobie doobie doobie," he stuffed his hands into his trouser pockets and strolled down the street.

And then Lily and Leo—oh, yes, most definitely Leo; how had she missed that before?—were alone. With the sun setting low behind her, he was bathed in a dozen hues of gold and orange, framed by the doorway and, thanks to the raised entry, standing even taller than usual.

Lily inhaled a shaky breath and questioned the wisdom in coming here tonight. She couldn't imagine what she'd been thinking yesterday to be so forward in inviting herself to his house. Oh, wait. Yes, she could, too, imagine. In fact, she could remember quite clearly what she'd been thinking yesterday to be so forward in inviting herself to his house. She'd been thinking that maybe the two of them could engage in some quiet conversation, move a little beyond the "Mr." and "Miss" phase, and then get naked and make wild monkey love.

It was all coming back to her now.

Thinking she should probably just make an excuse to leave and then run away, Lily heard herself ask instead, "Aren't you going to invite me in?"

For a moment, judging by the expression on his face, she honestly thought he was going to say *No* and slam the door in her face. Then he stood aside. "Of course. Please. Come in."

"Yes. Thank you. I will."

My, but the conversation was off to a good start, she thought. Any time now, they ought to be moving right into the polysyllabic stage, and after that, there would be absolutely no stopping them.

"I wasn't sure what to wear," she began as she moved awkwardly past him, for some reason suddenly unwilling to get too close. "I wasn't sure what we'd be doing." *Other than that wild monkey love thing, I mean, and I did put on some lovely under-*

things for that. "I guess when I—" *Might as well just say it.* "When I invited myself over, I didn't plan that far ahead. I was just thinking about yesterday afternoon ..." *Uh-oh.* "Um, about yesterday afternoon when ... um ..." *Oh, nicely dug pit, Lily.* "When, uh ..." she tried again.

"Yesterday afternoon in the pantry when I had my hand up your skirt?" he supplied helpfully. He closed the front door and leaned back against it, his posture seemingly benign, the fire burning in his eyes anything but.

She dropped her gaze to the back of her hand, furiously studying her fingernails. "Yes. Yes, that was it," she agreed, fighting back the heat she felt flooding her face. "I was thinking about ... that ... and I just sort of, um ... arrived early."

"Thirty-five minutes early," he pointed out unnecessarily.

"Well, I did say sixish, didn't I?"

"The operative word here being *ish*," he said.

"Actually, I don't think *ish* is a word, is it?" she asked, trying to steer the conversation into another direction. And at this point, *any* direction would be welcome. Even a silly one.

"Well, no, not a word, exactly," he conceded, still leaning back against the door. "But it does have a certain implication. When you tell someone *ish*, they form a definite impression."

"Yes, but that implication is ishish, at best," Lily said. Somehow, she found the fortitude to bring her gaze back up to meet his. "So when one uses *ish*, it means 'not specifically.' Therefore, when I said, 'sixish,' what I meant was 'not specifically six o'clock.'"

"Yeah, but you got here even before five-thirtyish," he said.

Lily gaped at him. "I most certainly did not. My

arrival was definitely *after* five-thirtyish."

"But way before sixish."

Lily inhaled a discontented breath and blew it out with *much* exasperation. "Oh, all *right*," she finally relented. "I'm early. I admit it. There. Is that what you wanted to hear?"

He smiled as he pushed himself away from the door and took the single step necessary to bring his body within a hairsbreadth of hers. "Actually," he said softly, "what I'd like to hear is an explanation as to why the memory of my hand up your skirt made you arrive here so much earlier than you said you would."

Gee, Lily would have liked to hear an explanation for that, too. One that didn't make her nipples tingle, anyway.

"But what I'd like even more," he added before she had a chance to say anything, lifting his hand to her sleekly arranged hair, "is to know how long your hair is."

Without even asking permission, let alone waiting for a reply, he found and deftly removed the long clip that held her French twist in place. Lily's hair came tumbling down past her shoulders, between her shoulder blades, to nearly the center of her back, the sleek shafts shining like blue-black satin.

"Wow," he said as he bunched a fistful in one hand. "I had no idea."

"Le—I mean, Mr. Freiberger . . ." she began.

But anything else she might have said dried up in her mouth, because slowly, leisurely, oh, so leisurely, he began to wrap her hair around his fist. Over and over again he turned his hand, winding her hair loosely about his fingers until they were nearly obscured by the long tresses. And all the while, his gaze remained fixed on the motion, as if he weren't quite sure why he was doing it, or what he would do when he couldn't wind any more around his fingers.

Then, just as she thought he would pull her forward, as quickly as he had begun the gesture, he halted it, lifting his gaze to lock with hers. "Leo," he said softly. "Call me Leo. Please."

She hesitated for a moment, not sure she could say the word aloud, not sure she could say *anything* out loud, because her entire body seemed to have shut down operation so that the thrill of heat winding through her would have a completely unhampered journey. He had simply been Mr. Freiberger, alleged bookkeeper for Kimball Technologies, for so long, Lily wasn't sure she could view him as anything else.

But somehow, running her tongue lightly over her dry lips, and in a very soft voice, she managed to utter the word, "Leo."

It was, evidently, all the encouragement he needed, because after that single concession to familiarity, he angled his head to the side, tugged lightly on her hair to bring her forward, and covered her mouth with his.

And then, Lily knew he would never be Mr. Freiberger again.

It was an extraordinary kiss, unlike any she had ever received from a man before, at once questioning and commanding, tentative and absolute. Leo kissed her as if he needed her for sustenance, for strength, for life itself. He cupped his other hand over the back of her head to urge her toward him even more, and with one little step forward, Lily was in his arms.

It was, she decided immediately, a very nice place to be, and how wonderfully convenient that she fit so well. She would have thought such a large man would intimidate her, would frighten her, would swallow her in one big bite. But Leo made her feel as if she were a part of him, returning after far too long a separation. Without hesitation, she curved her palms over the planes and angles of his hard chest, relishing every soft quiver of flesh as he moved. Then she pushed her hands up over his shoulders, and looped her arms around his neck. She, too, cupped a hand over the back of his head, threading her fingers through the short, silky strands of his hair, and pulled him downward. Then she pushed herself up on tiptoe, launching herself into the kiss.

Oh, my. It was even better when she helped.

Evidently, Leo thought so too, because a soft, contented sound erupted from somewhere deep inside him. He took another tiny step forward and slanted his head to the other side, to deepen the kiss. Lily opened to him willingly, and he slipped his tongue into her mouth, tasting her resolutely, thoroughly, wantonly. She heard another soft sound of satisfaction, and, not surprisingly, she realized that this time, it came from somewhere deep inside her. He just made her feel so . . .

Oh . . .

And she wanted to keep feeling that way. Forever.

"Leo," she murmured against his lips. She wasn't sure what she was going to say, but instinctively, she needed to slow down some. Not a lot. Just some.

But Leo seemed not to hear her, because he only claimed her mouth again, more insistently this time. He moved the hand entangled in her hair to cup her jaw, skimming the other down to the small of her back to press her against him. Lily indulged in another kiss for some moments more, then remembered that she had been trying to say something.

She just wished she could remember what.

"Leo," she tried again, doubling her fists loosely against his chest. "Please. We have to slow down."

This time he listened to her—sort of. He released her mouth, but left his hands where they were, then dipped his forehead to rest it against hers. He closed his eyes and took a few slow, deep breaths, as if he were trying to level off his heart rate. She knew that, because it was exactly the same thing she was doing herself. For long moments, they only stood there silently, heads touching, hands exploring, trying to match their respiration and steady their pulse.

And then Leo said, "Lily."

It was the first time she had heard her name spoken in his voice, and never before had she realized what an erotic connotation her name had. Of course, had anyone else been saying it, *Lily* wouldn't have sounded erotic at all. But Leo's dark, rich baritone was a sound that reminded her of good, mellow cognac warmed in a man's palm. And whenever she thought of a man's palm, she thought of his. And when she thought of his palm, she thought about how it would feel on her. And in his voice, her name came out sounding like a promise full of purpose, full of longing, full of impatience.

Instead of looking at him, she fixed her gaze on the hands she had splayed open over the nubby knit of his sweater. "Yes?" she asked quietly.

"Lily, I . . . I want to make love to you."

So much for slowing her heart rate. "Do you?"

She sensed, more than saw, him nod. "Yes. I do. Very badly."

"How interesting," she managed to reply. "I was

just thinking that *I'd* like to make love to *you*, too, Leo."

She braved a glance up at his face, only to find him smiling down at her. So she smiled, too, but for some reason, she was sure hers wasn't nearly as confident or as certain as his was.

"Well, well, well," he said. "Great minds think alike."

She chuckled low, but it came out sounding a bit tense to her ears, and she hoped he didn't hear how very nervous she was. "I miss you when you're not at Ashling," she said, wondering why she should confess such a thing.

"Do you?"

She nodded. "The house feels so empty without you there."

He lifted a hand to brush the backs of his knuckles gently over her cheek, and Lily's eyes fluttered closed so that she might better savor the sensation of his touch. Involuntarily, her lips parted a fraction, as if she couldn't . . . quite . . . get enough air. Or something. Deep inside her a curl of heat unwound and seeped into every cell in her body, and she found herself wanting him to move his hand lower . . . and lower . . . and lower still . . .

"That house would feel empty if you were entertaining the entire Arab Emirates," he said quietly. "It's much too large."

"Yes," she agreed, turning her head into the soft sweep of his knuckles. "It is."

"I like places that are a bit smaller," he told her.

"Me, too."

"A bit more cozy."

"Yes."

"A bit more intimate."

"Mm-hm."

"Like my bedroom, for example."

"Ah."

"What do you say, Lily?" he asked. "Would you like to come up and see my etchings?"

She opened her eyes slowly, taking her time to focus on his face. What she saw there heartened her some—he seemed to be no less nervous about what was happening than she was—but the coil of anxiety threading through her still prevented her from acting too rashly. Regardless of how much she wanted to ignore her troublesome, rational mind.

"I . . . I . . ." She inhaled a deep breath and released it slowly. "I don't know, Leo. This is just going so—"

"I like the way you say my name," he interjected. "And I like saying yours, too. Leo and Lily. Our names go together well, don't they?"

She hesitated only a moment before responding, "Yes. They do."

"I wonder if our bodies will fit together as well."

A little explosion went off in her belly at the roughness that edged his voice when he said what he did. He wanted her. Perhaps even as much as she wanted him. But he was leaving it up to her, she thought. Somehow, she knew instinctively that whatever she said, whatever she decided, he would go along with it.

For one long moment, she remained silent, unsure what to say. She opened her hands over his chest again, pressing her fingertips into the soft fabric of his sweater, searching, she suddenly understood, for his heartbeat. When she found it, she felt it racing beneath her fingertips, and she realized that he really was every bit as frightened and uncertain as she was. Somehow, the knowledge made all the difference.

Tipping her head back, she gazed up into his face, then curved her palm over his rough jaw. And then, very, very quietly, she told him, "I guess there's only one way to find out, isn't there?"

FIFTEEN

Leo's bedroom upstairs was furnished in much the same way as the lower portion of his home, Lily noted as she preceded him into the room. Muted earth tones, clean lines on all the furnishings, few accessories. Clearly, he preferred for his surroundings to be uncluttered, minimal, tidy. It was something she'd already noticed about him when he was working at Ashling. Where Schuyler's desk was normally piled high with all matter of unidentifiable refuse, Leo had always kept his things set well apart, and his things had always been stacked in an organized, orderly fashion.

She wondered suddenly if he felt the same way about his life, if he wanted to keep things organized and orderly there, too. If so, they could run into a few problems along the line, because Lily was by no means tidy and methodical in the way she went about doing things. Schuyler often wondered how she managed to keep everything together as well as she did, and he'd often remarked over the years how amazed he was that she'd run his life as well as she had. But Lily had a certain way of doing business, that was all. And that way just . . . worked.

Of course, her worries about a future with Leo might be completely unfounded anyway, because in worrying about such a thing, she was assuming the two of them *had* a future together. And that might not be the case at all. Not that Lily didn't think they were compatible, because they most certainly seemed to be, in virtually every area—intellectually, emotionally, spiritually, sexually. But she'd always been of the opinion that for a relationship to succeed, then there had to be things like love and devotion, and fidelity and loyalty, and trust and honesty.

Love and devotion, she figured she could manage with little effort. In fact, she was finding it difficult *not* to fall in love with Leo, and the devotion part just naturally went along with that. Fidelity and loyalty, too, ought not to be a problem, because why would a woman be unfaithful or disloyal to a man like him, seeing as how there were no other men like him on the planet?

Trust and honesty, though . . .

Ah, there was the rub. Because not only was she growing more and more certain that Leo was misrepresenting himself for some reason—she just wished she could figure out why—but she knew that she was misrepresenting herself, too. There was so much he didn't know about her. So much that, should he find out, he may very well never want to speak to her again. There were things in life that she had done, that she continued to do still, that were, at best, unethical. And if Leo found out about those activities, if he knew for sure what she had been doing, what she continued to do to this day, and if he realized she had been keeping the truth from him . . .

Well, then a future with him might very well be impossible. He seemed to be a man who saw everything in terms of black and white. And he seemed to be a man who demanded honesty from an individual, first and foremost. To try to justify to him the actions she'd performed that, although certainly orchestrated for good, decent reasons, were still pretty much unethical, and to try to explain why she had lied about it from the beginning, would be like trying to talk a policeman out of giving her a speeding ticket because she was taking a sick cat to the vet.

No, actually, it would be more difficult than that, she had to concede. Because Leo was like Schuyler in that, although he would certainly see the need to hasten an ailing pet to the doctor, he *wouldn't* be able to understand why Lily wanted—needed . . . *had*—to do the things she did.

When she heard the soft snick of the door latch behind her, the small burst of confidence she'd felt downstairs only moments ago fled. The good news was that in doing so, it took her distressing thoughts with it. The bad news was that, in doing so, it left Lily with only her instincts to guide her. And her instincts, although they always strove to do the right thing, had often led her into trouble.

She spun around to face Leo, crossing her arms over her torso in what she feared he might misinterpret as a defensive act. Then she wondered if such a thing would be a misinterpretation at all. But all he did was stand as he had stood at the front door only moments ago, leaning back against the door with his hands behind him, gazing at her with a look of unmistakable, but uncertain, desire.

"This suddenly feels very contrived," she said, blurting out the first thought that jumped into her head.

He seemed surprised by her statement. "Why? To me, it feels like something that's been a long time in coming. Something that's way overdue."

She scrunched up her shoulders and then let them drop. "I don't know, I just . . ."

"What?"

But she honestly didn't know what to say, so Lily said nothing at all.

He strode forward, slowly covering the few steps that separated them, almost as if he were giving her an opportunity to bolt, should that be what she wanted to do. In spite of her misgivings, though, Lily found that bolting was the very last thing she wanted to do. So she stood firm as he approached her and draped his arms casually on her shoulders, in a way that was anything but suggestive. And somehow, that made her feel better.

"But there is something I need to know before we go any further," he said softly.

What little reassurance she had begun to feel evaporated. "What's that?"

For a moment, he said nothing, only gazed down at her face as if reluctant to put voice to whatever it was he wanted to know. Finally, however, he asked straight out, "You and Kimball—are you involved? Sexually, I mean?"

She expelled a breath she had been unaware of holding and smiled. "No," she said readily. "We're not."

"But you were once upon a time."

She wasn't sure how he knew that, and maybe she didn't want to know, but she replied honestly and without hesitation. "Schuyler was my first, Leo," she said. "When I was nineteen. It didn't take us long, though, to realize that we made much better friends than we did lovers. But I'm glad for that brief intimacy with him, because I think it made our friendship stronger. We've both seen each other at our most vulnerable, yet we've never preyed on each other's vulnerabilities. That short time as lovers cemented our trust in each other as friends. Does that make sense?''

He nodded slowly. ''Yeah. In a way, I guess it does. I'm not sure how comfortable I am with the knowledge of the two of you . . . you know.''

''Hey, you asked,'' she reminded him.

He nodded slowly. ''And you answered.'' His tone of voice suggested he appreciated her doing so.

''Whatever Schuyler and I have, whatever we had back then,'' she said, ''it's not like this thing with you. It was never like this thing with you.''

''And just what, exactly, is this thing with me?''

She swallowed hard, reluctant to answer that question.

So Leo asked another one instead. ''What is it you want, Lily?'' he said softly. ''Forget about what you think is right or wrong. Forget about what you think you should do. Forget about what you think is proper. What you should think about instead is what you *want*.''

She did as he asked, and she wasn't much surprised by what she discovered. ''I want . . . you,'' she said softly.

He smiled, urging his arms lower down her back, circling her waist, pulling her close. ''Then take me,'' he said simply.

Well, if you insist . . .

But she said nothing, mainly because, at that point, no words seemed necessary. They were both adults, they were both unattached, and each was completely turned on by the other. There was no reason for Lily to deny him or herself what seemed to be the logical conclusion.

None.

Well, except maybe for the fact that she hadn't been entirely honest with him about something. A rather big something, too. But really, that and this had nothing in common, did they? What she was about to do with Leo had nothing to do with what she'd done where Schuyler was concerned. The two men were entirely separate, and her experiences—and duties—to each were completely unrelated. She could have this night, this time, this relationship, with Leo, and she could keep it apart from her activities where Schuyler and Kimball Technologies were concerned.

At least, she could for a little while. Until she was certain that things with Leo would work out. For now, she could be with him, and he'd never have to know what went on with Schuyler and the business. For now, she could lead both lives, and they'd never have to converge. For now, she could do this, she told herself. She could.

She could.

And then, when she was sure everything would work out between the two of them, she could tell Leo the truth. He would understand why she hadn't been completely truthful, she told herself. And he would forgive her. Because he would understand that she had done it out of a sense of duty and obligation. Surely a man like him would know all about something like that.

He dipped his head to hers then, and thankfully, every thought that was plaguing her scattered. Lifting her hands to his face, she cupped his jaws, relishing the warmth and roughness she encountered. She inhaled a deep breath and savored the scent of him, a mix of heat and musk and man. And then, as he covered her mouth with his, she tasted him. And he tasted . . . oh . . . So good.

"Leo," she murmured against his lips. The word came out sounding like a benediction, and he lowered his head again to receive his blessing.

Over and over, he brushed his lips against hers, each time exerting a little more pressure, each time claiming a little bit more of Lily for himself. She moved her hands to the back of his head, twining the short strands of his hair between her fingers, loving the way he felt in her hands, the way he responded to her touch. It had been so long since she had enjoyed any kind of intimacy with a man. So long since anyone had made her feel so feminine, so desirable, so cherished.

And then, as Leo opened his mouth wider, urging hers open, too, and tasted her more deeply, Lily realized that no one had ever made her feel like this before.

He released her waist and moved his hands lower, slowly urging them down over her hips and thighs, until he'd bunched two big fistfuls of her skirt in each. Then he moved his hands up again, back to her waist, pulling the fabric with him. Lily felt the cool air of his bedroom on the backs of her legs, and instinctively, to warm herself, she pushed her body into his. He moved one hand down again, fisting another handful of skirt, and brought it higher, too. Scooping the wealth of fabric under one arm, he dropped his hand yet again, this time palming her firm thigh over the cotton knit of her tights.

Damn. She knew she should have worn knee socks instead.

Leo didn't seem to share her concern however, because he expelled a soft sigh of satisfaction when he encountered the fabric. "God, I love a woman in tights," he said.

Somehow, she found the presence of mind to murmur, "Do you?"

"Mmm," he murmured back. "The only thing sexier than tights are those little cotton ankle socks. God, I love those, too."

"Come summer, I'll remember that," she said softly.

Immediately, she regretted the words, because they suggested that come summer, the two of them would still be engaged in this .... *thing* ... they were doing, and she worried that he would consider such an assumption presumptuous. She pulled back a bit, to see if she could gauge his reaction, but the expression on his face was one of complete, and delighted, anticipation.

"Come summer," he said, "I'll hold you to it."

She opened her mouth to say something else, but the hand on her thigh began to creep upward, and anything she might have said dried up in her throat. And when the fingers of that hand crept in between her legs, strumming along her sensitive inner thigh, all she could manage was a very soft "Oh . . ." as she tilted her head to the side.

Leo took advantage of her position to nuzzle the curve where her neck joined her shoulder, rubbing his lips over the tender flesh before dragging a few open-mouthed kisses along the column of her throat. When he did, he also inched his hand further up her thigh, moving his fingers into the heated juncture for a brief caress before continuing on to palm the firm globe of her bottom.

Lily nearly lost her footing at that single, swift touch, but Leo tightened his hold on her, pulling her up more intimately against himself. When he did, she felt the press of his erection along her belly, and she almost fainted again. My, but he was a healthy man, she thought. Not that she'd had a lot of lovers to compare him to, but it didn't take a genius to figure out that he was quite ... progressive ... in his ... thinking.

Impatient to do a little touching of her own, Lily dropped her own hands to his waist and thrust them without ceremony up under his sweater. Beneath her fingertips, she felt heat and ridges and soft springy hair, and she couldn't stop herself from skimming her open hands up and down and around his entire torso. The hungry touches seemed to spur Leo into action—not that he hadn't been acting already—because suddenly, his own caresses grew far more demanding.

The hand cupping her bottom moved upward, to the waistband of her tights, then dipped easily inside to immediately reclaim its place against her bare skin. In doing so, he pushed his fingers into the sensitive cleft, nudging one in particular more intimately against her. Again, Lily felt her legs go weak beneath her, so she pushed her hands higher, to his bare shoulders, in an effort to keep herself standing. When she did, the fabric of his sweater rose, too, exposing for her eyes what her hands had already discovered.

He was, in a word, glorious. All bump and sinew and satin. Helplessly, she nuzzled him, running her lips over one round, flat nipple, before laving it with the flat of her tongue and tugging it into her mouth for a taste. When she did, the hands holding her body clenched tighter, pushing her forward, so she tasted him again. And again. And again.

Gradually, she registered the fact that he'd released her skirt and was moving his other hand upward, but it wasn't until he was palming her breast with much possession that Lily moved her body so that she could more easily accommodate him. When she did, she moved her own hand lower, to the hard ridge beneath his trousers that attested to the depth of his desire. Flattening her hand, she rubbed her palm against him, hard, because she sensed somehow that that was the way he would like it. Again and again she moved her hand over him, feeling him ripen with every stroke. She was about to unfasten his trousers so that she could take him completely in her hand, when he suddenly—and completely—released her.

"What's wrong?" she asked as she stumbled away.

He caught her easily before she could fall, but didn't pull her back up against himself, as she had hoped he would.

"I need for you to be naked," he said succinctly, his eyes blazing, his breathing ragged. "Right now. I need for you to take your clothes off for me, Lily, because there's a lot more I want to do to you before we actually . . ." His voice trailed off, and he licked his lips. "Take your clothes off."

She told herself she should be offended by the command in his tone, but instead she only became more aroused. He wasn't demanding because he wanted to be in control, she realized. He was demanding because he really, really, *really* needed for her to be naked. Right now.

So, without hesitation, she crossed her arms over herself and gripped the hem of her sweater, tugging it up and over her head and releasing it in one swift, fluid move. She tugged first one boot, and then the other, from her feet, disposing of them near her discarded sweater. Then she hooked each thumb simultaneously in the waistband of her skirt and tights and pushed both to the floor.

And all the while, Leo stood there watching every move she made, without comment, without movement, but with quite a bit of interest. Then she stood before him clad in only a wisp of pale peach bra and panties. Meeting his gaze levelly with hers, tossing the long strands of her hair over one shoulder, she reached behind herself to unhook the bra, then let it tumble unheeded to the floor. His eyes widened at the sight of her bare breasts, but still he neither moved, nor spoke. So Lily tugged her panties off, as well, tossing them, like everything else, away without a care.

There was something unbelievably erotic about being completely naked with a fully dressed man, she thought. She would have sworn she would feel vulnerable and defensive and uncomfortable in such a situation, but something about standing so flagrantly in front of Leo made her feel powerful instead. For a moment, he only gazed at her, as if he'd never seen a naked woman before. And although Lily knew a man like him would have seen more than a few women naked, she could almost believe that she was the most important one of the bunch.

He began to stride slowly toward her then, and she suddenly felt less confident. He stopped when only a few scant inches separated them, and without a word, lifted his hand to fully cover her breast. Just like that, he claimed her, and just like that, Lily knew there would never be anyone else. His other hand easily covered her other breast, and he squeezed both gently before moving his hands behind her, through and beneath her hair, then down her back and over her bottom again.

Then he pulled her close, into the cradle of his thighs and said, "Now take my clothes off."

She wasn't sure she could manage such a thing, but she gripped the hem of his sweater and pushed it higher, until the placement of his arms hindered her progress. "I'm going to need a little help," she said, smiling.

He smiled back. "Oh, all right. As long as we can take up where we left off."

She nodded, not sure she trusted her voice.

When he lifted his arms above his head, she jerked the sweater up and over, and then it, too, joined the pile of clothes on the floor. Seeing their garments mingled that way made Lily feel warm inside, and she easily moved her hands to the zipper of his trousers.

"Take your shoes off," she said.

But she didn't release his zipper as he toed off each of his loafers and kicked them aside. That done, however, she pushed the zipper down, down, down, until a flash of bright red silk greeted her. She chuckled at the realization that all this time, beneath all his frumpy tweed and corduroy, there lurked skimpy little red silk briefs.

"Why, Mr. Freiberger," she said, "I didn't know you had it in you."

His salacious grin faltered a bit at her teasing comment, but he regrouped easily. "Yes, well, Miss Rigby, I'd rather have it in—"

She halted him with a chuckle and a kiss, pushing herself up on tiptoe, claiming his mouth in the most intimate way she knew how, tasting him as deeply as she could. He responded in kind, wrestling her for possession, pushing her body against his. To defend herself, she dipped her hand inside his trousers, beneath the waistband of his briefs, and cupped him lovingly in her hand.

He uttered a feral sound in response, then moved one of his hands to join hers, covering the back of her hand entirely with his palm. Slowly, he urged her hand lower, to the base of his stiff shaft, then moved both upward to the head again. Lily felt the first traces of his desire dampen her palm, and their next trip down his length was slick and warm. And this time, instead of encouraging her to move her hand back up, he pushed her fingers lower still, until she filled her hand with the rest of him and curled her fingers lightly closed.

"Oh," he said, pulling his mouth away from hers. "Oh, Lily."

He let her have her way with him for another moment, and she enjoyed another leisurely, thorough, damp exploration of him. Then with a sudden, quick gesture, he moved himself away. With one swift action, he shed his trousers and socks, then hauled her up and into his arms and carried her toward his bed. With one hand, he jerked down the spread and blanket and sheets, then he lay her on her back in the middle and followed her down. Before she could say a word—not that she necessarily wanted to say anything at all—he covered her mouth with his in a heart-stopping kiss. She circled her arms around his neck and to pull him closer, and he nestled his big body alongside hers.

He nestled one of his legs between both of hers as he kissed her, pressing his chest against her breasts. His soft hair tickled her sensitive breasts, and the heat of his entire body seemed to surround her. Instinctively, Lily arched her body against him, an action that pushed her against his leg. She gasped at the contact, then repeated it, again and again, until his leg was damp with her desire.

With one final kiss, he turned her onto her side, facing away from him, and spooned himself against her. She started to object, but he began kissing her along her shoulder and covered her breast with one big hand. Then she felt the hard length of him nestling into the cleft in her fanny, and she couldn't quite form the words to say anything at all. He caught her nipple in the V between his index and middle fingers, rolling the taut little pebble as he squeezed her tender flesh hard. His other hand had flattened against her belly, but now crept lower, down to the dewy curls between her legs.

She caught her breath as he furrowed her, dragging his fingers through her damp, heated folds, penetrating her with one long finger over and over again. Lily moved a leg backward, hooking it over his calf, and a second finger joined the first, plowing deeper and more insistently than before. She reached behind herself, cupping her hand over his head again, and for a moment, could only lie there as burst after burst of heat shot through her. Then, without warning, a white-hot explosion of sensation rocked her.

Before her orgasm could even begin to ebb, Leo turned her so that she lay on her back beneath him, then he knelt between her legs. In the next moment, he was sheathed in a condom and thrusting deep inside her, and the explosion that she had thought was ending doubled in its intensity.

Again and again he pumped inside her, and again and again she crested that wave only to ride it once more. Finally, when she thought she would die from the wanting, the craving, the needing, he lunged one last time against her, propelling himself deep, *deep*, inside her. As one, they cried out when he arched his back and emptied himself inside her. For one long moment, it was as if the two of them were suspended in space, unburdened by gravity or obligation or time. Then, slowly, Leo relaxed against her, withdrawing from her and rolling onto his back beside her.

All Lily could do was lie there motionless, with her eyes closed, wondering what had happened and why she suddenly felt as if she had no body, no mind, no soul. Then she remembered that she had just given all of them to Leo. Instead of alarming her, however, the knowledge of that comforted and gladdened her. Because she knew he had given freely of those things himself, to her, as well.

He turned his head and brushed a chaste kiss along her temple. "I'll be right back," he said before rising and making his way to a bathroom that adjoined his bedroom.

Lily wondered where he found the strength to move. She was overcome by a languid sense of peace and lethargy, and she never wanted to leave this place again. Never before had she made love to a man and felt so utterly full, so completely sated, so wonderfully right afterward. Yes, there were still things that she and Leo needed to work out, she thought vaguely, things she had to tell him and make him understand. But somehow, she was confident that he *would* understand. No two people could make love the way they just had and not be willing to make allowances for things they might not comprehend.

It was going to be okay, she thought. Whatever Leo was hiding from her, and whatever she was hiding from him, they would talk about it, and they would work through it. Whatever it took to make sense of things, whatever it took to forgive and move on, she was confident they would be able to manage it. They would both be honest with each other, and they would both understand. Of course they would.

Of course they would.

Leo propped himself up on one elbow to watch Lily as she slept beside him in his bed—*in his bed*, he marveled yet again—and couldn't help reaching out to touch her. With the index finger of one hand, he lightly traced her bare shoulder, drawing his fingertip along her collarbone, dipping into the elegant hollow at the base of her throat. She murmured something quiet and incoherent in her sleep, but didn't awaken. Reluctantly, he withdrew his hand, so that she would continue to sleep, so that he could continue to gaze upon her.

He would have thought that by now, he would have had enough of touching her, at least enough to get him through the night. They had made love twice, after all, the second time even more urgent than the first. But he simply could not resist reaching for her again, thumbing with feather-like lightness the fringe of dark bangs that brushed her forehead.

She lay on her side facing him, one hand loosely gripping his pillow, the other folded over her bare breasts. The sheet dipped low on her body, riding on the highest curve of her hip, and her skin shone like ivory in the pale light of the moon that filtered through the window beyond the bed. Her hair was a heavy black curtain of silk that spilled across her pillow and onto his, and, as if they couldn't quite help themselves, his fingers wandered into the dark tresses, sifting carelessly through them, threading lightly among them.

She was, without question, the most extraordinary woman he'd ever known. He still wasn't entirely sure why that was, but no woman had ever reached inside him and seized his heart the way Lily Rigby had. Certainly he'd met women as beautiful as she was—well, almost as beautiful—and he'd known women who were as much fun as she was—well, almost as much fun. He'd dated and made love to women who were intelligent, attractive, articulate and enjoyable. Yet none of them had come close to stirring up inside him the things that Lily Rigby had stirred up.

And she wasn't even honest.

He remembered all the things he'd learned from Eddie Dolan prior to her arrival, all the things that had made him want to turn around and run away from whatever it was that had sprung up between him and Lily. But whatever it was between them had grown much too large to be avoided. And really, in spite of everything, Leo had simply wanted her too much, for too long, to ever turn away from her.

So she'd hidden some aspects of her character from him, he thought now. So what? Nobody was ever entirely honest about themselves when they first met another person, were they? It took time to build a relationship—and for some reason, the eruption of the word *relationship* didn't bother Leo nearly as much as it usually did—and time for people to open up to each other. And, hey, it wasn't like he'd been entirely honest about himself.

But he still had work to do before he could come clean with Lily and tell her about who he really was, and explain why he'd misrepresented himself the way he had. As much as he hated to do it, he still needed to access her computer files without her knowledge, to see if they might offer him some insight into where Kimball—or whoever—had hidden the missing money.

Leo reassured himself that his motives in prying into her personal affairs were based on his suspicions about Kimball or someone else, and not about Lily. Because even though he'd started to feel a little edgy when Eddie had told him the things he'd discovered about Lily's past, even though she had motive and opportunity enough to rise to suspect status, Leo knew now that there was no way she could be capable of filtering millions of dollars from her employer.

Yes, she may be hiding some things from Leo, and yes, there might be some questionable reasons for why she had been doing so. But no woman could make love with the total freedom and lack of inhibition that Lily had shown and be a dishonest person. There was no way he would ever believe that a woman as giving as she had been tonight would be able to hide a theft of the magnitude that had struck Schuyler Kimball. She was, quite simply, not that kind of girl. He had good instincts, he reminded himself. And his instincts told him that although Lily was almost certainly hiding something, it wasn't something illegal or dishonest or immoral.

Regardless of the fact that the two of them definitely had things to talk about, things to straighten out, things to settle, Leo was confident that they would do just that. He'd never been in love before, and truth be told, he wasn't positive that love was what he felt for Lily Rigby right now. But by God, whatever he felt for her must be damned close. Because suddenly, he couldn't imagine ever having a life that didn't include her.

Once again, he reached out to touch her, a little more insistently this time. Gently, he moved her arm and covered her breast with one hand, thumbing the taut nipple to life. She moaned with pleasure as her eyes fluttered open, then she smiled like a woman who wasn't quite satisfied yet, and reached a hand toward him.

Yeah, Leo thought as he lowered his head to cover her mouth with his, they had some baggage to unload before they could be entirely free to enjoy each other. But he was certain that, eventually, they'd both work through all the things they needed to work through. Sure, they would.

Sure, they would.

SIXTEEN

Lily's room at Ashling was a lot like Lily herself, Leo noted the following day, when he entered her bedroom with all the stealth and silence of a sneaky little fink. As he closed the door behind him, he tried not to think about the fact that, in his need to perform his damned job, he might be potentially—and irrevocably—damaging any chance he had for happiness with Lily. Because if she caught him in here snooping around without her permission, especially after the night they'd just spent together, she was going to be just a tad surprised, just a tad peeved, just a tad totally unforgiving.

But it was four o'clock, he reminded himself, a time that she always, *always*, set aside for tea. Of course, usually, she enjoyed her tea perched on the edge of Kimball's big desk, flashing Leo with a breathtaking hint of thigh while he enjoyed a cup of coffee. But there had been a couple of occasions over the past two weeks when he'd been so immersed in his work, that she'd politely excused herself to take tea alone in the kitchen.

Today, he had feigned just such immersion. And

now, he was going to take advantage of her absence—and her trust—to delve into—and violate—her private domain.

He tried to forget about the way they had awakened beside each other that morning to enjoy yet another sexual encounter—using their mouths to please each other that time, he recalled with a wave of almost unquenchable need. They had showered together and breakfasted together, then had driven to Kimball's estate together—well, with Leo following on her bumper every mile, which sort of constituted together, since they'd been on their cell phones the whole way—and then they'd snuck in the back way just before dawn together.

They'd been like two teenagers who had stayed out all night when they'd been expressly forbidden to see each other, he thought. He hadn't had that much fun since he was a kid.

And they had giggled like kids as they'd tried to maintain their silence through the garden, had been forced to stop more than once so that they could enjoy another fierce, all too brief, embrace. Leo had nuzzled Lily's neck as she'd fumbled for the key to the back door, and they'd almost tumbled to the floor once they were inside, tempted to make love one more time. Instead, they had brewed a pot of coffee before Mrs. Kaiser, the cook, had even come in to work. Then Lily had gone upstairs to change into her Miss Rigby clothes, and Leo had gone to work.

Work, he muttered to himself now. *Lying and scheming and sneaking around* was more like it. Man, he was a creep.

Pushing the thought away, he crossed silently to the writing desk that was situated exactly where Halston Man had said it would be. Instead of being obscured by Beanie Babies, however, Lily's laptop was switched on and unfolded, as if she'd been using it very recently. It hummed softly in the otherwise silent room, the screen saver dancing almost eerily. It almost seemed as if she were inviting him to investigate, he thought, heartening some, as if she had absolutely nothing to hide.

He'd brought a stack of blank diskettes with him, just in case, and set them beside the state-of-the-art laptop before thumbing the mouse and scattering the screen saver. What appeared on the screen was a list of e-mails she had evidently recently downloaded, and he was surprised by the number and variety of senders. He shrank that screen and noticed that a variety of other programs were running simultaneously, and he moved the mouse to one titled *Receiving*, feeling sick as he did so. This was going to be too easy, he thought as the screen expanded.

And Lily was never going to forgive him for it.

His nausea doubled, however, when he saw what he had opened. He wasn't sure, at first, exactly what it was, but it appeared to be something pretty heavy duty for a social secretary to be concerned about. As he scrolled down, Leo's suspicions were confirmed. What Lily had running on her laptop was a list of Kimball Technologies' many suppliers, and all of the materials that were coming in that day. Okay, so that wasn't as heavy duty as he'd initially thought. It was still something that shouldn't concern a social secretary.

Curious, he pulled up her e-mail again and began to scan it, opening one or two for a flagrant read. The more he read, the sicker he became. Because he realized it wasn't Lily's e-mail he was reading. It was Schuyler Kimball's. Every last item was addressed to SKimball@KTech.com. And although the majority of it concerned business, much of it was explicitly noted as confidential. Several items clearly did not involve a social secretary where their need-to-know status was concerned. Nevertheless, somehow, and for some reason, Lily had accessed her boss's mail. God alone knew what she was planning to do with it.

He shrank the e-mail program again and pulled up the other programs that were running. Along with the one titled *Receiving*, there were others titled *Shipping*, *Production*, *P&L*, and *Personnel*. None of them seemed like the kind of thing that would find their way into the busy day of a social secretary. But all of them seemed like the kind of thing in which someone interested in, oh, say . . . stealing fifty million dollars would most assuredly take an interest.

His pulse pounding in his chest, in his throat, in his ears, Leo tugged open the desk drawer and found it full of diskettes. Full of diskettes that were each clearly labeled with what appeared to be bank account numbers.

Oh, Lily. Oh, no . . .

It was then that Leo forgot all about what had happened the night before. He forgot about his certainty that Lily was an honest woman. He forgot about how much his instincts urged him to trust her. He forgot about the fact that he had fallen in love with her.

And, pulling up a chair to seat himself at her desk, Leo scooped her diskettes out of the drawer, unbanded the blank ones he'd brought with him, and then he went to work.

It was going on six o'clock when Lily, surprised that Leo hadn't sought her out before now, went in search of the bookkeeper to see if he wanted to join the family for dinner. A long shot, to be sure.

After all, why would anyone want to join the Kimballs for dinner if their paycheck didn't require it? And seeing as how Miranda was insisting on bringing both Laurel *and* Hardy to dinner tonight, it could only bode badly for the evening.

Then again, judging by the fury and concentration with which Leo had been working when she'd stopped by earlier to see if he wanted to join her for tea, he would probably need a break by now. Not to mention a good laugh. And heaven knew dinner with the Kimballs always delivered in that respect.

Recalling his decline of coffee that afternoon, Lily tried not to feel stung by his unwillingness to visit with her. He did have work to do, after all, she reminded herself. Even if she still had no idea what that work involved. And just because the two of them had spent the better part of the night locked in each other's arms, in each other's bodies, well, that didn't necessarily mean that their work habits would change the following day, did it?

It didn't matter, she told herself as she approached Schuyler's office, growing warm with the anticipation of merely seeing Leo again. All that mattered was that the two of them had finally acknowledged and accepted the fact that they were meant for each other, and that now they could work toward building a relationship that would ultimately include honesty and trust.

"Leo," she said as she pushed open the office door and strode through to find him—

—gone.

Well, it hardly seemed prudent to extend an invitation to dinner now, did it? Telling herself there must be an explanation for why he had left Ashling without even telling her goodbye, Lily started to close the door, then noticed his suit jacket still hung on the back of Schuyler's chair.

Oh.

So he *hadn't* left Ashling without telling her goodbye. Well, of course he wouldn't, she told herself now. How silly of her. She was just feeling a bit unsure about what had happened the night before, that was all. In spite of her certainty that the two of them did indeed belong together, their budding relationship was still too new, too fragile, for her to be utterly confident of his feelings for her. It made perfect sense that she would worry about his abandoning her, even if such a worry were totally unfounded. Right?

She closed the door behind herself and wondered where he'd gone. He was probably looking for her, she thought. And if that were the case, if they both took to wandering around Ashling trying to find each other, it could be years before they stumbled upon each other again.

Well. He knew the rules and regulations governing dinner at the estate, she reminded herself, so eventually, he would find his way into the vast African landscape known as the dining room. She might as well go upstairs to change her clothes now, so that when the two of them did meet again—presuming Leo could remember where the dining room was, which, admittedly, was a big if— she would look her best. But she still couldn't help wondering where he had gotten himself off to as she climbed the stairs to her bedroom.

Much to her relief—well, her initial, short-lived relief, at least—she found him in her bedroom a moment later. She smiled at seeing him again . . . until she realized she'd found him in a place where he really shouldn't be. Not just because she hadn't invited him to explore her private realm, but because he was hunched over her desk, working on something on her laptop which—just guessing here—probably *wasn't* Free Cell.

Had she stumbled upon him in her room without her permission, she would have liked to think Leo was sneakily fondling her underwear, or perhaps had a fetish about her shoes. Instead, he obviously had a thing about her laptop computer. She just wished she knew exactly what it was.

"Leo?" she asked tentatively.

At her softly uttered query, his entire body jerked in the biggest, most unmistakable flinch she'd ever seen. She knew then that whatever he had been doing, it had claimed his complete and absolute attention, and that he knew full well he wasn't supposed to be doing it. Her heart began to pound rapidly behind her rib cage, her stomach rolled with uneasiness, and her mouth went dry enough that she had trouble asking her next, and perfectly logical, question.

"What are you doing here?"

She had no idea where she found the strength or energy to manage it, but Lily took a few steps into the room, trying to see past Leo in an effort to discover what he was doing. As she approached, she noted the scattered diskettes on her desk, and in a few more steps saw what was on the computer screen. It was a record of one of dozens of bank accounts, accounts that didn't concern Leo or his investigation of tax problems, or anything else having to do with Kimball Technologies at this point.

He hadn't turned around yet, hadn't acknowledged her presence in any way, save that one big body flinch when she'd spoken his name. But as she drew nearer now, he stood and turned to face her, placing himself menacingly between her and the desk, as if he were worried that she might hurry over there and try to sabotage whatever he was doing. Even though she was utterly confused by his presence and his silence and the expression of profound repulsion on his face, even though she felt wary and cautious inside, she tried to smile, tried to let him know that she was willing to give him the benefit of the doubt when it came to explaining himself.

Evidently, however, he wasn't willing to extend the same courtesy to her. Because instead of smiling back—even sheepishly—or offering an explanation for his presence in her room—even a lame one about fondling her underwear—Leo only frowned and shook his head slowly, his expression suggesting he was disgusted by the very sight of her.

"What are you doing here?" she repeated when he didn't answer her, the vast emptiness inside her spanning wider, growing colder, with every moment that passed.

"I'm sorry," he finally replied. But there wasn't an ounce of apology in his voice. "I meant to be out of here before you found me. Time just got away from me, I guess. That's what happens when I get really, really, *really* interested in my work."

"But what are you doing here?" she asked a third time, feeling her patience and her willingness to be fair gradually slipping away.

But again, he didn't answer her question directly. All he offered in response was, "Then again, I don't see any reason why *I* should be the one apologizing here. That should be your job. Not that I think an apology will ever come close to making up for what you've done. There are other, considerably more effective, ways to deal with something like this."

"What do you mean?" Lily asked, even more confused now. "Of course you should apologize. You came up here without my permission, without telling me, and you're prying into my computer files. In spite of all the free and easy information readily available on the Internet these days, this still qualifies as a violation of privacy. Where I come from, *Mr. Freiberger*," she added pointedly, "that qualifies as an offensive action, one that requires an apology."

"And theft, Miss Rigby?" he replied easily, his expression completely impassive now. "You don't find that offensive?"

Her stomach pitched a bit at his question, but she still didn't understand. "What are you talking about?"

Apparently tired of dancing around his reason for being there, he hooked his hands loosely, yet somehow threateningly, on his hips and told her, "I don't see why *I* should apologize when *I'm* not the one who's filtered off millions of bucks from my employer's profits this year. *I'm* not the one who's made it a habit to filter off millions of bucks from my employer's profits *every* year."

Oh, so he'd found out about that, had he? Lily thought. Well, that rather complicated things, didn't it? But before she could say a word about his discovery, he started talking again.

"Now, mind you," he went on, "I haven't had time to dig as deeply or go back as far as I'd like to in all these nice records you so helpfully made to keep track of your activities, but just how the hell long has this been going on?"

Lily didn't know what to say, wasn't sure what he wanted from her in response, had no idea what would be prudent when it came to explaining her actions. So she simply answered his question truthfully. "It's been going on since I started working for Schuyler," she said.

He dropped his mouth open in obvious surprise, as if he hadn't expected her to admit it. But what was the point in denying it? Lily thought. If he'd been delving into the files and diskettes here in her room—where she had never once tried to hide or mask her activities—then he knew everything there was to know. There was no reason to contradict any of it.

"It's been going on that long?" he echoed.

She nodded. "Yes."

"You've been filtering tens of millions of dollars annually from Kimball Technologies for a full decade?"

"Well, no, not that much," she told him. "When Schuyler first started the business, I could only manage a few thousand dollars annually. It wasn't until a few years later, when the business really started to take off, that I was able to turn it into millions annually. And then even more years before I could bump it up into eight figures."

For a moment, he only gazed at her in silence. Then, his voice reeking with amazement, he said, "My God, you actually sound like you're proud of yourself."

She lifted one shoulder and let it drop. "Well, I suppose there's a certain amount of pride involved," she admitted. "I mean, it hasn't been easy taking a bit here and a bit there, where no one would miss it. But I managed."

"You managed," he repeated tonelessly. Then, angrily, he added, "You managed to the tune of fifty million bucks this year."

She shrugged again. "Well, the last few years, Kimball Technologies has turned such an enormous profit, I couldn't resist. I knew nobody would miss the money. Not really. Where was the harm?''

"Nobody would miss it," Leo repeated, obviously extremely annoyed. "You thought nobody would miss the theft of fifty million dollars."

It hit Lily, then, finally, what Leo was implying, what he thought he'd stumbled onto in her records. A huge fist seized her insides and squeezed hard, and a hot wave of disbelief nearly overpowered her. "You think I *stole* all that money?" she asked, shocked to her very core that he would be capable of believing such a thing about her.

This time he was the one to shrug, but there wasn't an ounce of unconcern in his action. He gestured toward a pile of diskettes on the desk that Lily realized didn't belong to her. "I have every bit of evidence I need right there," he announced with absolute conviction. "All I have to do is take that to Kimball's board of directors tomorrow, and they'll have all the ammunition they need to fuel an investigation that will ultimately put you behind bars. I hope you look good in prison orange, sweetheart. 'Cause you're gonna be wearing it for a loooong time."

Lily shook her head incredulously, but all she could manage by way of a response was to repeat, more forcefully this time, "You think I *stole* all that money? From Schuyler?"

"No, I *know* you stole it," Leo stated without a bit of doubt. "And I have all the evidence I need to prove it right here."

She expelled a soft sound of distress. "Leo, you have no idea what you hold evidence of there. Just how far did you get while you were violating my personal files? Not far enough, apparently. If you'd just—"

"Lily, I have an extremely good idea of what I have evidence of," he interrupted. "Ferreting out this kind of criminal activity is what I do for a living. And hell, you didn't even bother to try and hide your tracks, that's how cocky you've been during this whole thing. You might as well have bookmarked it all into your favorite places on the Internet."

She expelled another soft sound of irritation, and tried again to explain something to someone who had clearly already made up his mind to convict her. "It was easy to find, because I wasn't trying to hide my activities," she told him. "There was never any reason to."

"Because you were so confident that you'd never be caught," he said. "Man, your ego must be right up there with your IQ."

She shook her head again, trying to ignore the sting of pain that knifed through her at his jab. "No, I never tried to hide what I was doing because—"

"Because," he interrupted her again, "you know your boss is in love with you, and that he would never suspect you, should the theft, by some wild miracle, be discovered by some troubleshooter who was really good at his job."

"No. You've got it all wrong. Schuyler isn't in love with me. He's never been in love with me, any more than I've ever been in love with him. Leo, listen to me. It was because—"

"Because, dammit, you knew I trusted you. And that I ... I cared about you, and you knew you could use that to your advantage."

Lily snapped her mouth shut, wondering why she'd even bothered to try and explain. Leo had made up his mind about her, and obviously thought she was more than capable of stealing money from her boss, her friend. He was also clearly of the opinion that she was the kind of woman who would exploit a man's affections for her without caring at all how he felt.

And here she'd been thinking he might be falling in love with her the way she had fallen in love with him.

Honestly. She should have known something like this would happen. She should have realized from the start that, eventually, it would all blow up in her face. How had she not seen this coming? And she thought she was so smart.

"You honestly think I've been embezzling money from Schuyler all these years and keeping it for myself," she said again, surprised that she managed to keep the bitter edge out of her voice.

"Yes, that's what I think. It's what I know," Leo concurred readily.

Too readily, Lily thought. He was going to accept the fact, utterly and resoundingly, that what he had uncovered in her computer was a network of embezzled funds that spanned nearly a decade. Embezzled funds that she'd kept for herself, because she was a greedy little pig who wanted more. He was going to accept without question that she was a thief and a cheat and a liar. That she wasn't to be trusted. That she cared only about herself.

In spite of the fact that he'd already drawn his conclusions, she said softly, "Think about this for a minute, Leo. Think about what you've found. You're obviously still in the middle of things there, and believe it or not, I *am* sorry I interrupted you before you were able to finish."

"Yeah, I bet you are."

"Think about it," she instructed him again. "If I'd embezzled fifty million dollars for myself this year alone, do you honestly think I'd still be here working for Schuyler? Wouldn't it make more sense for me to be down in South America doing my 'Girl from Ipanema' impression? There are infinitely more appealing places to live than Ashling, in spite of its beauty and luxury. And there are infinitely more appealing people that I'd like to surround myself with. Read my lips, Leo. If I were a greedy, superficial bitch who had fifty million dollars to call my own, regardless of how I'd come by it, I wouldn't be here."

Leo did read her lips. He couldn't help himself. He kept thinking about the erotic words those lips had whispered the night before, recalled the way those lips had felt skimming over every body part he possessed, over and over again. In spite of everything he'd learned about her that afternoon, he still wanted Lily Rigby. He still cared about Lily Rigby. God help him, he still loved Lily Rigby. He just wished like hell she were a different Lily Rigby. One who hadn't, oh, say . . . stolen fifty million bucks from her employer this year alone and lied her head off about God only knew what else.

"No, I haven't completed the investigation I'd like to complete," he agreed. "But I have more than enough here now to take to Kimball's board of directors and get things rolling. I've got nearly three years' worth of records that show where and how you've stolen the money—and you're damned good when it comes to stealing, Lily, I'll give you that—along with records of the banks where you put the money, once you had it in your greedy little hands.

"Of course," he continued, feeling his gut tighten when she made no effort to deny anything he said, "the money didn't stay in those accounts for long, and I haven't figured out yet what you did with it once it left. But a district attorney shouldn't have any problem at all getting the proper subpoenas to search the bank records for more concrete, more specific evidence.

"And now that *I* know what *I'm* doing," he continued relentlessly, "*I'll* be able to figure out everything I need to know, everything I've been hired to find out. I backed up quite a few of your files on my diskettes, and when I get home tonight, I'll get to the bottom of the rest of this. I promise you that."

"Someone hired you?" she asked, her voice lacking all life, all hope. Wearily, she added, "Will you at least tell me who?"

"Kimball's board of directors," he told her. There was no reason to keep that knowledge from her.

She nodded, as if the news didn't much surprise her. "I always told Schuyler they were smarter than he thought they were. That he shouldn't underestimate them. That a little knowledge was a dangerous thing where those guys are concerned."

Her words puzzled Leo, but they weren't important. What was important was that he'd finally figured out what the hell was going on. What was important was that he'd been so sideswiped by a beautiful face and a pair of great legs, that he hadn't performed his job as well as he could have— should have—performed it. What was important was that he'd been bested by Lily Rigby. A liar. A thief. A woman he'd grown to love.

"You're going down, Lily," he told her, gesturing toward the diskettes again. "It's over. Face it."

She went stark white at his assurance, and he could see that she knew he was serious. And he *was* serious, too, dammit. He really would encourage the board of directors to have her arrested and charged with embezzlement and fraud and breaking a man's heart. She was a thief, he reminded himself. She deserved whatever charges were brought against her, whatever the highest court in the land handed down.

He had to admit that he admired her coolness, though. Except for that one moment of fear that passed over her face, she showed no sign that she was worried. But then, she was a liar and a fraud, he reminded himself. Pretending and being a fake was what she did best.

In a very soft voice, she said, "Leo, I'm going to ask you to do me a favor."

He expelled a rough, heartless chuckle at that. "A favor," he repeated, unable to quite mask his amusement. "And what kind of favor would that be?" he wondered further aloud. "Although, I think I can probably imagine one or two things you might offer to do for me. Too bad for you, I've already had 'em done. By you, as a matter of fact. So don't be thinking you can bargain your way out of this by offering me sexual favors."

Her responding smile was gritty and held not a trace of good humor. He didn't like this side of her, this hard-edged, sarcastic, bitter one. Then again, he supposed he was the one responsible for bringing it out of her. No, that wasn't true, he quickly told himself. If she was feeling bitter and sarcastic, it was only because of the bad choices she'd made in life.

"You weren't listening," she said. "I'm going to ask *you* for a favor, not offer one up for your dubious enjoyment."

"Well, thanks for providing me with the opportunity," he said dryly, "but I don't do thieves and cheaters and liars."

She ignored his remark and instead said, "I'd like for you to give me a couple of days before you take what you've found to the board of directors."

This time Leo laughed outright. "Yeah, I bet you

would. God knows you can't pack all this stuff up and clear out your accounts in a few hours, can you? It'd be hell trying to line up a moving van for that much money by tonight, wouldn't it?"

"Actually," she told him, her voice surprisingly level in spite of the fact that he was doing his best to infuriate her, "very little of what's in this room— or in those bank accounts, for that matter—actually belongs to me, so packing and fleeing to a foreign country wouldn't be too much trouble for me. Especially if I cold-cocked you on the side of the head with a blunt object, which, quite frankly, holds a surprising amount of appeal right now."

He only grunted in response to that.

"But if you could hold off for a couple of days, you might learn something else of significance to add to your report," she said. "In fact, if you want to sit right down at the computer and keep going, I'll just turn right around and leave, and pretend I never caught you doing something so sneaky and underhanded in the first place. Because should you stay and investigate further, you might just be surprised by what you find."

He almost took her up on her offer. He was itching to see what else she had in her files, especially the ones he hadn't had a chance to back up on disk, and was certain that, given only a few more hours, he'd have a wealth of information to incriminate her more fully.

Then he remembered there was a two-way lock on her bedroom door—which, now that he thought about it, he probably should have used to keep her out—and that in leaving, she would no doubt lock the door behind herself, something that would give her a nice head start on leaving the country. Then again, he reminded himself, there was nothing that would keep her from leaving the country once he drove away from Ashling . . .

He still didn't relish being locked in her room, should she decide to do something like that. Although Leo could probably go out the window—it was only three stories, after all.

"Gee, thanks for thinking of me," he told Lily. He reached behind himself to scoop his stack of previously blank diskettes from the desk, palming them possessively. "But I think I'll just go with what I have here. As I said, it's more than enough to bring you to your knees."

God, he wished he hadn't said that. Because suddenly, he wanted very badly to bring Lily to her knees for an entirely different reason. Come to think of it, she'd been on her knees that morning when she'd—

Don't think about it, don't think about it, don't think about it, he admonished himself.

"Now if you'll just step aside, Miss Rigby," he added pointedly.

"Leo, please," she said softly, beseechingly. "Just give me a chance to explain."

He wanted so badly to give in, to sit right down and pull her into his lap and have her weave an intricate tale that would reassure him of her goodness and decency and love for him. But he knew better than to do that. What he'd seen in her files, what he'd discovered among all the numbers and activities and accounts was, quite simply, irrefutable evidence.

Lily Rigby had stolen money—a lot of money— from her employer. She'd put it into private accounts, then moved it out again, doubtless to buy herself some nice possessions she'd need in the not-too-distant future. She was a thief, Leo reminded himself. She was going to jail. And even though

Leo had made a lot of allowances for women over the years, incarceration was a bit more than he was willing to overlook.

"Step aside, Lily," he said again, more forcefully this time. "I have a lot of work to do at home tonight. You'll forgive me if I don't invite you over."

She said nothing after that, only moved aside to let him pass. Leo strode forward on legs that felt as if they would crumble beneath him any moment, amazed that he was able to carry himself at all. Moving mechanically and hastily, he returned to Kimball's office to retrieve his jacket and briefcase, then found his way to Ashling's front door. And as he stepped outside, into the dark and windy autumn night, it hit him that he'd never be coming back here as Leonard Freiberger again.

And he'd never be coming as Leo Friday, either.

Unfolding the collar of his jacket up around his neck to ward off the chill—though somehow, it wasn't the chill of the wind that bothered him most—he walked to his car, got in, and drove away.

Lily stood in her bedroom for a long time wondering what she could have done differently that might have kept Leo from leaving the way he had, might have kept him from thinking the worst of her, might have kept him from becoming such a stranger overnight.

Well, she supposed not funneling off all that money from the Kimball Technologies profits might have been a good start.

But if she hadn't funneled off all that money, then the entire last decade of her life would have been pointless. If she hadn't funneled off all that money, then her work for Schuyler would have been for naught. And if she hadn't funneled off all that money, then there would have been life-threatening repercussions that Mr. Leonard Freiberger—or whoever that man was that had just left—couldn't possibly have imagined.

She sighed, suddenly feeling more tired than she had ever felt in her life. *Whoever that man was*, she echoed to herself. More than all the other problems she had facing her right now, figuring out that one was the most pressing. Because whoever that man was, he was under the impression that she wasn't who she'd claimed to be from the start.

Of course, if she were honest with herself, Lily supposed she really *hadn't* been who she had claimed to be from the start. And now that she thought more about it, hiding her identity the way she had all these years probably hadn't been as good an idea as she and Schuyler had thought it was in the beginning. Naturally, their reasons back then had made sense. But now . . .

Now everything was a complete mess, she thought. And it was only going to get messier—a lot messier—before they cleaned it all up. *If* they cleaned it all up, she thought. Which, she had to admit, was a mighty big *if*.

She didn't bother to change for dinner before making her way back downstairs to the dining room. Frankly, eating was the last thing she had on her mind right now. That unmitigated feeling of fear pretty much filled her belly full. She and Schuyler had a long night ahead of them if they were going to salvage the tragicomedy that Leo had just put into play.

Unfortunately, when Lily arrived in the dining room, it was to find that, although the usual suspects had gathered for cocktails, Schuyler wasn't among them.

"Where's Schuyler?" she asked the room at large.

Everyone turned to stare at each other in curious silence, as if they'd just now realized Schuyler wasn't in attendance tonight. Finally, when it appeared Lily wouldn't receive an answer at all, Chloe spoke up.

"He's up," the teenager said.

"He went out?" Lily demanded. "Where?"

She shrugged. "Dunno. But he was *all* fine duded up. Big-time penguin suit. Mega roses."

Tuxedo and bouquet? Lily translated to herself, awed by the news. That made no sense. Schuyler didn't have any engagements this evening. None that he'd told her about anyway. And he told her about *all* of his engagements. In spite of her additional duties and activities, Lily was still an exceptional social secretary. And if Schuyler had had an appointment with a woman this evening—even a woman of the night—Lily would have known about it. How odd. Where could he have gone?

And wasn't it just like him to take off now, right when she needed him most?

"Schuyler," she said under her breath as she spun around to leave, "you'd better have an *awfully* good explanation for this when you get home."

SEVENTEEN

As he lifted his hand to knock on the front door of #3B in a South Philly brownstone, it occurred to Schuyler that, in all his years, he had never dropped in on a woman unannounced. Nor had he ever *wanted* to drop in on a woman unannounced. Nor had he ever brought flowers with him when he did drop in on a woman—announced. Nor had he ever actually wanted to hand pick and pay for the flowers he brought to that woman he'd never brought flowers to before.

Or something like that.

Hmmm . . . Call him overly analytical, but all of this seemed highly significant somehow.

He hesitated before allowing his hand to make contact with the door, surveying his surroundings again. The building was old, but sturdy, the paint in the dark hallway peeling, but clean. The mingling scents of Lysol, cigarette smoke, and cooked cabbage warred for possession of the air, but there was something surprisingly appealing about the smell. It reminded him of his childhood, something he would have just as soon not been reminded of.

In spite of that, however, as he stood at Caroline

278

Beecham's front door, a bubble burst inside him that was warm and soft and strangely reminiscent of affection. Though admittedly, it had been so long since he'd felt something like that, he wasn't entirely sure he was correct in his identification of the feeling.

The neighborhood Caroline called home seemed safe enough—though it was clearly, Schuyler fought off a shudder, *working class*—but he had instructed Claudio to remain parked at the curb and to stay with the car at all times. Certainly Schuyler wasn't anticipating any kind of trouble—not with anyone other than the resident of this particular apartment, at any rate—but he wanted to make sure he had an easy escape route, should something like escape become necessary this evening.

And where Caroline Beecham was concerned, escape was never far from the front of his brain. So far in their acquaintance—he hesitated to call it anything more—she had tried to strangle him, had called him stupid, had accused him of being unfeeling, and had seen him, dammit, at his most vulnerable. Which, granted, was none too vulnerable, he assured himself, thanks to that cool, steely armor he had erected around himself over the years, by God. Still, running away was looking more and more like a viable option where she was concerned. He wondered why he hadn't taken advantage of it already.

It was because of something in her eyes, he decided. Something in her voice when she spoke about the Van Meter Academy in general, and Chloe in particular. Something about the way she looked at Schuyler, too, that made him . . . curious . . . to know more.

He and Caroline—yes, he did rather like the feel of her first name rolling about in his head—had ended up spending the entire evening together last night, and not all of it had been used up discussing Chloe's health, education, and general well-being, either. For instance, Schuyler had discovered that, when she was a senior in high school, Caroline had been both the captain of her debating team and voted Most Likely to Appear with Staples in *Playboy*. For some reason he had yet to understand, she'd been much more proud of that first accomplishment than the second. In spite of all that, it was a combination no man would be able to resist.

It was really too bad about that high IQ business, though, he thought further. Too much intelligence was never good for a human being, male or female. In order for a body to hold that much sagacity, it became necessary to cut back on space for other things. Like a person's soul, for instance. Like a person's affections. God knows Schuyler had learned that for himself firsthand.

Caroline, however, seemed not to have been robbed as badly as others of his acquaintance, though, in that respect. And Schuyler was determined to find out why. She still seemed capable of caring about others—to a fault, really, because no one should be that concerned about the well-being of people who'd made bad choices from the get-go. Yet Caroline Beecham, for all her smarts, was working not to make her immediate surroundings more beautiful and luxurious and convenient, as Schuyler had always struggled to do. No, instead, she toiled long hours in an ugly, dark building, for little salary and less satisfaction.

It made no sense. Not when she had the kind of brain and passion that would have taken her anywhere. Caroline could be worth millions today, had she just chosen her career path better, could have gone to work for and with people who would have known how to exploit her resources. Had she chosen a route that included science and mathematics and technology, Caroline could be heading up a business that would be giving Kimball Technologies a run for its money right now.

But no. She had opted to study *education* of all things. Child development. Sociology. And all Schuyler could do was wonder, *Why*?

Only one way to receive an answer for that, he thought, rapping quickly on her front door. Just go ahead and ask. He'd meant to last night, at several points in their conversation. But as they'd sat in a deli near the school while Claudio parked the car two blocks away, as they'd shared a dinner of cheesesteaks and French fries and draft beer, Schuyler had found himself unwilling to put voice to such a thing.

Caroline was an enigma, and he'd encountered far too few of those in his life. Still, surely there was an explanation for why she was the way she was, an explanation that, once uttered, would completely remove the magic and mystery that clung to her. But last night, he'd wanted to enjoy that magic and mystery. Even if it only lasted one night.

He heard the slink of a chain on the other side of the door just before the deadbolt groaned in its chamber. Then the door flew open and Caroline stood on the other side, looking—

Wow.

Looking like a woman for a change.

Her hair, which had always been swept back from her face and fixed behind her head in a knot of something intolerable, cascaded down around her shoulders like a river of henna-stained silk. And instead of some colorless, shapeless dress, she was wearing what Lily had always referred to as "leggings"—and what Schuyler had always referred to as "those incredibly erotic things women wear in place of pants"—and a longish shirt—whose top two buttons weren't fastened, he noted with due interest—in a color reminiscent of a ripe strawberry. The fabric of each was a fleecy, sweatshirt material, something that suggested she was planning to stay in instead of go out, and he heartened quite a bit at the realization.

"Schuyler," she said, her soft voice tinted with more than a little surprise. "I mean . . . Mr. Kimball. What are you doing here?"

"Don't 'Mr. Kimball' me, you uncooperative wench," he said as he pushed through the door without awaiting an invitation. Had he waited for that, after all, he never would have made it inside. He halted just inside the door and turned toward her. "Call me Schuyler, like you did last night," he added. Then, impulsively, he dipped his head to hers and brushed a brief, chaste kiss on her cheek.

Immediately, she lifted a hand to touch her fingertips to the spot he had kissed, and her cheeks grew pink with the stain of a blush.

"Wh-why did you do that?" she asked as she closed the door slowly, reluctantly, behind him. "Why are you here?"

He shrugged. "Because I like you. Dammit. Where shall I put these?" He held up the roses—all four dozen of them—for her inspection.

She laughed a little anxiously. "I have no idea. I don't have anything big enough to hold all those." But she extended a hand gingerly toward the flowers, fingering one of the delicate red blooms as if it were spun glass. "I can't believe you did this. I can't believe you're here."

Yes, well, that made two of them.

She chuckled a little anxiously again before adding, "And you're dressed in . . . Why are you wearing a tuxedo?"

That, he thought, was a very good question. He only wished he had a good answer to go with. "Because I'm trying to impress you," he said. "There. I've admitted it. Dammit."

She laughed again, and he decided that he liked the sound very much. Hearing Caroline's laughter once or twice a day, he thought further, would go a long way toward making life tolerable.

"I'm . . . I'm at a loss," she confessed. "I . . . I don't know what to say."

Schuyler sighed. "Well, not to put words into your mouth, but how about something like, 'Thank you, Schuyler. Won't you stay for dinner?' "

She smiled again. "Thank you, Schuyler. Won't you stay for dinner?"

"I thought you'd never ask."

He extended the roses again, and, almost helplessly, she took them from him. She lifted the massive bouquet to her nose and inhaled their sweet fragrance, closing her eyes as she held the breath inside her. Something tightened inside him at seeing her enjoyment of such a simple act, and he marveled again that she had knocked him so thoroughly off-center. Funny, her coming out of nowhere like that, just when he least expected.

"I'm serious," she said as she cradled the bouquet in her arm as one might hold a sleeping infant. "I don't think I have anything large enough to hold these. I'll have to check. Come in, please," she added belatedly, gesturing over her shoulder. "But I don't want to hear a word about the clutter. You did show up out of nowhere, without warning, after all."

Yes, well, that made two of them, didn't it? Schuyler thought. It was only fair.

The clutter, he found, was actually quite nice. All the color that was absent from Caroline's office at school was present here in her home. One entire wall was covered with books, many of them novels, he noted. Another wall was virtually floor-to-ceiling windows that looked out on the back of a building beyond. The window seats sported dozens of multi-colored pillows and throws and . . . stuff, and there was a cat sleeping on each of the three, none of whom seemed at all interested in Schuyler's presence.

Which was fine with him, because he would just as soon pretend they didn't exist, either.

The sofa and chairs were an eclectic mix of style and color, each hosting more pillows, more throws, more . . . stuff. But thankfully, no more cats. On the walls were framed posters advertising a mix of genres on exhibit at the Philadelphia Museum of Art. The place was small, but cozy, the kind of apartment that invited Bohemian guests and arty conversation.

His gaze trailed after Caroline, who lifted the roses to her face again as she strode toward what he assumed must be the kitchen, skimming the soft blossoms against her cheek as she went. Schuyler could scarcely reconcile this woman with the one he'd gone to see at the Van Meter Academy the evening before. Certainly their conversation afterward had offered each of them an insight into the other that neither had had before, but this . . .

When Caroline was safely ensconced on her own turf, in her own domain, in her own home, she was obviously a different woman than the one she unleashed on the world. Because surely it couldn't have been anything he'd said the night before that made her so accessible now.

Could it?

A resounding clatter of metal striking metal snapped his attention around, and he realized she had disappeared from his view. So, rounding the counter that separated the kitchen area from the living area, he saw her stooped down, struggling to extract something from one of her lower cabinets. She squatted in front of the open door with both of her stocking feet planted firmly on the linoleum, her arms looking as if they were about to be consumed by whatever lived inside the cupboard. She tugged once, twice, three times, then lost her footing and fell onto her fanny. Schuyler smiled at the picture she made, so clearly unbothered at having someone view her in such a position.

She pushed herself back to a squatting position, dusting her hands on the part of her shirt that covered her bottom. "I think I have a big roaster," she said as she completed the action.

Schuyler refrained from commenting on that. Oh, no he didn't—he couldn't. "I don't think it's inordinately large," he assured her, tilting his head to one side to get a better view of her posterior.

But she seemed not to get the joke. She just nodded and said, "Yes, it is—it's *huge*. I think it would be perfect."

"I think it's already perfect," he told her.

But again, she didn't notice that they were discussing two entirely different things. Instead, she reached into the cabinet again and jerked hard, yanking a big, metal . . . thing . . . out of its jaws. Unfortunately, to win the war of the roaster, she had to concede the battle of the posture, and once again, fell backward onto her . . . roaster. And as she threw her head back without concern and blew an unruly curl off her forehead, Schuyler couldn't help but chuckle.

"Here," he said, moving forward, extending his hand. "Let me help you."

Without hesitation, she reached up and tucked her hand into his, letting him pull her up to a standing position. She tried to set the roaster on the counter as she stood, but he had tugged a bit too hard—though he really, honestly, truly hadn't meant to—and even when Caroline was standing, she just kept moving forward, until she had careened against him, coming to rest with her torso nuzzled against his.

Immediately, the big metal roaster fell to the floor with an almost deafening clatter. But all Schuyler heard was the sound of bells, rattling an alarm at the back of his brain.

As always, he ignored that alarm, and dipped his head to Caroline's to kiss her.

He had never realized what softness tasted like, what gentleness smelled like, what tenderness sounded like. Not until Caroline Beecham melted into him, curving her palms over his shoulders, curling her arms around his neck, threading her fingers through his hair. When she did, Schuyler intensified the kiss, cupping a hand under her chin and over her jaw, to tilt her head to the side and hold it in place while he plundered her mouth at will.

She sighed, a soft murmur of surrender, and he nearly lost himself completely to the sound. Without warning, he was overcome by a need to completely possess her, as if in doing so, he might transfer some of her warmth, her happiness, her ability to care, into himself. So what else could he do but end the kiss as quickly as he had started it, and take a step away?

"Well, that was certainly . . ." He took a deep breath and released it slowly. "Life altering."

Caroline blinked her eyes quickly, as if she were a mechanical doll, and wondered what on earth had happened to make the Earth tilt on its axis the way it clearly had. Then her gaze focused again, taking in the sight of Schuyler Kimball in a tuxedo, and she was surprised the Earth hadn't gone spinning completely out of its orbit and crashing into the sun. Because what else could explain the explosion of heat that rocked her as a result of one kiss?

She swallowed hard and had no idea what to say. "Ah . . . you like tomato soup?" she asked, uttering the first thought to brave entry into her brain.

"Tomato soup?" he asked. But he seemed to be not at all affected by what had just transpired between the two of them. "Well, I like the kind they serve at The Chart House. It's got leeks in it, and this funny little green herb that looks like fur. Do you make yours that way?"

She shook her head. "No, I open a can. I was about to have that and a grilled cheese sandwich for supper. How will that be?"

He kissed his fingertips before spreading them wide. "*Vive les tomates et la fromage.*"

She smiled. "Nothin' like home cookin'."

"Yes, that's what I meant," he said.

She still couldn't believe he was standing here in her apartment looking so . . . so . . . Wow. By the time their evening had concluded last night, she'd changed her mind significantly about Schuyler Kimball. But that didn't mean she felt as if she were up to the task of taking him on. Not even on her own turf this way. Nevertheless, he was here now, and she told herself she might as well make the best of it. Of him. Of herself.

Last night, she had realized that the man he presented to the rest of the world, the one he had been on the other occasions when she'd met him, wasn't the real Schuyler Kimball at all. On the outside, he was a wealthy, sophisticated, vaguely eccentric billionaire who cared about little other than his own satisfaction. Outwardly, he didn't seem as if he had a care, a heart, a soul.

But deep, *deep* inside, he did indeed have a heart. And a soul. And a care. He was simply too frightened to acknowledge any of them.

In many ways, he was like Chloe. In fact, he was like a lot of the children who came to Van Meter. None of them understood the source or comprehended the nature of the gift they'd been given. None of them could figure out the whys or whats or wheres or hows of it. And few of them knew quite what to do with the gift they had so arbitrarily received. That was part of the program at Van Meter, to teach the children how to handle and nurture and grow their gifts. And how to stay human in a world that tried to exploit them, a world that was becoming less human with every passing year.

Schuyler had never had the opportunity to learn how to do those things. No one had ever taken the time to teach him. And something inside Caroline responded to that lost quality about him. Certainly he was no child. And certainly she was drawn to him in a way that went far beyond her role as an educator. But she could no more resist trying to reach inside him to teach him about himself than she could resist performing the same gesture for one of her students.

And last night, at some point in the evening, as they'd shared a small table in the corner of a deli, bathed in the flickering red and green light of the neon Killian's sign, she'd made him laugh, a genuine, heartfelt laugh, and had broken through the first layer.

But there hadn't been time for more. By then, it was after midnight, and Caroline had needed to get home. So Schuyler had instructed his driver to drop her back at the school to retrieve her car, and then the two men had followed her home to make sure she arrived safely. Schuyler had walked her to her front door, even though she'd assured him such chivalry was unnecessary.

Chivalry, he'd assured her right back, had had nothing to do with it. Then they'd stood there awkwardly for some moments without speaking. And then he'd lifted a hand to a strand of her hair that had come loose from its knot, had wound it lightly around his finger, and had told her, very, very softly, goodnight.

He hadn't looked back as he'd made his way down the hallway to the stairs, and she had been certain she had seen the last of him. Even though she'd wanted with all her heart to spend a few more minutes with him—just long enough to see if she could notch another chink or two in his facade—she had thought for sure he wouldn't allow it.

But now here he was, of his own free will, and there was no way she would let him off that easily again.

"Had I known you were coming," she said, trying to pick up the thread of their conversation, "I would have been better prepared." She had thought she was talking about dinner, but somehow, the words came out suggesting something else entirely.

He seemed to understand that fully, because his gaze never strayed from her face as he responded, "Yes, well, that makes two of us."

She bent to pick up the roaster from the floor and settled it once again on the counter. Although it was black and unremarkable, it was all she had that would hold such an enormous bouquet. She could trim the stems and treat the roaster like a massive rose bowl, and when she was finished, it would make for a lovely centerpiece. She hoped. She withdrew a pair of shears from one drawer and began to snip the stems, one by one, nearly overcome by the sweet aroma of the blossoms, nearly overcome by the man who had brought them.

And she wished she knew what to say.

"They really are quite lovely," she began.

"Yes, they are," he concurred.

"And I appreciate your bringing them," she added lamely. "No one has brought me flowers for a long time."

"Haven't they?"

She shook her head and focused on the task she was performing, because she was much too frightened to meet his gaze. "No."

"Has there been no one since your husband?"

Her fingers faltered in their task, and she nearly snipped off her fingertip. "Ah, no," she said, still trying not to look at him. "No, there hasn't been. There was no one before him, either," she added quickly. For some reason, she needed for Schuyler to know that. She didn't know why it should make such a difference—or even if it *would* make a difference where he was concerned—but it was important that he understand how seriously she took something like physical intimacy.

But all he offered in response was, "I see."

She did finally glance up at that. "Do you?" she asked, meeting his gaze levelly. "Do you really?"

He nodded. "Yes, I do. And I think . . ."

"What?"

He shook his head. "Nothing. It's just not surprising, that's all."

"Does it make a difference?" she asked.

He seemed puzzled. "A difference in what?"

"In your reasons for being here."

He seemed to give that some thought, then told her, "No. It doesn't. My reasons for coming here are quite simple, actually."

"And just what would those reasons be?"

Neither his gaze nor his voice faltered the slightest bit as he told her, "I came to see you, Caroline. Because I missed you."

Her heart hummed at the way he offered up the admission so plainly, so succinctly. "You just saw me last night."

"Yes, and it was a long, long time ago."

This time her heart skipped a beat or two at his assertion, and she wondered just how seriously she should take what he said. He was a charming, handsome, wealthy man, she reminded herself. He was in no way the kind of man with whom she should involve herself. He couldn't possibly take seriously anything that might develop between them. There would be nothing lasting, nothing permanent with him. So why did she find herself so drawn to him?

For a long moment, they only gazed at each other in thoughtful silence, then Caroline returned her attention to the pile of roses on her counter. One by one, she lifted, snipped, arranged, until the roaster was full of the fragrant blossoms. At no time did she or Schuyler speak to each other. He only sat down on one of the high stools lined up along the counter and watched, very intently, every move she made.

When she was finished, she filled a watering can and emptied it into the roaster, then held the final product aloft in two hands. "There," she said, satisfied with her handiwork. "What do you think?"

"I think it's beautiful," he told her. "You have a way with flowers."

She smiled, then made her way to the kitchen table in the dining area that sat catty-corner to the living area. "Thanks," she said as she situated the bouquet carefully in the middle.

"Just like you have a way with kids," he added.

She made a few additional adjustments to the arrangement, then turned around to face him. "Thanks," she said again.

He rose from the stool and covered the few steps between them, then lifted his hand to run his thumb lightly over her cheek. "Just like you have a way with disillusioned, lonely billionaires," he added softly.

She had to tip her head back to look at him, because he stood a good half foot taller than she when she was in her stocking feet. She wanted to say something in response to his statement, but feared that whatever came out would simply be too revealing, too suggestive, too dangerous. So she said nothing at all, only lifted her hand to circle his wrist with loose fingers. Beneath her thumb, his pulse was pounding, something that was totally at odds with the cool, collected image he presented. She took heart in knowing that he was no more immune to the heat and awareness burning up the air between them than she was.

Gently, she removed his hand from her cheek, but not before he brushed his fingertips lightly over her lips. Impulsively, she kissed each as they passed, then knew the folly of her gesture when his pupils expanded with wanting. Hastily, she took a step backward, and retreated once again into the kitchen.

"I'll just, um . . . start dinner, shall I?" she asked, her voice faint and uncertain, and none too steady.

"Yes, why don't you?" he suggested. But he, too, seemed to be interested in something else other than the preparation of a meal.

Which was all the more reason, she told herself, why they needed to slow down.

Feeling more and more awkward with every passing moment, she opened all the cupboards necessary to gather the ingredients for their feast. But even after she'd amassed everything down to the salt shaker, she still felt as if something very important were missing. She glanced down at her clothes, at the very comfortable—but none too formal—shirt and leggings that were her at-home uniform. Then she looked back up at Schuyler.

"I can't believe you wore a tuxedo," she told him. "I feel horribly underdressed."

His mouth curled into a predatory smile, and his eyes flashed with a predatory fire. "Well, if it makes you uncomfortable, I could take it off," he told her, without hesitation, without batting an eye.

She shook her head quickly. "No. No, that won't be necessary." She had no idea what possessed her to do it, but she heard herself add, "Not yet, anyway."

He narrowed his eyes at her, then, with only a brief hesitation, reached for his bow tie and tugged it loose. Caroline opened her mouth to object, but something—something totally unmitigated and utterly confusing inside her—halted her from doing so just yet. She watched with what she hoped was only veiled interest as he shrugged off his jacket and tossed it over the kitchen counter beside him, then freed the top two studs of his shirt. His cufflinks followed, each of them clattering onto the counter with finality behind the studs he had already tossed there.

Finally, she found her voice. But all she could manage to utter was, "Schuyler."

Not surprisingly, he ignored her protest and reached for another stud on his shirt. Then again, she supposed what she'd said really hadn't been much of a protest at all. So she tried again.

"Schuyler."

"What?"

"You shouldn't . . . I won't . . . We can't . . ."

But no matter which way she tried to word it, any objection she might have uttered simply would not come. So Schuyler did. Slowly, as he freed yet another stud and tugged his shirt tail free of his trousers, he drew nearer. With fluid grace and clear intent, he covered the space of the tiny galley kitchen, until he stood in front of her, loosing the last of the studs. That one, he simply tossed over his shoulder without care, and it went sailing to the floor, skittering across the linoleum, right under the refrigerator.

Solid gold, she was certain, had now joined the dust bunnies, the stray cat kibble, and the petrified Froot Loops under her refrigerator. Somehow, the knowledge of that both aroused and comforted her.

"Schuyler," she tried yet again.

But he reached for her hand and tucked it beneath the fabric of his shirt, splaying her fingers open over the smooth, heated skin beneath. Soft coils of hair wound easily about her fingers, as if trying to entrap her, and hold her there against him forever. Every bump and ripple of flesh and muscle that she encountered felt as if it came alive under her touch. It had been so long since she had touched a man this way, so long since she had enjoyed even the most innocent intimacy with another human being. So long since she had *wanted* to share intimacy with another human being.

Telling herself she was foolish to do so, she closed her eyes and lifted her other hand to join the first, nudging it under his shirt, trailing her fingers over the same path her others had already traveled. He felt so good beneath her hands, so hot, so alive, so . . . She sighed deeply, then filled her hands with him, stroking, palming, caressing, enjoying.

A rough sound of satisfaction rumbled up from inside him, and Caroline felt it, absorbed it, through her fingers as well as her ears. When she opened her eyes, she saw that he was ravenous, and knew that the hunger blazing in his eyes was nothing more than a reflection of her own.

"We shouldn't do this," she told him. "It would be a terrible mistake."

"Why?" he demanded. He lifted his hand to her hair, skimming his palm over one long tress before winding it around his finger. "What would be so terrible about the two of us making love? I think we'd rather enjoy it."

"But it wouldn't mean the same thing for you as it would for me," she told him.

His gaze shot from the hair wound around his finger to her face. "Who says it wouldn't mean the same thing for me?" he demanded.

"It couldn't. Schuyler, I—"

"Don't," he interrupted her. "Don't try to analyze what this is about. It doesn't matter where it comes from, or even where it's going. This is about us, Caroline. You and me, right now, and the way we are when we're together."

"But—"

"For me, that's enough," he told her. "Because what's here right now, between you and me . . ." He inhaled deeply and released the breath slowly, raggedly. "God knows it's more than I've *ever* had with anyone else."

She held his gaze for a moment more, then forced herself to look away. Because if she didn't, she knew she would do something she really shouldn't do.

"But what's between us now," he continued, "isn't enough for you, is it?"

"I don't know," she told him honestly.

"Caroline, I . . ."

But whatever he had wanted to tell her, Schuyler halted himself. Instead, slowly, he unwound her hair from his finger and took a step away. When he did, Caroline found herself with her hands still extended toward him, but where a moment ago they had been filled with heat and life, now they groped for cool, empty air. So she dropped them back to her sides.

For a moment, Schuyler only stood there looking at her, and for a moment, she thought everything would be okay. Then a shutter fell over his eyes, and he turned toward the studs and cuff links scattered about her counter. With one swift, fluid gesture, he swept them all into the palm of his hand and dumped them in his trouser pocket. Then he scooped up his jacket and shrugged back into it.

He looked utterly and completely lost, she thought. His black hair hung restlessly over his forehead, and his shirt hung open over his bare chest. His collar was twisted and one of his cuffs stuck out of his jacket at an odd angle. More than anything, Caroline wanted to go to him, wanted to smooth him out and calm him down, but something in his posture forbade it. As if punctuating the image, he straightened then, lifting his chin almost defiantly.

"When you decide what will be enough for you, Caroline," he told her, "call me."

Without awaiting a response, knowing, she supposed, that she wouldn't have one to give him, he turned and strode easily through her living room, to the front door. Just as he had the night before, he left without once looking back.

And more than anything else in the world, Caroline found herself envying him his ability to do that.

EIGHTEEN

Lily was surprised when Schuyler returned to Ashling before nine o'clock. After all, he was alone when he did. What wasn't surprising, however, was that he was in a surly mood when he arrived. After all, he was alone when he did.

She intercepted him in the gallery as he made his way toward the east wing, matching her stride to his with no small effort. Boy, was he mad about something, she thought. And it was only going to get worse.

"We have a problem," she said by way of a greeting. But, because he didn't answer her, because he seemed to be focused on something else entirely, she offered nothing more until they reached his bedroom.

Bedrooms, plural, was more like it, she thought, as she invariably did whenever she came to his suite. As so many other areas of the house were, Schuyler's set of rooms was an utterly masculine retreat. The dark mahogany-paneled walls were interrupted only occasionally by even darker oil paintings of hunt scenes. All the furnishings were mahogany, too, as was the massive four-poster bed he claimed as his own. The carpet was an expansive Aubusson spattered with rich, deep jewel tones of ruby, sapphire, emerald, and amethyst, and the only light afforded this time of night came from a large, but none-too-bright, Art Deco lamp in the image of the sun that was fixed at the center of the ceiling.

On any other occasion, Lily might have found the room cozy in a macho, dark, film noir kind of way. But not tonight. Not when the house of cards the two of them had built together by hand over the last decade was about to come crashing down around them.

"Schuyler," she said when he remained silent. "Did you hear me? I said we have a problem."

He jerked off his tuxedo jacket and shirt—God alone knew what had happened to all the studs, because Lily sure wasn't going to ask him—and tossed both, without looking at them, onto an oxblood leather chair near the bed. His bare back gleamed like gold in the soft light before he disappeared into a walk-in closet that was roughly the size of New Hampshire.

"Who the hell cares?" he snapped from inside.

Lily curled her fingers into fists. "I care, Schuyler. Our man Freiberger is looking to send me up the river."

"What are you talking about?" he asked, still not emerging from inside the closet.

"If he has his way, I'm destined for stripes."

"Lily. Darling. You want to tell me something that makes sense now?"

Lily wondered where to begin, then decided she might as well just start with that crystal clear moment when her entire life exploded in her face. "When I went up to my room to change for dinner tonight, who do you think I found there?"

Schuyler emerged from the closet then, tying the sash of a flowing midnight blue silk robe over his bare chest and matching pajama bottoms. "The big, bad wolf?" he guessed.

She nodded. "Yeah, pretty much."

He sighed heavily, as if he really didn't want to be bothered by her this evening, then strode to the bar on the other side of the room and uncapped a bottle of cognac. "Join me?" he asked.

"You bet," she replied readily.

Lily, too, had finally changed out of her work clothes, but still considered it a bit early to be in her pajamas, so had opted for a pair of gray fleece sweats and an oversize, white man-style shirt. She'd pulled her hair to the crown of her head in a ponytail, and it tickled the back of her neck as she tossed her head to one side.

"I'm assuming," Schuyler said as he handed her a large snifter of cognac, "that this big, bad wolf is none other than our illustrious Mr. Freiberger?"

She nodded. "But I don't think his name is really Leonard Freiberger," she said.

Schuyler rolled his eyes. "Lily. Darling. That goes without saying. Did you honestly think it was?"

"I don't know," she said. "At this point, I have no idea what hit me."

Schuyler inhaled deeply again, and released the breath slowly. "So what happened?"

"He accessed my files, Schuyler. The ones in my laptop."

The snifter he had been lifting to his mouth stopped well short of completing the action. When he looked at Lily, she realized that he finally, finally, understood the magnitude of what had happened. "All of them?" he asked cautiously.

"Well, enough to think he's uncovered millions of dollars worth of fraud and theft."

Schuyler's entire body slumped forward. "Oh, fabulous."

"And he thinks *I'm* the one who's the thief."

That, at least, made Schuyler bark with laughter. "*You*? A *thief*? Oh, how wonderfully rich. Darling Lily steals millions. Film at eleven. What kind of idiot is the man?"

"One who has a little knowledge," she said. "And a little knowledge—"

"Is a dangerous thing," he finished for her.

"Especially in this case. I tried to explain—"

Schuyler's expression went utterly glacial. "You didn't. Tell me you didn't do that."

She hesitated only a moment before revealing, "He didn't give me a chance."

"Well, thank God for small miracles."

"But I would have told him the truth, Schuyler," Lily continued, wanting to make sure he knew where she stood on this. "I would have told him everything, if I'd thought he would listen."

This time Schuyler's expression punctuated his fear. "Lily, you can't do that. You can't tell him the truth. It would ruin everything."

"I may not have any choice."

"No. You promised me. Lily. You *promised*."

"But, Schuyler . . ." She exhaled a weary sigh. "He thinks I'm a thief."

"He'll get over it."

"No, he won't. He's not going to let this go." She might as well tell Schuyler everything. He'd find out soon enough. "He's preparing a report to take to the board of directors."

Once again, Schuyler's body slumped forward. "When?" he asked.

"I don't know," she said. "But I think it's safe to

assume it won't take him long to put it all together. Or, at least, put together what he *thinks* is going on. And the only thing worse than him telling the board what he thinks is going on is having them find out what's *really* going on. You know how they are. You know how they'll react. You know what this will mean to the company. We have to tell Leo the truth."

Schuyler nodded, then took a slow, thoughtful sip of his cognac. Then, after he had swallowed it, he thought some more. Finally, he gazed down at her and said, "Well, Lily. Darling. I guess you're right. I guess you and I are just going to have to explain things to dear Leonard Freiberger, aren't we? And we're going to have to hope like hell that he understands."

Leo was still feeling a little numb as he lay awake in bed that night perusing the file on the Rigby Gang that Eddie had left with him the day before. The more he read, the more he berated himself for his own stupidity. Because considering her background, then right from the start, he should have been able to ID Lily as the likeliest suspect in the theft of the missing Kimball millions. If he'd just been thinking with his brain instead of his—

He growled under his breath and enjoyed another long, cool slug of Anchor Steam. If he'd just seen past what she appeared to be to find out who she really was, then none of this would have happened. He would have fingered her as the thief right off, would have collected all kinds of accolades from Kimball's board of directors—probably some he'd never heard before from Thesaurus Man—and by now he would have moved on to the next client. He would be feeling proud of another job well done, satisfied that another crook was behind bars, convinced that he had done the right thing.

Instead of feeling sick inside every time he thought about Lily and how he had fallen for her so completely, so profoundly.

So stupidly.

He'd spent the better part of the evening going over the rest of the files from her laptop that he'd duped onto diskette. And what he'd found had only reinforced everything he'd already known to be true. Lily was guilty of stealing tens of millions of dollars from her employer over the years and putting it into private accounts all over the world. He just wished he knew what had happened to all the funds once she'd removed them again. Had she made investments? Had she consolidated the cash in one big lump in Switzerland? Had she bought real estate? Jewelry? Bonds?

That was the one thing he continued to have trouble understanding. Why she was still at it—she'd made deposits into some of those accounts as recently as last month. She'd filtered off enough money by now to live in incredible luxury for the rest of her life. So why hadn't she gotten out while the getting was good and retired with her ill-gotten gains? Was she so greedy that even scores of millions of dollars weren't enough to satisfy her? Had she been trying to go for a cool billion?

And, dammit, how could he have been so wrong about her?

Because Leo did have good instincts, by God. Yet not one of them had kicked in to warn him to be careful where Lily Rigby was concerned. Oh, there had been moments there in the beginning, when he'd first come to Ashling, when he'd suspected her of being up to something, of hiding something. But he'd thought that something had to do with fulfilling the billionaire's needs in an area other than social secretary. He'd certainly never considered her a candidate for the role of corporate thief. Even now, after all he'd discovered about her, the thought of Lily committing acts of theft and betrayal just didn't sit right with Leo at all.

But there was nothing else that would explain why she had been playing fast and loose with Kimball's billions for years. There was nothing else that would explain why she had taken money—and she clearly *had* taken the money—and hidden it in personal accounts. There was nothing else that would explain why she had lied and misrepresented herself to Leo.

Nothing.

Another long, thoughtful pull of beer left the bottle empty, and he was rising to retrieve a second from the fridge when the telephone on his night stand rang shrilly to stop him. Who the hell would be calling him at two A.M.? he wondered. Either it was another drunk who'd misdialed Yellow Cab—whose telephone number was only one different from Leo's—or else it was something important. In either event, he really didn't want to hear about it.

In spite of that, he snatched the receiver from its cradle and snarled, "What is it?"

There was a slight hesitation on the other end, followed by a woman's voice asking tentatively, "Leo?"

"Lily?"

He cursed himself for the wistfulness he heard in his own voice, then gave himself a mental smack for the curl of heat that unwound in his belly. Gripping the receiver brutally, he added, "What do *you* want?"

There was another slight hesitation on the other

end of the line, then she told him, "I need your help."

He couldn't quite halt the derisive chuckle that escaped him. "Again? Didn't you already try this once? Oh, wait," he went on before she had a chance to answer. "No, that was a favor you wanted earlier, wasn't it? Now you want help. Well, gee, isn't this just the biggest surprise I've ever had in my life."

Her voice was tinted with urgency and impatience when she said, "Just shut up and listen. The help I need is for Chloe, Leo, not me. Chloe's in trouble, and you're closer to where she is than I am, and I need for you to go get her. Please."

"Chloe?" he asked, his sarcasm dying a quick death, his concern rousing completely to take its place. "What's happened? What's wrong?"

"She just called here. To make a long story short, she's in a bar in downtown Philly with a man who's drunk and mean, and who's decided he's going to take her home with him tonight and make her his own. Am I making myself clear?"

"Shit," he hissed.

"I couldn't have put it better myself," she said succinctly. "She was with her friend Lauren, and the two of them evidently bit off more than they could chew, and now Lauren's abandoned Chloe, and she's all alone with this guy. She got away from him long enough to use the phone in the bathroom, but she doesn't think she can stall him much longer. Schuyler's gone out again somewhere, and I don't know where he is. I've tried his cell number, but he's not answering it. And even this time of night, it's going to take me a half hour to get into town. You could be at this place—"

"In fifteen minutes," he told her. "What's the name of the bar?"

"Smoky Joe's. It's on—"

"Oh, swell," he growled, interrupting.

"Do you know where it is?"

"Yeah, unfortunately I do. Look, a friend of mine lives a block away from the place. I'll call him before I go, and if he's home, he can run down and keep an eye on things until I get there. I'll be there myself in fifteen minutes," he repeated. "And don't worry. I'll make sure Chloe stays safe until you arrive."

"Okay. Thanks, Leo. I owe you."

You're damned right you do, he thought. *And not just for this, either.*

She hung up before he could say anything else—not that there was anything else to say. So Leo stabbed a finger down on the disconnect button, then punched in seven numbers as he struggled into a pair of blue jeans.

Thankfully, Eddie was home. "Yeah, whaddaya want?" he asked when he picked up the phone. He was clearly wide awake, which wasn't surprising, seeing as how the guy did most of his living at night.

Leo reached for a navy flannel shirt and thrust his arms into it, cradling the telephone between his ear and his shoulder as he buttoned the garment. "Eddie, it's Leo Friday. I need for you to do me another favor."

Smoky Joe's was a pretty awful place, Leo had to admit when he arrived there less than fifteen minutes later. And it was fairly typical of antisocial, misogynist dives. Its walls were composed of fake wood paneling that sported dozens of broken, dirty neon beer signs and posters of large-breasted women straddling big, nasty-looking motorcycles. The population of the place was overwhelmingly male. Though not necessarily human, he noted. Still, most of the patrons present could at least qualify for primate status. Probably. And the place smelled really bad, too. Like bad beer, stale sweat, and mean men.

Several of those mean men glanced up at Leo's entrance, many of them appearing to welcome any diversion he might provide. Especially if that diversion included an opportunity for them to either A) beat the hell out of some undeserving individual, or B) beat the hell out of some undeserving individual.

Leo tried to look mean in return, which wasn't all that hard to do, considering the day he'd had. And he breathed a silent sigh of thanks when he saw Eddie seated at the bar, looking totally incongruous in his Armani suit and Gucci loafers. Still, his large size and that broken nose of his, not to mention those dark, Mafioso looks, always kept him from being bothered much by troublemakers. So far, he looked as if he were just sitting there minding his own business, nursing a bad beer. When he noted Leo's arrival, however, he jerked his head silently toward a booth in the back of the bar.

Way in the back of the bar, Leo noted when he turned his gaze in that direction. Back where it was very, *very* dark.

He strode forward slowly, cautiously, praying like hell that no one would interpret his simple mobility as a sign of aggression. It seemed to take forever to cover the fifty or so feet between him and that darkness, and he was grateful when Eddie rose from his stool to cover Leo's back. He'd just stepped into the shadows when he heard the low, lethal chuckle of a man who was clearly drunk and amorous—or whatever it was that passed for *am-*

orous among men like this. Then he heard what sounded like the terrified whimpering of a young, and very frightened, girl.

"Chloe?" he called out.

"Here," she replied. But the word emerged as little more than a sob.

Leo moved forward again, slowly and cautiously again, until his eyes finally adjusted to the darkness. The first two booths he passed were empty. But in the last one, in the very corner of the bar, beneath the spastic half-light of a nearly burnt out Schlitz sign, he found what he was looking for. Unfortunately. Because Chloe was crowded into that booth, her eyes wide with terror, wedged between the wall and a very large, very menacing-looking man. He had shoved his face into her neck and was licking her throat, had unbuttoned her shirt and stuffed his hand inside her bra. He didn't even appear to notice Leo's arrival.

"Let her go."

Leo was surprised by the even, steady timbre of his voice, seeing as how, at the moment, what he wanted to do more than anything else in the world was rip the sonofabitch's hand off his wrist and turn it into chicken fingers. What he did instead was curl one hand into a tight fist, and cup the other—roughly—over the big man's shoulder to jerk him back.

Only then did the guy seem to realize that Leo had been talking to him. "What the hell is your problem?" he demanded. But he didn't release Chloe.

"I said, 'Let her go,'" Leo repeated as levelly as he could. "Because if you don't, I'm going to hurt you. Badly."

The man made a derisive face and snorted. "Who're you? Her old man? Tough. I got 'er now.

You can have 'er back when I'm done. Beat it."

"Oh, don't tempt me," Leo said, still masking his fury. "Because I'll be more than happy to beat it—right into a bloody pulp. I promise you that."

The man belched loudly and, clearly feeling put upon, pushed himself away from Chloe. She exhaled loudly and closed her eyes tight when he did, and two fat tears tumbled down her cheeks. As she had been the first day Leo had made her acquaintance, she was wearing about ten pounds of makeup and an outfit that was anything but appropriate for a fourteen-year-old girl. But her tears left white tracks on her cheeks as they washed the cosmetics away, and to Leo, she looked every bit her age. Immediately, she gripped the sides of her shirt and jerked it closed, then, crowding her body into the wall even more than it was already, she turned her face away.

"Get out of the booth," Leo told the man. "Now."

"If I get outta dis booth," he said, clearly unbothered by Leo's presence, "it's only gonna be for one reason. To knock you on your ass."

Leo smiled with feigned indifference. "I'd like to see you try it."

The man eyed him for a moment, obviously puzzled by Leo's concern, then asked again, "What the hell is your problem?"

"The problem is that you've got your hands on someone you shouldn't have them on," Leo said simply.

But he ground his teeth painfully in an effort to keep things as civil as possible. On top of everything else she'd been through tonight, the last thing Chloe needed was to see two grown men beating the hell out of each other. And he feared that any altercation that ensued between him and this big ape would spill over into the rest of the bar. God only knew what kind of chaos would result after that.

"Now go away," Leo added quietly, "and leave her alone."

"She's wid me," the man said. "*You* go away and leave *us* alone."

"Mr. Freiberger, no," Chloe said, jerking her head up, her expression frightened, beseeching. "Don't leave me here. Please."

As if he would, Leo thought. God. The kid honestly looked like she thought he would leave her here with this guy. Just what the hell kind of life had she lived before coming to Philadelphia?

Putting that thought on hold for now, he turned his attention back to the gorilla still seated in the booth. "She's fourteen years old, Humbert," Leo informed him. "A little young for you. Not to mention jailbait. But if you leave right now, I'll be real nice and pretend you never touched her."

The man laughed. "Fourteen. Yeah, right. Like I'm supposed to believe that. Lookit 'er." Following his own advice, he turned to offer Chloe a salacious perusal. "Ain't no fourteen-year-old looks that good, pal."

Leo opened his mouth to comment, but a third voice cut him off before he could say a word.

"Yes, well, if you think she's pretty, you should have seen her mother."

Leo snapped his attention around at the voice that came from behind him, and was surprised to see Schuyler Kimball standing just behind Eddie.

"Where did you come from?" he asked.

Instead of looking at Leo when he answered, Kimball took a few steps forward and focused on the scene in the booth. He frowned when he noted the belligerent expression on the ape man's face, then, when he saw Chloe crying, he went absolutely rigid. Funny, but Leo had never noticed before how big and threatening-looking Kimball was. But dressed in black trousers and a black turtleneck, with every muscle he possessed flexed that way, he cut a pretty damned intimidating figure.

But as furious as he obviously was, all the billionaire said in response to Leo's query was, "As luck—or, perhaps, irony—would have it, Freiberger, I was on my way to see you, hoping we might have a little chat. Then Lily darling called me on the cell phone to alert me to this other matter. I wasn't far from here. It was just a matter of having Claudio turn the car around."

That was when Leo noted that Kimball wasn't alone. Behind *him*, shadowing Eddie, stood another man—or something—who was even taller than Leo was. Gee. Suddenly the odds seemed much more workable than they had when he'd first entered Smoky Joe's.

"Oh, great, another one," the ape man said when he saw Kimball standing by Leo. He turned to Chloe. "Just how many men are you doin', sweetheart? You must be better than I thought. I can't wait to get between your sweet—"

He never finished what he was going to say, because Kimball lurched past Leo then and reached into the booth, grabbing the man by the throat and squeezing hard.

"Your next word," he said in a surprisingly calm voice, "may be your last. If I were you, I'd think very carefully before I chose it."

The man's eyes bugged out, and his face began to grow purple, and Leo wondered if he should step in and intercede before Kimball killed the guy. Nah, he decided. No reason to be hasty. Might as well let this thing run its course.

"Now then," Kimball continued in a benign voice, loosening his grip just the tiniest bit. "You were saying . . . ?"

The man had reached up to circle both of his beefy hands around Kimball's wrist, but he hadn't managed to alter the billionaire's grip one bit. He uttered a feral, guttural sound, then surrendered to Kimball's fury and loosened his hold. Roughly, raggedly, he somehow managed to mutter, "Who the hell *are* you?"

Kimball gritted his teeth in a way that made Leo take an involuntary step backward. In a voice that chilled him further, the billionaire announced quite clearly, quite threateningly, quite adamantly, "I'm her *father*, you bloated, revolting pig. And if you *ever* come near my daughter again, I will kill you. With my bare hands. And I shall take great pride in committing the act. Do I make myself clear?"

The ape man stared into Kimball's face for another moment, and Leo was pretty sure the guy's bowels were about to fail him. Sure enough, the instant Kimball loosened his grip, the man scrambled out of the booth and through a door nearby that was labeled in peeling letters, *Res ro ms*.

Kimball, however, didn't move. He only stood bent over the table with his white-knuckled fist gripping nothing but air. Chloe continued to cower in the corner, her shoulders shuddering in silent sobs, her face turned away, her entire body shrunken into a ball. Then slowly, very slowly, Kimball's fist unclenched, his fingers uncurled. But instead of dropping his hand to his side, he moved it toward Chloe's hair. For a moment, his hand only hung suspended there without touching her. Then he cupped his hand over the crown of her head in much the same way a father would if he were trying to comfort his daughter.

Chloe's head snapped up at the contact, her face a mess of running mascara and rouge. Still cradling her head in one hand, Kimball reached into his pocket and withdrew a handkerchief, which he used to wipe away the worst of her tears and makeup. Awkwardly, Chloe reached up and took the scrap of silk from his hand, then blew her nose indelicately into it.

"I'm sorry," she said in a very small voice. "I didn't mean to—"

"I understand," Kimball said, cutting off her explanation before she could even begin to offer one. His voice softened some as he added, "Believe it or not, Chloe, I do understand. And I'm sorry, too. We can talk about it on the way home."

Chloe started crying harder then, as if in doing so, she were releasing years' worth of pent up emotion. But somehow, she managed a brief smile through her tears. Kimball brushed his hand over her head one more time, then extended a hand toward her to help her out of the booth.

"We'll talk later," he said to Leo, the statement in no way inviting comment. Then, to the other men present, he added, "Gentlemen, if you'll all excuse me, I'm going to take my daughter home now."

Without a word, the big man who'd accompanied the billionaire into the bar extended Kimball's coat, and Kimball draped it around Chloe's shoulders. Then, after only a small hesitation, he dropped his arm around her shoulders, too. Gently, he led her toward the exit with the massive bodyguard right behind them. And all Leo could do was stand there watching them go.

Unbelievable, he thought. Kimball really had come through.

"Thanks, Eddie," he said to the man who stood

gaping as he watched the scene conclude.

"No problem, Leo," he replied. "What can I say? I got a soft spot for kids. I'd like to have a couple of my own someday."

Leo started forward, more than a little anxious to rid himself of Smoky Joe's for good, but he halted mid-stride when the door to the bar opened again, and Lily Rigby came stumbling through.

Her long black hair was half-in and half-out of a ponytail caught at the top of her head, and an over-size leather bomber jacket hung open over gray sweats and a big, man-style shirt. She'd accessori-zed the ensemble with her enormous hiking boots, and, as a result, she didn't exactly look like a Vic-toria's Secret model. In spite of that, every male eye in the place—which was pretty much every eye in the place period—homed in on her, and she gazed about the room with much apprehension.

"Yikes," she said to the room at large, obviously not having seen Leo standing back in the shadows. She glanced around at her surroundings—and her companions—and went pale. "Um, hi. Nice place you've got here," she muttered. Smart woman that she was, she clearly sensed immediately that she shouldn't be there alone, and she quickly turned to go back out the way she'd come in. Unfortunately, another of the bar's missing link patrons entered behind her, halting when he saw her, blocking her way.

"Ah . . . okay," she said, spinning around again, evidently trying to make the best of a fast degen-erating situation. She cleared her throat discreetly when two men at the bar rose and began to ap-proach her. Then, once again, she directed her com-ments to the entire room. "I wonder if you . . . lovely gentlemen . . . could help me out. I'm look-

ing for someone. Have any of you . . . lovely gentlemen . . . seen, um . . ."

She faltered a bit when the first of the two lugs
from the bar stopped within a foot of her. Then,
suddenly, she brightened.

"My husband?" she finished. "Have any of you
seen my husband? He's a big, hulking guy, about
six—" She hastily sized up the man nearest her
before continuing, "Uh, six-five." She cleared her
throat again when another man began to approach.
"He weighs about, ah, two-fifty? Two-fifty-five?
And he has big, beefy fists and hair all over his
back. And no neck. None whatsoever. He, uh . . .
he carries a switchblade in his sock. And . . . and
numchuks, too. His name is, um, Rocco. Rocco Cor-
leone. Do you happen to know if he's come in here
tonight?"

The man nearest her reached out a hand to clamp
it over her shoulder, chuckling evilly as he did.

"Did I mention that he's also insanely jealous?"
she added halfheartedly as she recoiled from the
man's touch. "And that he's out on parole for killing a man who tried to sell me some encyclope-
dias?"

"Here I am, honey!" Leo called out from the back
of the room, wondering when he had decided to
intercede on behalf of a criminal. Probably because
she was a really cute criminal, he thought. That
was why.

He took a step out of the shadows, tugging Eddie
Dolan along for the ride. "And I brought my
friend, Vito, with me," he added as the two of them
strode forward. "He's in town visiting his godfather."

She was obviously more than a little relieved to
see him. "Oh, darling!" she cried in a pretty convincing June Cleaver voice. "I'm so glad you're

here. It's your Aunt Sybil. She's got an ingrown toenail again, and you know you're the only one she'll let near her with a pair of tweezers.''

"Damn," Leo said blandly. "Oh, well. Duty calls. Gentlemen?''

He made a dismissive gesture with his hand, hoping the men who had formed a ring around Lily would let them all leave with their lives—and limbs. Evidently, the guys at Smoky Joe's had bigger fish to fry that night—or else they were stupid enough to believe that bit about Eddie's godfather— because, as one, they parted to allow Leo and Lily and Eddie through.

Leo pretended that his heart wasn't pounding in his throat as he passed through the throng, nudging Lily ahead of him, hoping like hell that Eddie would pull up the rear. The moment they were outside, however, he grabbed her by the upper arm and propelled her forward as fast as he could, toward Eddie's apartment building at the end of the block.

But Lily struggled free and stopped dead in her tracks. "Chloe," she said.

"She's safe," Leo told her.

Her entire body seemed to relax at his assurance. "Oh, thank God. Where is she?"

"She's with . . . her father," Leo said.

Lily eyed him warily. "Schuyler made it in time?''

Leo nodded. "The guy came through. Big time. He and Chloe are going to have a lot to talk about during their ride home.''

Lily nodded. "Good. As bad as this was, maybe, ultimately, some good will come of it. Now then," she added quickly, "how about the two of us make an example out of them and do likewise?''

He studied her in confusion. "What do you mean?"

"How about the two of us do a lot of talking on the way to your place? And even more after we get there?"

He shook his head adamantly. No way was he going to let her take advantage of his emotions right now. No way was he going to let her talk him into doing something he knew better than to do. No way was he going to let her get under his skin again. No way was he going to set himself up for that kind of fall.

"Forget it, Lily. It's over."

She expelled an impatient breath, running a restless hand through her bangs. "Leo, you have got to give me a chance to explain," she told him.

"No. I don't."

She dropped her hand in front of her, curling it into a fist. "Yes, dammit, you do." She snarled at him. Actually snarled, he noted. How incredibly . . . arousing. "You *will* give me a chance to talk about this before you take your findings to the board. You *will*."

"Why would I do something like that?"

"Because I deserve the opportunity, that's why. You know I do, Leo. You know it."

"Hey, kids, if I'm interrupting something here . . ." Eddie began, edging backward a bit, in an obvious effort to free himself of what was promising to be a pretty rabid confrontation.

"You're not interrupting anything, Eddie," Leo snapped. But he kept his gaze fixed on Lily. "Nothing except the usual farce that is my life, anyway."

"Oh, well, in that case," the other man said, jutting a thumb over his shoulder, "I think I hear my mother calling."

"Wait," Lily said, reaching out to curl her fingers

around the other man's arm to prevent his flight.

Leo became unaccountably jealous at the sight, curling his own fingers into loose fists, before he remembered that he wasn't letting Lily Rigby under his skin again. He wasn't. He *wasn't*.

"Mr. Dolan," she continued, her voice much softer than it had been when she'd been addressing Leo, "I can only assume that you're the friend Leo called to help out. Thank you for what you did tonight, helping Chloe."

Eddie bunched up his shoulders and let them drop. "Don't mention it. I just hope everything works out okay for the kid."

Lily nodded. "Look, why don't you come to dinner at Ashling tomorrow evening?" she said. "It's the least we can offer you after your contribution tonight." Before Eddie could respond, she added, "And bring your friend Leo with you, would you?"

Eddie smiled, letting his gaze wander between Lily and Leo. "Yeah, okay. I think he's available."

"Eddie . . ."

"But ya know, Miss Rigby, he don't got the greatest table manners in the world. You sure you want him?"

Lily smiled, too. "Yes, I want him. And he'll have you there to keep him in line, won't he?"

Eddie smiled back. "Yeah, well, one of us will keep him in line, anyway."

She turned to face Leo again. "Will you come?" she asked him, her voice urgent now, instead of threatening. "And will you wait until after dinner tomorrow night to confront the board of directors? I promise you, Leo, it will all make sense to you after tomorrow night. You just have to give me the chance to explain."

He didn't want to. As Leo stood there in a spill

of yellow lamplight on the street corner, he told himself not to go for it, not to give Lily the chance she was asking for, because she was a thief and a liar, and she didn't deserve an opportunity to mess him up again.

But her eyes were so big and so beautiful and so full of earnest need that he couldn't quite find it within himself to refuse her. It was only one more day, he told himself. Less than forty-eight hours. The board of directors would be no worse off hearing his report in two days, should he wait until then to get it all prepared.

God, he was such a sap.

But maybe, just maybe, if he gave Lily the chance she requested, she would tell him the truth. And better still, he thought—*hoped*—further, maybe, just maybe, that truth would even make sense.

NINETEEN

As Schuyler's dark limo rolled down rural county roads toward home, he studied the young girl seated across from him, who, thankfully, had finally stopped crying. Considering the wash of tears she had released since they'd left that abominable place, he supposed that at this point, she was pretty much dried out. Now Chloe simply stared numbly out the window at the swiftly passing darkness outside. Whatever she had been through tonight, it had humbled her greatly. It had terrified her. It had humanized her. And now, Schuyler knew, her life was going to be even more difficult than it had been before.

His daughter.

How extraordinary.

Of course, he'd known since the day she arrived at Ashling that she was his daughter. Her eyes were identical to his, and he'd learned quickly that she'd been cursed with the same kind of brain. But something other than that, something more immediate, more profound, something he would be hard pressed to explain, had made the inescapability of their blood relationship even more clear to him.

Something in Chloe had spoken to him that day. Without words. Without expression. Even without thought. He had discovered within himself the existence of some previously unfelt emotion, the genesis of which had occurred that very day. Because as he'd gazed for the first time upon the young girl whom a now forgotten social worker had introduced as his daughter, Schuyler had known—had *known*—down to the very depths of his soul, that she was, quite simply, his.

And the knowledge of that had terrified him.

So he had turned from it. He had tried to deny it. He had made every effort to wish it away. Unfortunately, when one was "gifted"—he still curdled at that word—with the kind of brain capacity he had, one could never banish knowledge completely. And the recognition of Chloe's relationship never hovered far from his consciousness. Still, until tonight, he had never acknowledged it to anyone but himself. And now, of course, he realized how foolish he had been in thinking he could maintain that status quo.

Chloe was his daughter. He was her father. And now, he was going to have to deal with that, beyond the physical, genetic repercussions. Whether he liked it or not, from this day onward, he was going to have to accept the emotional ones, as well. Somehow, he was going to have to join the two without harming either structure. And he was going to have to try to make Chloe understand why he hadn't bridged the chasm between them before now.

To do that, he would have to make allowances, would have to offer explanations, would have to try and make sense of it all. He didn't relish the

coming days and weeks and months and years, but
he understood now that he could no more avoid
them than he could stop the sun from rising in the
morning. Reality, it would appear, had intruded
into his perfect life, and would taint it for the rest
of his days. He would have to be human now. He
had no choice. And he would simply have to make
the best of it.

"When I was fourteen," he said suddenly, softly,
noting with dubious satisfaction the way Chloe
flinched at the sudden sound of his voice in the
otherwise silent car, "I had a friend who was much
like your Lauren. His name was Jason, and I didn't
like him much. But there are times in life when
intimacy is bred with those who offend and annoy
us the least. Plus, my mother detested him, something that went a long way toward cementing my
friendship with him. He was not, shall we say, a
good influence. Nor was he particularly reliable."

Chloe's face was still turned to the window, but
she glanced his way as she said, "What happened
to him?"

Schuyler crossed one leg over the other and
flicked at a nonexistent piece of lint on his trouser
leg. "I have no idea. I like to think he's in a Turkish
prison somewhere, but something tells me he
doubtless became either a highly successful CEO
or else is, at this moment, holed up in Montana
somewhere plotting to overthrow the government
with a band of hired ex-Green Berets. He wasn't a
very nice person."

There was another brief bout of silence, then
Chloe remarked, "But you were friends with him."

"Yes. I was," Schuyler conceded. "For a time. I
remember one night in particular—when I was
fourteen, as providence would have it—when Jason convinced me to do something I shouldn't have

done. Actually, that night wasn't the first occasion upon which he did that. It was just the first time doing something I shouldn't have done backfired on me.''

Chloe hesitated only a moment before asking, ''What happened?''

Schuyler inhaled deeply and released the breath slowly, trying to keep at bay memories of that night that remained far too fresh for his tolerance. ''To make a long story, whose details I'd prefer not to discuss, short, I ended up alone, facing down five young men who had exceeded their genetic potential in the brawn and ugliness departments. Unfortunately, they weren't likewise gifted with brains, and any effort I made to talk them out of doing what they wanted to do failed most profoundly. To put it simply, they beat the hell out of me that night.''

Chloe turned her head then, to face him fully, but in the dim light of the car, he had no idea how to gauge what was going through her head. Especially since she said nothing in response to his assertion.

''They broke my arm, my wrist, three fingers, and two ribs,'' he said. ''I received a minor concussion, and had to have five stitches under my chin. If you ask me nicely, when we get home, I'll show you the scar. I am, after all, rather proud of it.''

''Why?''

He sighed again and uncrossed his legs, leaning forward to weave the fingers of his hands together between them. Then he waited until he was sure Chloe was looking at him full on before he continued. ''Because, my dear daughter, it's a very effective reminder of how close I came to submitting with much success to my own feelings of self-destruction." He leaned back in his seat, and this time, he was the one to stare out the window at the swiftly passing darkness.

"I hated myself when I was young," he told her, surprised at how easily the words came. "I hated being different from everyone else. I hated standing in the middle of a crowded room, pretending I felt comfortable, when I knew I would never be comfortable around anyone. I hated being able to easily comprehend things that baffled other people completely. I hated seeing things differently, understanding things differently, feeling things differently. And I hated knowing that no matter how hard I looked, I would never, ever, find anyone who was like me, anyone who shared the same thoughts and feelings I claimed myself. And I hated knowing that, even though I was surrounded by people—people who cared about me, even—I would essentially be alone forever.

"There were times, Chloe," he continued more softly, "when I wanted to die instead of having to go on with the rest of my life feeling the way I felt, knowing the things I knew. And because of that, I frequently cast myself into situations that might, somehow, achieve such a goal for me, when I couldn't go about doing it on my own."

This time he did turn to look at her again. "At best, I wanted to create some understandable, identifiable reason for why I felt so angry and resentful and dissatisfied all the time. I needed an excuse for why I was so utterly unhappy. Talk about your rebel without a clue . . ."

In the brief slash of a passing street lamp, he saw that she was gazing right at him. Intently, and with full understanding. Then the shadows fell again, something that made it possible for him to continue.

"Life is dangerous for people like us, Chloe," he said, forcing a weak smile. "We think too much, we comprehend too much, we feel too much. Some days, it's exhausting just trying to get through to the end. But that doesn't mean we have to submit. I'm only now learning that. Hopefully, it won't be such a hard lesson for you, or one so long in coming."

"What—" She stopped when her voice came out sounding rusty and dry, then cleared her throat before trying again. "What happened to you that finally made you feel better about yourself? When did you start thinking that maybe things would be okay?"

Schuyler didn't hesitate at all this time before answering. "Lily happened," he said. "She was the first person to come into my life and treat me like a human being. Not a troublemaker. Not a brilliant mind. But a person. At first, I didn't quite know what to make of her when she did that. Then, I allowed myself to love her for doing it. More than I've ever loved anyone, I suppose. Until recently," he qualified. "At first, I mistook that love for the kind of love that a man feels for a woman he wants to make his wife. But soon I realized that it was actually something else entirely."

"What?"

"It was the love one feels for a friend—a true, genuine friend—that he knows he will have forever. No matter what happens. No matter how many people, or how many mishaps, or how many miles come between them. No matter how many hardships or injustices occur. Lily is a constant in my life. For a long time, I thought she was the only constant I would ever have. She's never cut me any slack, and she's never coddled me. Nor has she ever dismissed or overlooked me. When I met her, it was the first time I felt a kinship with anyone. And that has never changed."

Chloe seemed to think about that for a moment, then said, "I need to find someone like that."

Schuyler hesitated for only a moment before assuring her, "You have."

She gazed back at him in thoughtful silence for a long time, but again, the shadows in the car prevented him from deciphering clearly what she might be thinking. Then, as softly as he had spoken himself, she said, "Do you still feel like you'll never meet anyone who's like you are? Who feels and knows and understands the same things you do?"

This time when Schuyler smiled, the gesture was heartfelt. "No, I don't feel that way anymore," he said. "Because I have a daughter, and she and I are of one essence, one soul, aren't we? I don't know why I didn't see or understand that before. Some big brain I've turned out to be." He hesitated briefly before adding, "And, perhaps, there might be someone else who—"

He stopped himself before saying any more about Caroline, before speaking out loud what was still much too new and uncertain for words. "I have a daughter," he said again, knowing that, at least, *was* certain. "I'll always have a daughter, I hope. And you, if you want one, will always have a father in me."

"I want a father," she said immediately, plainly, genuinely. "I want you."

Something inside Schuyler opened up wide, filling with warmth, with light, with a giddy sense of well-being. For a moment, he also felt that old ripple of terror rising, and with no small effort, he forced it back down. It was going to take time, he knew, before he would be any good at this parenting thing. But with any luck at all . . .

"Well, then," he said. "I suppose we're off to a reasonably good start, aren't we?"

Lily had never been more nervous about dinner in her entire life. Of course, that wasn't surprising, seeing as how her life—and the lives of so many others—pretty much depended on this dinner. She'd even shirked her professional duties to go shopping that day, so that she would have something reasonably appropriate to wear that was neither the cocktail dress of a hostess, nor the workday suit of a social secretary.

No, tonight, Lily intended to dress as—and be—exactly what she was. So she had found her way to the very top floor of Bloomingdale's, and had selected a lovely, deceptively conservative Ungaro suit in smoke-gray velvet with pearl buttons. She fastened a string of exquisite pearls around her throat, fastened two more in her ears, then scooted her feet into black, low-heeled pumps. She swept her hair high on her head, applied only a minimal amount of makeup, and then, satisfied that she could successfully play her role to the public for the first time, she left her quarters to go down to the dining room.

Leo hadn't yet arrived, but the rest of the usual suspects, save Schuyler, were there. Mrs. Puddleduck, looking as morose as usual in tepid brown, hovered over her young charge, though not quite as militantly as usual. That was probably because Chloe herself looked small and tired, her bright fuschia dress making more obvious the pale undertones of her complexion. Her eyes were smudged by faint circles, attesting to the late and difficult night she had suffered, but she stood straight and tall, and she was smiling faintly at something Miranda said, so perhaps things were on the mend there.

Lily was certain Schuyler *would* be there for her tonight. She was certain because she had made it abundantly clear to him earlier that, if he wasn't there for her tonight, then she would make kielbasa out of him.

Inhaling a deep breath—the last she would take as Schuyler's secretary—she strode purposefully to the bar on the other side of the expansive room. And, seeing Janey Kimball standing nearby wearing her usual straw chapeau and dainty gloves, not to mention a lilac gown that was positively gossamer, Lily decided to try flexing a little muscle.

"Janey. Darling," she said. "Fix me a martini, would you?"

Without turning her head, Janey dropped her mouth open in outrage at the suggestion—nay, the command—that she should perform a service for someone other than herself. Then she jerked her head around to look at Lily, and whatever words she had been about to utter were squelched before making themselves known. She swept her gaze over Lily from head to toe, then up again, then down again, and then fixed on her face for some moments. And then, almost imperceptibly, Janey nodded.

"All right," she said, surprising Lily. She pivoted around to the bar. "I suppose I could do that."

Miranda Kimball, too, seemed to notice something different about her son's secretary, because she crossed the room in a graceful, and abundant, flow of purple satin, pausing to stand in front of Lily. But she said nothing at first, only gazed in steady perusal at the woman she had scarcely heeded before.

Then she tilted her head to the left a bit and said,

"What was that, Joan?" After a brief pause, she smiled and nodded. "Yes, I think so, too. Lily does look divine tonight, doesn't she?" Then, to Lily, she added, "Miss Crawford thinks you have a very powerful aura about you this evening. And you do. It's very . . . potent."

Well, Miss Crawford would know, Lily thought.

Janey extended a martini to her then, and she took it with a quick nod of thanks. She was about to respond to Miranda's comment, when she suddenly felt the presence of an aura that was infinitely more important, infinitely more potent. She sensed, more than saw, Leo enter the dining room, and when she turned to gaze at him, her heart nearly jumped out of her throat.

Because, like his friend Eddie Dolan, who stood at his side, Leo was dressed in the most elegant, most sophisticated—most erotic, most sexy—tuxedo that Lily had ever seen. His hair was slicked back dramatically, as if he had just stepped from a fabulous forties film, and he had a white rose affixed to his lapel. It was identical to the one Mr. Dolan wore in his own lapel, so Lily was certain it was Leo's friend who was responsible for the adornment, and not Leo himself. Added to that, he seemed in no way comfortable in the formal attire, and that, more than anything else, made Lily go hot all over with her love for him.

He had a lot to atone and apologize for before the night was over, she reminded herself. But gosh, he was awfully cute.

The two men strode forward—Mr. Dolan with considerably more finesse than Leo—but she scarcely noticed the other man at all. As they drew nearer, Leo lifted a hand to the black tie at his throat, tugged at it viciously, and muttered something to his friend that sounded like, "I still can't believe I let you wrestle me into this penguin suit."

"Mr. Dolan," she said, extending her hand toward him, deliberately excluding Leo from the greeting just to tick him off. The gesture worked really, really well, too, because he frowned and refused to look at her. "I'm so happy you could make it this evening." She turned to Leo then, as Eddie Dolan's huge hand swallowed hers. "And you brought Mr. Freiberger—or whoever he is—with you. How nice."

Leo was still trying to wrangle his tie when he glanced up at her, then back down at his tie, then back up at her again. Immediately, his fingers stopped worrying the length of black silk, and he narrowed his eyes at her suspiciously. He, too, dropped his gaze downward to survey her, then back up again, inspecting her attire and her . . . aura. Or something. But instead of being impressed by what he saw, as the others so clearly had been, he frowned.

Before he could remark, however, Janey Kimball forced her way into the small group and eyed Eddie Dolan with *much* interest. "Can you spell *onomatopoeia*?" she asked him without preamble.

To his credit, Mr. Dolan seemed not to be at all surprised by the query. He furrowed his brow and rolled his eyes upward for a moment, as if concentrating very hard. Then, "Nope, sorry," he said. "I can't."

Janey brightened some. "Do you know what it is?"

Again, he seemed to think hard before answering. "Yeah, my Aunt Peg suffered from it real bad. A couple doses of Pepto-Bismol always cleared it right up, though. But she was a great old broad, Aunt Peg, in spite of her affliction."

Janey's smile in response to that, Lily noted, could have lit up eastern Pennsylvania for the next two millennia. "Lily," she said, "aren't you going to introduce me to our guest?"

Lily made the necessary introductions, marveling at how Mr. Dolan, too, seemed inordinately eager to make Janey's acquaintance. Then the two of them strode off toward the bar, leaving Lily to contend with Leo on her own.

"You look wonderful," she told him, unable—and unwilling—to keep her feelings to herself on that score. A wave of uncertainty washed over her, though. In spite of recognizing this man, she was beginning to feel as if she'd never really met him at all. "I just wish I knew who you really are," she added softly.

His expression revealed nothing of what he might be thinking. And all he said in response to her assertion was, "Yeah, well . . . that makes two of us. And you don't look so bad yourself," he hurried on before she could comment on his remark. He didn't sound much pleased by his observation, however. "Different, though," he continued, scanning her from head to toe again. "I just can't say exactly how."

Ah, well, she thought. He'd figure it out soon enough. Hey, he was a smart guy, after all.

"Is your name really Leonard?" she asked.

He winced, but nodded. "Yes. My name really is Leonard. But, please, call me . . . something else."

"Well, then, how about Mr. Freiberger?" she asked, not quite able to mask her sarcasm entirely. "Could I call you that and still be correct?"

"No," he told her.

"Because that's not really your name, is it?"

"No."

"And you're not a bookkeeper, either, are you?"

"No."

When he didn't volunteer the information she was so inexpertly skirting around, Lily asked him flat out, "Who are you then? Really? And what brought you to Ashling to begin with?"

"That's a question I'd like to have answered myself."

They both turned then to see Schuyler approaching. He, too, was dressed in a flawless tuxedo, his fingers curled around the stem of a martini glass streaked with cool condensation. He covered the few feet left between them, then fixed his attention entirely on Leo.

"You've disrupted my entire household since you came to Ashling, Mr. Freiberger, and I think the least you could do is tell me why."

"His name isn't Mr. Freiberger," Lily said.

"Yes, I know," Schuyler conceded, still looking at Leo. "But it will do for the next few moments, until we get this all straightened out." He glanced down at his watch. "Dinner won't be served for another half-hour. Shall we retire to the library for this? It could, after all, get ugly. No need to ruin everyone's appetite."

Leo turned a questioning gaze to Lily. "He knows about this?"

Lily nodded. "Of course he knows. He and I were up all night discussing it. And between the two of us, we hope we can make you understand something very important."

Schuyler turned away from Leo then for the first time, and gave his full attention to Lily. He opened his mouth to say something, then took in her attire and her new attitude. Then he smiled. "Why, Lily, darling. You wear it well. Something tells me that perhaps we should have done this years ago."

She smiled back. "I only hope it doesn't all blow up in our face tonight."

Leo was obviously becoming impatient, because his voice was tinted with irritation when he said, "Would somebody care to enlighten me as to just what the hell you two are talking about?"

For another scant moment, Schuyler and Lily gazed at each other, both knowing that everything was about to change, and trying to preserve, for one or two final moments, what had been a way of life for them for so long.

Then, after a quick sip of his martini, Schuyler turned back to Leo. "Freiberger," he said, "you might want to fix yourself a drink before you join Lily and me in the library." He smiled wryly. "Methinks you are going to need it, old man."

And without awaiting a reply, he spun on his heel and strode confidently out of the dining room without a backward glance.

"He's right, you know," Lily said, lifting her own drink for Leo's inspection. "Help yourself, and we'll see you shortly."

And without awaiting a reply, she spun on her heel and strode confidently out of the dining room without a backward glance.

TWENTY

This was too weird.

As Leo watched Lily trace the steps of her employer in exactly the same manner in which the billionaire had strode out of the room himself, a wave of déjà vu washed over him. Man, it was as if one of them was a shadow of the other, something that frankly gave him the creeps. And because of that, he had no qualms about following their instructions regarding a drink. So when he approached the library a few minutes later, he was armed to the teeth with a Scotch and water, and he wasn't afraid to use it.

There. That oughta hold 'em off.

Kimball's library was, like the rest of the house, a study in conspicuous consumption. The fifteen-foot ceiling was a gridwork of elaborate, stylish molding, and the shelves were crammed with books, many of them leather bound. The furnishings were likewise overwhelmingly leather, and the mingling aromas of old books, and tanned hide, and mellow Scotch made Leo feel just so damned grateful to be alive.

As he stood in the doorway looking in from the

334

hall, he saw Lily and Kimball on the far side of the
room, framed by the massive Palladian window behind them and, beyond it, the illuminated land-
scaping outside. Their heads were bent in quiet
conversation, and they seemed to be both troubled
and resigned about whatever they were discussing.
Neither had noted Leo's arrival, so he took a minute to study them in private.

Even if they weren't lovers anymore, there was
an intimacy between them with which Leo wasn't
sure he would ever be completely comfortable.
Then he realized that in acknowledging such a feeling, he was allowing himself to think that he and
Lily had a future together, and that simply wasn't
the case at all. Whatever she had to tell him tonight,
even if whatever that was excused or explained
what she had been doing with Kimball's company
over the years—and that was a pretty major *if*—he
wasn't sure it would be enough to repair the damage that had been done to their newly generated
feelings of trust and affection and fidelity for each
other.

The damage had occurred in the roots of their
relationship, and had cut deeply into those roots
before their affection—okay, their *love*, he admitted
grudgingly—for each other had had a chance to
fully blossom. And that kind of wound almost
never healed completely. The flower of their affections would have to be awfully sturdy to sustain
such a blow.

And when the hell he had decided to become
such a friggin' poet, Leo would never know. In addition to everything else Lily had done to him—
made him fall in love with her, crawled into the
center of his heart and rearranged all the furniture
there, tied him up in knots—she'd made him

whimsical. Dammit. He was never going to be the same.

He couldn't get over the change in her this evening. He just wished he could identify how, exactly, she had changed. There was an air of command about her that hadn't been there before, an unmistakable confidence in who and what she was. But precisely who and what she was still remained a mystery. As did so much else.

"So?" he said as he ambled into the room, feigning a casualness he didn't feel. "You have my undivided attention. Convince me not to take what I've found to the board of directors of Kimball Technologies, Inc. Tell your boss why you've been stealing money from him for years, and see what he has to say about it."

To Leo's surprise, Kimball didn't bat an eye at the allegation. Instead, he smiled as if Leo had just reminded him of an old joke he had enjoyed years ago.

"Yes, Lily, darling," he said, turning his attention to his secretary. "Do tell me. I'd love to hear all about it."

"That's funny," she replied, smiling in much the same way Kimball was. "You never wanted to hear about it before. You always told me, 'Lily. Darling. I don't want to know. Just do what you have to do.' "

"Yes, well, there was a reason for that, wasn't there?"

"Not a very good one."

"Lily. Darling. You—"

"Would somebody please tell me what the hell is going on?" Leo interrupted. He was getting tired of the by-play between employer and employee.

But instead of offering the explanation Leo had demanded, Lily turned to look at him full on and made a request—or was it a command?—of her own. "Before I spill my guts to Mr. Not-Freiberger, I'd like to know more about him," she said. "So, please tell us all about yourself, sir."

Leo inhaled a deep breath and released it slowly, but he never took his eyes from hers. Really, she was the one who owed the more important explanation here, not him. In spite of that, he supposed what she was asking wasn't unreasonable. And he really did want to clear the air about himself. Why? He still wasn't sure. But somehow, it seemed essential that there be no lies or misconceptions left between them.

"My full, *real*, name is Leonard Gustav Friday," he said.

"Gustav?" she echoed with the first genuine smile he'd seen from her all evening, obviously delighted by that scrap of knowledge. "Really?"

Leo wasn't nearly as delighted by it as she was, but he replied levelly, "Really."

She smiled coyly. "What *were* your parents thinking?" Before he could answer that he had no idea, that he had often wondered about that himself, she hurried on, "And tell me, *Mr. Friday*, what is it you do for a living?"

He hesitated, then said evasively, "I'm self-employed."

"As?"

Another hesitation, then, "I guess you could say I'm a private investigator."

"Could I say that?" The revelation seemed to surprise her for a moment, but then she nodded, as if it all suddenly made sense.

"What I investigate, though, is mostly white-collar–type crime that's financial in nature," he explained. "When businesses think money is disappearing too fast and too suspiciously, they call me in to find out where it's going."

"And that was what happened here," she guessed. "Schuyler's board of directors finally became suspicious?"

He nodded again. "You got a little too greedy this year, Miss Rigby. Fifty million bucks is kind of hard to hide."

"I don't see why it would be," she said mildly. "They didn't notice the sixty million the year before."

He gaped at her, his eyes widening. "Sixty?" he asked. "I only accounted for forty-two that year."

"Yes, and you only accounted for fifty from last year, didn't you?" she asked. Then she smiled, a teasing little smile that made his heart both hum with delight, and crinkle with distress. Because as nice as that smile was, it didn't quite reach her eyes, which remained cool and flat and angry. "Guess you're not as good as you thought, are you, Mr. Friday?"

Leo couldn't believe what he was hearing. "You mean there's more than fifty million dollars missing?"

"There's more than fifty million gone from the Kimball profits of last year, yes," she corrected him.

"What's the difference?"

She shrugged, completely unconcerned about the fact that she was confessing to an enormous amount of illegal activity. "The difference is that when something is missing, no one knows where it is. When something is gone, that may not necessarily be the case."

"And of course, you know where all the money is," Leo said bitterly, "because you took it."

"Oh, yes," she assured him. "I know where every last penny went, and yes, I'm the one who

. . . appropriated it. You didn't quite find all my records, Mr. Freiber . . . Mr. Friday. Otherwise, this conversation wouldn't be necessary."

He deflated some at her readiness to discuss the particulars of her theft. Somehow, he'd been holding on to a thread of hope that all of this would come to make sense. Clearly, she just wanted to taunt him with her success, with the fact that she had so thoroughly outsmarted him, with the overwhelming amount of cash she had been able to collect. "So you're not denying any of it?" he asked halfheartedly.

"No. I'm not."

"You really did take the money."

"I really did funnel it off, yes."

"And what did you do with it?"

"Oh, I bought all kinds of things, Mr. Friday, you can't possibly imagine." She waved a hand breezily through the air as she continued, "I bought clothes and cars, stocks and bonds, real estate and houses—"

Leo grew sick to his stomach hearing the particulars of her shopping list. "You can stop there, Miss Rigby, I get the idea."

But she obviously wasn't quite finished yet. "I also bought some wonderful meals and entertainment. Oh, and athletic equipment, and college scholarships, and hospital equipment. In fact, I endowed an entire hospital wing one year. That was kind of fun."

Certain he was misunderstanding, Leo asked, "What?"

"And then there was the Best Chance School I started in West Philly. That's one I'm rather proud of. A full ninety percent of the students have gone on to become college graduates. It's really quite unprecedented."

A loud buzzing began humming at the back of Leo's brain, gradually growing louder and louder, threatening to drown out his rationality. "I'm afraid I don't understand, Miss Rigby . . . uh, Lily."

"No, I know you don't, Mr. Friday. That's why I'm trying to go slow. Now then. After the Best Chance School, there was the chair I endowed at Penn State for the School of Social Work. After that came the endowment for the International Educational Fund for the Children—or IEFC, as it's more familiarly known—which has built schools in twenty-three countries so far."

"Lily?" Leo interrupted, trying really, really hard to stay on track, but not quite succeeding in that particular quest.

"Wait, I'm not finished yet," she interrupted him right back. "There have been the annual—and anonymous, of course—donations to things like Habitat for Humanity, Amnesty International, PETA, the United Way . . . oh, the usual . . . and also quite a bit given to fund awareness campaigns for a variety of social causes. All in all—"

"Lily?" Leo tried again.

"Really, Mr. Friday, if you keep interrupting me, we'll be here all night. I have a full decade's worth of charitable donations to account for, and it's going to take some time."

"Charitable donations?" he repeated. "Are you trying to tell me that all that money you skimmed from the Kimball profits has gone for *charitable donations*?"

She nodded, smiling again, the gesture not quite so brittle as it had been before. "Yes, that's right."

"You expect me to believe that you've *appropriated*, as you said, scores of millions of dollars from your employer, and it's all been given to other people?"

"Well, only people who deserved it," she qualified.

He narrowed his eyes at her, hopelessly lost now. Thinking—praying—that Kimball might be able to shed some light on the situation, Leo turned to the billionaire, who stood beside Lily, sipping his martini without a care.

"Kimball?" he said in an effort to claim the man's attention.

"Yes, Friday?"

"Would you, uh, care to help me out here? I seem to be kind of—"

"Befuddled?" the billionaire supplied helpfully.

"Uh, yeah. That'd be a good word for it."

Kimball sighed dramatically. "It's actually quite simple, Friday, if you think about it."

"Is it?"

The other man nodded, then took a few steps forward, pausing beside one of the leather-bound sofas to strike a nonchalant pose. And then, very clearly, very matter-of-factly, he said, "Leo. Darling. Lily runs the company. She always has."

Leo opened his mouth to reply, but absolutely nothing emerged. He could only stare in silence at Schuyler Kimball, feeling certain that he must have misunderstood.

Seeming to take pity on his inability to speak, the billionaire flicked a piece of lint from his lapel and continued with a careless explanation. "She's been the one in charge of Kimball Technologies from the start. We just never exactly got around to telling anyone about it, that's all."

If Leo had thought he was confused before, he had been mistaken. Because with this newfound knowledge, he was suddenly, completely, utterly . . . well, still befuddled. "I'm afraid I'm not following you."

Kimball sighed again, even more dramatically. "I was afraid of that," he muttered. He glanced down at his watch. "Damn. Dinner will be served in fifteen minutes. Let's see if we can make this quick, shall we?"

"Oh, that would be fine with me," Leo assured the other man. "Let's just make it understandable, too, okay?"

Kimball took another step forward, rounding the sofa that was situated perpendicular to the fireplace and facing an identical one on the other side of a wide coffee table. "Have a seat, Leo," he said, following his own advice. "No sense standing on formality."

Leo obeyed the billionaire's instructions, not because of any feeling of obligation or courtesy, but because the command was the first statement that had made sense all night. Lily, too, crossed to the sofas, but instead of aligning herself with Kimball on his, she sat at the opposite end of the one Leo occupied. Somehow, that went a long way toward making him feel as if maybe they would recover from all this.

Depending on just what the hell *all this* was. Unfortunately, the answer to that was looking murkier all the time.

"Schuyler's intention to create Kimball Technologies started in an apartment we were sharing at the time," Lily said. "All the creative power, all the design work, even the labor, he performed himself. I kept track of the paperwork and records for him, more as a favor to him than anything else." She offered the billionaire a brief smile, then turned back to Leo. "Schuyler, for all his brilliance, can't even balance a checkbook, let alone keep track of a business. Even a small one. So the responsibilities for that fell to me. Because he was my friend, and because I was well suited for running a business, I was happy to take them on."

Leo shook his head slowly, unable to believe he was hearing what he was hearing. "Are you trying to tell me that, all these years, it's been you, not Kimball, who's been running Kimball Technologies? That you're the man in charge?"

Lily nodded, but smiled sadly at his wording. "I'm afraid so."

Finally, Kimball jumped in. "She's been the CEO of Kimball Technologies in everything but title," he said without a trace of resentment. "When I decided to go into business for myself, Lily was, quite simply, the best man for the job. She still is." He threw her a look of weary resignation. "I don't know what I'll do without her. I don't know what the company will do without her. Lily, darling, I wish you'd reconsider."

She shook her head and smiled with something Leo could only liken to melancholy. "Schuyler, you know what's going to happen when word of this gets out. If you keep me in charge, the stock will plummet, the board of directors will be outraged . . . It's better I quit now, before things go sour. You'll find someone to take my place. Someone with a Y chromosome to make it all more palatable to everyone."

Leo gazed at both of them in silence for a moment, completely at a loss for something to say. Finally, he managed to get out, "You, uh, you'll excuse me if I have just a little bit of trouble believing all this. Not that you couldn't run the business," he hastened to add when he saw her expression change to one of prim offense, "but because keeping something like this a secret all these years would be next to impossible."

"Not really," she said, her pique evaporating,

once she understood his objection. "What would probably have been impossible, at least where the American business and financial communities are concerned, would have been launching Kimball Technologies with a woman in charge. A girl, really, was what they would have considered me," she amended. "Because I was only twenty-one at the time."

"I'm sorry, but I'm still not following you," Leo said.

She exhaled a quick breath. "No one would have taken us seriously, had mine been the face they saw as the one in charge when we approached businesses for investment. A young woman, they would have all assumed, would never be able to cut it, wouldn't have the sense or the wherewithal to build a business from the ground up. A young *man*, however," she added, dipping her head toward Schuyler, "well . . . that was perfect. A young hotshot mechanical designer with a brilliant mind, fresh out of college? Schuyler was all the rage.

"We used the prejudices of the business community to our advantage," she said. "The reason it was so easy to keep secret the fact that I was running things was because no one ever bothered to question Schuyler's position. We said he was the CEO, and he was, in fact, the CEO—on paper. Then we let them assume whatever they wanted after that. We let them assume he would be the one in charge, the one with the final say, when in fact, I was the one making all the decisions and keeping the business running. And, naturally, everyone did indeed make that assumption. It was a very effective smoke screen."

"But—"

"No, no buts," she interrupted him. "The hard fact of business is that women simply are not given the same treatment or recognition that men are. And I wanted Kimball Technologies to be a rousing success. Maybe even more than Schuyler did. In order to accomplish that, *I* needed to be the one who was in charge, but we needed for other people to *think* that Schuyler was. Otherwise, it never would have worked."

"But why would you be content to stay behind the scenes that way?" Leo asked. "Why would you let Kimball take credit for your hard work?"

"Well, for one thing, Schuyler was working every bit as hard as I was. He was just doing it in a different area. And for another thing, I got something out of the arrangement that was far more important to me than recognition for my contribution."

"What's that?"

"Money," she said succinctly. "And lots of it."

Leo's gut twisted again when he heard her say it flat out that way. So she really was driven by greed. She really had been motivated by personal gain.

"It's not what you think," she said calmly, clearly having read his nausea on his face. "The money I wanted—and received—from the arrangement was never meant to make my life better. Well, not in the way you're interpreting it. All of that money, Leo, every last nickel, went to worthy causes. And in seeing it distributed that way, I did, in fact, receive quite a lot of personal gratification."

"But she never received any money," Kimball threw in. "No more than was required for her to live on." He smiled at her in a way that said he would never, in a million years, understand her, but would always, always respect her decision. "She's an odd duck, is our Lily," he continued.

"Always wanting to do for others, never letting anyone do for her."

"What's so odd about wanting to help other people?" she asked

"It's odd because so few people share your opinion," Schuyler said.

"Oh, you might think so, Schuyler," she responded, "but you haven't met the people I have working with different charities. You'd be surprised how many people *do* care."

Kimball sipped his martini, feigning—somehow Leo knew he was faking it—boredom. "Yes, I think I would be surprised," he said.

"I'm not going to get into this with you tonight," Lily said. But there was something akin to amusement mixed with the bemusement in her voice. "You already know my stand on this. Whether you believe it or not, there really are some things in life that are more important than money."

Kimball rolled his eyes, and Leo got the feeling that this was an old argument with the two of them. "Very easy for you to say, Lily. You grew up with every comfort a person could have. Mondo houses, private academies, convertibles on your sixteenth birthday, cotillions, yachts, and Chateaubriand for dinner every night."

This time Lily was the one to roll her eyes, something that only reinforced Leo's conviction that they were playing out an old scene. "Converti*ble*," she corrected the billionaire. "Singular. I only got *one* convertible for my sixteenth birthday. Which, I'll remind you, got repossessed three months later. Along with everything else we owned. And we did *not* have Chateaubriand *every* night."

"Oh no?" Kimball asked.

She shook her head, but smiled devilishly. "Only Wednesday was Chateaubriand night."

"And I suppose you're going to tell me you ordered pizza from Domino's every Friday night."

"Of course not," she retorted with a haughty sniff. "We had Cook whip us up a prosciutto-and-shitaake pizza from scratch, just like any other self-respecting Main Line family would."

"*We* couldn't even afford Domino's in *my* family."

"Yes, yes, yes. So you've said a million times. And you couldn't afford ice cream, or new shoes, or a basketball, or a dog, either. Tell me, did you also have to hike barefoot for ten miles through five feet of snow to get to school everyday?"

Kimball shook his head before enjoying a thoughtful sip of his martini. Then he replied, "No. We couldn't afford snow."

"Poorboy," she said with a warm smile.

"Debutante," he retorted just as fondly.

The two of them exchanged a look that held a wealth of affection and understanding behind it, a look that made Leo wish he'd known Lily for as long as Kimball had. But he was beginning to realize that, although she shared a bond with the billionaire that was different from the kind of relationship she would ever have with anyone else, the one she shared with Leo was—and would always be—no less important.

"Besides, I've never needed anyone to do anything for me," she added imperiously, lifting her chin. "I've managed very well on my own."

"So you have," Kimball agreed. "But, Lily. Darling. You really are going to have to do something about your solitary status. And Mr. Friday here does seem to be a decent sort." He turned to throw Leo a meaningful look. "You are a decent sort, aren't you, Leo? Do assure me that I haven't misjudged you most profoundly."

"Depends on what you mean by 'decent,' " Leo said, his brain still buzzing from everything he'd learned here in the last several minutes.

"You won't take your findings to my—our—board of directors just yet, will you? You'll let me and Lily have a word with them first, yes? They do, after all, require a certain . . . handling. Surely you noticed that about them."

Leo didn't answer. Frankly, he had no idea what to say. He still couldn't quite believe that Lily Rigby had been instrumental in building Kimball Technologies into a multi-national, multi-billion dollar industry. He still couldn't quite believe that she had given all that money away—*given it all away*—to people and charities and organizations who might see their lives and situations improved as a result.

Could he?

"Just tell me this," he said.

"Anything," Lily assured him, and he knew that whatever it took to straighten all this out, she was willing to do it.

"Everything the two of you have done—the structuring of the business, the appropriation of the money, the donations to all the charities . . ."

"Yes?" she spurred him further.

"Has it been legal? Ethical? Moral?"

"It has most assuredly been legal," Lily told him. "We have all the documentation and records to prove that. And it's all moral, too," she continued. "We never lied to anyone, Leo. We just let them assume what they wanted to assume. Schuyler and I were a team from the beginning. We just never told anyone for sure that *I* would be the one making the final decisions and that *I* would be the one running things. They all drew their own errone- ous—and sexist, I might add—conclusions. So none of it was illegal or immoral."

"How about ethical?" he asked.

She and Kimball exchanged glances that were none too casual.

"No, I don't suppose it was ethical," she conceded. "But it *was* necessary."

"Why?" Leo asked. "I mean, you've told me why it was necessary to put yourself in charge and keep that part a secret, but what about all the charitable donations? Why did you have to keep all that a secret? What was the big deal with giving away millions of dollars annually? I would have thought that would just make Kimball look better in the eyes of the public."

"Well, it *was* quite a lot of millions," Lily reminded him. "Considerably more than the average corporate philanthropy."

"So?" Leo asked, thinking it a very good, if very succinct, question.

Kimball was the one to supply the explanation this time. "So I didn't *want* to look better, that's why. I didn't want it getting out that I was a bleeding heart philanthropist. Especially since it's Lily, and not me, who's the bleeding heart philanthropist here."

Okay, so as explanations went, that one left a lot to be desired, Leo thought. "Why wouldn't you want to be viewed as a blee . . . as a philanthropist?" he asked.

Kimball exhaled a long, impatient breath, then, as if that hadn't been enough to dispel his restlessness, he rose and paced to the fireplace, setting his empty glass on the mantle. For a moment, he only stared into the dance of flame that leapt and crackled and shifted from gold to orange, from blue to red.

And then, without warning, he spun around, his eyes livid with discontent. "I absolutely detest poverty and anything even remotely associated with it," he fairly spat at Leo.

"Well, gee, color me idealistic," Leo said, struggling to mask his surprise at the other man's vehemence. "But I don't think you're alone in that view."

"No, you don't understand," the billionaire said. "I abhor it. I find it revolting. It sickens me."

"Again," Leo muttered, still mystified, "that's not unusual, Kimball, trust me. A lot of people feel that way."

"Yes, but few of them lived it the way I did."

"Still . . ."

"Still," Kimball interrupted him, "you can't possibly appreciate what it means to be needy unless you have truly experienced it first hand. *Needy*," he repeated in a voice that punctuated his revulsion. "It's such a nice little word, isn't it? Needy. It's almost cute. I won't subject you to a gratuitous, maudlin description of what my life was like growing up. Just know that all the Mother Teresas and op-ed pieces in the world could never do justice to what poverty really is. And once I rose above it, I *never* wanted to be associated with it—tainted by it—again. Not even to help alleviate it. I don't want to go back there, Friday. Ever. I don't want to look at it, I don't want to hear about it, I don't want to know it exists. I paid my dues in the poverty department. Trust me on that. I am *done* with it."

The venom in his words was almost scorching, Leo thought. He had no idea how to reply. His family had never been rich by any stretch of the imagination, but they'd never really been poor, either. So since he had nothing to offer by way of understanding, Leo only remained silent and waited for the billionaire to answer the question he'd asked.

"When Lily and I launched Kimball Technologies, we struck a bargain. Actually, Lily gave me an ultimatum. She demanded that a specific percentage of our earnings each year go to charitable organizations and to people who needed help. Frankly, I wanted no part of that. But because I needed Lily, I agreed to her demand, so long as no one—*no one*—ever found out where the money was coming from. Even that first year, when we ran the business from our apartment and were barely able to turn a profit, she took the allotted percentage and gave it to the SPCA.

"It was easy then for her to hide the origins of the money she extracted, because it was just the two of us. Even when we added a few more people to the fold, there was never any indication to alert anyone to the fact that Lily had skimmed money from anywhere. But for the last several years, I know it's been difficult for her. Still, because she'd promised she would always keep me out of it, she managed it."

He smiled then, a genuine smile of warmth and good humor, and the fury that had been present a moment ago all but faded. And when he turned his attention to Lily, even that little bit of leftover anger disappeared completely. "We had no idea then that we would be able to take the company as far as we did," he said softly. "We hoped for it, certainly, but I don't think either of us ever even imagined we would go as far as we've gone. Had we given more thought to it, we probably wouldn't have organized things the way we did, and I probably wouldn't have demanded the secrecy that I demanded. But we were young and full of dreams. I suppose I should be grateful we've gone as long as we have without being found out. We've had a good run, but still . . . It's not going to be the same now."

"Why not?" Leo asked.

"Because darling Lily, in her infinite wisdom, has arrived at the conclusion that the business will suffer with her taking the helm in public, not just because she happens to be a woman, but because she is so prone to giving away the profits. I've tried to talk her out of abdicating, but she won't listen to me."

"The board of directors, Schuyler," she said softly. "They'd never go for having your social secretary take charge, and they'd certainly never allow for the . . . distribution of funds . . . that I prefer. And with the bickering that would ensue, the company would suffer significantly and, probably, irrevocably."

Leo had to concede that she could very well be right. In spite of that, and although he had no idea what possessed him to do it, he heard himself say, "Maybe if you let me talk to the board of directors first?"

Lily and Kimball both turned their attention fully upon him, their faces bearing identical expressions of, well . . . befuddlement. Leo heartened considerably at the realization that he wasn't alone. Then he remembered that he had Lily. Darling Lily. And he would never be alone again.

At least, he was pretty sure he had Lily. Probably, he had her, anyway. He was sure she'd forgive him for being such a sneaky little fink. Eventually. She'd come around . . . once he'd groveled and begged and prostrated himself before her and promised to do anything—*anything*—to make up for being such a jerk. Of course, that was assuming she still wanted *him*, too, an assumption that was, at this point, more than a little iffy.

"What do you mean?" she asked.

"Well," he began, focusing on his connection to the board of directors for now, instead of his tenuous position with Lily. He tried not to be too smug as he continued, "I've sort of established a rapport with the guys on the board, and—"

"A rapport?" she repeated. "With the board of directors? Oh, now there's a dubious distinction if ever there was one."

"Needless to say," Leo continued, ignoring the comment, "I think I . . . you know . . . bonded with a couple of the guys, and—"

"Oh, my," Lily interrupted him again. "You bonded? Truly? This just keeps getting better and better."

"And, *anyway*," he plodded on, "I think maybe, between the three of us, with a little time and effort, we might be able to work this thing out, that's all. If you want to give it a shot, I mean. As long as you guys haven't done anything illegal, and as long as you've got all the proper documentation to uphold everything you've done, and as long as you could make the formal transition of power from Kimball to you fairly painless for the big boys . . ."

He scrunched up his shoulders and let them drop. "Well, they might come around to your—our—way of thinking. Hey, your record speaks for itself. I don't know a lot about boards of directors, but status quo seems to hold a lot of appeal for them. And if you removed Lily from her position, it could mess with that status quo. Big time."

No one said a word for a moment after that. They all simply regarded each other with varying degrees of skepticism, and speculation, and . . . hope.

Kimball was the one to finally break the silence. Without moving from his position by the fireplace, he said, very softly, "Lily. Darling. What do you think?"

She hesitated a moment longer before replying, "I think you're both being overly optimistic."

"Well, it wouldn't be the first time that's happened, would it?" Kimball said.

"No, that's true," she agreed. But still, she didn't concede either victory or defeat.

"C'mon, Lily," Leo said, throwing his weight into the ring. "You know you don't want to step down from your position. I can see it in your eyes. You love being the man in charge. And think of all the good you could do once you're recognized as the driving force behind the business. If you leave the running of Kimball Technologies to someone else—someone with a Y chromosome—you know the first thing to go, in favor of the bottom line, will be the charitable donations."

She nodded slowly, sadly. "Yes. I do know that."

"Then you can't let the big boys win."

She inhaled a deep breath, clearly anxious about deciding one way or the other. "I don't know . . ." she began.

"At least try, Lily," Leo said. "You can't give it all up without even trying."

"Well," she finally said, "it would be awfully difficult for me to watch someone else undo the network I've worked so hard to put together. And I really would hate to see all that excess money going to pad the pockets of a bunch of greedy, rich businessmen when it could be putting food into the mouths of families who are infinitely more deserving."

She brightened some as she turned her attention to Leo completely. "And seeing as how you've got such a good *rapport* with the board," she added meaningfully, "I'd hate not to take advantage of it.

But, Leo, perhaps it would be beneficial, too, to ask your friend, Mr. Dolan to come along when we address the board. And ask him to wear one of his double-breasted suits of Italian manufacture, would you?"

Leo smiled. "Hey, I'll even have him eat some garlic and pesto before the meeting."

Lily smiled back. "I think that would be an excellent idea. Schuyler," she added, turning toward her cohort, "what do you think?"

He glanced down at his watch. "I think, Lily, darling, that it is now seven o'clock, and therefore a very opportune time to break for dinner." He lifted his glass from the mantelpiece and strode toward the door. Over his shoulder, he called out a question that really required no answer. "Shall we continue this conversation afterward?"

TWENTY-ONE

Schuyler left the library feeling only marginally better about the state of things in his universe. Certainly the business area was much improved over what it had been less than an hour ago, even though they still had a ways to go there. But things weren't so ideal on the personal front.

He had telephoned Caroline that afternoon, both at the Van Meter Academy and at home, hoping to catch her and talk to her and try to explain what he himself still didn't quite understand. It was just as well he hadn't reached her, he supposed. Because he really had no idea what to say to her. That hadn't stopped him, however, from leaving a message on her home answering machine, asking her— no, begging her—to come to dinner at the house tonight.

And now he couldn't quite slow his embarrassingly rapid pace as he covered the distance between the library and the dining room. When he arrived, however, it was to find himself awash in his family, with no sign of Caroline Beecham to be had. He deflated some at the realization that she hadn't come, but for some reason, his attention remained fixed on the collection of women who populated the dining room.

His family.

How extraordinary.

Funny that he had never really considered them such in more than a denotative sense, not even when he'd been a child growing up. He'd never felt as if he had one iota of anything in common with his mother or his sister, and he'd never really known—or cared to know—his father. And now he had a daughter with whom he was discovering some semblance of camaraderie. Family. Strange, that. Stranger still was the odd little trickle of warmth that wound through him at the knowledge that he did indeed have such a thing to claim as his own.

Really, he thought, he was going to have to try harder to understand the comings and goings of his life, if he ever hoped to make sense of anything.

"Schuyler."

And speaking of things that made no sense . . .

He turned slowly at the sound of his name uttered in a voice he had feared he would never hear again. His heart pounded in his chest, his blood rushed through his veins, his breath caught in his lungs. Because Caroline strode down the gallery . . . albeit at a speed that would have put her in third place behind a glacier melting and a sloth awakening. It seemed to take forever for her to reach him, and when she finally did, she still halted with a good five feet of space separating them.

That was okay, though, Schuyler thought, for now. Because standing as she was, he could drink his fill of her visually, and visually, she was a magnum of Perrier-Jouet just waiting to be savored.

Her hair was once again swept up behind her, but not in the severe, pinching fashion she normally wore. No, in fact, several breezy little tendrils cascaded around her face, nearly to her shoulders, and the rest looked as if someone had just carelessly piled it atop her head. It was almost as if the removal of one little pin would send the whole arrangement tumbling down.

Oh, yes. Schuyler *much* preferred this style to the other.

She had bypassed her usual bland wardrobe colors and had opted for a sapphire blue gown that hugged her lush form in a manner that would have made him jealous, had her dress not been an inanimate object. Oh, hell, yes it did make him jealous, and he itched to remove it so that he might be the one hugging her form instead.

Later, he promised himself. But not *much* later.

"You look absolutely edible . . . uh, incredible," he said by way of a greeting. "Well, you know what I mean."

She smiled at him, and those few little bits of uncertainty that were still settled in his belly dissolved. Just like that. "You don't look so bad yourself," she said, nodding toward his tuxedo.

"Well, that goes without saying," he agreed.

She took a step forward, almost reluctantly, then another, and another. Schuyler crooked an elbow when she was still a foot away, and the gesture was evidently enough to encourage her to take that final step. Looping her arm through his, Caroline paused for a moment beside him, and it was all Schuyler could do not to scoop her into his arms and carry her upstairs and make dinner out of *her*.

"I was afraid that you wouldn't come," he said, not sure when he'd decided to reveal such a thing.

"Were you?" she asked.

He nodded. "And then I was afraid that you would."

She parted her lips slightly, as if she couldn't quite get enough air. "And now?" she asked. "How do you feel now?"

He gave that some thought before answering, and was surprised by what he discovered. "Now," he said, "I think everything—*everything*—is going to work out exactly as it should."

She smiled again, but this time the gesture was one of understanding. She said nothing to comment on his remark, but then, no comment was really necessary. So Schuyler covered her hand with his and tugged her forward, and together they entered the dining room.

He was still focused entirely on her face when he slowed his pace, urging them both to a standstill at the center of the room. "Everyone," he said in a voice of urgent announcement. "I'd like for you to meet Caroline. Caroline," he added, still looking into her eyes, "I'd like for you to meet everyone." And then, just to make sure everyone—including Caroline—knew what was what, he forced his gaze away from hers and to the audience that had gathered. And then he added, in a surprisingly carefree voice, "Everybody be nice to her. She doesn't realize it quite yet, but she's going to be my wife. Oh, and let's not hold dinner for darling Lily and Leo," he hastened on before she could correct his assumption—not that she would correct it, because it was in no way erroneous. "Something tells me they're not going to make it. Not for dinner, at any rate."

In the library, Lily rose to follow Schuyler as he fairly raced out the door—honestly, what *was* his hurry?—but Leo's soft voice halted her from making a clean escape.

"What's your hurry?" he asked.

She narrowed her eyes at him, suspicious of his ability to read her mind. It was more than a little unnerving. Nevertheless, she supposed there was still far too much left unsettled between them to let it go just yet.

In spite of that, "I'm hungry," she told him.

He smiled, a *very* predatory smile, but there was a lingering uncertainty darkening his eyes. Good, she thought. He should feel uncertain. The sneaky little fink. Call her a liar, would he? He was the one who had manufactured a completely false persona from the start. Call her thief, would he? He was the one who'd stolen something. Her heart. Damn him. Call her greedy, would he? He was the one who consumed something whole. Her love. Good thing for him she had such a charitable nature. She was willing to forgive him. Eventually. But not until she had him exactly where she wanted him.

On his knees. *Begging* for forgiveness. Among other things.

"Hungry huh?" he asked. "What a coincidence. I'm hungry, too."

Yes, but were they hungry for the same thing? she wondered. Experimentally, she suggested, "Then it would probably be a good idea to join the others in the dining room, don't you think?"

"Oh, you're hungry for *food*, are you? That's too bad. I had something else in mind myself."

Ah-hah, she thought. So they *were* hungry for the same thing. That was going to make the rest of the evening infinitely easier to plan. After she finished with that business of bringing him to his knees, of course. But all she said in response to his assertion was, "Oh?"

He nodded. "Yeah, I'm in the mood for a veritable feast, myself. A real smorgasbord, as a matter of fact. All-you-can-eat."

"I see."

He rose from his seat, too, unbuttoning his tuxedo jacket with much nonchalance. "Not as much as you're going to."

Lily's heart began to hammer, and her very skin began to hum. "Why, Mr. Friday. I do believe you may be making a sexual overture toward me."

He nodded. "You got that right, boss lady."

Ooo. She did like the sound of that.

"And if you think the overture is good," he added, "just wait until you see the first act."

"Mmm," she murmured noncommittally. "I hope there will be lots of gratuitous sex."

"Oh, you can count on that."

"Then I think I'll like the first act very much indeed. And the second. And the third. Of course, that's assuming that *you* are the one playing opposite me in that act, something that, right now, is very much in question."

His smile fell. "Oh."

"You see," she began mildly, "I don't normally make it a practice to have sex with a man who's accused me of lying, and stealing, and being greedy."

He winced, flinching visibly at her charges.

"Did I do that?" he asked.

Lily feigned consideration. "Mm, yes, I believe you did. I distinctly recall you resorting to name calling at one point. A thief, you called me. A liar. Kind of interesting, seeing as how *you* were the one who lied about his identity—"

"That wasn't lying," he interjected with an almost convincing look of surprise. "That was practice. I was planning on being a bookkeeper named Leonard Freiberger for Halloween, and I was just trying out my costume on you. Pretty convincing, huh?"

Lily eyed him with much skepticism, then continued, "You lied and then violated the privacy of my bedroom—"

"Oh, now see, there you go, making assumptions again," he interrupted once more. "I just went up to your bedroom to fondle your underwear, that's all. Your computer was making a funny noise, so I decided to see if I could fix it, then suddenly . . . boom . . . all this information just sort of appeared, and I made the perfectly innocent mistake of thinking you were, you know, stealing money from your employer. It could have happened to anybody."

"Mm."

He inhaled a deep breath and released it slowly. For a long moment, he said nothing, clearly struggling to find something to excuse, or at least explain, his actions. Then, evidently deciding there were no words to accomplish such a thing, he simply told her, "I don't know that I will ever be able to apologize enough for thinking the worst of you the way I did."

Okay, that was a good start, Lily thought. But not quite enough to appease her. What else was he willing to do?

"And I'm not sure I can even explain why I was so ready to think the worst of you the way I did. Unless it was just because I was—"

"What?" she demanded.

He hesitated again, then confessed, very softly, "Because I was terrified of you."

Oh, well, that certainly got her attention. "Terrified?" she echoed incredulously. "Of me? Why?"

He took a step forward, then seemed to think better of the action, and halted. "Because it scared me, how quickly I fell in love with you."

Ooo, *now* they were getting somewhere. But instead of making it easy on him, Lily said, "Go on."

He sighed again, with a little less anxiety this time. "I've never felt about a woman the way I've found myself feeling about you. You just . . . you're inside me, Lily. And I know you'll be there forever."

Yes, that was good. "Go on."

"And maybe, as a last-ditch reflex of self-preservation," he continued, "I jumped to conclusions about you in an effort to put the brakes on those feelings. Funny thing, though," he added, his voice softening more. "Even when I was trying to tell myself you were a liar and a thief, I never really believed myself. I knew, deep down, that you just weren't capable of something like that."

She nodded, but said nothing, just waited for him to go on. Because she knew he wasn't finished yet.

"I'm sorry I lied to you," he said.

There, that was what she'd been waiting for.

"I could try to excuse myself by saying that I was only doing my job," he went on, "but that's a pretty lame excuse. Still, Lily . . . I was only doing my job. And I am sorry for misleading you."

This time Lily was the one to sigh, in acceptance, in resolution. "I guess we both rather misrepresented ourselves, didn't we? Neither of us was entirely honest. Which means that we can't afford to make that mistake in the future. For the rest of our lives, Leo, let's promise to always be truthful, okay?"

He paused a telling moment before asking, "So then, we do have a future?" He was obviously still not quite sure where he stood with her.

"Oh, yes," she promised him. "We definitely have a future. A really long and full one."

He smiled at that, looking extremely sexy and suave and sexy and sophisticated and sexy and handsome and sexy and hot and . . . did she mention sexy? He must have only used water to slick back his hair, because it was dry now, a single, unruly lock falling down onto his forehead. His eyes were lit with a raucous gleam, and the black tuxedo enhanced every elegant line of his body, every ripple of hard muscle he possessed. She couldn't wait to get it off of him. Something told her then that they would very likely be spending the rest of the evening in the library, in front of the fireplace, performing all kinds of maneuvers that were wanton and lascivious and hedonistic and—

"You really are one smart lady," he said, scattering her thoughts.

"What was that?" she asked absently, hoping her lascivious intentions didn't show. "I'm sorry, I was calculating the weight of the sun."

He chuckled as he shook his head. "You just . . . you're not like any woman I've ever met. And I . . ." He shrugged. "I love you, Lily. I don't want to lose you."

The warmth in her belly curled and dawdled through her midsection to points beyond. "I love you, too. And you never will lose me. Now then," she proposed, taking a step toward him. "About that hunger we both seem to be experiencing . . ."

He glanced toward the library door, then lifted a finger in that direction. "Does, um, does that door have a lock?"

She nodded. "A really big one. Schuyler's safe is in here."

"That's all I need to know."

Quickly and deftly, he crossed to take care of that particular matter, while Lily strode to the Palladian window and tugged the heavy draperies closed.

She reached for the top button of her jacket as she spun back around, and by the time she'd returned to the sofa, she'd freed all but one of the buttons. Beneath, she wore a brief camisole of silver silk, and the soft fabric danced and glittered in the firelight. Leo, too, had made short work of his jacket, which he'd tossed onto the sofa beside Lily's. Now, as she watched, he pushed the suspenders of his trousers over his shoulders and went after each of the buttons.

"Hurry," she said, reaching for the zipper at the back of her skirt, pushing that to the floor and kicking it aside. Beneath, she wore tap pants to match the camisole and smoky thigh high stockings. She started to toe off her high heels, then, feeling devilish, decided to leave them on for now. Because judging by the way Leo was looking at her . . .

He halted his movements at the sight of her, the fire in his eyes leaping higher, burning hotter, than those in the fireplace beside him. "Oh, Lily," he said softly, his voice a mere caress. "You are so . . ."

"What?" she asked, suddenly overcome by uncertainty.

He grinned *very* salaciously—something that went a long way toward dispelling that uncertainty—but shook his head slowly, teasingly. "I just don't ever think I'll get enough of looking at you."

She grinned back. "Oh, please, Leo. You'll have decades to look at me." She took a step forward. Then another. And another. "Right now," she purred, "I want you to touch me. All over."

He extended one finger toward her, tracing it over the slender line of her collar bone, then down her breastbone, to the lace of her camisole. "Hey, you're the boss," he told her, his voice low and husky.

Oh, yes. She most definitely liked the sound of that. "In that case, Mr. Friday," she said, her own voice none too loud or smooth, "you'd better do exactly as I say."

He lifted his head to meet her gaze, but his eyes were full of playfulness and teasing. "Yes, ma'am."

"Then again," she said softly, eyeing his half-open shirt, "there's a lot to be said for doing things for oneself."

Quickly, easily, Lily unfastened the rest of his buttons and tugged his shirt free of his black trousers. Beneath, he wore an old-fashioned undershirt without sleeves, his dark hair springing from the neckline, the salient biceps revealed by the style gilded with gold in the firelight. One side of his face lay in shadow, but she could see that his eyes were now dark with desire. She cupped one hand over his rough jaw, and his eyes fluttered closed. Then she raked her thumb gently over his lower lip—so incongruously full and soft compared to the hard planes and angles of his other features—and he uttered a quiet sound of pleasure.

The touch encouraged him, because the hand hovering at the lace of her camisole dipped down over the garment, and he covered her breast with sure fingers, nudging the soft fabric back and forth over her already sensitized flesh. His other hand joined the first, cupping her, palming her, owning her, until Lily felt her knees going weak. He must have sensed her infirmity, because he suddenly scooped her into his arms and carried her over to the leather sofa.

He lay her down and covered her body with his, pushing her camisole up as he came, fastening his mouth to her breast without warning, and with a hunger unlike any she'd known a person could feel. It was as if he were trying to inhale her, sucking her deep into his mouth, laving her with the flat of his tongue, teasing her with the tip, before mouthing her completely again. Lily tangled her fingers in his hair, gasped at the fever of sensation that rocked her, and silently begged him for more.

She felt his fingers at the waistband of her tap pants, and then, suddenly, the soft kid leather of the sofa beneath her bare bottom. Without slowing his assault on her breast, Leo pressed his fingers into her naked thigh, urging her legs apart. Willingly, she allowed him the access he demanded. So he dragged his open mouth down her torso and flat belly, nuzzling the dark curls between her legs before dipping his head lower to taste her more intimately, more thoroughly. The fingers she had wound in his hair flexed tighter, and interpreting her action as a demand for more—which, indeed, it was—he buried his mouth against her.

Oh. It was so . . . *oh.*

Over and over again he devoured her, suckling, laving, plowing with his tongue. He cupped her bottom in both hands to push her higher, to facilitate his onslaught and drink his fill of her. A tight coil inside Lily wound tighter still, until she feared it would implode into a billion flaming pieces. Then, slowly, that coil began to unwind. Wider and wider, faster and faster, until she was insensate to anything but a white-hot explosion of unmitigated joy. Wave after wave pummeled her, until she could scarcely breathe, could scarcely think, could scarcely feel.

When she finally did catch her breath, if not her thoughts, she opened her eyes to find Leo positioned above her, grinning with much satisfaction, something she found odd seeing as how she had been the recipient of such utter bliss. He had shed his shirt, but still wore his trousers, and instinctively, she reached for the fastening at his waist.

"Now," she managed to gasp. "I want you inside me now."

"That may cause some problems," he said. But in direct contrast to his statement, his voice held surprisingly little concern.

Which was really neither here nor there, because Lily wasn't listening anyway. She was too busy cursing the inventor of the zipper, and the manufacturers who couldn't make it unzip at the speed of light. Once it *was* free, however, she shoved both of her hands inside his trousers, filling her fingers with him, stroking him, rubbing him, until he was ripe and erect. He growled something unintelligible under his suddenly ragged breath but didn't discourage her actions. Not until she curled her fingers around that most sensitive part of him with loving possession. And then he jerked backward. Fast.

"Lily," he tried again. "Did you hear me? I said me being inside you right now could cause problems. I didn't exactly come prepared for a party tonight. If you know what I mean."

So muzzy-headed was she, thanks to his skillful, savage, loving, that she had no idea what he was talking about. Nor did she honestly care.

And he finally seemed to realize that, because he told her flat out, "I don't have a condom."

"I don't care," she told him right back, voicing her thoughts out loud.

"I do," he said adamantly.

That sobered her for a moment, because, quite simply, she wasn't sure how to interpret it. But since tonight was a night of revelation and truth-telling, she decided she might as well go for broke. "Leo," she said, "I want to marry you."

He smiled, then lifted a hand to her damp forehead and swept her hair back from her face. "Good. That'll work out well. Because as luck would have it, I want to marry you, too, Lily."

A great weight that had settled in her stomach, a weight she had scarcely acknowledged before, dissolved then. In its place burst a bubble of delight that tingled and traveled to fill every empty place inside her. "Ah, that's, um . . . that's good. You're right. This will work out very nicely indeed."

He kissed her briefly, almost chastely, then pulled back. "And someday," he added, "I want to have children with you. But not yet," he went on when she opened her mouth to say more. "I'm selfish, and I want to have you to myself for a while, and you have a lot of work to do with Kimball Technologies. We have years ahead of us to make babies, Lily. But right now, all I want is you."

She drew her hand along the length of him, slowly, seductively, and he hissed out his satisfaction at the touch. "But you didn't—" she objected.

"Oh, believe me, I've had a very nice time tonight," he told her. "And it's not over yet. In fact, with your hands in my pants that way, I think we could come up with one or two ways to take care of my . . . condition."

Lily nodded. "Or three or four. I'd like to try a variety of different things. I'm kind of funny that way."

Leo nodded, too. "I like variety. Variety is good. We can do variety. Over and over again, if you want."

"I want," she told him.

"Well then, Miss Rigby," he said as he lowered his head to hers once again, "I'm your man. It looks like we have a full night—and a full life—ahead of us."

EPILOGUE

"**O**rder! Order, please, ladies and gentlemen. We have a lot to cover today."

Leo smiled as he watched Lily from where he stood unobserved at the entrance to the boardroom of Kimball-Rigby Technologies, Inc. The company had moved into its new—and much less ostentatious—digs last spring, and he had to admit that he liked the new environment much better. The boardroom was surrounded on two sides by windows that offered a spectacular view of the Philadelphia skyline beyond, and sunlight poured into the room to brighten every last inch of the place. Plants hugged every windowsill, and the soft pastels of the walls and carpet were very soothing, and not a little feminine. It was vastly different—and vastly improved—over the last boardroom Kimball Technologies had claimed.

Seated at the head of the table, surrounded by her board of directors, Lily looked like exactly what she was—the leading businesswoman in the country, and the CEO of a corporation known for its cutting edge technology and its limitless philanthropy. This year alone, she'd been featured in *Forbes, Inc., Working Woman, Cosmopolitan*, and *Cigar Aficionado* magazines—that last one still bugged the hell out of Cohiba Man—and she had made appearances at dinners for the United Way, Planned Parenthood, and NOW. She was, as he had always known, a force to be reckoned with. It was something a few of her directors—the male ones—still didn't quite get.

"Denise," she said to the woman seated next to her, the one Leo had come to think of as Silk Woman, "how are we coming on the Denby acquisition?"

"Moving right along, Lily," she said. "Smooth as silk."

"Excellent," Lily replied. "Angela?" she added for the benefit of the next woman down the line, the one seated between Halston Man and Versace Man, whom Leo had dubbed, for reasons that were obvious, Mousse Woman. "What's up with Richard Steiner? Is he coming around?"

"He will," Mousse Woman said with conviction, touching a finger to her permanent wave—but not too hard. "Don't you worry about a thing."

Versace Man and Halston Man looked a bit miffed for some reason, but kept their comments to themselves. Leo shook his head and bit back his laughter. Lily sure had shaken things up in the last five years. Sure there had been some problems in the beginning, after she and Schuyler had gone public with their arrangement. The billionaire had put Lily firmly in charge of the company, so that he could focus on all the research and development that he'd always enjoyed most. A lot of the old boy network hadn't liked that much. But Lily and

Schuyler had stood firm, and they had stayed a team.

A very effective team, too, not surprisingly. Because it hadn't taken them long to recover from the brief downturn the company had initially suffered. And now that she was unhampered in her position, Lily was able to function in a way that outpaced even her earlier performance. The company was growing by leaps and bounds. And nothing would stop them now.

A cry of dissension erupted then, something that turned every head at the big table in Leo's direction. Leo himself scarcely noticed, however, because he bent down over the stroller beside him and picked up a blue-flanneled, three-month-old Andrew, rocking him gently to quiet him. But Andrew would have none of it, clearly had something else on his mind, so Leo shrugged and threw Lily a resigned look.

"Oh, bring my sweet baby boy over here," she cooed, reaching for the top button of her high-powered executive blouse.

On her other side, Cohiba Man blustered and coughed and started to object.

Lily rolled her eyes. "Look, Cyrus, if I've told you once, I've told you a million times. That breast-feeding policy *stays*. You do *not* want to challenge me on this."

As quickly as he had started to object, Cohiba Man settled down. He reached inside his jacket and lifted his cigar to his mouth, then, obviously not thinking clearly, reached back once more for a lighter.

"And that no-smoking policy holds, as well," Lily told him.

He opened his mouth to protest again, but she narrowed her eyes at him fiercely. "There's an opening in the Abu Dhabi office that I need to fill," she reminded him.

He shut his mouth, then shoved the unlit cigar into his pocket with his lighter.

Leo chuckled again as he carried little Andrew to Lily for his lunchtime feeding, but no sooner had he placed the baby in her arms than another hungry cry erupted from the stroller. Figures, he thought. Julia always had to have whatever her twin brother was having. He retraced his steps to the stroller and extracted the other baby, then glanced down at his watch.

"Look, Lily, I have to be in Haddonfield in thirty minutes to meet with the carpenters," he told her. "Can I leave the twins with you for the afternoon? Schuyler and Caroline and the baby have already left to go visit Chloe at Juilliard. And don't forget— the New York Symphony is performing her piece at the Met this weekend. I want to be out of Philadelphia early Friday morning to be sure we get there in time."

Lily nodded as she gazed down with undisguised and unadulterated love at the tiny boy nestled to her breast. "No problem. Let Marvin take Julia for a few minutes. He's great with her."

Leo surrendered his daughter to Charlton Heston Man, who cuddled the little baby in his arms and, in that voice of God, stated quite adamantly, "Cootchie. Cootchie. Coo."

"She's beautiful, isn't she?" said Thesaurus Man beside him. "Delicate. Well-favored. Bonny."

"Just like her mother," Leo agreed, adding to himself, *strong, commanding, smart*.

Yeah, things had worked out pretty well, all things said and done, he thought. Life didn't get much better than this. He moved to stand behind Lily, ostensibly to give her a quick kiss goodbye.

But as he leaned forward, he couldn't help whispering a few choice, and very erotic, promises into her ear. She chuckled low as she nodded and murmured a single word in response. "Tonight."

So Leo brushed his lips over her cheek one final time, and bid her a very reluctant goodbye. And as he left the boardroom, he heard the newest board member, the one who'd begun working just this week, Scarf Woman, ask, "So that was Lily's Mr. Rigby, huh? Very cute."

He halted just outside the door, to see what the response would be. "No, no," he heard Silk woman pipe up, her voice laced with good humor. "That was her man Friday."

Smiling to himself as he headed out, Leo conceded that that was certainly true.

Dear Reader,

If you love westerns the way that I love westerns, then you won't want to miss Connie Mason's latest love story, *To Tempt a Rogue*. When Ryan Delaney—the third Delaney brother—leaves the family ranch on what he hopes will be a great adventure, he never expects to get mixed up with Kitty Johnson. Is Kitty really running from the law, or is this a case of mistaken identity? And as passion flares between them, Ryan must determine if he's thinking with his head...or his heart.

Lovers of contemporary romance won't want to miss Hailey North's delightful, delicious *Pillow Talk*! Meg Cooper has always believed in what she calls "possibles," but is it possible to become engaged to a stranger for only two weeks? Sexy, wealthy Jules Ponthier woos Meg with promises of this "innocent" proposition—but how long can she resist this irresistible man? If you haven't yet become a fan of Hailey North, I guarantee this will make you one.

Karen Kay has thrilled countless readers with her sensuous, unforgettable love stories with Native American heroes. Her latest, *Night Thunder's Bride*, highlights her heartfelt brand of storytelling as a young pioneer woman must become the wife of Night Thunder, a Blackfoot warrior.

Eileen Putman makes her Avon debut with the wonderful *King of Hearts*, a Regency rake who is plucked from a hangman's noose and unexpectedly rescued by Louisa Peabody, a golden-haired beauty who seems to be the only woman in England who can resist his many charms.

Until next month, enjoy!

Lucia Macro
Lucia Macro
Senior Editor

AEL 0699

Discover Contemporary Romances at Their Sizzling Hot Best from Avon Books

HER MAN FRIDAY   *by Elizabeth Bevarly*
80020-9/$5.99 US/$7.99 Can

SECOND STAR TO THE RIGHT *by Mary Alice Kruesi*
79887-5/$5.99 US/$7.99 Can

HALFWAY TO PARADISE   *by Nessa Hart*
80156-6/$5.99 US/$7.99 Can

BE MY BABY   *by Susan Andersen*
79512-4/$5.99 US/$7.99 Can

TRULY MADLY YOURS   *by Rachel Gibson*
80121-3/$5.99 US/$7.99 Can

CHASING RAINBOW   *by Sue Civil-Brown*
80060-8/$5.99 US/$7.99 Can

LOOKING FOR A HERO   *by Patti Berg*
79583-3/$5.99 US/$7.99 Can